Love and pa
– what mo
want?

POSSESSED
BY THE
SHEIKH

A collection of two atmospheric stories
brought to you by two brilliant, much
loved authors

We're proud to present

MILLS & BOON®

SPOTLIGHT

a chance to buy two bestselling novels by favourite authors every month – they're back by popular demand!

POSSESSED BY THE SHEIKH

The Playboy Sheikh
ALEXANDRA SELLERS

The Sheikh and the
Runaway Princess
SUSAN MALLERY

MILLS & BOON®

*This collection is first published in Great Britain 2007
Harlequin Mills & books Limited,
Eton House, 18-24 Paradise Road, Richmond, Surrey TW9 1SR*

POSSESSED BY THE SHEIKH © Harlequin Books S.A. 2007

The publisher acknowledges the copyright holders of the
individual works, which have already been published in the UK
in single, separate volumes, as follows:

The Playboy Sheikh © Alexandra Sellers 2002
The Sheikh and the Runaway Princess
© Susan Macias-Redmond 2001

ISBN: 978 0 263 85672 9

064-0307

*Printed and bound in Spain
by Litografia Rosés S.A., Barcelona*

The Playboy Sheikh

ALEXANDRA SELLERS

ALEXANDRA SELLERS

is the author of over twenty-five novels and a feline language text published in 1997 and still selling.

Born and raised in Canada, Alexandra first came to London as a drama student. Now she lives near Hampstead Heath with her husband, Nick. They share housekeeping with Monsieur, who jumped through the window one day and announced, as cats do, that he was moving in.

What she would miss most on a desert island is shared laughter.

Readers can write to Alexandra at PO Box 9449, London NW3 2WH.

For Nick
for love's sake only

Prologue

A pair of green eyes filled the screen and smiled a challenge into the room. His stomach tightened and he caught his breath.

"This is her now," said a voice behind him.

"I know it is," said Jafar al Hamzeh. His mouth was firm with conscious control as he gazed at her. The eyes looked straight at him, into his soul.

The irises were pale green, delicately traced with darker green and russet and then bordered by a smooth, fine circle of deep emerald. The whites were pure and clear, the eyes themselves wide and slanting slightly up at the corners under straight, fair eyebrows.

He had seen those eyes close like this, and they had filled his whole world. When she had lain above him, his arms around her, and he had been consumed with a pleasure-pain that he thought would annihilate him. Or the world. He hadn't known which. Hadn't cared.

Then her eyes had been as close as this. He was aware of a deep, primitive jealousy now that the others in the room were seeing her so intimately. If he had given way to it, he would have stood up and tossed them bodily out of the studio.

The camera drew back to reveal the wide, straight forehead, smooth cheeks, the straight, slightly flat nose. Then further, and her generous, half-truculent mouth trembled into a smile. Thick, pale blond hair in a wave above her eyes fell back from her forehead and down in a luxurious tumble over one shoulder and arm.

He had lain tangled in that hair, had stroked it and threaded his fingers into it. He could feel the memory of it now on his fingertips, a sensuous silk. Its perfume was suddenly thick in his nostrils. He closed his eyes as the familiar yearning swept him.

"Very unusual beauty."

"Real individuality…"

Behind him the voices murmured, but he scarcely heard. Onscreen, she spoke briefly, turned and walked away from the camera. She was wearing a short, tight skirt that outlined her hips, showed the slender legs. Her voice was low and resonant, as always, and amused, as it had been when he last heard it. She spoke over her shoulder, a half smile toying at the corner of her mouth, then swung her head so that her hair slid from her shoulder and tumbled down her back.

He felt it like a touch. His skin burned.

The door opened and closed, and she was gone. Just the way she had walked out of his life. A smile, a shake of the head, and the sound of a closing door.

He ached now the way he had then, for the door to

open again, for her to come back, to say she had changed her mind.

"Here's another," said a voice.

She was there again, this time in a bikini, on a beach. She was eating ice cream, totally absorbed in it, while all around her men ignored reality to watch her and dream. A man capsized a boat. His passengers waved and shouted from the water, and the lifeguard leapt to attention, but it was her that he had seen. A volleyball game collapsed in mayhem as she strolled in the sunshine, her hair blowing, her beautiful body warm with female curves. A hot dog vendor drove his cart off a pier.

She is mine, he told them all.

"Fabulous," murmured a voice.

There were murmurs of agreement, but Jaf said nothing. He watched her lick the cone and mime a satisfaction that was almost sexual. He had seen that look on her face before, too, but she had not been miming then. He was sure of that.

The ice cream manufacturer's logo flashed and froze onscreen above her upturned face. "Well, I don't think we could find a better addition to the harem, could we?" a man said, as if he had a choice. As if it had not been a foregone conclusion from the beginning. "I think she'd be a gift to please any sultan. How about it, Jaf?"

He smiled and nodded. Going along with the pretence. "Fine by me," he said. As if it hardly mattered to him. As if they didn't know.

She had smiled at him before she went, half mocking, challenging him. *Do your worst,* she had said.

She would see what his worst was. A gift for the sultan first, but she would be his, all his, in the end.

One

She clung desperately to the slippery surface of the mahogany chest and rode the swell as a wave lifted her. Behind her the next wave broke with a tumbling hiss, and she gulped in air as it washed over her.

Ahead of her was the long white coastline. Beyond, miles of blinding green sea.

The sun was fierce. The salt stung her eyes. Her pale hair floated around her in the water and clung to her cheeks like rich seaweed. The long skirt of her dress, open down the front to free her legs, trailed behind her in the waves, green on green. Her legs kicked through the sparkling water, searching for a footing. As if the sea were a passionate, impatient lover, another wave rose over her and grasped her in its rough caress.

At a little distance, hidden from view behind a rocky outcrop, he sat astride a white horse, watching.

Jealousy burned in him as if he saw another man make love to her.

Her kicking foot touched ground then, and she stood upright in waist-deep water and let the wooden chest go to be pummelled and tumbled up the white sand beach by the surf.

As she struggled through the breakers, they rushed and dragged, the sea trying to pull her back into its arms. She stumbled once, and staggered, almost losing the battle, but the sea missed its moment, and she righted herself.

Still he watched, motionless, as if waiting for a sign.

The sea's froth bubbled around her as she moved, dragging her skirt back to reveal her legs and then rushing forward with it again, as if in sudden anxiety to preserve her modesty. As she came unsteadily out of the sea it danced and hissed around her slick, glowing thighs, then her knees, then her rippling calves, and finally her ankles, while her dress alternately hid and revealed her flesh.

It was an erotic and evocative striptease. His body tormented him as he imagined his hands, his mouth, his body stroking her as the waves did, reducing her to the panting exhaustion that made her breasts heave.

With a sensuous sweep, she lifted one arm to drag the long, water-soaked hair off her neck and shoulders and toss it to fall down her back. Her firm young breasts pressed against the low neckline of her dress as she moved, and her forearm showed soft and female under the green fabric.

His mount snorted and tossed its head, and he laid a hand on its neck. "Wait a little," he murmured. The horse obediently stilled.

At a point barely beyond the water's reach, in grateful, graceful exhaustion, her hands lifted high, her head fell back, and she opened her mouth with a cry of triumph and gratitude and dropped to her knees on the sand. Then she collapsed onto her back, her arms outstretched, to drink in sun and air and life.

A stronger wave rolled up the beach under her legs, lifting the skirt of her dress in a bubble and then dropping it to one side, revealing her legs again, one knee a little bent. His body hurt with the need to kiss her where the water kissed her.

The horse reacted instantly to the permission of his knees and leapt forward into a gallop. Sand flew up under its hooves. His keffiyeh and his white robe streamed out behind and his white-clad legs blended with the horse's back as if they were one creature.

They pounded along the beach together, horse and man, spattering sparkling water that caught the bright sun so that they seemed to spread diamonds in their train.

She must have felt the thunder under her back but, as if too exhausted to react, still lay without moving. Then he was almost upon her. He pulled the horse to a standstill as she turned her head against the sand to look up.

Her eyes found his face. Her mouth fell open in complete shock. She leapt to a sitting position, all trace of exhaustion gone. Totally disoriented, she cried, "What are *you* doing here?"

He smiled grimly, one eyebrow raised. "This is my land," he informed her.

"Your land?" she repeated in blank amazement.

"I told you you would come to me in the end," he said.

* * *

"What the devil's going on?" demanded Masoud al Badi, of no one in particular. "Where did that white horse come from? Where's the black horse? What the hell is Adnan doing?"

The assistant looked up from the shooting script and shrugged expressively. "I went over the scene with him, and he was on the black horse then."

The director turned his eyes back to the couple on the beach. "Isn't that Adnan out there with her? Who the hell is it? Where's Adnan?"

"I'm here," said a sheepish voice as a man in the same white desert garb as the rider came out of a nearby trailer. "It's Jafar al Hamzeh." He shrugged helplessly. "Sorry, Mr. al Badi, he said—"

"*Jaf?*" exploded the director incredulously, whirling to stare again. "Is he crazy?"

As he watched, the distant female figure struggled to her feet and started running wildly along the beach. Her naked feet left small, perfect white imprints in the wet sand as she ran.

"*Allah*, he's panicked her! She'll break her ankle!" the director cried.

A buzz ran through the set at the sound of the name, and the crew was suddenly alert. Wardrobe people and makeup artists and gofers appeared at the doors of different trailers as if someone had waved a magic wand. Jafar al Hamzeh, Cup Companion to Prince Karim, was not only rich and as handsome as the devil, he was also, at the moment, the tabloids' favourite playboy.

Things got interesting when Jafar al Hamzeh was around. If he had taken an interest in the film's star…this could be quite an adventurous shoot.

Down on the beach, the rider remained still, seated

negligently on the horse, one fist against his hip, the other casually gripping the reins, in a posture so purely, physically arrogant it was like watching a hawk or a big cat. Letting his prey run a little, his attitude said, for the sake of better sport.

The director stood as if tied, staring, while the tiny green-clad figure raced wildly down the beach. He lifted his bullhorn and shouted, but they were too far away. His voice would be feeble against the surf.

He turned and glanced around him for inspiration. Catching sight of the actor in the white desert robes, he gestured imperatively. "Adnan, get on your horse and—"

"Oh, my God!" someone gasped, and Masoud al Badi turned again.

The rider had spurred his horse to action at last. The white beast responded eagerly, leaping forward to the chase, and within moments was close behind the running woman. He did not slacken speed.

The director cursed helplessly into the bullhorn.

"Jaf! God damn it, *Jaf!*"

Those watching gave a collective gasp as, in the distance, the horseman now dropped the reins against the horse's neck. Like a trick rider in the circus, he leaned sideways out of the saddle, clinging with his knees, while the horse, galloping perilously close to the fleeing woman, moved abreast of her.

"Is he trying to run her down?" Masoud demanded furiously.

She screamed something, turning to flail her arms at him, but to no avail. The horseman's hands caught her firmly around her slim waist and he lifted her effortlessly as he straightened in the saddle. Suddenly she was sitting in front of him on the horse, being held tight in one ruthless arm. With the other he captured the reins again and urged the horse forward.

"Put me down!" Lisbet shouted wildly. "Are you trying to kill me? What the hell do you think you're doing?"

"But you dared me, Lisbet," he murmured, his face alight with a devilish smile. "When a woman dares a man of spirit it is because she wishes to provoke him to action. But she must beware. The action may not be exactly what she wished."

Lisbet gasped in outrage. "Do you imagine I wanted you to—! How did you get here, anyway? How did you know where we were?"

He smiled down into her face, showing all his teeth.

"Do you take me for a weakling, who waits for circumstance to assist him? You are not so foolish!"

Her heart was beating uncomfortably fast. At this it kicked hard. "What do you mean?"

Jaf laughed and encouraged the horse, forcing her to cling to his chest for balance. The white horse galloped effortlessly along the perfect, smooth sand with his double load. Water diamonds splashed up around them and fell back into the glittering sea.

"What do you mean, you didn't wait for circumstance?" she repeated, more loudly.

"You will learn what I mean," he said.

Once they were lovers, but that was long ago. No, not in a previous life, though such is always possible. They had met almost a year ago, when her friend and his brother were struggling through suspicion and misunderstanding towards love.

There had been no suspicion or misunderstanding

for Jaf and Lisbet. Not at the beginning. For them to look had been to love—or at least, to desire. And from desire there had been nothing to bar the rapid progress to completion.

Of a sort. But soon he came to feel that sexual completion was not all that he wanted. He had wanted, in the words of that still echoing song, to get inside her head.

She had not wanted him there. He would hold her head between his two powerful hands in the moment when passion was about to drag them away from shore and into those unfathomable depths—he would cup her head, as if it were one of the precious, paper-thin jade cups in his late father's treasury of antique art, and gaze into her eyes, watching for a sign that what swept his heart also touched her. But she would only laugh and turn her head away or, if his hands were too insistent, close her eyes as the pleasure his body made for her coursed through her.

When he became demanding, she had warned him. "Don't dream about me, Jaf. Don't look at me and see the mother of your babies. That's not who I am."

It drove him wild. Of course when he looked at her he saw the mother of his sons and daughters. He saw the grandmother of his grandchildren.

"Come with me to Barakat when I go," he pleaded, for soon he would have to return. "A visit. See whether you could live there. We would live there for part of the year only. It's a beautiful country, Lisbet."

She had smiled in that way that infuriated him— remote and untouchable. "I'm sure it is. Anna loves it there." Anna was her friend, who had married his brother—once love had conquered, as it must. "Maybe I'd love the country, too. But that's not the point, is it? It's not about Barakat versus England. It's about marriage versus freedom. And I did warn you, Jaf. Right at the start.''

''Freedom!'' he had exclaimed impatiently. How could she be so blind? ''What freedom? The freedom to grow old alone? To be without children to comfort you?''

A look he did not understand had crossed over her face then, and her eyes became shuttered. ''Exactly,'' she said cheerfully, her voice belying the expression on her face. ''The freedom to grow old alone, without children to comfort me. We're mismatched, Jaf. If you would just face that simple—''

His hand urgently clasped her neck to stop the words in her throat. ''We are not mismatched,'' he growled. ''We are the perfect mating that others only dream of.''

She had the grace to blush. ''I didn't mean sex.''

He stared at her, shaking his head, until her gaze fell. Then he said gently, to the top of her bent head. ''Sex is only one of the ways in which we are matched, Lisbet. Do you think I do not know how you struggle to hide from me? Do you understand that what I am saying means that such hiding is unnecessary?''

She had looked at him then, smiling defiantly. ''You're imagining things, Jaf.''

But he knew that he was not.

TWO

Lisbet kicked her heels futilely at the horse's powerful, rhythmically flexing shoulders. She was sitting side-saddle in front of Jaf, one hip tilted against the low pommel. In spite of his imprisoning arm, it felt precarious, and she was forced to cling to him for stability.

"Where do you think you're taking me?" she cried.

"My home is a few miles away," Jaf told her.

Lisbet gasped. "Your home! Are you crazy? Take me back to t—"

His dark eyes met hers with hard anger. "Do not speak to me in this tone, Lisbet."

She quailed, then forced her courage up. "I'm in the middle of shooting a film, Jaf!" she cried. "You've already wrecked a scene we were hoping to get in the can in one take! Take me back to the set!"

"When I am through with you," Jaf agreed, his

voice grating against her already electrified nerve ends.

Her blood surged up under her skin at the pressure of his unforgiving hold against her waist. Her body told her it had been long, too long. But she wasn't going to admit her weakness to him.

"When you're—how *dare* you? What are you planning, Jaf? Rape? Let me go!"

He laughed. "Do you pretend that rape would be possible between us? How long has it been, Lisbet? Have you counted the days?"

"No, I have not!"

"The weeks?"

"Stop this horse!"

She reached for the reins, one hand still of necessity clinging to his chest, but he simply knocked her hand aside.

"The months?" he prodded. "I want to know, Lisbet."

"It's over six months!" she snapped. "And I was not coun—"

"How much over six months?" he demanded relentlessly.

"I have no idea!"

"How much?"

"It's seven months and three weeks, damn you!"

"And how many days?"

"How the hell am I supposed to know?"

"You know."

"I do not know!"

"Then I will tell you. Four days. It is seven months, three weeks and four days since you told me to do my worst, Lisbet. Did no instinct warn you that it might be dangerous to come to my country so soon?"

"You call nearly eight months *soon?*" she gibed. "I thought you'd have forgotten my name by now."

"You were disappointed that I did not come after you?" he inquired softly. "Ah, Lisbet, if I had known…"

She stiffened, feeling the silky edges of the trap he had laid for her.

"No, I was not! After all your ranting, I was relieved."

"Liar!"

"Don't speak to me in that tone of voice, Jaf!" she snapped furiously.

He laughed. "Ah, my fire spitter! I had almost forgotten the delights of tangling with you. But we will have the pleasure of learning them all again."

"Spitfire," she said coldly. "If you're going to insult me, at least get your English right."

"Spitfire?" he repeated. "Isn't the Spitfire an aeroplane?"

"A fighter plane," she told him sweetly. "And as for the delights of warfare with me, the little Spitfire defeated the Luftwaffe, so don't get your hopes up."

He raised surprised eyebrows. "You call this war?"

"What would you call it?"

He shook his head, and she felt the muscles of his arm bunch as he drew on the horse's reins. The horse slowed.

Ahead of them a high ridge of rock erupting from the sand stretched into the sea, barring their path—one of the isolated fingers of the distant mountain range that brooded over the scene, as if, in this desperately hot, inhospitable climate, even the mountains yearned and reached for the sea.

He drew the horse to a walk, and they entered the

shadow of the ridge with relief. Lisbet put both her hands above his on the reins and now he allowed her to pull the horse to a standstill.

"One way or another, I'm going back to the set," she announced.

His jaw clenched with the possessive ferocity that had made her run the first time. "Not one hour to spare for your ex-lover?"

"While I'm working? I'm a professional, Jaf," she said. "Don't expect me to fall in with your amateur, playboy attitude to life."

His eyes glinted with an indecipherable expression. "Ah," he said. "So you didn't forget me entirely."

"It was a little difficult to forget you entirely!" she snapped. "You're in the tabloids every week."

"One of the benefits of fame I hadn't foreseen," he observed blandly.

Now he believed she had been following his career in the papers, she realized with irritation. It would have been better to pretend she knew nothing of his new status as the tabloids' favourite bad boy.

But she couldn't stop herself complaining, "That's a heady lifestyle you've got yourself. I was particularly entranced by the gold-plated limousine."

He shrugged disparagingly. "Par for the course in these parts."

"Nice for some. But I have a job to do."

Her hands on the reins, she guided the horse into a 180-degree turn. Jaf allowed it, but when she tried to spur the horse to move, it froze into immobility.

She was startled to see how far they had come. She had expected to see, in the distance, the cluster of trailers, equipment, umbrellas and people that marked the filming location, but the sand was empty. They were

alone. A thrill of fear shivered through her. In this
barren landscape and merciless, unforgiving climate,
she was at his mercy.

Just what she had always feared.

"Damn it!" Lisbet exclaimed, urging the reins, and
nudging the horse's foreleg with her bare heels. The
horse might as well have been carved of wood. "Move
damn it!" she cried. And then, "What have you done
to this horse?"

He laughed, showing white teeth. His eyes sparkled
in a way she remembered they had even in London's
damp. Here in the harsh sunshine the look dazzled her.

"Firouz and I have been together for six years," he
said. "If you understood me as well as he does…"

Lisbet gritted her teeth. "It would be better if *you*
understood *me!*" she snapped. "Now, are you going
to get this horse to move and take me back to the set,
or am I going to get down and walk?"

It was a long way in such heat, and if she did not
get lost, she would get sunburn, if not actual sunstroke.
She could feel the prickle of drying salt on her skin
and knew that the sea had washed off some, if not all,
of her protection.

"You can't walk in the sun," he told her, looking
down at her bare legs, the rise of her breasts in the
revealing neckline of the costume. It was a look she
remembered all too well. Her skin tingled under the
drying salt. "You are nearly naked. My house is cool
inside. It is among trees, a date plantation."

"Take me back," she said stonily, kicking futilely
at the immovable horse. Her eyes scoured the horizon
for some sign that someone was coming to her rescue.
"They must have called the police by now. They must
think you're a kidnapper."

"But that is what I am," Jaf pointed out.

"What have you done to Adnan?" she almost shrieked.

"Your imagination is very vivid, but perhaps that is a professional necessity for an actress," he said. Lisbet ground her teeth. She had never had an easy time controlling her temper around him. "I have done nothing to Adnan Amani except ease his financial worries for the immediate future."

"You *bribed* him to let you take his place?" she cried, outraged.

"Would you prefer that I had knocked him on the head and tied him up? Violence should always be a last resort," he chided.

"Of course I wouldn't prefer—" Lisbet began heatedly, then realized that he was succeeding in putting her in the wrong. She heaved a breath.

"Take me back to the set."

"On one condition."

"To hell with your condition!"

"You must have dinner with me this evening."

"Dinner! If that was all you wanted, why didn't you come to Gazi and Anna's? You must know I've been staying there!"

Coming to the Barakat Emirates to shoot the movie a week ago, she had naturally stayed with Anna and Gazi. It would have been natural for Jaf to visit them, but he made no move to try and see her. "We usually see him once or twice a week," Anna had said apologetically. "He must be very busy."

Lisbet had been half relieved, half anxious. If there was going to be a meeting, she wanted to get it over with. If not, she'd have liked to be certain of that.

He laughed. "Did you miss me?"

"I never expected you to come. Why would you want to see me? Why do you now?"

"What I have to say to you is not for public consumption," he said.

Her heart pounded. She was afraid of him in this steely mood. She remembered how hard it had been to shut him out of her life. It had taken all her determination. "I'm not interested," she said stonily.

"You do not agree to come?"

"We finished months ago, Jaf. It's over and it's going to stay that way."

He seemed to make no move, and yet the horse lifted a delicate foreleg and stepped around in place, till it was facing the rocky ridge and the sea again.

"My house is beyond this point," he said. The horse moved into the sea. "It is well protected. Once we are there, no one will reach you except with my permission."

"Let me down!" she cried.

She struggled, but he held her tight, and the horse moved faster. She could not risk jumping, especially when she couldn't be sure of the surface under the water. If her foot landed on a rock, if she fell or the horse kicked her...

"Now, or tonight, Lisbet? One way or another, you will see me." The horse was moving into deeper water, on a heading around the thrusting finger of rock.

She could feel determination in him. Her feet were now brushing the surface of the water. Her body skittered with nervous anticipation.

After the months of silence, she had begun to believe that he had forgotten her, forgotten all his protestations of love. During the past week of waiting every night on tenterhooks for him to turn up at dinner, she had been convinced. And now, suddenly, here he was, angry, unforgiving, punitive.

She felt disoriented. She suddenly felt she didn't know him. He was in his own country, on his own territory, taking her she knew not where. She was a foreigner, and he was influential here.

"All right!" she exploded, furious at her own capitulation.

The horse stopped instantly. Jaf frowned into her eyes. "You will have dinner with me tonight?"

"Yes, I'll have dinner with you, damn you! But not at your house. I'll go with you to a restaurant, and that's final. So if you were expecting more than dinner, forget it! A face over a meal is all you'll get."

His head inclined with regal acceptance, making her feel like a rude peasant in the presence of the lord of the manor. "But of course," Jaf said, as if she had made an indelicate remark. "What else?"

Firouz turned in place and began to pace back out of the water, as precise as a circus horse.

"Just as long as you realize there'll be no sex for dessert," Lisbet said defiantly.

"Do *you* realize it?" Jaf said.

They met two dune buggies halfway. Jaf laughed and reined in. "Your rescuers are only a little late," he said.

"Lisbet, are you all right?" the director demanded, piling out of one of the vehicles in half-crazed concern. "Is everything okay?"

They had galloped in silence, Jaf's chest against her back, the horse moving powerfully under her thighs, in a twin reminder of masculine might. Lisbet was filled with such a churning of conflicting and varied emotions she couldn't find words.

One of the grips was there to help her down, but the dark, stocky director pushed him aside and solicitously reached up for her himself. She slipped out of Jaf's strong hold and down onto the sand, and only when his protection was gone felt the loss.

Jaf's face was stone as he watched the movement drag the dress of her skirt up around her hips, revealing the full length of her legs and the lacy underwear.

Masoud, glancing up at Jaf, let her go a moment too quickly. Lisbet staggered a little and then straightened.

"No, everything is not all right," she informed the director in quiet fury. "Do you know this man? I won't work while he's on the set," she said, storming off towards the dune buggy.

She was hoping for an argument, because Jaf was certain to lose. But she might have known better. She had taken no more than two steps when there came the sound of hooves. Involuntarily, Lisbet turned. Jafar al Hamzeh, his robes flying, magnificent on the white horse, was riding back the way they had come.

Minutes later, Lisbet slammed into the welcome if erratic air conditioning of her trailer. Tina, her dresser, wide-eyed with unspoken curiosity, fluttered in anxious concern while she struggled with the buttons on her costume.

"You've been in the sun too long! Is your nose burned? I *told* Masoud, less than half an hour and then we need to reapply the sun block!"

Lisbet was suddenly exhausted. Her meeting with Jaf seemed to have drained her of energy. "Save it, Tina. I want a shower," she said, stripping off the torn costume.

Then she was under the cooling spray. Cast and crew had all been asked to use the fresh water sparingly, since it had to be trucked onto the site, but Lisbet forgot that as she held her face to the cool stream.

If only other things could be so easily forgotten.

She had met Jafar al Hamzeh when he came to ask for her help. Her best friend, Anna Lamb, was in trouble and needed her. Naturally, she had agreed to go with him.

There was an immediate spark between them. He made no secret of his attraction to her. That evening, having given Anna the help she needed, Lisbet had had to leave for work—shooting an exterior scene for an episode of a television series, on Hampstead Heath. Jaf had driven her to the location and then stayed to keep her company—all night.

She would never forget the electricity of that night. Sitting in the deeper dark behind the floodlights, bundled up against the chill, she and Jaf gazed into each other's eyes, talking about nothing and everything, while she waited to be called. Each time she went on set to do a take, she feared he would have gone when she got back, but he was always there, waiting.

There was a connection between them like a taut, singing wire, and over the course of that long night, the electric charge got stronger and stronger till Jaf was more blinding than the floodlights.

He had taken her home in the limousine, and she had invited him in for coffee. As they entered the darkened apartment he kissed her, suddenly, hungrily, as if he had let go a self-restraint of banded steel. It was their first kiss, and it exploded on their lips with fiery sweetness. The thought of it, even now, could make chills run over her skin.

She would never forget that first time, making love with Jaf as the sun came up over the damp roofs of London. Not if she lived to be a hundred.

Afterwards, she had worried that, coming from so different a culture, he would think her cheap, despise her for such ease of conquest. He left her with a passionate kiss in the morning, saying he would call her soon, and her fear whispered that for him it had been no more than a one-night stand.

The limousine was waiting for her at the curb when she left the television studio that evening. Her heart leapt so hard she staggered. It took her—or perhaps, she had told herself, giggling, in the lush, leather-lined splendour of the Rolls, *swept* was the more appropriate word—to the Dorchester Hotel.

No one at the Dorchester even raised an eyebrow at her grubby sweatpants, the frayed sweater, the ragged bomber jacket, her shiny, just-scrubbed face, the hair caught up with a couple of jumbo clips, the extra-long scarf taking three turns around her neck.

"You might have given a girl some warning!" she protested, when Jaf opened the door on the penthouse suite. He was standing in an entrance hall bigger than her whole flat.

His smile made her drunker than champagne. "What should I have warned you about?"

He put out a hand and drew her inside, and before she could begin to answer his mouth closed on hers, hungry and demanding.

Later, they lay lazily entwined in each other, while he stroked her back, her hip, her thigh. Above them, a huge skylight showed them the stars. His hold was light, and yet he seemed to protect and enclose her. She had never felt so safe.

They looked up at the stars, and he complained at how pale they were, compared to the sky in Barakat.

"Once, when I was very young," Jaf murmured, "I was with my grandfather as he examined a collection of diamonds. I can still see those stones dropping onto the black velvet cushion my grandfather had set down. They sparkled with black fire. They dazzled my eyes."

"Mmmm," she said, as his hand painted little sparkles of electricity along her spine.

"My mother said afterwards, though I don't remember that part of it, that I absolutely insisted on touching them. All I remember is that I was lifted up and put my hands out, and my grandfather dropped diamonds onto my palms. It was a moment that thrilled me beyond description."

Lisbet smiled, picturing him as a little boy, trembling with delight. "I wonder why it had such impact."

"Because I thought I was touching the stars, Lisbet," he said softly. "That is what the stars are like in my country. They are diamonds. I really believed that my grandfather had brought down stars and a piece of sky. It was a moment of almost mystical ecstasy."

Lisbet smiled, touched and charmed by the image. She turned her head and looked up at the night sky. "Yes, I see."

Jaf's arms tightened around her. He gazed down into her upturned face and saw starlight in her eyes. For a moment there was pure silence.

"I have never had such a feeling again until now," he whispered, lifting one hand to her cheek. "Till now I never touched the stars again."

Three

"**H**e's here," Lisbet's dresser said breathlessly, tapping and entering the trailer that was Lisbet's living quarters for the duration of the location shoot. Tina was trying to disguise her excitement, but still her tone of voice irritated Lisbet.

"You sound like a pensioner meeting the Queen," she muttered.

"Funny you should say that. When I was twelve I met Princess Diana. It was the most exciting moment of my life," Tina said with a grin. "I've met plenty of celebrities since then, but in this business the glitter goes fast. Nothing's ever had quite the impact. Until now."

Lisbet knew she was joking, but couldn't help responding in a repressive tone, "What's so hot about Jafar al Hamzeh?"

"Hey, you're the one who's going to have dinner with him!"

Lisbet shrugged. No one here was aware that she had known Jaf before, and she had no intention of letting them know.

Tina gave her a look. "You do know he's one of Prince Karim's Cup Companions, don't you?"

"Yes, I know."

But Tina was in full swing. "So's his brother Gazi. In these parts that's sort of like being a rock star, except that they also have political clout. Rashid—one of the grips—told me that the tradition of the Cup Companions goes back a very long way, to pre-Islamic times, but in the old days they were just the guys the king relaxed with. They were deliberately excluded from the executive process. Nowadays, they form what amounts to the prince's cabinet. Most of them have specific responsibilities, and they all have a lot of influence, right across the board. And they're as loyal as it gets, to each other and the princes."

Lisbet wanted to shout at her to shut up. But she concentrated on her lipstick and did not answer.

"He's rich, too, Lisbet—stinking rich, since his father died, according to the scuttlebutt on the set—and, they say, very generous. Also spending mad. Those stories in the press aren't all scandalmongering, apparently. He's going through his inheritance like water over a falls. He dropped half a million barakatis in one sitting at the casino a couple of nights ago, and got up completely unfazed. If you play it right, you could dip your bucket into the flow and put something away for a comfortable old age."

She paused, but Lisbet was still carefully outlining

her lips in a pinky beige. Tina frowned. With that out-fit, her lips should be wine-red.

"And incredibly sexy, on top of it. What about the way he galloped after you on the beach—woo! We were all practically fainting. And when he actually picked you up on the fly—I swear I got sensory burn from here. What did he say when he had you on the horse?"

"Nothing much." Lisbet set down the lipstick brush and sat back to examine the result. "Certainly I don't recall hearing any apology for risking my life in a circus stunt."

Tina manifestly disbelieved her indifference. She waggled her eyebrows.

"Well, anytime he wants to perform a stunt with me, he's welcome!" Tina said. "Did you know he was on the Barakat Emirates' Olympic equestrian team in 1996, and they got a gold? And in his wild youth, when he was at university in the States, he spent his holidays in a circus or rodeo or something."

Lisbet knew it all, but she wasn't going to have everyone on the set raking over her ancient affair with Jaf if she could help it.

"A rodeo would be just the place for him. The wonder is why he ever left," she said. She got to her feet and checked herself in the mirror. She was wearing a knee-length tunic top over pants, all in a soft knitted oatmeal silk, a few shades darker than her hair.

"You've got to be joking!" The dresser was un-stoppable now. "The man oozes sensuality. He re-minds me of those old French movie stars. Belmondo. Delon. *Je t'aime, moi non plus.* Ooooh." Tina picked up the matching calf-length silk coat and held it as

Lisbet slipped her arms into the sleeves. "I wish it were me he was after. Yum!"

"He is not after me!" Lisbet said irritably. She shrugged into the coat and reached for her evening bag. Tina's litany was only making her more nervous. She wondered why she had capitulated to his ridiculous ultimatum. She should have realized he couldn't make it stick.

Maybe she just couldn't resist seeing him one more time.

"Silly me, I thought he was," Tina corrected herself in a tone of extreme irony. "He was just warning you off his land, then, was he? Did you know he owns the whole stretch of beach along here?" she added in parentheses. "We're on his land."

Lisbet concentrated on her reflection. Her leather sandals and handbag matched the oatmeal silk, and her long hair was held back with a tiny braided ribbon of the same colour. She had chosen the outfit carefully, for its cool, undramatic elegance. It was the furthest thing from deliberately sexy, she told herself, that you could find.

Her earrings were thin squares of beaten gold. With them she wore a gold chain necklace...and on the third finger of her left hand, a large pearl ring.

"You look fabulous!" Tina said, hoping her tone disguised her faint disappointment. She began unnecessarily brushing Lisbet down, and tweaked a fold of her coat. She wished Lisbet had left her hair loose or worn a touch of colour. Anyone would think she was deliberately dressing her warm sexuality down, but Tina couldn't believe anyone would act in such a stupid and self-defeating way.

It must be nerves. Because Lisbet, as her dresser
had quickly learned, had a craftsman's eye for what
suited her. She could always add just that personal
touch to a costume that made it her own, giving it a
flair the camera loved. That was Tina's yardstick for
what made a star.

But as the actress moved to the door Tina blinked
and took a second look. Maybe Lisbet knew what she
was doing after all. She supposed Arabs were as sus-
ceptible to the Ice Maiden myth as other men, and the
hinting motion of Lisbet's body under that silk might
just drive a guy wild.

At first she had given herself up to the passion that
consumed them.

They had a devastating, emotionally tormenting,
crazily passionate time together. Like nothing she had
ever experienced. Sometimes she felt drunk, so drunk
she was reeling. Sometimes she felt that Jaf had her
heart in his hand. A word, a look, had a power over
her that was completely outside her previous experience.

It frightened her. Not just his possessiveness, but
her own response to it. And she had plenty of reason
to fear having her life taken over.

It touched Lisbet on an old but ever tender wound.

It had been out of motives of love that her father
had deliberately got her mother pregnant, in order to
put an end to her promised stage career and keep her
with him.

That had been a long time ago, when the morality
of the swinging sixties hadn't quite reached the small
Welsh mining village where the young lovers lived.

Gillian Raine had won a place at drama school and was waiting for the summer to end before leaving for London and another life. Her lover, Edward MacArthur, had already done what every man in the village did—he had started work down the coal mines.

The cautionary tale of her mother's murdered dreams had been burned into Lisbet from a child. How he had pleaded with her to stay home and marry him. How she had had to give in when she learned she was pregnant... *Never give up your dreams, girls,* her mother had warned them.

As they grew into teenagers, the story became clearer. Then Gillian told her daughters how that life-changing pregnancy had occurred. Told them of the fateful night when Edward had asked her to turn her back on drama college, stay at home and marry him....

Gillian had resisted all Edward's pleading and, when he knew he had lost the argument, he began to kiss her.

Her daughters, educated in the new model of the world, had asked breathlessly, "Did Dad date rape you, Mama?"

She had laughed impatiently. "No, no, don't you see what I'm trying to tell you? He was such a lover, your father, he just—girls, he just kissed me till..." She sighed. "Always before we'd used protection. That night he had none. But he was so passionate. I forgot everything, I wanted him and I didn't care. A few weeks later I cared, right enough. When I told him I was pregnant I saw that he'd meant to do it."

She had given up her dreams, married her lover, settled down to the grind of life as a miner's wife and produced a string of children.

And never ceased to regret the life she might have had.

Lisbet had listened closely to the terrible warnings. She didn't want a life like her mother's. Always regretting what she hadn't done. *If it hadn't been for you lot, that would be me up there,* she would say when they sat around the television watching the latest costume drama.

Still, life had been more or less happy before the closure of the mines. Until then her father had come home at night exhausted and black with coal dust, maybe, but he was a man who held up his head. A man who made his wife smile with secret anticipation over the dinner table when he gave her burning looks out of those dark Celtic eyes.

Lisbet was just approaching her teens when the great miners' strike was called, the prime minister infamously sent in the mounted strikebreakers, and an era came to an end. When the dust and blood cleared, the coal mines were finished, and so was Lisbet's father.

More than his mine was gone, more than his job. His faith in British justice and fair play, and much else besides, was destroyed. His vision of himself had been shattered.

He had never worked again, except for casual labour here and there. It was his wife who went to work now, an even deeper shame for a man like him. Gillian worked in the little fish and chip shop, practically the only enterprise that survived the economic disaster that had engulfed the village, and came home smelling of cigarette smoke and half-rancid cooking fat, her hair lank and her once-beautiful face shiny with grease.

Her husband had hated the fact that his wife now had to work, without having the will to get up and change his life. He was a failure in the first source of pride he had, and it unmanned him completely. He began to drink.

The only bright side had been that there were no mines now for Lisbet's brothers to go down. Their choice was different—join the ranks of the unemployed, or leave their village.

The MacArthurs were all bright. They had all gone on to higher education, in those days when, thank God, students from poor backgrounds were still being given full study grants. They had all worked hard, done well, gone on to good jobs.

Lisbet was always the special one. Lisbet, inheriting her mother's beauty as well as her taste for theatre, had gone to a prestigious London drama college, with the weight of both their dreams on her shoulders. There she had left behind her musical regional accent and her father's name. She chose her mother's maiden name as a stage name, and Elizabeth Raine MacArthur became Lisbet Raine.

At graduation, she had won the most coveted prize, the Olivier Medal. Since then, she had worked steadily, mostly in television, getting bigger and better parts as time went by.

Lisbet knew at first hand that real security lay only in oneself. Not in marriage or a man. Not in letting someone else run your life according to their own tastes. The only real security was to become someone on your own merits. Only achievement lasted. Her mother was living proof that in the end you could count on no one but yourself.

For a woman, love was full of pitfalls. So, very soon after her affair with Jaf began, Lisbet was thinking of her independence. She didn't want any misunderstandings about her expectations—or Jaf's.

He bought her jewellery for her birthday, a beautiful gold bangle studded with rubies and diamonds. She was thrilled, but said with a smile, "It'll come in handy to pawn next time I'm between jobs." And she laughed when he furiously said that of course she would apply to him if she were ever broke, all the rest of her life.

"Oh, sure. And how will I get to you through your staff and what will I say when your secretary says you don't know the name and can I tell him what it's about?"

"I will forget nothing about you," Jaf said, kissing her with ruthless passion. "From the first moment I saw you, there is not a moment I will forget."

She thought he was the most wonderful, thoughtful lover a woman could have. But that only increased her risk. "Your lies are liquid honey," she told him softly. "So sweet, so delicious."

"You don't believe it because you don't *want* to believe it," he had railed at her. "You avoid commitment by pretending to think that I am not serious, Lisbet. You tell yourself it is impossible for a rich and influential man to love you and you ignore the fact that your friend and my brother have married!"

On one level, it was true. When Anna and Gazi married, it shook her badly. Marriage was not for her, and she had been deeply dismayed by the yearnings that had surfaced as she stood beside her friend during the sweetly moving wedding service.

Maybe that was the first moment she understood that her affair with Jaf was a very dangerous liaison, and would have to end.

When Lisbet opened the door of her trailer, the first thing she saw, a few yards away down one of the metal roads that were temporarily crisscrossing the desert sand, was a Rolls. The chauffeur, in polo shirt and trousers, was wiping down the immaculate paintwork while chewing industriously on a toothpick. The limousine was a spotless, creamy white. The bumpers and handles—all the trim that should be chrome— were gold.

So it was true. She hadn't believed it, reading about the car in the papers. It was a long way from the Jaf she had known.

But maybe he'd just known that a thing like the gold-plated Rolls wouldn't go over very well in laid-back Britain.

A large number of the crew seemed to be lounging in doorways and under awnings, with no apparent purpose. Lisbet frowned and shook her head in disbelief as she realized that they were actually hanging around to watch the meeting between her and Jaf.

This afternoon's little drama had ignited people's imaginations.

The director, Masoud, was standing by his office trailer, talking to someone. The other man stood with his back to her in a black kaftan and keffiyah. It was the kind of dress worn, at times, by every male from waiter to prince in the Barakat Emirates.

Lisbet paused for a moment in the doorway, gazing at him. She had never seen Jafar al Hamzeh in Eastern clothing before, unless you counted this afternoon's Lawrence of Arabia getup, but she knew it was him.

He seemed to have sensors on his back, too, because he instantly straightened and turned around and stared along the tiny "street" to the door of her trailer.

Jaf stood motionless, just looking, as she stepped out of her trailer and moved towards him. Her hair was drawn back to reveal the soft curves of her cheek and throat, the delicate sculpting of her ears, where beaten gold glowed in the late-afternoon sunlight. Flowing silk just darker than her hair brushed her body with every movement, simultaneously revealing and cloaking the curve of arm, thigh, breast. Blood rushed to his hands, burning him with the sensual memory of those curves.

Lisbet, under the intensity of his gaze, half stumbled, her fingers automatically spreading to steady herself. Jaf came to meet her, while the chauffeur stowed his polishing cloth and opened the door of the sumptuously appointed, gold-plated limousine. He was still resolutely chewing the toothpick.

The elegant Rolls-Royce emblem had been removed from the nose of the car, and Lisbet's eyes were irresistibly drawn to the grotesque gold statuette that took its place—a full-breasted, naked woman in a kind of swan dive, her back arched and her hair streaming out behind her.

Well, she had seen a picture of it, but she hadn't believed it.

"And some people say Arabs have no taste!" she marvelled.

"Out here this counts as the stripped-down model," Jaf assured her.

"So I see." She bent forward to peer inside the car. It was a vision of luscious white leather, burnished wood, Persian carpets, and more gold trim.

"What a lot of buttons!" she exclaimed in mock wonder, catching sight of a large panel of gold-plated switches on the armrest. "What do they all do?"

"I can only say it would be inadvisable to push any without prior notice."

She couldn't help laughing at that, but Jaf's mouth suddenly lost its smile. He gazed at her with an unreadable expression that held no humour.

"Get in," he said.

Sudden, superstitious fear pulsed in her. She'd never seen this side of him. She'd never seen him dressed like this. Here in his own country—on his own property—he was a stranger to her. A man who owned a gold-plated car.

She didn't have a clue what he wanted from her tonight. But he looked as if he meant to get it.

She stood helplessly at the car door, battling with herself. She half felt she should refuse to go with this stranger, but her heart was beating with excitement and anticipation as well as nervous fear. His presence still affected her physically. Probably it always would.

He didn't repeat his command, giving her nothing to kick against. The chauffeur was standing there expectantly, and everyone was more or less discreetly watching. Mostly less. After a moment Lisbet obediently bent and got in.

For all the ostentation, the leather seat was silky smooth, divinely comfortable. She slipped over to the right side as Jaf followed her inside and the door closed after him.

Masoud, the director, lifted his hand in farewell, and members of the crew stared unabashedly now as the car backed and turned, and carefully started along the metal slats of the temporary road.

They had scarcely moved beyond the immediate area of the movie camp, where desert stretched all around them, when Jaf reached out to grasp her wrist. Lisbet's breath hissed with surprise.

"What is this?" he asked softly, lifting her hand. Left hand. His voice was deep, and running with dangerous undercurrents. Like the sea.

"You can see for yourself, a pearl solitaire with diamond chips."

He gave one slow blink, silently watching her. It was totally unnerving.

The sun was setting over the water. It had taken on a rich glow, painting the sea with thick gold. On the other side of the sky, behind the mountains, darkness approached. A portent, maybe.

Jaf remained silent, his eyes burning into hers. In spite of herself she was compelled to speak.

"An engagement ring, Jaf," she said, a little more loudly than necessary.

He didn't move, but now she was nervous of him. His eyes darkened all at once, in a way she knew.

He touched a switch, and the window beside him rolled smoothly down. The fine sand dust caused by their passing swirled gently into the car.

Lisbet gazed at him in puzzlement, blinking as his grip tightened on her wrist. Then he lifted her hand, dragged the ring down the length of her finger, and flung it out the window.

He didn't speak a word. His hand dropped to the panel and the window glided silently up again.

Lisbet's heart seemed to stop. Whorls of furious excitement exploded into a dance over her skin. "How *dare* you?" she choked.

He gave a contemptuous flick of his chin in the direction of the vanished ring. "It wasn't even genuine. Is the man a fool? Are you?"

Lisbet bit her lip. She had borrowed it from the costume mistress's collection only an hour ago. She'd thought it looked pretty good, but she ought to have known that Jaf would know the difference at a glance.

"I know it's not real!" she improvised wildly. "We're both stretched financially at the moment, but he said he wasn't having me coming out here to sheikh country without some badge of possession on my finger."

Jaf stared at her, so bemused she almost laughed. She was doing her best on the spur of the moment, but she had to agree, it was a pretty feeble story.

"And who is this fool who expects a cheap *souk* ring to be enough to hold his claim to a woman like you?"

"His name is Roger," Lisbet said furiously.

"Roger what?"

She gave him a look, her lips firmly closed. He released her hand at last, and she pulled it back to her lap. It was pins and needles up to her elbow, as though his touch had cut off the blood supply, which was ridiculous.

"Six months ago you were not the marrying kind," he reminded her harshly.

"People change."

He was stretched against the upholstery, one arm along the back of the seat, the other elbow propped against the armrest, but she didn't make the mistake of thinking he was relaxed. His tension shimmered in the air.

"And how have you changed, Lisbet?"

The ring had been the impulse of the moment, like putting on a magic talisman to avert the evil eye. She should have known he wouldn't let it pass without question.

But she wasn't exactly rehearsed in the role of adoring fiancée.

"Could we change the subject, please?"

"You don't like to talk about him?"

"Not to you."

"Does Roger understand that he is marrying a woman with no heart?" His anger was being ruthlessly kept in check. "Does he give up the desire for children for the sake of possessing you?"

The Rolls was still creeping along the steel road. There was no other way to travel along such a surface, but Lisbet's claustrophobia was intensified by the dead slow pace. Long purple-grey shadows stretched out from the dunes over the rippling surface of the sand.

"Roger and I are perfectly agreed on what we want from the future, thank you!"

He smiled, but it was the smile of a tiger. "Poor Lisbet."

"What does *that* mean?"

"You will never be happy with a yes-man."

"Roger is not a yes-man!"

"Then he is a fool. A man who does not want children is a fool, or a liar."

She thought of her father, and her heart hardened. "All men aren't as primitive as you, Jaf."

His eyes flashed dangerously. "Be careful. You might make me imagine that you are speaking from your desires rather than your observations."

"Is that a threat?" she demanded shrilly.

His hand moved and his fingers caught the errant little curl of hair at her temple that could never be tamed. He stroked it around his forefinger while little jolts of electricity rushed down her temple and jaw and shot into her body.

"I only say what you should already know."

Lisbet gritted her teeth. What a fool she had been to come out with him thinking to find protection in a cheap ring! She slapped his hand away.

"I think you're confusing me with someone else."

"I could prove to you that I am not."

"No, you could not!" Lisbet said quickly.

"Too loyal to Roger to fan an old flame?"

"Of course!"

"Did you tell him about me?"

"Briefly, along with several others."

One eyebrow flickered.

"Does he know you're seeing me tonight?"

Lisbet hesitated for a fatal moment. "Yes," she said. She knew it sounded like a lie.

He nodded, as if to himself. "Did you plan it, then, Lisbet? You are engaged to another man, and yet you risked coming here, living at my brother's house. What did you tell yourself? That I could be put off by a ring from the bazaar and a distant fiancé?

"But no, you knew better than that!" he answered himself. "What was in your mind? Another quick, meaningless affair? Is that what you planned for when you came? A little reprise of passion with a barbarian before going back to marry a safe man, a man from your own culture? Did you hope I would be too hungry for your body to turn away from the crumbs you offer? Did you cast me in the part of the beggar at the gates, Lisbet? You mistook me."

His lips smiled. But as his black eyes met hers a shiver of danger traced her skin. As if she were looking into a cave where a wolf lurked in the darkness.

"Do you tell yourself that I still want you, Lisbet? Do you imagine that it is impossible to kill a love such as mine?" His voice grated over her soul, rough and sharp together. "Or did you hope to find that I had now developed a taste for heartless passion like yours?"

The tirade was more than she could stand. With a silent cry she launched herself at him, both arms lifting, to beat him or strangle him, she hardly knew.

But Jaf was an Olympic-level sportsman, and his reflexes were well honed. His hands snapped out and caught her wrists in midair, and suddenly everything changed. His eyes darkened as he drew her close and held her wrists in an unbreakable grip.

"Do not push too hard, Lisbet," he warned harshly.

She could smell the scent that was uniquely Jafar, his cologne, his sweat, his skin, and it reminded her of moments of pleasure so extreme she had wept for joy.

"Let go!" she cried.

"A woman so concerned for her freedom should be careful before she provokes a man."

"All right, I'm sorry! Let me go!"

For answer, he dragged her wrists together and slowly, agonizingly, pulled them in against his chest, trapping them there as he wrapped his arms around her, drawing her close. Her heart leapt into her throat, choking her. A trickle of sweat moved like a tear down her temple and cheek.

"Let you go?" he repeated, in a hoarse whisper. His lips were almost brushing hers as he spoke, sending tendrils of sensation into her flesh, little harbingers of pleasure to come. "But I did let you go. If you really wanted to be free of me, Lisbet, why did you come to my country?"

Four

His mouth came down on hers, ferocious with hunger. Her heart fluttered, her blood surged. Heat like the noonday sun scorched her skin, leaving it parched and thirsty for the balm of the very touch that burned her.

His hands seemed to turn the silk of her clothes to flame, so that every twitch of her skin met more burning. His lips were unforgiving, his tongue hungry and demanding. His arms pressed and held her, imprisoning and protecting her at the same time.

Everything was contradiction, except for the central joy of hunger assuaged. That was why she couldn't move, couldn't struggle. Tell the man who has been lost in the desert not to drink. Tell the woman who was shut up in darkness not to gaze at the sun. Tell an escaped prisoner not to dance.

Jaf lifted his mouth at last and drew a shuddering breath. Released from that punishing, tormenting kiss,

Lisbet regained a little self-control. She pushed him away. She could feel tears burning her eyes without understanding what had summoned them.

"Was that supposed to be some kind of punishment?" she cried.

Jaf's eyes narrowed dangerously. "Punishment? Is that what my kiss is to you?"

Lisbet turned angrily away.

"Answer me, Lisbet! The touch of my mouth was distasteful to you?"

The lie wouldn't get past her throat.

"You think so, anyway!" she cried.

"*I* think so? What would make me think that you had changed so completely? You, the woman who melted for me as woman has never melted for man before. I hear your cries in my dreams, Lisbet, even now. And I wake to weep that you are not there. And you pretend to think that I know my touch is a punishment to you?"

She was shaking, and held her hands tightly in her lap. "I didn't say…" she began, but couldn't find any words.

He sat back into the corner, his arms spread, facing her, like a judge. His kaftan was fading into shadow now. The keffiyah stood out, circling his head. His eyes fixed on her face, locked with her gaze. In every way he seemed a stranger.

She managed to turn away, and stared out of the window. The last rays of the setting sun washed the clouds in pinky gold, and the dunes threw long navy shadows now that made the desert seem a haunted, magical place. Above, the sky was turning a deep shade that could only be called purple.

He had told her she would love the desert.

"Is that what you wanted me to believe when I received these?" he demanded, after a long, charged silence. He lifted his hands to the neckline of his robe and pulled it open, reached inside and extracted something flat and black.

Her heartbeat quickened a little, and she caught her breath as he opened the wallet and dragged a little sheaf of papers from it. With a flick of the wrist, he tossed it into her lap. The air caught it and half a dozen slips of paper showered over her.

She felt his anger like a little electric shock. Lisbet reached a shaking hand to one of the pieces of paper and drew it up, straining to see it in the gloom. Then another.

They were all identical. Personal cheques, made out to Sheikh Jafar al Hamzeh, and signed by Lisbet Raine MacArthur.

It was Jaf telling her that he wanted to set her up in a flat that was the beginning of the end.

Bit by bit, Jaf had been proving himself every bit as possessive as he was passionate. Now he wanted to own the home she lived in. If she allowed that, in a certain fundamental way she was admitting that he owned her. He would always have the upper hand.

Except for the fact that it didn't seem big enough when Jaf was there, she was comfortable in her current home. She was renting a large studio flat on the top floor of an Edwardian house in North London. It was a bit out of the city centre, but as a space it was great for the money. All her friends said so. She was lucky. She might not be so lucky another time.

If, for example, she and Jaf disagreed over something, and the only option was for her to go. She might have a hard time finding so good a place at short notice.

So she was adamant. Thanks for the thought, but she would stay where she was.

Not long after, as luck would have it, she was given her notice on the studio. The house had been unexpectedly sold to people who wanted to restore it to a single-family dwelling. And suddenly Lisbet was facing a bleak midwinter hunting for somewhere new.

She soon discovered just how lucky she had been. The rental market was at a peak, and her money wasn't going to go as far this time around. And after a dry two months on the work scene, Lisbet didn't have any money to spare.

Of course she wouldn't ask Jaf for help. By that point she had turned him down so often Jaf had given up talking about buying her a place. She regretted her decision only in weak moments.

After a couple of depressing weeks spent in fruitless apartment hunting, Lisbet realized that her best option for the moment would be to share. Eventually she found a wonderful apartment share in a breathtaking apartment with a view over Primrose Hill, an area she really loved.

For the owner it was little more than a pied-à-terre, the agent explained. A lawyer who did a lot of work in Hong Kong, she was sharing because she preferred to have someone in the flat full-time. She wanted someone responsible, someone who would take care of her plants and the beautiful furnishings and works of art.

Lisbet could scarcely believe her luck when she landed it. Sacrifices would have to be made, of course. It was more than Lisbet could comfortably afford at the moment, and her own bedroom was the smallest room in the place. But the flat itself was an absolute dream, beautifully decorated, with wonderful light and a terrace filled with plants.

Jaf was less than delighted. "How will we make love in that tiny bed?" he asked. "It is even smaller than the one in your flat. I don't see how you can be happy in such a room. You haven't even met your roommate."

"You're spoiled," she told him. "You have no idea how ordinary people live. I'd be happy in a broom cupboard in a place like that. Are you kidding? I'll have that huge place to myself at least three weeks of every month! Even if I can't stand her, for a place like that I could put up with Godzilla himself one week out of four."

So he shrugged and stopped objecting, and helped Lisbet with the move. She had to sell most of her own furniture rather than put it in storage, because she couldn't afford both storage fees and the rent, but she wasn't going to worry about that.

It wasn't till she'd been living in the place for a week that Jaf gave her the title deeds in her name.

It had all been a hoax—the Hong Kong lawyer, the sharing one week a month—it had been just a game to entice her to sell her furniture, make the move, to get her to the point of no return.

But if he was expecting trembling gratitude, his plans backfired. It had exactly the reverse effect of what he had probably designed. Maybe he had meant it for the best, but Lisbet was furious at this calculated interference in her life, casual undermining of her self-determination.

If she didn't actually feel trapped, she certainly felt

how easy it had been for him to force his will on her. And without her being at all aware of it till it was done.

Jaf couldn't see it. All he had done was circumvent a misplaced pride in her. She needed a place to live. He had provided it. What could be wrong with that? If self-determination was her thing, well, the flat was hers outright. She had the freehold. There were no strings, nothing that compromised her ownership. He had not done this to gain a hold over her, but to make her more secure. He had liberated her in the most fundamental way. Why couldn't she see it?

But the feeling that he was willing to go to such massive lengths to get his own way—and the ease with which he had achieved his ends—unnerved her in some fundamental way. She felt shaken, disturbed.

She already knew that a man who tried to undermine your self-determination was not to be trusted. In a wild flight of imagination, she realized that, stooping to tricks like that, it wouldn't be all that difficult for Jaf to get her pregnant. And then it would be her parents' story all over again.

So the first thing she did, when he gave her ownership of the fabulous flat, was show Jaf the door of it.

Lisbet sat for a moment, staring down at her own handwriting. After a moment she gathered up all the cheques. Then she sat with them in her hand, not looking at him.

"What was the message you intended me to take from this?" Jaf demanded roughly.

At that her chin went up. "This is the amount of

rent I had agreed to pay the owner to live in that apartment.''

''Well?''

Here, in this context, her actions suddenly seemed petty and ungenerous, even to herself. But it had not seemed that way in London, when each succeeding month in which he did not cash her cheques only made her more determined to make her point.

''No matter whose name is on the title deeds, the apartment is in fact owned by you,'' she said. ''I'm merely sticking by the deal I made before I moved in.''

''You knew there was no need,'' Jaf said.

''And you knew I felt there was a need! Why didn't you cash them?'' she demanded hotly. ''How do you think I felt about that? If we're talking about offending—''

''A need to repudiate my gift? Yes, I see. When did you meet Roger?''

''Ro—?'' Lisbet began in confusion, then gasped. She had almost fallen flat on her face. ''I'm not going to answer that.''

''Does he make love to you on the bed I bought for you? On the sheets that I gave you? Does he kiss you on the pillow where your head lay beside mine and we laughed? Is that why you sent me this *rent?*'' He flicked the little bundle in her hand. ''To salve your conscience for what you were doing?''

''This conversation is illuminating,'' she said brightly. ''It proves I was right, doesn't it? You manoeuvred me into that flat for one reason—to control me! Did you want me to feel too guilty and beholden ever to take another lover, Jaf? Our relationship was over. Should I have given up all other men forever because I was living in the flat you had manipulated me into? Or would a few years of celibacy have been enough for your ego? How many, exactly, would satisfy you?''

''I did not buy the flat to control you!'' He bit out every word.

''But having bought it, you're furious that it didn't have that effect?''

''Don't be a fool!''

''Meanwhile, here you were having a wonderful time with your gambling and your gold-plated Rolls. Isn't there a song that goes, 'You don't want me, but you want me to go on wanting you'?''

She held out the cheques.

''Please cash them,'' she said levelly. ''Thank you, but I don't like feeling like a kept woman.''

Jaf reached out and took the little bundle, ripped the cheques into pieces, pushed the window control again, and tossed the scraps into the wind. They whipped into a little whirlwind and then were lost against the vastness of the desert as she watched.

''If you send me another cheque, Lisbet,'' she heard him say in a dangerous voice, and her eyes moved to meet the black fury of his gaze, ''I will deposit a million pounds into your bank account. Then you will feel what it is to be a kept woman.''

They were approaching a small town, where a picturesque cluster of domed roofs sheltered in the protection of a palm forest. The limousine slowed and turned off the highway onto a rough, unpaved road. A few yards along, they pulled into the courtyard of a small building. There was a sign in Arabic script over the door.

"Is this where we're eating?" Lisbet exclaimed in surprise. She had been expecting that he would take her to one of the big expensive hotels, like the Sheikh Daud in Barakat al Barakat, where the producer had dined her on the first night of her arrival.

"The food is excellent," Jaf said, in a voice that said he had regained his self-control.

There was a tiny vestibule, and then the room they entered was dark, the walls and ceiling hung with swaths of exotic fabric and carpets in deep, rich shades. It was lighted with kerosene lamps, one on each of the low tables and a larger one hanging from the centre of each of the circles of fabric that draped the ceiling.

It was like entering a nomad's tent, quiet and mysterious. Lisbet smiled involuntarily as a dark-haired, heavyset woman came out through a curtained doorway with a cry of pleasure.

"Marhaba!" she cried, approaching Jaf with exuberant delight and stretching out her arms, then clapping her hands together and bowing her head in welcome, talking all the while. *"Assalaamu aleikum!"*

"Waleikum assalaam, Umm Maryam."

They chatted like old friends for a moment, and then the hostess turned and smiled at Lisbet. *"Assalaamu aleikum. Ahlan wa sahlan!"*

"Salaam aleikum," Lisbet returned with a smile, using up her entire cache of Arabic. But fortunately the woman didn't appear to expect any further response. She turned and led them along the room past several groups of diners who paused in their meal to stare, up two steps of a raised wooden platform at the end, and through a doorway in a partition of intricately arabesqued wood.

Lisbet reached out a hand to trace the birds and flowers frozen in permanent grace.

This area contained only two tables. With its lower ceiling, it felt enclosed and private. One kerosene lamp hung from the centre of the ceiling, giving subdued light. The hostess pulled out the low table to expose the cushions piled neatly on the floor and against the wall.

Lisbet sank down and Jaf slipped into a cross-legged posture beside her before helping to draw the table back into position.

Their hostess, meanwhile, lifted the lantern chimney and set a match to the wick. After a moment a little glow made the table their own special place.

Lisbet realized they were as intimate here as they could be anywhere.

"They have no printed menu," Jaf murmured, as the hostess disappeared. "Will you trust me to choose?"

She nodded.

His eyelids came down in lazy approval, and he smiled. "Good," he said, as if her permission had wider implications.

"My food, tonight," she told him evenly.

His nearness was making her skin hot. She could smell the scent of him, and she only had to close her eyes for that scent to take her back to moments whose memory melted her like a wax candle in a furnace. She lifted her chin and bit her lip to keep her eyes open, her guard up.

He looked as though he would have answered, but their hostess came through the little doorway with a tray. She set two generous glasses of rum-coloured liquid in front of them.

Lisbet picked it up and sipped. She blinked at the unexpected taste. "What is it?"

"Date juice with pine nuts," Jaf said, sipping his own. Lisbet took another sip, nodded and smiled at the hostess, miming enjoyment. Now she could recognize the flavour as dates. It was strange and different, but curiously pleasant.

Meanwhile, the woman, standing with the tray under one arm, was discussing the finer points of tonight's menu choices with Jaf. Lisbet listened absently to the strong Arabic consonants.

It felt odd to let him decide for her like this. But she was helpless without the language, and there was a strange comfort in having the decision taken out of her hands. It was almost like being a child—not that she had had much experience of that. Fate had given her an adult sense of responsibility very early.

"Do you like lamb?"

"As long as it's not a whole roast lamb, I can probably do justice to it."

"It's steak that's rolled and stuffed with dried fruits, herbs and spices, and baked in ashes. One of the specialties of the house, as well as being a traditional Barakati dish. No one does it better than Umm Maryam's mother."

"Her *mother?*"

"Yes, this is a family restaurant. Umm Maryam is the third generation. It was started by her grandmother."

Umm Maryam, understanding that she was under discussion, smiled at her. After a moment the meal negotiations drew to a close. The hostess made a couple of additional suggestions and Jaf nodded, and then with a smile she was gone.

The silence and peace of the place settled around them. Lisbet felt their mood change. Jaf seemed suddenly softened. His eyes lost their punishing glint.

"Do you come here much?" In London they had found several great little restaurants together, but if the newspapers were right, his tastes were very different here at home. Now it was only the most expensive, most popular *in* places for Sheikh Jafar al Hamzeh, whether they served good food or the place was hideously over-hyped.

"Would you have preferred to sample the night life of the city? We will do that after our meal."

"I wasn't lamenting the Sheikh Daud." Not by a long way. "I was just surprised."

He gave her a deliberate look, then spoke close to her ear. "I hope I will never lose the power to surprise you, Lisbet."

His voice caused little pilot lights of memory to puff into life, waiting for the signal to ignite her blood. He had said that once before. When she had been lying by his side, trembling in the aftermath of a pleasure so profound she had felt fundamentally changed. He had refused to stop until she was worn out.

"I think you just altered my DNA," she had murmured, half tranced with the mix of pleasure and sheer exhaustion. Every muscle twitched and trembled spasmodically.

That was when he had whispered it. *I hope I never lose the power to surprise you.* He'd said "hope," but his tone of voice had said he meant to make very sure of it.

She had responded only with a faint smile. Even her face muscles had been worked to overload.

Refusing to meet his eyes now, Lisbet shook off the

heaviness the memory provoked in her limbs. "You certainly surprised me today," she admitted wasp-ishly. "What a mess you caused!"

Jaf lifted his eyebrows. "Was it so serious, what I did? It was only one scene."

"It was the master shot for a very difficult scene. Why did you do anything so crazy?"

A smiling young woman stepped through the door-way with their first course on a tray. She greeted Jaf with unabashed pleasure and set down several dishes to a rapid fire commentary before smiling shyly at Lis-bet and disappearing.

"But I wanted to see you, Lisbet," Jaf murmured, picking up a large sprig of basil and munching it into his mouth bit by bit like a rabbit.

Which was totally inappropriate because, Lisbet was slowly coming to realize, with Jaf, *she* was the rabbit. The one who was hypnotized and then devoured whole.

Five

"There were easier ways," she said repressively, struggling to subdue her body's response to that simple statement. "You wrecked the day's filming. I don't know how much that little stunt will end up costing. No one could get back on form afterwards. You must have known it would cause disruption."

Jaf grinned. "Don't you know that I am mad, bad and dangerous to know?"

It was what a tabloid paper had called him a few weeks ago.

She took a mouthful of herb, watching him. "Why?"

He had taught her to eat the fresh herbs and bread in London, in the early, carefree days of their romance. Lisbet was surprised by the sharpness of memory that accompanied the taste on her tongue.

He grinned. "But for your sake, of course. I have gone mad for love, Lisbet."

"That's not what they say," she told him. "They say getting your hands on such a massive inheritance is what did it."

"Do they? Who says that?"

"Who doesn't say it?"

"Fools without romance," Jaf said dismissively.

He was being flippant; he didn't mean her to believe it. But there was an edge of something underneath the flippancy.

"Why are you courting publicity, Jaf?" she asked curiously.

He shrugged. "No Cup Companion has to court publicity, you know that. We are a natural resource."

It was true, but still, he had seemed to know exactly how to avoid being noticed when they wanted privacy in London. Now every move he made was reported. There had been a sea change in him.

"You may not have to, but today you certainly did."

"It won't do the film any harm." Jaf shrugged. "The prepublicity will probably be worth the price of a lost day's shooting, as I'm sure Masoud will see, once he's calmed down."

And then they were discussing the film, and suddenly the animosity between them died and it was like London again, with Jaf listening with the close interest he had always shown in anything that concerned her, and Lisbet confiding everything to him.

She was thrilled to be working with Masoud al Badi, a director whose last film had won the Palme d'Or at Cannes, and several other prestigious awards. This was a relatively low-budget film, but that was no problem, Lisbet told him, where there was a good script and good actors and no need for special effects and name stars.

And the part was brilliant, a perfect opportunity for her, if she had the talent to stretch to it. Lisbet was alternately terrified and thrilled at the challenge facing her.

"Why were you in the sea today? What is the story?"

"Don't you know about Rose Dumont, the bandit?"

"Tell me."

He had said that a couple of dozen times before. Jaf loved stories—he came from a nation of storytellers—and Lisbet had got into the habit of telling him the story of virtually every script that she read for.

"The screenplay is loosely based on her memoirs. Rose Dumont was the undutiful daughter of a rich London merchant. She didn't 'take' during her first social season, in about 1860, because she was too independent, too outspoken, and didn't suffer fools gladly. And she absolutely refused to go through the humiliation of a second season. So she was packed off by her family to India, where it was thought she would have a better chance of finding herself a husband."

"And did she look on it as an adventure?"

"She did. In her memoirs she wrote that she toyed with the idea of turning herself into a man on the ship, but she was too closely supervised to be able to put her plans into execution. Still, she was convinced that anything could happen, and she was right. She never got to India. Just off the coast of the Kingdom of Barakat, as it was in those days, Rose's ship was attacked by pirates. In the battle she was lost overboard. A piece of flotsam saved her.

"Rose got to shore—in the scene you interrupted today—and was immediately captured by a desert tribesman. But she put up such a powerful, spitting resistance to his advances that he got frightened that maybe she was one of the djinn—they're the people made of fire, you know, as humans are made from earth, and it can get tricky for humans to mess with them—and decided that instead of making her his own wife, he ought to offer her to the king."

Jaf scooped up another little cluster of herbs. "A djinn," he said thoughtfully, looking at Lisbet from lazy eyes, as if a new idea had occurred to him. "I never thought of that."

She ignored him. "Well, so he carried Rose to the palace and told the king he hadn't touched her, and the king accepted the gift, and Rose was dispatched to the harem. There she was left 'to languish among women' as she laments. Rose had always hated restriction, and she hated being in purdah. She wrote that she found life in the harem 'almost as limiting' as life in Victorian England," Lisbet reported with a grin.

She bent to pick up another morsel of hot flatbread with a little cube of goat's cheese, and set a sprig of herb on top before popping it into her mouth.

"She was bored, so she occupied her days learning Arabic—she had a quick ear and had whizzed through French and German in the schoolroom—and got fairly fluent.

"Most of the women in the harem were completely uneducated. But a few were very highly educated and skilled, and some, like herself, were foreign captives, and she allied herself with them. And between them these women began to plan an escape."

Jaf's eyebrows went up. "Where did they think they would go?"

"They bribed one of the eunuchs, and he agreed to help them. Bit by bit he took their valuables and jewels to the market and sold them. With the proceeds, when they had enough, they planned to buy a boat and hire a captain. They were going to set sail and take their luck."

"Very courageous," Jaf interjected, his eyebrows still up.

"In the middle of all this, something happened. After almost two years, one night the king suddenly remembered the gift the desert tribesman had brought to him, the foreign woman with the unusual colouring, and he sent to the harem for her."

Jaf gave her a look. "Lucky king, to have such power," he murmured.

Lisbet had to close her eyes. She swallowed. "Rose doesn't go into detail for her Victorian audience, but she does obliquely hint that she had learned certain skills from the eunuchs. 'I took Queen Esther as my guide,' she wrote. Maybe you know that Esther learned tricks from the eunuchs that allowed her to impress Ahasuerus, the King of the Medes and Persians, when she was finally summoned to his bed."

"I have not heard this story before."

"It's in the Bible," Lisbet said. "Ahasuerus is called Artaxerxes in the history books. Anyway, whatever Rose actually did that night, and on succeeding nights, the king fell in love with her, eventually becoming completely besotted with her."

"Of course."

Lisbet pressed her lips together and resisted her response to his teasing. "Do you want to hear this story or not?"

Jaf's eyebrows shot up again. "What am I doing wrong?"

"Never mind. Just don't interrupt so much, okay?"

Obediently he closed his mouth, but there was still a wicked glint in his eyes. Lisbet shook her head and looked away to take another bite of food.

"Rose suddenly found herself in the position of being the king's favourite, and life in the harem changed dramatically for her. She had power. She got a new apartment in the harem. She gave birth to a son, and received even more honours. She began to get gifts from people who wanted her to intercede for them with the king.

"This was a great advantage, because it meant the women could sell the stuff and make their escape that much sooner. And then one day, just when their plans were reaching fruition, Rose made the discovery that she was happier than she had ever been, right where she was.

"She had fallen in love with the king. They would talk long into the night about everything from affairs of state to astronomy. He consulted her and listened to her. She'd never met her intellectual match in a man before, and here he was. And she had a lovely baby son. Rose was enjoying life more than ever before.

"The other women were still desperate to escape, of course. And so Rose was faced with a choice."

She paused, and Jaf shook his head.

"A choice? What was there to choose? She had a husband and a child. What could weigh against that?"

Lisbet looked at him. "He wasn't her husband, Jaf, he was her owner. And the alternative was freedom."

She saw fury blaze in his eyes.

At that moment, the smiling young woman arrived with their second course, the lamb. A wonderful aroma came with her, and it was so mouth-watering that Lisbet completely lost track of her story.

"Ohhh, it smells delicious!" she cried, as a plate was set before her. The meat practically disintegrated at one touch of her fork, and the scent of the mix of herbs and spices was out of this world.

For a few minutes they ate in silence, for in the Barakat Emirates eating is a serious business and there is no social compulsion to make conversation over a meal. When conversation began again they talked mostly about the food. But when the main course had been cleared away, Jaf returned to the story of the film.

"You were telling me about Rose," he said.

After much soul-searching, Rose had decided to escape with the other women.

"She knew that one day she would fall out of favour with the king. Her happiness was entirely dependent on his will. She wanted to have a life where she controlled her own destiny. And she felt she couldn't disappoint all her friends who had worked and planned for so long.

"The day came when the eunuch returned to the palace to report that the boat and a captain were ready. The eunuch had arranged the departure for a date when the tide would be going out early in the morning, so the women could escape by night and go straight aboard.

"On the appointed night the women collected in Rose's apartments, where they dressed in men's clothing. When the palace was asleep, the women kissed their sleeping children and prepared to go."

"They didn't take their children?"

"They couldn't. It would have been too much of a risk. Rose says she almost relented as she bent over her sleeping son and kissed him for the last time."

"This must be fiction. Do you believe this, Lisbet? That a woman leaves her child for such a reason? Could you do such a thing?"

"They were in a situation they hadn't asked for, Jaf. They hadn't come to the harem willingly, had they? None of them went to the king's bed voluntarily."

"Except Rose."

She ignored that. "The eunuch let them out of the harem and led them by secret ways out of the palace and into the city. They trooped down to the shore, but when they got there, the eunuch mysteriously disappeared."

"Ah."

"Yes. The captain of the boat matching the description the eunuch had given to Rose denied all knowledge. They had been betrayed. Rose never was certain whether it was the eunuch's doing, or whether the eunuch himself had been taken in by the captain, and murdered under cover of night as they crept along.

"But the sun was coming up and they had no time to think about it. As soon as the alarm was raised in the palace they would be searched out and put to death. Rose had brought her remaining jewels with her, and they used them to buy horses and weapons. And instead of escaping by sea, they fled inland, into the desert. Eventually, she and a number of women managed to set up camp in a ruin by an oasis."

Jaf looked faintly incredulous. "And they survived there?"

"They became bandits, rivalling the notorious Abu

Tariq, who controlled a huge slice of the Barakati desert. He was the grandfather of the Selim who was grandfather of ex-Prince Jalal, by the way.''

Jaf's eyebrows climbed into his hair. ''And how did Rose manage to survive in a desert controlled by the great Abu Tariq?''

''She says that after one encounter Abu Tariq left them alone, and they had an unspoken agreement to divide the desert in such a way that Rose was left exclusive control over a small territory. She doesn't say exactly how they came to that agreement, but it's possible she used the same arts she'd used on the king. Some historians have suggested that Rose gave birth to the man who was later the father of Selim.''

Jaf smiled. ''Is this being billed as a true story?''

Lisbet believed it, or most of it, but she only shrugged. ''It's what Rose published in her memoirs. Some people at the time debunked her story, too, but then in 1958 someone did some research on the story in Barakat and found references to a band of women bandits in the desert at that period.

''They were noted for their ferocity, apparently. The records say the women had control over a certain segment of the caravan routes. People used to double the guard over that part of the route, because the women bandits terrified people even more than Abu Tariq's gang.

''And they are mentioned as having been finally wiped out in about 1890, which is the date Rose gives for her return to England.''

''She returned?''

''She got homesick in middle age. So she passed leadership of the gang over to a younger deputy, and travelled back to the port with one sidekick. She saw a European traveller, and robbed him of his baggage. Then she passed herself off as an Englishman. She had plenty of valuables to barter for passage back to England, the proceeds of her bandit life.

"Her memoirs are fascinating, but she doesn't go into as much detail as I'd like. The book was hugely popular reading among women for a decade or so, and she was a heroine, but her story was pooh poohed a lot. There were discrepancies in it."

"What did she do, back in England?"

"Took up the cause of women's votes, of course!" Lisbet laughed. "Actually her life wasn't by any means over. In the First World War, when she was quite old but still very fit, she worked as a battlefield nurse. She died in the flu epidemic of 1919."

"Alone, and childless."

"Yes, but the film doesn't end there."

"How does it end?"

"On her deathbed, Rose remembers a particular moment in her bandit life. It's not in her memoirs— the story has been changed quite a bit for the film. She and a few of her band come upon a young man who's become separated from a hunting party. He defends himself so bravely for one so young that they decide to take him prisoner.

"Then the king and his companions ride to the rescue, and the bandits realize that he is the Crown Prince. Rose suddenly understands that the boy is her own son. So it's very poignant, because she sees her other life—the might have been. She would have been mother of the Crown Prince, perhaps mother of the king one day. Without identifying herself, she demands the young prince's sword as ransom, releases him and gallops off with her women."

"And the king lets her go?" Jaf asked.

"He doesn't recognize her."

Jaf was shaking his head. "Impossible," he said.

She bit her lip. "Why is it impossible?"

"How could he fail to recognize the woman he had loved?"

"Fifteen or sixteen years," she pointed out weakly.

He reached out to stroke that tiny tuft of hair that just hugged her temple. "Even a hundred years would not be enough to wipe away the sound of your voice, Lisbet, the scent of you, the way the colour of your eyes changes with your mood." He dropped his hand.

"A man may stop loving, but he can never forget."

Sheikh Jaf's Film Flam

Jafar al Hamzeh, bad boy Cup Companion to Prince Karim, apparently wants to be a movie star, and he believes in taking the direct route. Yesterday the handsome sheikh galloped onto the set of Masoud al Badi's latest film while a scene was being filmed in the Barakati desert, threw the English star, Lisbet Raine, over his saddle, and...

Lisbet tossed the paper down without reading any more, stood restlessly and moved to the little trolley to pour herself a cup of coffee. She stood sipping as she gazed at the scene around her.

The house, high on a forested escarpment that lined this arm of the bay, faced south along a white sand beach and curving shoreline. It was a fabulous view, and the air was wonderful. A soft breeze rippled the skirt of her turquoise sundress against her calves. Mental cobwebs didn't stand a chance here.

"You're staying with us, of course," her friend

Anna had said. She was the first person, after her mother, whom Lisbet had called to give the news that she had landed the female lead in Masoud al Badi's latest film and would be coming to Barakat to do the location shooting. "It'll be wonderful to have you for a long visit."

Lisbet was thrilled to be here in Anna's new home, of course, but there was pain mingled with the pleasure. To see Gazi and Anna so happy in their marriage, planning a future together, was lovely. But every intimate smile they exchanged, every quick, loving touch, reminded her that this was something she herself might have had, if only...

But she had made the right choice, even if not for the right reasons. Jaf wasn't Gazi, a fact the newspapers delighted in pointing out. He didn't have his brother's stability. Life with Jaf would have been no more secure than life with her father. Last night had proved that.

"Good morning!"

Anna was leaning over the flower-covered balcony above. As Lisbet looked up, blinking in the sunlight, Anna lifted a hand in greeting and then turned and started down the beautiful, centuries-old stone staircase.

When she arrived on the terrace the two friends kissed and exchanged morning chitchat as Anna poured herself coffee and sat down in the delicious shade of the huge umbrella that protected the table.

Her eyes fell on the headline, and she made a little face. "What's Jaf been doing?"

"You haven't heard about yesterday yet?" Lisbet had arrived back with Jaf very late, when the household was already asleep.

"I know Gazi got a phone call from Jaf that had him hopping."

"Was he trying to suppress the story? Wasted effort."

"Gazi can do most things when it comes to publicity," Anna said, bridling a little. "But I know with Jaf damage limitation is difficult. The press really love to write about his escapades."

Lisbet blew on her coffee and sipped. "Well, and there are moles on any movie, and mobile phones work out there. Within half an hour of Jaf galloping onto the set, half a dozen journalists at least had the story."

She nodded at the stack of newspapers on the end of the table. "Wonderful how he timed the stunt just in time for the Sunday gossip glut."

Anna opened her eyes. "Jaf galloped onto the set?"

"Rode his white steed into the middle of a scene we were shooting, chased me down the beach when I freaked and ran, did a flying pickup that could have killed us both, and kept on going, with me clinging on for dear life. You'll catch flies like that," Lisbet advised her friend in a matter-of-fact voice.

Anna's lower jaw was halfway to her chest. "You—he—what? I don't believe it!" she babbled, though she clearly did, every word. Her hand reached mechanically for the tabloid with the screaming headline.

"Hey, you're checking my story against the *Sunday Mirror?*" Lisbet chided with mock indignation. "*I'm* the eyewitness!"

But Anna couldn't tear her eyes away from the story, which was illustrated by a fuzzy long shot of a galloping horseman. It might or might not have been a still from yesterday's film.

"Oh, I wonder how Gazi's going to feel about this! Everyone knows Prince Karim's warned Jaf to stop courting publicity." She looked up. "If he's stripped of his title, it will be a deep family shame, you know."

"Is it likely?"

Anna shrugged.

"This isn't exactly a hanging offence, is it?" Lisbet found herself saying. "Now that I've cooled down about it, I begin to see that he's done us a big favour. I'm sure a film doesn't often get prepublicity as good as this."

Anna laughed. "Maybe you should have married him, after all. He could make you famous."

"Thanks. In those immortal, always relevant words, I'd rather do it myself."

"Sorry, darling, of course you would!" Anna's eyes dropped to the story. She read for a moment, then gasped on laughter. "Did you really refuse to work as long as Jaf was on the set?"

"I was pretty peeved," Lisbet admitted.

"'The actress was, in effect, throwing the wealthy sheikh off his own land. The producers may count themselves lucky that he has not returned the favour. The movie location is being leased from the arts-loving Cup Companion at a nominal sum,'" Anna read aloud.

She tossed aside the paper as a servant silently approached across the tiled courtyard. "Morning, Mansour. What would you like for breakfast, Lisbet?"

"Let's have something lazy. I'm not called today."

When breakfast had been decided on, Anna stood up and moved to where a dozen European newspapers were neatly stacked at the end of the table. She flipped through them.

"Not many have actually put it on the front page. They're more concerned with the drugs pipeline." She held up the *Times* for Lisbet to read the headline.

Barakati Heroin Connection Baffles Scotland Yard.

Anna picked up the *Sunday Mirror* again. "This looks like the worst one," she said, and slipped it well down in the pile. "That way Gazi doesn't have to see it first thing," she said, smiling conspiratorially at Lisbet. "Let him concentrate on the heroin. It's less personal."

Lisbet's heart gave one spasmodic beat. It must be nice to care about someone like that, wanting to protect them.

"Jaf came in with me last night, by the way. He said it was too far to go home."

"I know he spent the night here. He's with Gazi in his office right now."

"Is Gazi very worried about him?"

Anna sat down again. "He doesn't say much about it. He reads every story that's printed, but when I try to get him to open up—" She shrugged.

"Does he talk to Jaf about it?"

"Not in front of me. I don't know what they're discussing now. As you saw, Jaf hasn't been here for a while."

"Oh, he said that was on my account," Lisbet said.

"Really? I must admit I was a little surprised. I thought he'd come the moment he knew you were here."

"I told you he wouldn't," Lisbet said quietly. Still, she had spent the week in unconscious expectation. Maybe that was why she had been so thrown by Jaf's appearance on the beach. There had to be some reason for the blind panic that had descended on her when she looked up and saw his face.

"Sometimes I wonder if all this would be happening if you had married Jaf," Anna commented, shaking her head. "It was when he got back here after you two broke up that all this started to happen, you know. Sometimes I wish—"

Lisbet lifted a hand to stop her friend. "Then he must have been pretty unstable in the first place, Anna. Don't wish it on me. I don't want to be anyone's sole moral support. And if you'd seen what I saw last night…"

"How was dinner?"

"Dinner was fine. It was the gambling afterwards that really opened my eyes. We went to the Shalimar Gardens."

The Shalimar Gardens, as Lisbet had quickly learned, was an extremely luxurious casino, recently built on the grounds of the Sheikh Daud hotel for the entertainment of wealthy foreign tourists. It was one of only two casinos in the country.

"Oh, damn," Anna said softly. "Oh, Lisbet, please don't mention that to Gazi! What happened?"

"He gambled, he popped champagne, he tipped wildly, he lost."

"How much?"

"I have no idea. A fortune. He was just a totally different person. A caricature. I hated the whole scene."

"Shhhh!" Anna hissed sharply. "Here they come."

Lisbet turned her head. The two brothers, in light-coloured shorts and dark polo shirts, were just emerg-

ing from the house. Both had strong bodies and powerfully muscled legs with fine, bony ankles.

Jaf was laughing at something Gazi had just said,
his head thrown back. The sun burnished his thick,
ruffled hair and darkly tanned skin.

"Cor! They are a gorgeous pair, aren't they?" Lisbet exclaimed, in stage Cockney.

"Phwooah," Anna agreed.

When they arrived at the table, Gazi bent to kiss his
wife, his hand cupping her head with an intimate, protective hold that made Lisbet bite her lip and look
away.

Jaf headed for the coffee trolley, poured himself a
cup, turned and looked straight into her eyes. His gaze
had an unreadable glint. Her heart kicked a little protest as he approached, but he only pulled out a chair
on her right and slipped into it.

"So, have you told Roger all about your date with
your ex-lover?" he asked.

Anna's interest was instantly caught. She glanced
over, but the warning in Lisbet's eyes stopped her curious question in her throat. Lisbet couldn't be sure
whether Jaf had intercepted the look or not.

"I just got up," she protested.

Jaf laughed. "In that case, why not save the con-
fession till tonight? Might as well be hanged for a
sheep as a lamb. Let me show you a bit of the country
today."

Six

It was a beautiful country, as he had promised. First he took her to the Bostan al Sa'adat—The Garden of Joy—where inside a high wall enclosing several acres of land there were fountains and canals, and every kind of plant and tree and bird imaginable. It was very peaceful.

"Boy, they knew something about stress relief, didn't they?" Lisbet marvelled.

"This garden was endowed by King Daud over sixty years ago, at the time of his marriage to his beautiful, foreign first wife," Jaf told her as they wandered behind a tiny waterfall. "It took twenty years to complete."

Then they visited the fifteenth-century Great Mosque, and the tomb of Queen Halimah, in the city centre, said to be among the most perfect surviving examples of classical Islamic architecture in the world.

It was the first time Lisbet had ever seen anything so beautiful up close. Her mouth was permanently open with wonder.

At the entrance to one room, which was completely covered in a mosaic of tiny mirrored tiles, she paused, breathless with astonishment.

The room was filled with light that had no discernible source. The room simply glowed, as if endless reflection were enough in itself to produce light.

"It's like being in the centre of a diamond!" Lisbet whispered.

She wondered if he was remembering all the times he had described these architectural wonders to her, and promised that one day he would bring her here. She certainly could not forget. It had happened mostly when they lay in bed after lovemaking. They were always close at such times, and his descriptions of the wonders she would see became a part of the soft lovers' chat they shared.

But if it bothered him that, though he was showing these things to her as he had promised, they were no longer lovers, he gave no sign.

He drove her out into the desert, where they visited an ancient ruin so worn by time it might almost have been a natural geographical feature. Lisbet was entranced again, for a completely different reason.

"This must be just the kind of place Rose Dumont and her women took refuge in! They had an oasis, though, of course."

There was no water here. The arched, crumbling, mud-brick walls were as dry as the sand dust that blew against them. The ruin was a potent reminder of the limited importance of individual lives.

"'My name is Ozymandias, king of kings,'" she

recited. "'Look on my works, ye Mighty, and despair.'"

"No one even knows that much," Jaf said. "There is no king's name here."

"How old is it?" she demanded, walking around every inch of the walls and trying to imagine the people who had lived here. The sun burned down on the empty vastness that surrounded them, making the air dance. Lisbet thought she could almost see the ghost of the original building in the shimmer.

Jaf shook his head. "It's virtually impossible to date such a ruin accurately. Mud brick was used for millennia. And arches, too, go back to earliest times. All identifying detail has been worn away by time."

She stood under one crumbling arch, looking out over the endless stretch of desert. A light wind blew the long skirt of her rich aquamarine dress, grabbed at the broad brim of the protective hat she wore.

"Someone stood here once," she told him, in an imaginative half-trance. "I can almost feel her. She stood here looking out over the desert while a storm blew, waiting for someone to come back."

What a harsh, inhospitable land this was, but it had enormous drawing power. Its magnetism was a tangible thing.

"Just like a sailor's sweetheart, waiting and praying was all she could do. But for her the sea and the storm were made of sand."

"And did he come back?" Jaf asked, in a low, rough voice.

The whisper of heartbreak seemed to touch her mind. "I don't know," Lisbet murmured, shaking her head to try to free herself of the strange impression. "Maybe not."

"And still she waits," he said. "You feel her presence after hundreds, perhaps thousands of years. How can *you* sense the mind of such a woman, you who waited no more than weeks? Do you claim to have a heart that understands such loyalty?"

Her breath trembled at the passion his voice struggled with. Against her will her heart caught fire. Her lips were dry. She couldn't speak.

"What have you done to us, Lisbet?" he demanded, his voice quiet, but intense enough for a brand. "What have you destroyed, with your foolish resistance? I loved you enough for a dozen lifetimes, but that was not enough for you. What did you want, Lisbet? What more did you want, that you were so eager to kill my love?"

She tried to swallow, but her throat closed.

"Look at me."

It would be fatal to look at him in this mood, she knew it. Lisbet kept her eyes firmly on the distant dunes, where the early-afternoon sun was already painting faint shadows. How mysterious the desert was, with its ripples and waves. Like a solidified sea.

"Look at me, Lisbet," he commanded again. He was close beside her now, his voice against her ear. He lifted a hand to her chin and drew her head around to face him.

"I didn't want *anything* from you!" she cried furiously, finding her voice at last. "I told you, what I wanted was to be free to be myself. You wanted to own me, and I didn't w—"

In furious silence his mouth smothered hers. Liquid fire seared her lips, sending a spear of flame along every limb, and into her heart—a stabbing, sudden heat as powerful as the first time they had kissed, almost a year ago.

It was a punishing, tormenting, hungry kiss, but irresistibly it summoned up her own wild, half-buried hunger. With a helpless moan she opened her mouth under the onslaught of his, and his tongue pushed into the moist cavity savagely, ferociously, driving a storm of desire pell-mell into her blood.

It lasted moments only. With the same suddenness, Jaf lifted his mouth, and his arms fell away. Lisbet closed her eyes against the rush of emptiness.

"The wind is blowing harder," he said in a harsh voice. "We'd better get back to the city."

"Coffee, Ahmad, and would you toast me one of those, please?" Lisbet said, pointing.

Behind her in the canteen tent, conversation was picking up again. It had parted like the Red Sea when Lisbet appeared, and no prizes for guessing what everyone had been discussing.

She picked up her coffee cup and toasted bun with a murmur of thanks and, giving a little general wave, stepped out into the early-morning sunshine to walk slowly back to her trailer. Sometimes she ate her breakfast in the canteen, but not today. She would only put a crimp in the conversation.

Tina was already waiting in her trailer, nursing her own cup of coffee.

"How was your date?"

"We ate, and then we went to the casino," Lisbet replied shortly, sinking into a chair as she pried the plastic lid off the cup. Yesterday's *Mirror* newspaper lay on the table. *Film Flam.* What a ridiculous play on words.

Taking a bite of her toasted Danish, Lisbet licked her fingers and picked up her coffee.

"The casino?" Tina demanded.

"The Shalimar Gardens. Very, very," Lisbet murmured, waving her hand expressively.

"Did he win? Did you play?"

"No, twice."

"Wow, not even one bet?"

"Jaf was leaving enough behind for both of us."

"I guess you saw the story," Tina said, nodding towards the paper as she zipped open a garment bag.

Lisbet nodded.

Her costume was lifted out of the bag and hung; the same one as on Saturday.

Lisbet set down her coffee cup and picked up a tissue to wipe the butter from her fingers. She stood up.

"Have you got the right costume? I thought we got that scene in the can Saturday."

"That's not what the call sheet says this morning," Tina told her.

"Was there a problem with the rushes?" If there was a problem, it had something to do with Jaf and the way he had stormed the set, she was sure. But she decided not to suggest it to Tina.

The dresser shrugged expressively. "Mine not to reason why."

"Damn." Lisbet shook her head. "I hope I'm not going to have to do that water thing again."

There was a tap on the door, and the director entered on her call. "I'll be retaking some of the close-up and medium shots today, Lisbet," he said.

"So I hear," she said. "What happened, Masoud?"

He scratched behind his ear. "We're going to be doing it with a white horse."

"A white horse!" she repeated, surprised.

"The scene will be slightly different, too. You run from Adnan when he rides up and he gallops after you and picks you up."

She gazed at the director. "Do you mean you're going to shoot something like what actually happened when Jaf—"

"It looked very good in the rushes. Very, very good. The white horse—everything looked very good. We want to capture that chemistry if we can."

Stunt people, of course, were doing the close-ups of the actual pickup. Lisbet spent the morning kicking her heels while the scene between her and Jaf was played and replayed for the cameras.

The afternoon was spent largely on one sequence. This entailed Lisbet leaping up from the sand and running along the shore while she turned and shrieked defiance over her shoulder, pursued, first, by the cameraman on a dune buggy, second, by the cameraman on the back of the white horse, and third, by Adnan on the horse and the cameraman on the dune buggy behind him.

It was a high-spirited horse, and at various times it took exception to Lisbet's curses, her hair, the camera, a grip, the clapboard, the dune buggy, and anything else that came in its way. And every time it did it spoiled the shot.

Lisbet lost count of the times she started up and plunged along the beach, only to hear the calm cry of "cut" behind her.

And after each attempt, someone had to come and

rake the sand clear of footprints, hoof marks, and wheel treads, and pump seawater to smooth it down.

Each time Lisbet retreated to the shade of an umbrella to have sunblock reapplied and drink ice water while she waited for the next take. Since her costume tended to dry on her within a very few minutes, it had to be damped down before each take.

The afternoon was tedium itself.

But no one thought of complaining, least of all Lisbet. Masoud al Badi was a brilliant director, and he was known for his moments of inspired madness on the set. If anything, she felt honoured to be part of a vision she could not understand.

By the time Masoud was satisfied, Lisbet had run herself nearly into heat exhaustion, her skin felt toasted, and her voice was hoarse. She collapsed into the dune buggy and was chauffeured up to her trailer. "Just throw me under the shower and turn it on," she said to Tina as her dresser worked on the thousand tiny buttons running down the back of her costume.

"There's no water," Tina warned her, grimacing apologetically. "Someone forgot to bring in the truck yesterday, and no one realized it till the tank ran dry an hour ago. They've called for an emergency supply, but it won't be here for at least an hour."

So when Jaf showed up a few minutes later suggesting drinks and dinner at his house, Lisbet didn't put up any argument at all.

"The sky here is just the way you described it," Lisbet smiled, leaning back to look up at the stars as they walked along the beach.

"Did I tell you about the sky?" Jaf murmured, as if he had forgotten.

She knew she was a fool to be disappointed. Why should he remember now, when he no longer loved her? Maybe someone else's skin was his velvet sky now.

"Once, you did," she said.

The limousine had driven again in the direction of Umm Maryam's restaurant, then along the side road through the forest of date palms, till the road came to an end at a high white wall and a massive pair of gates.

His house was even more beautiful than his descriptions of it, long months ago in England. Like many homes here, it was built around a central courtyard with a pool and fountain. The courtyard was partially latticed over to protect against the harsh sun, and the branches of trees had been trained over the lattice, giving a delicious, dappled shade.

Dinner was served in a long room with arched windows overlooking the courtyard, and paved with a mosaic in a carpet design of the most intricate workmanship, in pink, brown, black, red and white marble.

Jaf's conversation had been only slightly barbed, keeping her on edge without actually attacking her.

For their coffee they moved out under the stars beside the pool, where the fountain burbled gently in the darkness. The pattern of glazed tiles on the floor and the raised sides of the pool had been worn by the passage of centuries, but was perhaps more beautiful in age than it had ever been.

The air was perfumed by flowers. A night bird sang. It was as idyllic as he had promised.

Except that he did not love her.

After coffee, Jaf took some cubes of sugar in his hand and they went out to the stables. Firouz pushed his head eagerly against his master's chest, accepted the small sweet tribute. A mare, too, put her head over the stable gate and whinnied softly.

"Oh, aren't you a pretty one?" Lisbet crooned, stroking the soft nose.

"Shall we ride?" Jaf asked. It was another of the things he had told her they would do, in London. Lisbet couldn't resist the beauty of the night, and five minutes later, bareback, barefoot, they were riding down towards the sea.

They galloped along the water's edge, then dismounted and, dropping the reins, left the horses and walked splashing through the cool water as the waves whispered up the sand.

The stars were breathtaking, and so numerous it was difficult to pick out the major constellations from among the wild sparkle. And Lisbet was reminded of the moment when he had described the night sky and the stars to her. A moment he had forgotten.

"It sounded like something out of a dream," she said. It seemed like a dream now, the rich, sensuous purple-black, so spangled with glittering lights. *So soft your fingers long to touch it,* he had said.

"How did I describe it to you?" Jaf prodded gently, and Lisbet bit back a rueful smile and shook her head. She was a fool to have let him see how much she remembered.

"I said that your skin was like the night sky," he said, in a rough, purring voice. "Didn't I? Velvet, so that one longed to touch it. Is that what I said?"

His voice brought back the physical memory so sharply she choked on a gasp, remembering how he had stretched out beside her, stroking her trembling body to quiescence after half killing her with sexual pleasure.

Beautiful, he had breathed, running one strong, sensitive hand along her quivering thigh. *Only the night sky in Barakat is as soft as your skin, Lisbet.* And then he had told her about his grandfather's diamonds.

Now her skin was melting with the memory, with the heat of the evening, the burn of his voice. She closed her eyes. "Yes," she whispered, "that's what you said." And now she was burning up with yearning.

"Your soul, too, I described, do you remember?"

She couldn't answer. The pressure in her throat was almost intolerable, and she didn't know what would come out if she parted her lips.

"I said your soul was pure and burning, like the stars, isn't that what I said?"

She bowed her head, and if he wanted to take it as a nod, he could.

"How wrong I was, Lisbet. But I am not the first man to be blinded by beauty."

A breeze caressed her bare legs and shoulders, stirred her hair, and sensations of painful delight quivered through her, as if the wind were his body and arms.

"You remember it—our time together?" he demanded, as if the question were torn from him. "You remember what I said to you, how you responded?"

Lisbet bit her lip in the attempt to keep her emotions at bay.

"You remember," he murmured in a rough, tortured voice. "You can remember such love, and then lie to me about belonging to another man."

She gasped.

"You are surprised. But such a shallow, empty lie, Lisbet—why should it have convinced me for longer than a day? Why did you say it? Were you so afraid of my love? But there is nothing to fear anymore.''

She opened her mouth on a soundless sigh.

''You have come to my home, where I dreamed of seeing you, where I knew that our love would reach perfection. But you come too late. How can it be that you are here at last only when my love is ashes in my mouth?''

She looked at him, not understanding the pang that pierced her. This was what she wanted, wasn't it? Freedom to be herself. To be alone.

''Then what are we doing here?'' she asked, her voice catching in her throat.

He laughed, but without joy. ''I did not say I do not want you. That did not die with my love. I want to make love to you, Lisbet,'' he said with rough urgency. ''It is like thirst in the desert.''

And he would know. His voice caressed her like silken water, his need beat upon her like waves, drowning her in the flood tide of her own need to love and be loved by him.

''My arms long to hold you, my mouth to taste you, Lisbet. My hunger is the hunger of a thousand wolves. But now it is the kind of wanting you wanted me to feel. It is wanting without a heart. Isn't it so? Now you will be happy, even though such love is a travesty. Let us make love on this new bargain. We will mate as animals, thinking of nothing but pleasure.''

''Jaf,'' she pleaded. ''You know—''

He was suddenly fiercely angry. ''No!'' he rasped. ''I know nothing!'' He wrapped his arms around her in passionate abandon, and she felt his mouth ravage hers. His wild, angry passion thrilled through her like flame, burning up everything except hunger.

"Jaf," she moaned, on fire for him.

"Say it!" he commanded. "Tell me it is all you want!"

The world tilted, and somehow she was on the sand underneath his long, hard body, the stars a wild curtain of diamonds above their heads. On the horizon a fat orange moon was lifting out of the water, pouring liquid red-gold over the shifting ripples, colouring it till it looked like the desert sand.

His touch was everywhere. Where his hands grasped her, her flesh grew hot, her blood thundered. "Tell me!"

It was impossible to resist him any longer. His wildness infected her at the deepest level of being.

And as if his anguished passion were a burning brand setting her alight, now, at last, Lisbet recognized the love she had hidden deep inside. Set free by the flames of the remorse and regret that swept her, as surely as if he had burnt down a prison that held her, love stood up without disguise for the first time.

She was breathless with the discovery, and with the anguish of knowing that it had come too late.

"Tell me!" he cried again, and the torment in him was like fuel on the flames, so that it seemed that soon there would be nothing in the world but love.

But what she wanted to tell him now, he no longer wanted to hear.

Seven

He lay over her, his hand stroking her with a trembling caress, rough and urgent against her arm, her breast, her hip, her cheek. Then his fingers locked in her hair, his eyes lost the glint of starshine, and she had only time for the tiniest indrawn breath before his mouth smothered hers.

His body came down hard against her now, angry, urgent, punishing, passionate. His sex pressed painfully against her groin. His kiss pushed into her mouth, starving, ruthless.

Her fingers locked in his thick hair and she pulled her mouth away from his, gasping against an upsurge of need that swamped her. Was this what she had feared? This deep, unrelenting passion? She moaned with the hopeless understanding that had come too late.

"This I can give you," he said hoarsely, hearing

her cry. "This is what you want from me. Show me how much you want it, Lisbet!"

He let her go to kneel above her on the damp sand of their bed. She was weeping with need, with the hunger of long months, with the joy of discovery and the pain of loss. She called his name desperately, not the Jaf who was with her now, but the Jaf she had known, the man who had loved her and offered his heart without reserve.

"I am here," he answered roughly, dragging up her skirt so that the moonlight painted her legs and hips, outlining the tiny sliver of lace that was all that barred her body from him. Of their own accord his fingers caught the lace and drew it down her legs and away.

With quiet ferocity he pushed her thighs apart and bent down between them, grasping her hips. His mouth tasted her flesh, and his hands felt the quivering response.

He knew her so well. He knew every inch of her, every atom. All that she was. She had closed her heart and her throat on the words he had wanted to hear, but she could not now refuse him her body's response.

His tongue found the tender bud, his mouth enclosed her in warmth. His hands clasped her thighs' smooth muscle. He felt the pleasure he made for her build in hungry ripples, felt her fingers clench in his hair. Heard her breathing quicken to a moan.

He lifted his head. "Oh!" she cried in soft disappointment.

"Tell me, Lisbet," he said. "Is this what you want?"

"Jaf," she protested on a sigh. She both wanted and did not want it. She wanted the loving Jaf she had known. Now that his heart was no longer hers for the asking, she saw what a jewel she had spurned.

He lowered his head again. Stroked and rasped her with his determined, angry tongue. Tendrils of fire curled out from under his mouth, honey melted under his fingertips to spread sweetness through her body under her skin.

His hands stroked the tender skin, kneaded the flesh of her thighs, her abdomen, her hips, and every touch sent heat and delight shivering through her. His mouth, his tongue, toyed and toyed with her pleasure, building it by the slowest imaginable stages.

No effort was necessary, no clenching or straining. He knew her body perfectly. She felt her pleasure slowly tense, like a wild animal preparing to leap, and then, without effort, it was there, spiralling and flooding through her, the sweet, sweet burning that only he could give her.

"This is what I offer you now, Lisbet. Is it what you want?"

"Jaf!"

His hand stroked her moon-kissed abdomen, molten gold turning to silver-gilt as the moon climbed higher up the sky behind his head. His elbows kept her legs apart, opening her to his eyes and his kiss. She was half fainting with hunger for him to complete what was begun.

His mouth lowered again, and he smiled at the convulsive tightening in her thighs. The suddenness of his heat and his tongue drew her breath in on a tiny gasp, but he heard it even against the shushing of the surf, and it was like whiskey in his blood.

A larger wave frothed up the sand, running under his feet and legs and up under her knees, adding the water's contribution to her fever. Her hips lifted, seeking the release that his mouth promised. She moaned a tiny moan, like soft wind against a rock, and it burst in her again, an explosion of molten delight. Her body arched and trembled, and sank down again onto the sand.

She locked her fingers in his hair and tried to pull him up into her embrace. He lifted his head, and she felt his dark gaze touch her, though the moonlight blinded her.

"Say it, Lisbet," he commanded, his voice rasping her nerve endings as surely as, a moment ago, his tongue had.

"Jaf, please!"

"Yes, I please. I will, Lisbet. Only tell me, and I will do all that you desire and more."

"What do you want to hear?" she cried, knowing the answer.

"That in this way, if no other, you are mine."

The plain, flat statement was loaded with hunger and possession, and her response sliced through her like a newly sharpened sword. She turned her head helplessly from side to side.

"What do you want to prove?" she pleaded.

"When it is true, you will tell me," he said, and his mouth came down again.

Pleasure rippled through her body, pleasure like a thousand silver bells on a string pulled into shivery motion by his touch. Their delicate tinkling music built to a slow clamour in her blood, and she was wild for the deafening crescendo when it came.

His tongue rasped along her abdomen, brushed down a thigh, then to her inner thigh, tormenting her with its nearness. His hands kneaded her thighs, pushing them with a rough and hungry passion that made the stars go out.

"Please," she begged.

He looked up. "Do you want me to stop?"

She stretched her hands towards him, begging for his embrace. She needed him against her breast now, her arms around him, loving and holding.

His eyes closed slowly, like a cat's, and he bent his head again.

This time her response was sudden and wild, shaking her like a tree in a whirlwind, drawing helpless cries from her throat. Pleasure stormed through her, leaving her alone and trembling.

"Jaf!" she cried on a high, yearning wail, and held out her desperate arms. "Please, please love me!"

It struck him like a blow. He was helpless in the face of such a cry. He tore and kicked off the sea-soaked fabric that clung to his body, then, painted in moonlight and shadow, lifted himself over her.

She moaned her wild expectation and lifted her hips to meet the hungry, dangerous thrust of his. He pushed his way home with a suddenness that rocketed sensation into every cell, drew away and pounded home again.

The deeper pleasure that had teased and beckoned hammered out of her blood with a wild, crashing, blinding heat that robbed her of breath, of voice, of sense.

She flew high, aware only of the distant thunder of his body beating into hers, the high, melting heat and light that was both the moon and not the moon, the shivering surrender of her heart to a pure pleasure she had never known existed.

"Jaf!" she cried, for that pleasure was freedom from fear. "Love me, Jaf, please love me!"

It fountained up in them, a mingled joy and torment, love and anguish, light and darkness, for opposites are the hallmark of the One. The stars burned into supernovas, blinding them both, and then winked out.

The sky was just beginning to lighten beyond the broad door that stood open onto the courtyard. Lisbet could see a white flower against the shadows.

Her body was both sore and languid with the memory of pleasure. He had pushed her, held her, made her muscles stretch and clench and then shiver into a thousand shards as joy rushed through her blood, again and again.

Allahu akhbar. Allahu akhbar.

In the distance the village muezzin was calling the faithful to prayer.

Her back was against Jaf's chest, and she could feel his heartbeat, strong and steady, through her system. He had burned his anger out at last, and sex had been the flame. She thought of the moment when, lying on the beach, she had felt the beat of love in her heart and understood, too late, what she had lost.

Thrown away, she amended. She had let fear rule her, and this was the result. So her heart told her.

Was it fear? her head replied. Or was it some deeper instinct that had known he would just repeat for her the experience of her father? In London she had seen no sign of his gambling, his profligacy. But perhaps the signs had been there for her unconscious to read.

Whatever the truth, she could not see the way forward from here. She loved him, now, when he no longer loved her.

And if she tried to win back Jaf's love, knowing what she now knew about him, she was a fool. A gambler was little better than a drunk.

No way was she going to marry her father.

She knew more about herself, too. When she had split up with Jaf, she saw now, she had been half hoping he would pursue her. She hadn't really wanted him to accept her decision.

She wasn't sure now what she had wanted to prove if he did come after her. But she had successfully hidden her disappointment from herself when he did not, and that had allowed her to come to the Barakat Emirates imagining she could meet him without risk.

Had she been lying to herself all the time?

As the honey of the night's lovemaking still flowed through her cells, sweetening every sense, Lisbet could see no way forward.

Slowly the light increased. The white rose revealed itself as pink, and the leaves behind turned from black to green. She lay without stirring, letting thoughts wander through her head, till the golden rays of sun streaking across the tiles of the courtyard told her it was past time to rouse herself.

Jaf's hand was locked on her hip, possessive even in sleep. Lisbet tried to slip away without disturbing him, but his arm unconsciously lifted to embrace her, drawing her back.

She turned her head to watch him in sleep. He was on his side, naked except for the sheet lightly draped over the prominent bone structure of his hip. The taut flesh fell away under the hipbone, creating a cave of shadow where his sex lay hidden.

He had a strong build, his upper body all muscles, neatly tucked and folded one into the other. His legs, too, she remembered from the night. He was a man at a peak of physical perfection, and his agile endurance had worn her out.

He had said he had nothing to offer her now but sexual pleasure. If there was ever a man who could make that addictive for her—she was looking at him.

An Olympic sportsman, too, she reminded herself, and with a sigh allowed herself to be drawn in against the warmth of his body. She was a fool, but…not yet, oh, not yet.

He awoke because his flesh was stirring into life. His mouth against her ear, he whispered, "Good morning," and his hand stroked down her arm from shoulder to elbow.

"Good morning," she responded with a slightly wary smile. "Sorry to disturb you so early, but I've got to get moving. I'm due on the set."

His eyes closed, he smiled and nodded, stroking her thigh with intoxicating firmness, as if to underline his ownership. "When?"

"About an hour," she murmured, stretching involuntarily as he continued to caress her still pleasure-swollen flesh. Foolish to think she could have sufficient control to resist his lovemaking when she was actually in his bed.

"We can take the horses. It's faster," he said, his hand sliding over her breast, down her abdomen, to the nest of hair below. Melted sugar flowed just under her skin in the wake of his touch, and then, anticipating, in advance of it.

"All right," she murmured, agreeing to the unspoken part of his proposition, and with rough precision, he drew her thigh up over his hip and threw off the sheet, opening her body and legs to his lazy exploration.

His hand moved to tempt the cluster of nerves lurking hungrily under the still-damp thicket. Lisbet grunted a little in surprise at the speed of her own arousal, arched her back, and sighed the suddenly peaking pleasure out through her toes.

The sight and sounds of her ready response aroused him, and he wrapped his arm under her back and rolled her over, drawing her up to kneel over his body, making her legs straddle his hips, her full, lush breasts catching an errant ray of sun. Then he lifted his flesh to hers and, with a sigh of deepest satisfaction, thrust home.

Stay me with flagons, comfort me with apples: for I am sick of love.

Sheikh Jaf To Be In Movie

Sheikh Jaf's impromptu appearance in Masoud al Badi's new movie, now being filmed in the Barakati desert, will make the final cut, according to sources. Apparently the scene that was involuntarily filmed when Jafar al Hamzeh invaded the set and galloped off with Lisbet Raine, the film's star, is so hot the director wrote it into the film.

Jaf's house was quite a bit closer than Gazi's to the location, and almost at once they fell into a routine. The gold-plated limousine would pick her up at the end of the day's filming and take her back to Jaf's house, where she would bathe and refresh herself and then, usually, they made long, delicious love as the last rays of the sun were drawn down into the sea.

That was their quiet time. When they got up, it was

sometimes to a meal prepared for them in the house and served at the table in the courtyard. But more often than not, Jaf would want to eat out. And then, inevitably, the "public" Jaf would take over, and he would be anxious to hit the high spots.

They went to expensive places like the Sheikh Daud, now, where they were certain to be noticed by the clique of foreign journalists who hung out in one of the bars there.

It was very different from their time in London, where Jaf had always seemed to want her to himself, where it sometimes seemed they could have talked forever. But those lovers' conversations were a thing of the past.

And no matter how Lisbet tried to change events, they almost always wrapped up the night at the casino. And Jaf almost always lost.

The Shalimar Gardens was quiet, discreet and very expensive. It was intended for the amusement of the wealthiest foreign tourists only. The Barakat Emirates might have a secular government, but gambling was still severely restricted and frowned on in the country.

Barakatis were discouraged from going into the casinos, which made Jaf's appearance there that much more noteworthy. The fact that he was throwing away the fortune he had so recently inherited from his father was becoming household gossip.

Everyone disapproved, including Lisbet, but Jaf was deaf to disapproval.

"Jaf, it's so *boring!*" Lisbet would complain. "Whether you win or lose, where's the excitement? It's just standing around waiting for the ball to drop in the right hole. Why don't you take up golf? At least you have some control over the ball!"

"Come on, Lisbet," Jaf would cajole her. "It's my turn for a run of luck. Any day now."

Of course she could refuse to go with him. But she was sure he dropped more money if she wasn't with him. And, although she hated to admit it, she wanted to be with him, wherever he was.

It was her father all over again. Both men, Lisbet realized fairly soon, had collapsed under a blow of fate. The fact that her father had experienced sudden unexpected loss, and Jaf sudden expected gain, had not made any difference to their responses, though she knew who she respected more. Each of them had changed from being a useful human being to lying around doing nothing, fixated on a game over which they had no control, and drinking too much. Neither of them had even tried to make something better of the hand life had dealt them.

Worst of all, she found, was that her attempts to prevent Jaf's worst excesses were nothing more than fodder for a hungry media. Sheikh Jaf's "troubled affair" with the star of the first joint British-Barakati film was a hot item in the Sunday papers back home.

But she was foolish to worry so much about what was going to prove no more than a brief affair. If there was one thing that was now totally clear, it was that, whatever the media thought, Jaf had no serious, long-term intentions towards her. He never talked of the future now, never made demands, never used the word *love*.

It was just the perversity of life that she now yearned for him to do so. *Life is suffering.*

The only way Lisbet could cope was by ruthlessly reminding herself how impossible a long-term relationship would be with Jaf, and pretending that she wasn't falling daily more deeply in love with him.

Eight

Meanwhile, the country was eagerly preparing for the first state visit by the newly crowned Sultan and Sultana of neighbouring Bagestan.

Bagestan was one of the country's nearest neighbours, and an old ally. It wasn't long since the citizens of the Barakat Emirates had watched enthralled as the ruthless and unpopular dictator, Ghasib, had finally been driven out of Bagestan and the sultanate restored in the shape of the old sultan's grandson. Scenes of the Bagestani people, first staging silent protests outside the palace, and later cheering deliriously as their new sultan rode through the streets, had played endlessly on Barakat television.

Everyone knew that the princes of the Barakat Emirates had done all they could to aid in the restoration. After all, the old sultan's three grandsons had all been Cup Companions in Barakat.

The Barakatis had been almost as thrilled by the restoration as the Bagestanis themselves. And now the sultan and sultana had chosen to make the Barakat Emirates the destination of their first official state visit, both in recognition of this help and support, and as a signal of the return to the old ties that had historically bound the two nations prior to Ghasib's coup.

Numerous events were scheduled, but the one everyone wanted an invitation for was the Royal Grand Reception being held by the three princes in the magnificent Queen Halimah Palace in Barakat al Barakat.

All the Cup Companions would be there, of course, including those of the sultan and sultana, as well as the titled, the successful, the movers and shakers of the country. In addition, from the census lists of every city, town and village in the country, names would be drawn at random, and the lucky ones would receive an invitation to attend as the representative of their area.

It was the occasion of the century. A once-in-a-lifetime experience of history in the making. People would talk about it to their grandchildren. There was practically no one in the country who wouldn't give up their hope of Heaven to attend.

One evening, Jaf surprised Lisbet by handing her a large, thick envelope addressed in Arabic.

She felt its importance in the weight of the beautiful linen paper, the lushly embossed crest on the back flap, and sat without opening it for a few breathless moments.

"What is that written on the front?" she pressed.

"My name, and yours. Open it."

"What is it?" Lisbet whispered, afraid to guess, when she had lifted the flap to reveal a thick, luscious, gold-embossed card with an ornately engraved seal stamped into red wax. The flowing Arabic calligraphy was a work of art in its own right.

Jaf smiled. "Our invitation to the Royal Grand Reception for the Sultan and Sultana of Bagestan. When Karim asked, I said you'd like to be included."

"Oh, Jaf!"

Lisbet felt as if she'd stepped into a dream. She gazed down at the invitation. She was even more thrilled than she would have imagined. The event to mark the culmination in freedom of thirty years of struggle by an oppressed people!

She had a more personal interest, too, as Jaf already knew. She had known Dana Morningstar as a fellow actress in London. How interesting to meet her now, as the Sultana of Bagestan!

"Thank you!" she breathed, even more moved because it would have been so easy for him to deny her this pleasure out of his anger. "And he agreed I could go, just like that?"

Jafar laughed. "In truth, it's more of a royal command than an invitation. The old forms still apply between monarch and Cup Companion, and that extends to consorts. If you decide you don't want to go now I'll—"

"Decide I don't want to go to the celebration of the century?" Lisbet laughed half-hysterically. "Oh, but—Jaf, everybody will be...what will I *wear?*" she cried.

He smiled, as if he had been waiting for just this question, and got to his feet. "Come," he said. "Let me show you."

He led her to the large, pleasant, book-filled room he used as an office. In the shadowed interior he pulled a book from a shelf, reached in to pull a latch, and drew a section of shelving open to reveal a door. Keying in a code, he pushed that open, too, while she watched.

A light came on automatically, and he gestured to Lisbet to enter.

It was a tiny, square room, lined with steel. A small baize-covered desk had stools on either side, and a lamp. There were several doors set into the steel walls.

"I think you know my grandfather was a collector," Jaf remarked, moving to one of the safe doors while Lisbet perched on one of the stools at his command. Her heart was beating with a sense of mystery and excitement.

"He had a particular fondness for the jewellery of the Jalal Period."

That was the name, Lisbet knew, given to the two or three centuries of extraordinary flowering in the fine arts named for the reign of the great King Jalal, grandson of Queen Halimah. Perhaps the most important piece of the period was the famous Cup of Happiness, now in the possession of Prince Omar of Central Barakat. She had seen a picture of that in the paper.

Drawing open a steel door, Jaf reached inside to lift out several velvet boxes and a small wooden chest and set them on the table.

"Some of these treasures have been in our family for many generations, but it was my grandfather who really expanded it into a collection. It was a passion he transferred to me. I loved to look at the collection even as a young child, and my grandfather taught me a great deal as I grew older.

"He knew that any hope for his collection lay with Gazi and me. At his death he left it in trust only to my father, and thereafter the collection was to be divided. He left to me the pieces that comprised the Jalal Collection, and the remainder to Gazi.

"My father was forced to keep the collection intact, but he cared little for it and added nothing to it during his lifetime. I hope to do more with it."

Standing over her, Jaf lifted one of the boxes, opened it, and placed it before her on the table.

Lisbet was prepared to be stunned, for anything beautiful in Barakat was always measured against the Jalal Period, but at the sight of what was lying on a bed of maroon velvet she felt the blood rush in her ears.

It was a single, massive emerald pendant, its deep, rich green intricately engraved, on a chain of the most delicately and precisely formed diamond, emerald and ruby florets.

Lisbet had never seen anything so beautiful in her life. The modern jewellery that Jaf had given her in London simply couldn't compare. The piece glowed with beauty and the rich lustre of age, and the workmanship was unbelievably intricate and delicate. The little florets were so perfectly shaped her heart melted at the sheer beauty.

"It was a Golden Age for such arts," Jaf murmured, setting the case to one side and opening another. "Craftsmen of this calibre no longer exist."

The next box revealed a worked gold pendant set with a large square central ruby, a surround of diamonds and emeralds, and a milky-white pearl drop pendant.

Lisbet suddenly thought of the pathetic "pearl" ring

she had hoped to fool him with, and almost laughed to think of her own stupidity. Trying to fool a man who had a collection of jewels like this!

She glanced up at him, her eyes laughing. "No wonder you threw my ring into the desert," she said.

He returned her look with one of dark intensity. "Not because the pearl was false," he reminded her.

As the next case was opened, her eye fell on a strand of polished emerald beads that was breathtaking in its simplicity. Lisbet caught her lip between her teeth and shook her head.

An intricately worked flower brooch composed of petals of ruby, emerald and diamond was next. A ring carved from a single piece of ruby, inlaid with gold and set with emeralds. Earrings, forehead ornaments, bracelets and armbands were laid before her till she was dazzled by the sparkle and drunk with their beauty.

"This piece is called the Concubine's Tears," Jaf told her softly, opening a box to reveal the last piece: a circular pendant composed of ranks of tiny, tear-shaped rubies fanning out from a central emerald, all inlaid in worked gold. An inner and an outer circlet of emeralds bordered them. A large teardrop emerald hung quivering below. The necklace was a narrow chain set with cabochon-cut rubies and emeralds.

"Like the Cup of Happiness, it is the work of King Jalal's great Parvani jeweller, Nazim Gohari."

They were by no means the showiest stones. But something in its very delicacy seemed to catch at her throat. "Oh, how beautiful!" Lisbet whispered inadequately. "I've never seen anything so lovely! I'm almost afraid to touch it."

He smiled down at her, not surprised that she should

have understood that this was the prize of the collection, in spite of having none of the showy stones that the other pieces boasted. Works by Nazim Gohari were rare outside of the palace treasuries of the three princes of the Barakat Emirates. A few were in museums.

"Why is it called the Concubine's Tears?" Lisbet asked, still gazing at the piece, and feeling that perhaps it was because the concubine in question had wept when she saw a thing of such beauty. The workmanship was unimaginably fine.

"The piece has a history. It was ordered by Jalal from Nazim Gohari for his favourite concubine, Kumar al Nahar," Jaf told her, while she lifted the piece this way and that in the light.

"Kumar al Nahar was a most beautiful woman, with amazing accomplishments for her young age. It was said she could sing, recite her own poetry, write a beautiful calligraphic hand, and play several instruments. She also regularly stumped the king with her philosophical arguments and deep knowledge of the Quran.

"It's said that while in the market on a shopping expedition with her women one day, the king's favourite went to the shop of a silk merchant. The merchant had with him his nephew, whom he was training up in the business.

"Kumar al Nahar and the young man fell instantly in love. She ordered some silks to be brought to the palace, and the young silk merchant duly arrived in the harem.

"The two embarked on an affair that was full of peril, for if the king found out he might have them both put to death. But they fell more and more deeply in love, so deeply that they took wild risks to be together, putting themselves at the mercy of those who might easily violate their confidence and bring doom on their heads.

"Rumours reached Jalal's ears, but he loved the concubine so much he preferred to give Kumar al Nahar the benefit of the doubt. And he chose that moment to show his favourite increased favour. He ordered for Kumar al Nahar bigger apartments, enlarging her entourage and increasing her household.

"Meanwhile, rumours began to circulate about the young merchant, and angry citizens stormed his uncle's shop, for fear of King Jalal's wrath. The young man was forced to flee the city suddenly, without being able to see his beloved one last time to say farewell.

"Kumar al Nahar received a hurried, desperate message from her lover wishing her goodbye forever, and was inconsolably grieved. When the king next requested a visit with her, she accepted and prepared for his coming, but with a heart weighed down with sorrow.

"When the king arrived, she sat by him while food was served to him and her singers and dancers performed for him, and did her best to hide her grief.

"The king presented the jewel to Kumar al Nahar, and when she looked on its perfect beauty, her heart was assailed with the memory of her perfect love and her terrible loss. She fell unconscious, alarming the king and all who saw her.

"When she recovered consciousness she began to weep uncontrollably, tearing her hair and calling to heaven in her grief. Then she swooned away again.

When they tried to revive her, it was discovered that she had died.

"A friend of her lover in the city sent a messenger to the young man to inform him of her death, but the messenger returned saying that the young man had also died, on the same day as his beloved."

Jaf stopped speaking, and there was silence in the little room.

"Such beauty should be shared with the world. It would please me to have you wear this jewel—or choose any of the others—to the reception for the sultan," Jaf said, as calmly as if he were offering her a drink.

Location shooting was finally completed, and the movie crew moved into newly built sound stages just outside the capital, Barakat al Barakat, for the interiors. Jaf and Lisbet began to spend their time at Gazi and Anna's house, because it was so close.

They were a close-knit family, Lisbet discovered. In spite of Jaf's bringing disrepute on the family name, Gazi spoke to him with respect, and he consulted him, and listened to his advice, as often as the reverse.

Gazi and Jaf had together supported their sister, Nadia, through a difficult divorce recently, and Nadia was now living in the house with her baby daughter, Safiyah, while she waited for her lover to come and claim them.

Ramiz Bahrami had been Nadia's first love, as Lisbet already knew, but their father had forced her into marriage with another man. After three brutally unhappy years, Nadia had met Ramiz again by chance, and the predictable had happened.

That had been difficult enough. But then Ramiz had

disappeared, leaving her pregnant and at the mercy of a suspicious husband. Nadia and her baby had only just managed to escape.

All this Lisbet had learned months ago, back in England, on the day she and Jaf had first met. She had been astonished, on her arrival in Bagestan, to learn that Nadia was still loyally waiting for her lover to return to her.

"Hasn't she learned her lesson?" Lisbet asked Jaf with a dry cynicism born of her own dilemma. He looked at her gravely.

"She trusts him because she loves him, Lisbet. Perhaps it is something you could learn from her."

She swallowed and bit back the truth. It would serve no purpose.

"Are you two going to get married this time?" Anna asked her one day. Nadia was in the pool with Safiyah. The baby's ecstatic screams as she splashed made a pleasant background to their conversation.

Her mouth firm, Lisbet shook her head. "Jaf doesn't love me, Anna. This is an interlude only."

Anna stared. "Did he tell you so?"

"Yes. And anyway, Anna, don't wish it on me. Jaf's a compulsive gambler."

"What if he reformed for your sake?" Anna pressed. She would love to have Lisbet married to Gazi's brother, but not at the cost of her happiness. It was a dilemma.

"He won't do it for my sake," Lisbet said, swallowing hard. "He's easy enough on the surface, but scratch Jaf and he's still very angry and unforgiving underneath. He says his love is dead and I believe him."

They sat in silence for a moment. "Oh, Lisbet," Anna said at last, and Lisbet bit her lip hard.

"Well, that's life, isn't it? I should be grateful, and one day, no doubt, I will be. Life with someone like Jaf would be no picnic."

That was what she said. But that wasn't how it felt. Picnic? Her heart was convinced life with him would be a perpetual banquet.

Physically, Jaf was the lover to die for. His body gave her a pleasure that every day seemed more melting, more overwhelming than the day before. In every physical cell she felt daily more alive.

But Lisbet's heart pined for the love that had once been hers. She missed the intermingling of their souls that had once occurred. In London she had accepted that part of their lovemaking without realizing what it meant.

She remembered nights in London, when, the limousine following at a discreet distance, they had taken long walks in the rain, beside the Thames. Then he had been the perfect lover, if she had not been too afraid to realize it.

In the darkness, their souls seemed to merge. Then she had felt, without allowing herself to form the words, that she had found the other half of herself.

Jaf had believed it. "I knew it the moment we met," he had told her one rare, crystal-clear night, when the stars had appeared. They had left the hotel and gone for a long walk through the park and then across Westminster Bridge. Traffic was light, and in the middle of the bridge they had paused to look out over the river and the city.

"Even before that, when we spoke on the phone, I

had a sense of something momentous happening. When I saw you, I knew. As if an angel came out of a cloud and spoke in my ear. *Here she is.*"

She could not speak when he talked like this.

"Look at the stars!" he had commanded her, and she couldn't disobey. "Here in London you do not see the stars as they really are. The lights of the city blind us to true light. In my house in the desert the stars show you what they really are. Sparks from God's presence.

"Each star is a reflection of the divine light, do you feel it?" Jaf demanded.

She bit her lip without speaking, wondering where this was leading.

"God is unknowable, and yet is in the world. The mystics say that God begins as perfect emptiness and radiates presence through many levels of being until the material level is arrived at. That is how everything in the world is said to be One.

"And it is there, where the material world manifests, that Being for the first time divides into masculine and feminine.

"The division, they say, causes a deep yearning in the soul's two halves. And that is what humans are searching for—to restore the Divine Soul to unity. We go through the world, yearning for the perfect fit that is our other half, so that in our being together, the Divine Soul is unified again."

He stopped and turned her to face him, his arms encircling her with the rough ownership that both thrilled and terrified her.

"Do you see the truth of it, Lisbet?" he demanded, gazing down into her starlit face with a passionate hunger that shook her.

"It sounds wonderful," she choked, her heart almost too full to speak, because in the face of such knowing how could she argue that the world was not God's habitat as much as the heavens?

"Yes," he told her urgently. "And you, Lisbet, you are my other half. You and I were one soul in that moment before Creation tore us apart. And now, *Alhamdolillah,* we have found each other."

When she looked back on such moments now, she could not understand herself. What had made her drive such love away? Who was the real wastrel—Jaf, who only threw away money? Or she herself, who had thrown away something infinitely more precious?

Nine

At Lisbet's request, they went back one Saturday night to Umm Maryam's restaurant to be away from the prying eyes that now seemed to follow them whenever they appeared together in public. She was hoping that, for once, he would be happy with a quiet evening.

At the end of the meal they were alone in the little upper room. Jaf's arm was around her, holding her protectively into his shoulder, while he lazily ate with his other hand. They were sharing a single dessert composed largely of nuts, spices and honey, that was called Happiness in Arabic. Lisbet could believe it. In the main room musicians were playing a curious collection of zithers and strangely shaped guitars. In the little enclosure they were very private.

"Mmmm!" Lisbet exclaimed, taking a last mouthful of the heady but too-fattening mixture. "Diet tomorrow. This is impossible to resist."

Jaf slipped the tiny spoon into his mouth and ate another mouthful, turning the spoon over to catch every drop with his tongue. His eyes were half-lidded with sensual response as he licked an errant drop of spiced honey from his lower lip.

"It tastes like you," he murmured, close to her ear.

The honey in her stomach seemed to catch fire, and rush out through her blood and nerves to every part of her. "Jaf," she protested on a whisper. She had no control now over her response to him. He could melt her with a word, a look, the slightest caress.

His arm tightened around her, his hand clasped her hip with the urgent possessiveness that both thrilled and frightened her. One little part of her mind was always monitoring such moments, and whispering warnings. She could never be sure whether he still blamed her, as she blamed herself.

What if, when the time came, he refused to let her go? He was a man of influence here. Suppose he could prevent her leaving the country? There was a fierceness in him sometimes that made her wonder how safe she would be if Jaf were her enemy.

Then, as if the universe were laughing at her fear— or was it hope?—he let her go, drew his arm up and consulted the gold watch on his strong, dark wrist. "The night's still young. How about looking in at the Shalimar?"

Lisbet's heart plummeted. The look in his eyes now was the one she dreaded: rueful determination, as if he hated the compulsion that drew him there, but still gave in to it.

"No," she said quietly. "I don't want to go to the casino tonight, Jaf."

He nodded. "All right. Shall I drop you at Gazi's,

or would you rather stay at the house tonight? I can join you later wherever you are.''

''Jaf,'' she said, in a low, tormented voice.

''Lisbet, don't say it.''

''Please,'' she begged, exactly as she had heard her mother plead, when her father was going to the pub. ''Please don't go.''

''I won't stay long,'' Jaf promised. As her father had promised.

She closed her eyes. But she was as helpless against the urge to plead with him as he was against the urge to go. ''Please stay with me, Jaf. Please don't go to the casino tonight.''

His eyes were black with an unreadable emotion. ''Not tonight,'' he said. ''Soon, Lisbet. This won't last forever.''

Next time, her father used to say. *Next time, I swear.* Or he would agree, take off his cap, and sink down in front of the television. But half an hour later he'd be gone. Nothing swayed him. Even when there was no money to buy food for his children, there was money for drink.

She looked at Jaf now, and wondered why it was that people are driven to repeat their worst life experiences, over and over. ''You're fooling yourself if you think you ever loved me,'' she said harshly.

A dark, almost frightening expression crossed his face. His jaw clenched so that the muscles bulged. He lifted a hand to stroke the hair from her cheek, tucking it behind her ear with a trembling restraint that made her eyes burn.

''I loved you more than you can dream of,'' he said roughly, his voice shaking. ''You are asking for something that I can't give you, Lisbet. Not now. Trust me. Why won't you trust me?''

"That's what my father said," she told him. "Every night. Sorry, but I used up all my blind, stupid trust before I was fifteen. You can call this whatever you like, Jaf—a passing phase, a mood—but please don't ask me to take you on trust while you continue in it. If you were really to be trusted, you would stop this insane compulsion now.''

He closed his eyes and breathed deep, letting her run to a standstill. Then he looked at her with dark, stern eyes.

"Lisbet, you are quick to judge. You question me and my motives so readily. Do you ever question yourself? Do you ever ask yourself whether it is right for you to lose all your ability to trust because of this experience with one man?''

"My father," she pointed out.

"Yes, he was your father! Even so, Lisbet. The universe is bigger than one man. You cannot throw away all your trust because one man was weak!''

"I'm not judging you by my father, though, am I? I'm judging you on your own actions. I'm making a decision based on my prior experience, I grant you. A man in the grip of an obsession isn't to be trusted, that's the plain and simple truth.''

Somehow she felt as if her words were the doom of their affair. She thought, *However long it takes me to finish it, this is when it ended.* Hot tears welled up. She bent her head, blinking them back.

"I was obsessed by you once, but no more," Jaf said harshly.

"I meant gambling.''

"That is nonsense! I am not addicted to anything.

I pay money to be entertained, as everyone does. I pay more for my entertainment than most people, that is all. I *have* more money than most people.''

''Not for long, at this rate.''

''So, it is because I might one day be poor that you feel as you do? You do not wish to share the bed of a lover who is a poor man? What excuse will you make for yourself when the next man comes along?

''It is too late for us, Lisbet, but if you do not work to free yourself of this fear, you face nothing but emptiness.''

His words were broken glass scraping her heart. It was the first time he had said it. *Too late.*

''You're just trying to put me in the wrong!''

''And you are making up stories for yourself, so that you can run from life. It is an excuse! You look for excuses! You ran from me in London, and what was your excuse then? That I gambled? No, because you never once saw me gamble before you came here. What was your excuse then, Lisbet?''

She hated this. ''You know what it was. And it wasn't an excuse.''

''You tell me. Put it in words, Lisbet, if you can.''

''You were being too possessive.'' She shifted uncomfortably, because she did not want to admit to him how much she regretted her actions. ''You were trying to—own me.''

''Own you!'' he exploded. ''I loved you. I wanted you to be my wife. I wanted to spend my life beside you. This is what the whole world does, Lisbet, if they are lucky enough to find the person they seek!''

''It wasn't something I ever wanted,'' she said stoically. ''I made up my mind when I was fifteen that I'd never get married, never have children.''

He shook his head. "At fifteen, a child's brain is not even fully developed, so it is not surprising that you made such a wrong and life-denying choice then. But are you going to base your whole life on a decision made by someone with so little experience of the world? One day, if you live, you will be eighty, Lisbet. What will that old woman think of the child's opinions of life?"

He was right, and perhaps she recognized it in some part of herself that was only just coming into awareness. But confrontation is not hospitable to subtle knowing, and besides, Lisbet was afraid to give away one of her supports out of fear of undermining the other. She was very sure of her ground there.

"Any woman of eighty would tell me I'm making a mistake getting involved with an inveterate gambler," she said, in a flat voice.

"You are talking like a fool."

Anger came to her rescue. "When I was a kid, there were times we went hungry because my father had taken the housekeeping money to buy beer. I'm not letting myself in for that again!"

Jaf laughed, a long, loud peal that, for a moment, stopped the conversation in the outer room of the restaurant.

"So that is your reason? You are afraid of going hungry? What about your own career, Lisbet? You are a professional, working woman. Can you not hope to feed yourself?"

"That's not what I mean, and you know it!" she cried furiously, because he was making her feel small and stupid. "Although let me point out that when my father had drunk his way through his dole money he quite often moved on to my mother's earnings.

"What I am talking about is the sense of betrayal I felt, knowing my father cared less about me than he did about his next pint of beer! A child is very capable of making those connections, you know. You can't protect yourself against loving your own father, you can't stop that hurting, no matter how often it happens."

He sobered suddenly, looking at her with an open, deep, understanding gaze. "Ah, I begin to see," he said, lifting a hand to stroke her hair back from her cheek. "Yes, now I understand you better. Lisbet, I am not your father. It is not as you think. If I could tell you—" he began, but Lisbet, terrified by the melting of her heart, shook her head so violently, her eyes squeezed shut, that he stopped.

"If you aren't an addict," she said, "it's simple enough. Don't go to the Shalimar tonight."

"Lisbet, is it beyond your comprehension that the world may not be exactly as you imagine it to be?"

"Otherwise, drop me at Gazi's, please."

Black flames burned up behind his eyes and she held her breath and sent up an urgent prayer that she would win.

"Fine," he said, pushed the table out, and got to his feet.

The next day the Sultan and Sultana of Bagestan arrived at Barakat al Barakat port in the magnificent royal yacht. The city was alight with happiness and goodwill. Cheers rang in their ears and streamers and fresh flowers poured out on their heads as the royal couple drove up from the docks to the Queen Halimah Palace, accompanied by the three princes of the Barakat Emirates and their wives, all in open cars, with thirty-six mounted Cup Companions as escort.

Everyone was crazy with delight at the pageantry. Something always came over the citizens of Barakat when all three of their princes appeared in public together, and this day the delirium hit an even higher pitch.

It wasn't merely that so many Barakatis had family connections in Bagestan that they took the restoration personally. People also instinctively felt that the restoration made their own monarchy more secure. President Ghasib had interfered in the affairs of Barakat for years before his downfall, secretly trying to destabilize the reign of the princes.

And even now there were dissidents and extremists who didn't know when they were well off. In addition to everything else, the fact that there was no Ghasib in the background, fuelling discontent and financing dissent, lifted a burden of fear from the country's heart.

So the Barakatis were almost as ecstatic as the Bagestanis over the restoration, and the fact that the sultan and sultana were young and magnificently handsome only added to the joy and the sense of rightness. It was a heady time. Sirens blared, flags waved, blossoms rained down on the royal couple's heads, and the cheering never stopped.

Anna and Lisbet dressed for that evening's glittering event in a kind of stunned disbelief. Who would have guessed, a year ago in London, that these two friends would be standing together in a place like this, getting ready to meet princes and sultans?

"Are you *sure* we're not dreaming?" Anna said

once. "Could it be that I'm actually still in that hospital in London, with a concussion and a bump on my head, imagining all this?"

"Probably. But then, where am I?" Lisbet pointed out. "*I* didn't have an accident. I got home safely that night."

"Are you sure? Can we be absolutely certain that a taxi didn't run us both down?"

Lisbet paused dramatically. "Now you mention it…no."

"Well, then, there's only one thing to do."

"Carry on enjoying ourselves till we wake up," Lisbet agreed.

They certainly weren't likely to have any rude awakenings tonight.

"Is that from the Jalal Collection?" Anna squealed in breathless admiration as Lisbet lifted her necklace from its velvet bed.

Of course she had chosen the Concubine's Tears.

"Isn't it wonderful? Jaf insisted. He said this was a once-in-a-lifetime occasion and if we couldn't take the risk, what was the point?"

"I guess the gambler mentality has its good side," Anna joked.

"It must be worth millions. I'm going to be terrified of losing it all night long."

When they had finished dressing, the two friends stood side by side in front of the mirror, gazing at themselves.

Their outfits, Anna's white and Lisbet's green, fitted with all the perfection that only hours of painstaking cutting and fitting on the part of a top dressmaker could achieve. Each wore a king's ransom against hair and skin that glowed almost as richly as the jewels themselves.

Anna's jewellery was a stunning sapphire-and-diamond set that Gazi had bought for her in London. In a creamy, sleeveless, calf-length tunic over the flowing Barakati pants called *shalwar,* with her black hair and dark blue eyes, and her warm golden skin, she was a vision.

To set off the magnificent ruby-and-emerald jewel at her throat, Lisbet wore emeralds at her ears, but nothing else was necessary. Her eyes, darkening to match, appeared to be two more precious jewels.

Her strapless silk dress, in a rich deep green to match the emeralds, clung to her body, the fabric drawn together at the hip. The skirt was slit on one side to reveal a matching gold-spangled panel of transparent georgette behind which the tanned skin of her leg was tantalizingly visible when she moved.

Around her shoulders she carried a stole of the same gauzy fabric, also spangled with gold.

Anna shook her head in admiration of her friend's green-on-green beauty.

"Look at you, Lisbet, you're way out of the ordinary," she breathed. "You've always been a beauty, but there's just something about you now. You have real charisma. And I don't believe Jaf doesn't still love you."

To her surprise, Lisbet's eyes clouded.

"What's wrong?"

"Nothing. Jaf went gambling again last night, that's all. But I already know he's not going to give it up, so if I'm disappointed, I'm a fool."

Last night she had locked the bedroom door against him for the first time in their relationship. It had taken her hours to fall asleep, but she hadn't heard him try her door in all that time.

"Did it make you happy, to sleep alone?" he had asked this morning, in a voice that made her skin twitch.

She had steeled her resolve. "I would have been alone most of the night anyway, wouldn't I? You must have had a very good night at the tables."

Immediately afterwards he had gone out on business with Gazi and the men had returned only in time to dress for the reception.

"I don't say you're not right, Lisbet, but you know, I asked Gazi about it, and he swears Jaf will be okay. He says there's absolutely no question he'll give up all his crazy ways if you give him time."

"How much time is he going to need, did Gazi mention?" Lisbet asked dryly.

"I know, I said that—why doesn't he just give it up now? And all Gazi could say was, he won't just yet."

A choke of mirthless laughter escaped Lisbet. "Men. What a club."

"I know it looks like that, but—I don't know, Lisbet. Could there be something going on we don't know about?"

Lisbet gave her friend a look. "Oh, sure. The instructions in his father's will mean he has to gamble away half his money in order to keep the rest?"

"Well, no, but…Gazi did once say that there would be things he couldn't tell me about. He said, *You need to know that I am a Cup Companion, and that there are some secrets not even a wife can be told.*"

"I'll just bet there are. And one of them is a secret family propensity for risk-taking."

Anna made a face. "I guess I'm being too far-fetched. And maybe Gazi is just saying that about Jaf to keep me from getting stressed just now."

Lisbet caught it immediately. "Why especially now?"

Anna smiled a slow, happy smile that spread all across her face. "I have to tell you first, Lisbet. I'm pregnant."

"Oh, *Anna!*" Lisbet embraced her friend with little thought for the perfection of their clothes and hair, smiling and exclaiming. "There couldn't be better news!"

A year ago Anna's life had seemed nothing but tragedy. What a transformation there had been.

Anna was blinking hard to protect her makeup from the happy tears. "Gazi's over the moon. So you see how much we'd both like it if you two could sort things out. Wouldn't it be lovely if our kids could grow up together?"

Lisbet was silent. The old, automatic rejection would not come to her lips. She looked at Anna's still-flat tummy and thought of the child growing there, and all she could feel was a pang of yearning.

All the old certainties were shifting. But to what benefit?

It is too late for us, Lisbet.

Ten

The "pleasure gardens" of the Queen Halimah Palace were a masterpiece of architecture. They had appeared in several books and photographic studies, but no photograph could have prepared Lisbet for the staggering beauty she saw.

There were water steps and cascades, arches and pillars, fountains and pools, cloisters and colonnades, pavilions and pergolas, all in the most beautiful workmanship and materials—marble, sandstone, walnut, cedar, mirror and painted tile. There were citruses and plane trees and cypresses, roses and box hedges and pomegranates.

Everywhere she turned a new vista opened up, whether it was a double phalanx of cypress lining a water channel descending through several levels, a spread of lush tropical foliage, a row of scalloped arches, or a spacious, shaded cloister. It was completely magical.

And the assembled guests were every bit as breathtaking and beautiful. The Barakati world had pulled out all the stops. Not merely the jewellery, but the clothes, were the most luxurious possible: the traditional costumes of Parvan, Barakat and Bagestan were lushly embroidered tonight with gold and silver thread, mimicking the royal court of the Golden Age. The fabrics glowed in the flaming torches and lamps that illuminated the gardens as the sun set.

The food, too, was simply out of this world. There were skewers of delicately grilled chicken, salmon, or lamb, tiny pastry cups filled with delicious pastes of aubergine, tomato, peppers, onion, courgette and unknown others, intricately carved raw vegetable flowers, pastry envelopes wrapping a delicious mix of savoury herbs and cheese, tiny mounds of delicious bulgur-and-parsley salad on miniature lettuce leaves, toothpick kebabs comprising no more than a mouthful, balls of spiced minced lamb, mushrooms stuffed with rich, spicy cheese, vine leaves wrapped around savoury rice; the scent of cumin, coriander, cardamom, cinnamon.

Instead of wine, a fascinating variety of drinks was on offer—the date juice she had already learned to like, a light, tangy yogurt drink, a variety of delicious and unusual mixes of fruit juice.

And all in an endless procession, carried by beautifully costumed, dark-eyed children ranging in age from ten to about sixteen, all clearly proud of being chosen for this duty and on their mettle.

Groups of musicians playing every variety of Middle Eastern instrument were tucked into corners, under

trees, by fountains, under cloisters, in pavilions. The
music they played travelled hauntingly on the evening
air, and as Lisbet and Jaf moved through the pleasure
garden, they would lose the sound of one orchestra
and a moment later come into range of another.

It was a night she would remember all her life.

Jaf wore the traditional ceremonial dress of the Cup
Companions: the flowing white pants called *shalwar*
worn under a richly coloured, high-necked silk jacket
belted with a jewelled strap holding a glittering scabbard, and bedecked with a thick double rope of pearls
thrown over one shoulder and caught high on the left
breast with a fat jewelled pin. The Cup Companions
could wear almost any colour of jacket. Tonight Jaf's
jacket was indigo, and his eyes were black.

She had never seen him look so heartbreakingly
handsome.

Jaf returned the compliment. When she and Anna
had come down the beautiful old stone staircase to the
terrace where the men were waiting, for a moment
neither Jaf nor Gazi had spoken a word. But the expression in Jaf's eyes had been enough. And as he put
an arm around her to shepherd her out to the car, she
had felt him tremble.

The hostility of last night and this morning was forgotten, and now they stood together in the glory of
the royal court and knew that, whatever happened between them, this night would never pass from their
memory.

A young boy with a tray full of delectable tidbits
paused by them. Jaf bent over the tray with frowning
concentration.

''What do you recommend, Afif?'' he asked the
child in English.

Without hesitation, the child indicated the bowl on the right.

"Take the sall-mon, please, cousin," he said.

"The salmon?" Jaf obediently picked up one of the little sticks and popped it into his mouth. "Very tasty," he approved. "Is the other not so delicious? Nonetheless, it seems to have been eaten."

"It is not called *nonetheless,* it is called *breast of chicken,* and people like it so much that my tray has become unsteady. That is why I asked you to eat from the bowl on this side," the child informed him gravely.

They laughed and helped themselves to the little skewers of salmon, and the child nodded solemnly and moved on.

"Why did he call you *cousin?*" Lisbet asked, wondering if it were a translation of some kind of formal title used between children and adults.

"Because we are cousins," Jaf told her with a smile. He gestured with a hand. "All the children serving tonight are from the royal family or the families of the Cup Companions. It has always been thus."

"And will they grow up to be Cup Companions in their turn?"

"Some will, no doubt."

"Did you do it?"

"My grandfather was advisor to Sheikh Daud for many years. As a child, I served at many such occasions. But I do not remember one of such magnificence as this.

"One day, *insha'Allah,* my sons and daughters will serve in this way. It is an important training for those who are born to rank, to teach them that service is both a duty and a privilege."

Lisbet couldn't speak just at that moment, so filled was she with the ache of hopeless yearning. She had given up her chance to be a part of this. Anna's child, probably, would one day learn the simple truth about service in this way, but not her own child. She thought of Jaf as a father, holding his child close, and her heart clenched with yearning.

It is too late for us, Lisbet.

For perhaps the first time, she looked at the spectrum of human life and saw that it was a continuum, a passing on from one generation to the next—of duties, of wisdom, of information, of genes. Long ago, unhappiness had caused her to decide to isolate herself from the continuum, to have the thread of what she was stop with her. She had thought of childhood as too full of suffering to pass on to others.

But childhood was more than suffering, even her own. The bonds she shared with her brothers and sisters and her mother had supported them all through the hard times.

She was the one who had taken their father's downfall hardest. Lisbet now remembered, with a little shock, that as a young child she and her father had been very close. Perhaps because she had been his first daughter after two sons, she was closer to him than any of the others.

Had that made the betrayal that much harder to bear? That he would not give up drinking even for her? There was a host of memories in her mind suddenly, of moments when she had tried to use her power with her father to sway him from his chosen course. Like her mother, she had failed.

Looking back now, Lisbet could see that on each of those occasions her father had already been drunk. She had been pleading with beer, not Edward MacArthur. But how could a child have understood that? Even many adults could not distance themselves in such cases.

"What are you thinking about, Lisbet, that your eyes have gone so grave?" Jaf's voice softly broke into her musing.

She looked up into his eyes, her heart in turmoil. If she had given in to love when it was first offered, would she now have the power over him that she had never had over her father? Or would it be a repeat?

She would never know. *It is too late for us.*

Those words would drive her to an early grave, and then be written on it.

Gazi and Anna were coming along the torchlit marble path running beside the channel of flame-spangled water which led from a pool under a beautiful pavilion down to the fountain where the couple stood.

Jaf consulted his watch. "It is our moment to be presented to the sultan and sultana," he told her, as the other couple arrived.

Anna and Lisbet exchanged glances. However democratic your principles, there was still something that thrilled to the idea of meeting a sultan.

"Lisbet's met the sultana before, haven't you, Lisbet? In her previous incarnation as an actress in London," Anna said as the two couples moved off, arm in arm. Gazi turned a curious glance on Lisbet.

"Gazi wasn't there when you told me, remember?" Anna prompted.

"About three years ago we did *Midsummer Night's Dream* together in the Park," Lisbet explained to Gazi. "She played Helena and I was Hermia. We had a great time, but right afterwards I went on tour and we lost touch. I wonder if she'll remember me.''

They passed from the smaller side garden into the huge, brilliantly lighted square, bordered with trees, where the magnificent pillared pavilion stood. In front of it was a pool from which a fountain jetted up, the water catching the light from the thousand torches and multiplying it into a million shards.

The pavilion was reached by a short, broad flight of stairs. The four royal couples were standing at the top, and people were moving slowly up and down. Two ranks of men in the glittering ceremonial uniform of the Palace Guard lined the stairs looking very ornamental, but Jaf informed her in an undervoice that they were among the best trained bodyguards in the world.

''Those scimitars on their hips aren't merely ornamental, either, however jewelled the scabbards. Security here is a lot tighter than it looks.''

Lisbet was startled. Security had looked pretty tight to her. Guests had passed into the palace only after a search by a handheld metal detector, which had reacted hysterically to every bit of metal anyone wore.

''Really? Why?''

''Because there are still some who would be very happy to cause the downfall of the princes of Barakat. Ghasib was not the only man in this region with an agenda. Look up there.''

She followed the direction of his glance. Above them, on the roof of the pavilion, she could just make out several dark shapes.

''The secret service has mounted one of the biggest operations in its history to cover this event.''

Jaf's office as Cup Companion, Lisbet knew, was the rough equivalent of a Minister for the Arts, with the particular focus of fostering cultural exchanges between West Barakat and the world. She wondered how he knew so much about the operation.

"Are you part of it?" she asked.

"All Cup Companions constantly take some part in the protection of the princes," he said. His hand unconsciously rested on the handle of his own gorgeously bejewelled sword.

"Is your sword real, too?"

He smiled. "It is the sword of my ancestors. Fine *jawhar* steel, still beautiful and deadly. You would call it *damascened.*"

They moved up the steps in the wake of Gazi and Anna then, in the flickering torchlight that lined both sides of the staircase. At the top the *talar,* or balcony, was bathed in a golden glow from a series of beautiful cut-crystal and bronze lamps.

Lisbet gazed up at the royal couples on the *talar* above her as she mounted the steps. It was a sight to take the breath away. She simply stopped breathing in the face of such beauty and majesty. However many photos one saw, nothing could equal seeing five ruling monarchs—for the sultana shared executive power with her husband—together in one place. The sense of real power was palpable and overwhelming.

They were all magnificently dressed in brilliant colours, gold, and jewels that sparkled richly in the golden light. They were all instantly recognizable to anyone who read the paper or watched television.

But recognizing them and meeting them in person were two very different things, Lisbet found, as she made her first curtsey and was presented to the prince to whom Jaf was most closely connected.

Prince Karim, dark and clean-shaven, wore a sapphire jewel on his turban and pearls over his shoulders. The Great Seal of Shakur, a magnificently carved emerald clasping his arm just above the elbow, glowed with green fire against his cloth-of-gold jacket.

There was no sign of his disapproval tonight, no distance between the prince and his erring Cup Companion, a fact Lisbet noted with relief.

Beside the prince, Princess Caroline was wearing an emerald in the middle of her forehead that made her beauty look other-worldly, but her smile seemed very real, and so did her interest in Lisbet and the film.

Next, Prince Rafi, dark and smiling, with a thick moustache, exuded warmth and charm. He wore a ruby in his turban, and at his hip carried the Sword of Rostam in its intricately jewelled ceremonial scabbard. Beside him, Princess Zara, her eyes glowing with warmth, wore white gold-embroidered silk with diamonds and rubies.

She, too, spoke to Lisbet about the film.

"We like to think Rose Dumont set up her headquarters in the ruins at Iskandiyar," she said. "We were hoping the film could be shot there, did you know? But it just wasn't possible to let it be used as a location at the moment, with the museum still being built."

"I'm very much looking forward to visiting Iskandiyar while I'm here," Lisbet responded.

"Well, Jaf must bring you. Jaf, do you hear that?" She reached out and put her hand on Jaf's sleeve. "Will you bring Miss Raine to the site sometime soon? Call first to let me know, so I can be sure to be there."

Prince Omar, tall and erect, with the neat pointed beard that was his trademark, wore in his ceremonial gold turban an emerald that matched his haughty green eyes. Prince Omar was intimidating, until his face softened when he looked at his pregnant wife.

Princess Jana, a warmly tanned redhead, was wearing a wonderful gold outfit that matched her husband's ceremonial jacket and turban, and glowed like one of the hanging gold lamps behind her head. Her neck was wrapped with half a dozen strands of the most luscious pearls Lisbet had ever clapped eyes on.

Then they were approaching the Sultan and Sultana of Bagestan. A voice announced, "His Excellency Jafar Zaki ibn Bassam al Hafez al Hamzeh, Miss Lisbet Raine," and Lisbet found herself looking up into the smiling eyes of a magnificent creature she could barely recognize as Dana Morningstar.

The sultana was wearing a breathtaking outfit of deep purple-and-turquoise silk and silk georgette, encrusted with gold embroidery and spangled over with gold diamanté and hundreds of minuscule gold mirrors. Nestling in her black hair was a circlet of gold and diamonds.

Beside her the sultan looked compellingly imperious and majestic in cloth of gold and a blinding array of pearls and emeralds.

"Lisbet!" the sultana cried with a smile, and bent forward to kiss her cheek. "I heard you were coming tonight. How wonderful to see you again! What's it like working with Masoud al Badi? I always wanted to work with him."

Lisbet grinned. "Very rigorous," she said, and Dana laughed. The two women chatted together for a moment almost as they would have, Lisbet reflected wildly, meeting in a rehearsal room in London.

Against this backdrop the conversation seemed utterly incongruous.

But the pressures of the occasion meant it had to be curtailed. "Ash," Dana murmured, leaning into the sultan's shoulder to interrupt his low-voiced conversation with Jaf, "Lisbet is an old friend."

As Sultan Ashraf Durran ibn Wafiq ibn Hafzuddin al Jawadi Bagestani's imperious dark eyes fell on her, Lisbet's curtsey was completely instinctive.

"Your Majesty," she murmured. No wonder the Bagestanis had wanted the man as their sultan! No wonder they had risked life and freedom, taking to the streets to demand his homecoming.

He said something, and Lisbet replied without knowing what either of them was saying.

Then Dana said, "Lisbet, every minute of our schedule is full while we're here. But when you've finished on the film, or if you get a break, will you come to Bagestan and stay with us for a few days? I'd love to really talk!"

"Good evening, Miss Raine," said a voice, and Lisbet turned to see a white-haired stranger in formal court dress standing beside her. She hadn't seen him before, but he was clearly a man of importance. He carried himself like a man used to power.

After their presentation, the foursome had strolled into one of the smaller pavilions on the grounds, where Lisbet and Anna had been enthralled by the architecture, paintings and furnishings.

Built on a square, with a ceiling of intersecting, descending domes, the main room of the pavilion was divided by a double circle of marble pillars that held up the pattern of domes.

A myriad exquisite Parvani and Persian carpets, all hand knotted in silk or fine wool, flung as if at random over each other, covered every square inch of the marble floor. More carpets hung from the walls, alongside silver-and gold-embroidered silk tapestries that glittered and glowed in the warm light of a thousand crystal lamps.

In every corner was the green of tall, leafy plants and trees. Here and there fountains played.

The guests relaxed on cushions and divans as richly coloured and embroidered as the hangings and the carpets, while the endless supply of tidbits borne by the children continued.

Stationed at one corner of the room, a small orchestra playing traditional instruments provided a haunting background to the buzz of conversation.

Jaf's attention had been caught by someone, and Lisbet had wandered out of the main room into a smaller area, examining the paintings and hangings.

Now she was standing in front of a portrait of King Daud, the princes' father. She looked up as her name was spoken. She and the stranger were alone in the small hall.

"Hello," she said, arching her eyebrows enquiringly.

But he did not introduce himself. "You are interested in our late king?"

"He had a very dramatic life, didn't he?"

"Ah yes. He, too, loved a foreign woman."

"Like his sons."

"Not only his sons. Are not you loved in this way?"

He smiled, but she was not fooled. Malevolence exuded from him like an acid mist, little drops that burned wherever they touched her, parching her lungs when she breathed. Lisbet would have liked to walk away. But something held her there. Perhaps his very malevolence.

"Do you think so?"

His eyes fell on her necklace. "Even a man as foolish as Jafar al Hamzeh does not allow any ordinary woman to wear the Concubine's Tears. Do you know the value of what you wear around your neck?"

She was conceiving a powerful dislike of this man.

"On the other hand, maybe he wanted it seen tonight. Maybe I was just the handiest neck."

He stared at her for a long moment, then nodded.

"You are a wise woman," he said, in carefully modulated admiration. "You understand that Jafar al Hamzeh is a poor risk. Gambling, drinking—how can such a man be counted on? We hear that you try to turn him away from the evil."

"Is that what you hear?"

"Forgive me if I take the privilege of my white hairs to tell you, Miss Raine, that if it is his rehabilitation you desire, you go the wrong way about it. A man like Jafar al Hamzeh will not be induced to stop gambling because a woman—however pretty she is— asks him. It is a sickness. There is only one cure for such a disease."

"And what would it be?"

He smiled and tapped the air with a forefinger. "Did I not say you were a wise woman? So many young people fail to understand how much grief would be saved if they would listen to the advice of their elders. It is a modern epidemic. But you understand."

The forefinger moved again. "The only way to treat this foul disease is to let it run its course. Turn your energies in the opposite direction, Miss Raine. Only when Jafar al Hamzeh has utterly wasted his inheritance and ruined himself can he begin to live his life as a sober, sensible man.''

She didn't waste her time getting indignant.

''I have seen it many times. The efforts of mothers, even, fall on desert ground with such men. Only the delivery of a deep shock allows such behaviour to change. Even Western psychiatrists are now learning this wisdom. You can help.''

Behind her the music floating from the main room added its own thread to this surreal scene.

''But if I encourage Jaf to gamble away everything, where will that leave me?'' she pointed out in gentle mockery. ''The deep shock may also allow him to reject me for my betrayal.''

''Ah, but you will recover, you will move on! I understand you and the business you are in.'' His voice dripped with unconscious contempt. ''Such as you do not expect to choose a partner for life, isn't it? A new movie, another leading man. It would be too much to expect more from such a lifestyle.''

With a little shock Lisbet understood that this was not an idle conversation. She also saw, with a clarity that frightened her, that here was a man with an agenda.

''In that case, why should I care what he does?'' she said, racking her brains for some clue as to what he could want. ''Should I bother trying to reform him if there is no long-term benefit to me?''

A look of quickly suppressed triumph crossed his face. He laughed admiringly.

''Very true. But consider, Miss Raine—if Jafar al Hamzeh faced his ruined life, took stock, and returned to the straight path to live as Allah intended, how his friends would rejoice! They would be very grateful to the one who had made him see the error of his ways. You need have no fear of losing anything by this course, I assure you."

"I see," she said. "That would make all the difference, of course."

He nodded, completely missing the irony. He looked at her for a long moment, and then, as if they had understood something, took out a slim wallet, extracted a tiny gold pen, wrote a number on a card.

"You will know better than any other at what moment the shock has been delivered. On that day, call that number. You will not be sorry."

Her eyes still on his face, Lisbet lifted her hand automatically and accepted the card.

You're wrong, she mentally told the man. *I'm not nearly as smart as you think. It's taken me all this time to realize that you aren't my enemy, but Jaf's.*

Eleven

Lisbet tossed and turned till the sun came up. Only when the room was light did she finally fall into a fitful sleep, and when she awoke a few hours later, Jaf was gone.

She got up and staggered to the bathroom, where she stood for five minutes in a cold shower. *Nice to have been to such a blowout and not have a headache afterwards,* she thought absently. *There's something to be said for not having wine shoved at you at every turn.*

The only headache she had was from the blast of malevolence she had absorbed from the stranger. In retrospect, Lisbet shuddered. How could she have stood beside the man for as long as she did? She had dreamed of him as some kind of alien, nasty and sinister, with yellow eyes.

He seemed to her the kind of man who never gave

up, who would go on and on, a step at a time, till he got what he wanted. The fact that she refused to help him would disconcert him not a bit, she was sure. He would just wait for another opportunity.

And it was Jaf he was after. He wanted Jaf's ruin. The thought of such a man being bent on such a mission terrified her. Like a vulture, hovering, waiting, till his victim was too weak to resist.

And that was only half of what had kept her awake by Jaf's side last night. The other half was finally facing how deeply entangled she was. The nameless threat from the stranger had caused things to crystallize.

She loved him, deeply and completely. It would be like tearing her hair out by the roots to leave him.

For the first time, Lisbet understood that her mother had been half complicit in the pregnancy that had scuttled her chances of a different future. There had been a part of her that wanted to stay with her lover.

And for the first time she could see that, however hard life became, what had held her parents together was love. It was like looking at one of those graphics where dark and light markings seem meaningless, but if you look long enough an image suddenly appears.

And she must always have known it, unconsciously. The reason she had been so terrified of Jaf owning her was that she loved him. She had learned the lesson of her mother's life unconsciously, and it had guided her actions without her being in touch with her motives.

It was herself she was afraid of. Herself, and love.

And, she reminded herself, the man who had offered her a bribe to bring about Jaf's downfall.

It was late when she got down to the terrace, where everyone usually ate breakfast. Gazi and Jaf, she learned from the maid who refreshed the coffeepot, had gone out on business. Anna was in her studio, working. Nadia had taken the baby into town.

Lisbet waived breakfast out of deference to last night's gorging, and took a quick swim in the pool. With perfect timing, there was a delay in filming just now, while one of the harem sets was being rebuilt. There would be no filming for at least a week.

Thank God, Lisbet thought. She would have had a hard time concentrating today. But she pulled out her script and settled to trying to work on her lines for the scenes to be shot as soon as filming resumed.

Her attention wouldn't fix on Rose Dumont. Again and again she found herself mulling over the events and discoveries of last night. Strange how something so magnificent as the reception could be so overshadowed by a two-minute conversation. Strange how blank her mind was whenever she tried to think of the future.

"Are you ready for a drink of something?" Anna's voice broke into her thoughts after a couple of fruitless hours, and Lisbet turned gratefully to see her friend striding across the terrace to where she sat.

Anna was wearing a blush-pink swimsuit, her white terry robe flapping on the breeze. She was warmly tanned, her skin glowed and Lisbet couldn't help comparing this happy vision to the woman she had been a year ago. Then she had been too thin, depressed and listless, grieving over the man who had walked out on her and the stillbirth of her child.

Now her manner said she had everything to look forward to. Anna had never seemed happier. If only the same road to happiness were open to Lisbet.

She supposed it was just typical of anyone with a damaged childhood that she had somehow managed to repeat her mother's experience. Falling for an addict. If she did have children with Jaf, she would be giving them the same childhood that she had suffered through—the kind of responsibility-laden time that wasn't childhood at all. Always nervous about what Daddy was going to do. Trying to stop him from indulging in his addiction because it hurt everyone so much....

No, on the day she discovered she was pregnant with Jaf's child, if she ever did, she wouldn't feel the unalloyed joy that Anna clearly felt. For her there would always be mixed emotions. Her happiness would always have echoes of guilt and foreboding.

And if, as seemed more likely, Jaf never loved her again, how long would she grieve? Would she ever love another man the way she had finally realized she loved him?

Anna was carrying a big pitcher filled with creamy-white liquid, and two glasses, which she set down on the little table at Lisbet's elbow.

"This kind of thing drives the staff crazy," she confided with a grin. "But I think if you let yourself be waited on *all* the time, you get soggy. Okay if you're born to it. Piña colada, your favourite."

"Mmmm."

Anna filled the glasses and sat down. A tendril of yellow blossom from the wall stretched towards her in the breeze, and she caught it in one hand and brought it against her cheek, sniffing the perfume.

"Isn't this terrace heaven? Even on a boiling hot day like today, it's pleasant here. Is Jaf's place nice? I've never been there."

They chatted about houses, but the topic foremost in both their minds was last night, and it wasn't long before they were discussing it.

Lisbet managed to forget her worries in the excited postmortem of the evening.

"Well, we've gossiped over lots of parties on lots of mornings after in our day," Anna observed, after the subject had been thoroughly washed, wrung out and hung to dry. "But I think today we've peaked."

"You're right. It really was the party to end all parties. When we're sitting in our 'sheltered accommodation,' Anna—"

"Side by side in our comfort shoes and our E-Z loungers—"

"Complaining that no one makes piña colada the way they used to—"

"They will say of us—"

"*This* was our finest hour!"

Something else she would remember about the past twenty-four hours, Lisbet thought. She drained her glass of the deliciously sweet piña colada and set it down, suddenly grave.

"Something happened last night, Anna."

"Jaf proposed!" Anna cried.

"Nothing like that. It was quite frightening, actually." Lisbet embarked on the brief narration of her conversation with the stranger. When she had finished, Anna sat frowning and gnawing her lip.

"What did you make of it?" she finally asked.

Lisbet breathed deep. "I've been trying to work out what he really wanted. I keep thinking of the way he commented on the necklace. Do you think it could be something to do with the Jalal Collection? That would be a reason for wanting Jaf's financial ruin, wouldn't it? He might assume that Jaf would have to sell the collection cheaply if he lost big at the casino.''

Anna shrugged. ''Maybe. But I think Gazi would buy the collection if it came to that. Jaf has talked about giving it to a museum, and that would be okay with Gazi, but sell it to a private collector? I don't think either of them would like that.''

''The man who talked to me may not know that.''

''True...'' Lisbet could see that Anna wasn't convinced but couldn't find any concrete objection. ''One thing mystifies me—why this man assumed you would agree to do it.''

''I think it was just contempt. I'm a Western woman, I'm an actress, I'm sleeping with Jaf without being married—doesn't it follow that I'm totally corruptible?''

''Mmmm. But it's also possible, isn't it, that he's trying to spook Jaf?''

''You mean, said what he said hoping I would pass on his comments to Jaf?''

''*Have* you told him?''

''He was gone when I woke up.''

''Gazi, too. They both have a lot to do with the royal visit,'' Anna said. ''But they'll be back for lunch. Are you going to tell him?''

Lisbet looked out over the turquoise expanse of the sea. The heat was intense today, but the breeze was pleasant, as Anna said. A huge cruise vessel was sailing past. ''I'm almost afraid to. Do you think I should?''

Anna sat in silence for a moment, tapping a finger against her lips.

Lisbet recognized the signs and was silent, letting her think.

"Last winter, when it was all happening with Nadia—Gazi told me something. I can't tell you any details. But I have a feeling you should tell Jaf about
this immediately. It may have much broader implications than appear on the surface."

"Where did you think you had seen him earlier?"
Jaf asked.

"Jaf, there were so many people!" Lisbet protested.
"When he spoke to me, I had the feeling I'd seen him
before, that's all. I can't be certain."

"But not spoken to him? You hadn't been intro-
duced at any point?"

"No. I'd remember that voice."

"You said you felt he was someone important,"
Gazi said. "Can you say why?"

She closed her eyes, trying to visualize the scene
and her first reactions to the man. They waited in silence.

"At first I thought it was just because he had an
aura of power," Lisbet said. "But I think maybe there
was something else, too, something I'd seen earlier—
maybe one of the princes talking to him in a certain
way? I have the vague recollection of seeing something like that without really noticing it."

She had told Jaf about the meeting when the men
came home for lunch. Jaf's reaction was convulsive.
He had questioned her briefly and urgently, and then
called Gazi. Now Lisbet and the al Hamzeh brothers
were in Gazi's office going over the incident in minute
detail.

"How sure are you that he didn't come into the
pavilion after your conversation with him?"

"I'm almost certain he wasn't in the main room. I

was looking around for him because I wanted to point him out to Jaf.''

Gazi tapped the white card with the phone number against his thumb. ''Is there anything else at all you can remember, Lisbet? Any clue?''

''I really think I've told you everything.'' She had been racking her memory for every detail of the man's appearance for the past half hour. ''Jaf, can't you tell me what this is about?''

It seemed that Anna's suspicions were on target. The way Jaf and Gazi were reacting told her there was more than petty malice against Jaf involved. They were like wild animals, every sense alert at the approach of an enemy. Then she mentally amended that. Their attitude wasn't that of victims, but hunters. They were lions who had scented their prey.

''I am not sure how much we can tell you at the moment, Lisbet,'' Jaf said. ''We will have to consult, and get permission before telling you anything.''

She blinked. ''Permission?'' She had never heard of Jaf asking anyone's permission to do anything. Except one. ''Do you mean you have to talk to *Prince Karim* about this?''

The brothers exchanged glances. Gazi grinned. ''And all this time I thought you chose her for her looks.''

Jaf's eyes rested on her with a look that made her heart skip. ''I chose Lisbet for her soul,'' he said.

How could one heart be made both lighter and heavier by the same remark?

''Lisbet, we have to swear you to secrecy,'' Jaf told her that evening. The three of them were in Gazi's office again, looking out over a shaded nook of the terrace.

"It's a question of national security and I have to ask for your word not to speak of it. Anna and Nadia know some of it, but it would be dangerous to talk where you might be overheard. Do you agree?"

There was a kind of thunder in her ears. "You want to tell me national security secrets?" she breathed.

The men nodded, and she looked from one to the other.

"Why?"

Again the brothers exchanged significant glances, and Gazi clicked his tongue admiringly at his brother.

"You want me to do something," she said. "That's the only reason I can see for my needing to know anything."

"We want you to help smoke this man out of hiding," Jaf said. "You are the only one who has seen him, Lisbet. We think you've talked to the man at the top, or very close to the top."

Her heart was pounding hard. "The top of what, exactly?"

"Of an ongoing conspiracy to topple the monarchy of the Barakat Emirates."

"Oh, God!" she cried. "And how could I help?"

"By leading me along the road to ruin and then calling the number he gave you and demanding your reward," Jaf told her simply.

"As far as we know it started about twenty-five years ago," Jaf told her later, as they walked along the beach under the stars. "When a beautiful young woman appeared at the palace demanding to speak to the king. No doubt she had been raised on stories of the old courts, where the king held regular days of justice at which ordinary citizens could speak. Her name was Nusaybah. Perhaps you know the story of Prince Jalal.''

Lisbet nodded. She had read the story in a magazine at the time his identity was discovered. Jalal was the posthumous son of Prince Aziz al Quraishi who, with his brother the Crown Prince, had died in an accident before he could marry Jalal's mother. Only the king had known of his grandson's existence, but although he had educated the boy at great expense, he had left absolutely no provision for him on his death, hadn't even revealed his existence to the three sons—the present princes—to whom he left his kingdom.

Jalal had gone into the desert with his followers and become a bandit, demanding territory of the princes, thinking that they knew who he was. Only when, in desperation to be heard, he had taken Princess Zara— then Zara Blake—hostage, was the truth revealed.

''Yes, that is the story the public believes,'' Jaf told Lisbet now, as the soft sound of waves tumbled up the shore. ''But it is not the full truth. Last year Jalal was confronted by men who told him that the old king, his grandfather, had never known of his existence. Someone who was deeply opposed to the Quraishis, someone within the palace, had seen in Aziz's unknown young son a future weapon against the ruling family.

''It was this man who had taken charge of Jalal's education, who had seen to it that the princes never knew who he was, who had caused him to be spurned and become disaffected. The plan was to overthrow the princes and install Jalal as a puppet. But when the plan was revealed to him Jalal would have no part of it.''

Lisbet's mouth opened in a gasp of comprehension. "Is *that* why Jalal gave up his titles and left the country? I thought he renounced it all for love."

Jaf smiled, his face reflected in moonlight. "Love formed a part of his decision. But Prince Jalal was also determined not to spend his life, as he put it, 'a focus for every sect that is disenchanted with the state of the country.'

"Those who had invested so much in Prince Jalal have not given up on their dreams of power simply because no puppet prince is now available, however. They are looking for other means to achieve their ends."

Lisbet nodded. "Like what?"

"At the moment, we have learned, they plan to subvert one of the Cup Companions. We do not know exactly for what purpose at the moment."

"How have you learned that?"

"Ramiz Bahrami is undercover with this group."

"Ramiz! Is that—do you mean Nadia's…"

"That is why Nadia waits so patiently for him," Jaf said softly. "She knows that a higher duty makes its demands on him."

"Ohhhh."

His eyes watched her gravely in the starlit darkness. "I, too, Lisbet."

"You? You're working on this?"

"I am deeply involved with the attempt to expose these people before they can achieve their ends."

Her lips were dry. She licked them. He was trying to tell her something. What was he really saying here? A bird cried from the trees in sudden, sharp alarm. Shivers of unnamed dread started along her skin.

"And does all this have something to do with that man who talked to me last night?"

"We hope so. We think so."

"What is your involvement, Jaf?"

"I am proving myself a worthy target for subversion. A man who is in the grip of a passion like gambling may be a man whose loyalty can be purchased."

Twelve

Lisbet closed her eyes as a dozen tiny clues clicked into place. The ridiculous, gold-trimmed car that did not seem like the Jaf she knew. The reluctant determination to go to the casino. The crazy way he bet.

"It was all a setup," she breathed. "It's nothing but a front."

He was listening closely for her reaction. "It is."

"Oh, God, and I fell for it! What a *fool* I am! That Rolls…" She closed her eyes, shaking her head. Opened them. The nervous bird shrieked out again.

"And all the money you're losing at the tables—where does that come from?"

"Prince Karim restores my losses. The Shalimar Gardens is a Crown property."

They walked in silence, their feet pressing white shapes into the dark sand, while she absorbed it.

"I really should have guessed, shouldn't I?"

His mouth was just slightly twisted. Bitterness, perhaps.

"But then, trust is not your strong suit," he said.

The words flicked her painfully. "Admit that your disguise is very good!" she cried indignantly. "You were in the papers for months with your extravagance and your lifestyle."

"You had known me for months before that, Lisbet. You chose to ignore your personal experience of me in private to accept the public face I was presenting. Isn't it so?"

"Not until I got out here and saw it for myself," she protested hotly. "Did you expect me to ignore the evidence of my own eyes?"

"I asked you to trust me."

"And *I* asked *you* not to gamble!"

"I told you I would give it up soon."

And suddenly there they were again, arguing.

"Oh, right! That and a bus pass will get you to Hammersmith! Everybody in the world is going to give up something soon!"

"Except you, Lisbet. You are not going to give up mistrust, are you? How can you blame me now, when you have been told—"

"Me blame you? It's you who are blaming me! All I said—"

He caught her shoulders. "There is no time for this luxury, arguing. We must know if you will help us."

"Of course I'll help you!" Lisbet snapped. "If you knew me as well as you think I should have known you, you'd know that!"

He gritted his teeth to contain his retort. "Then let us begin."

* * *

For the next week Lisbet lived the wild life of a rich man's pampered mistress. Jaf took her on wildly extravagant shopping sprees, ostentatiously buying her jewellery and clothes, brought a top London hair stylist in on a flying trip at enormous expense to do her hair, took her yachting, even ordered her her own monogrammed Rolls.

That was during the day. At night, inevitably, they wound up at the Shalimar Gardens, where Lisbet encouraged Jaf to gamble on her wildest hunches.

Pictures were taken of them, whatever they did. The papers loved this new twist of events, and everyone they talked to had a story to sell. Staff at the casino were interviewed and talked about the amount of champagne they consumed, the wild betting, how Sheikh Jafar seemed to be completely taken with the beautiful English actress.

Of course the journalists discovered that they had begun this affair long ago in London and that Lisbet had been the one to break it off. They printed every detail of the relationship they could dig up, and then some, including the fabulous flat in Primrose Hill.

The stories printed grew wilder and wilder. One said that the couple made love with Lisbet wearing jewellery from the fabulous Jalal Collection. Another suggested that Jaf had financed the film on condition that Masoud al Badi cast Lisbet in the lead, on purpose to bring her to the Barakat Emirates where he could woo her again. One even said the model for the gold statuette on the Rolls had been Lisbet herself.

In the King's Pavilion, seven men sat on cushions around the plashing fountains whose noise would hinder any attempt to eavesdrop on their conversation. Three of the men were the Princes of the Barakat Emirates—Omar, Rafi, and Karim. Three more were their Cup Companions, Hashem al Makin, Arif al Rashid, Jafar al Hamzeh. The last man, older than the others, was the Grand Vizier, Naseh al Rajulu Daulati.

"So we have him," Omar was saying.

"It is far from certain," Hashem al Makin informed them. "I will remind you all that we've had to carry out any investigations with the utmost caution, for fear of tipping off some unknown member of the conspiracy.

"Having said that, the phone number given to Lisbet Raine is a mobile phone registered to a woman named Rima Bokhari. She lives in al Fakri area."

"Al Fakri! And she has a mobile phone?" exclaimed Rafi.

"Exactly. However, enquiries uncovered the fact that the woman has a widowed daughter, named Afra al Haziya. This latter woman is rumoured in her own neighbourhood—which is somewhat more upmarket than her mother's—to be the mistress of a government official.

"Surveillance presented huge problems, since anyone of whose loyalty we could be completely certain would probably be known by sight to the target. With more time, we could, of course, be more certain. However, two sightings have been made in the neighbourhood. It is enough of a coincidence to be noteworthy at the very least."

"Who was it?"

The Cup Companion paused with unconscious dramatic instinct to glance at his audience. "Yadeth al Najaz."

The name fell among them like a brick through a

window. The six listeners took in one collective breath, and the splash of the fountain grew sharply loud, as if their silence had become somehow more complete.

"How certain is this?" Karim was the first to speak.

"Not certain at all, Lord. He was seen in the street behind this woman's house. There is a back door to the garden in that street."

"There's never been a whisper about Yadeth al Najaz's loyalty," Rafi said. "He's been around as long as I can remember."

"He became Father's Cup Companion before we were born, didn't he?" Omar mused. He turned to the Grand Vizier. "What can you tell us about him, Khwaja?"

The older man sat for a moment, marshalling his thoughts.

"Yadeth al Najaz must by now be nearly seventy years old. As you know, he is of the Najazi tribe, hereditary enemies of the Quraishi. Forty years ago, the climate among the tribes was much more volatile than it is today, and the Najazi were the ringleaders.

"Yadeth al Najaz was very highly placed within the tribe. I believe it was on the advice of Nizam al Mulk, my predecessor, that your father appointed him Cup Companion. Several other appointments were made at that time, in the effort to calm the hostility of the Najazi and convince them that there was no room for tribal hatred within a modern state.

"I always suspected that Nizam al Mulk was not entirely sanguine about the experiment. He advised your father never to put any of the Najazi men into positions of real influence or give them his deep confidence.

"That is why Yadeth al Najaz was appointed to palace administration—a nonpolitical role. He became Chief of Staff of all the palaces on the death of Mustafa al Nabih and served in that position until the death of your honoured father. And after your succession, of course, he was made *Sadin al Qasr* of Queen Halimah Palace."

The Queen Halimah Palace was the seat of the Barakat Emirates' joint government.

Omar stroked his neatly pointed beard. "Well, he would certainly have been in the right place at the right time. When Jalal's mother came to the palace demanding to see the king, it is very likely that he would have been called. And who better than he to intercept the mail thereafter?"

"The *Sadin al Qasr* also had full access to palace letterhead."

"And he had a ready-made grudge," added Karim. "Motive, means, and opportunity, all staring at us."

"Has Miss Raine had an opportunity to identify him?" asked Omar.

"One of the strangest coincidences is the lack of any photograph of Yadeth al Najaz over the past forty years," said Jaf. "We're trying to take a photograph covertly. Meanwhile, Lisbet has seen an old photo and certainly doesn't rule him out."

"Well, I think we can take it as a working hypothesis that we've found our man," said Omar.

"What was his original motive for not relaying the news of Jalal's existence to Father, I wonder?" Rafi mused. "He can't have conceived of the whole scenario at once. It must have grown over time."

"Think of the joy your father and Queen Azizah would have felt, if they had discovered that, against all the odds, they had a grandson," Jafar al Hamzeh suggested. "It may be that it began in no more than simple malice."

Karim nodded. "And perhaps a gut feeling that the boy could be used somehow, sooner or later."

"Well, it's time his career was stopped," Prince Omar said, with steely precision. He turned to Jaf. "You and the admirable Miss Raine seem to be doing a first-class job with the bait. Could you spring the trap anytime soon?"

"Now's as good a time as any," said Jaf.

On the evening of the day chosen for the final act of their drama, Jaf and Lisbet lay in the tangled sheets of his bedroom at Gazi's house, looking out over the bay. They had made love with a passion that took added urgency from the approach of danger. Now they talked calmly about what they were about to do.

"Tribal rivalry?" Lisbet repeated in astonishment.

Jaf nodded. "It's the only thing that makes sense. The Najazi-Quraishi feud has been going on for centuries. Only a Najazi would be capable of planning something against the royal house that was going to take a quarter of a century to come to fruition.

"And by the same token, when Jalal destroyed Yadeth al Najaz's hopes in that direction by refusing to take part, he would be perfectly capable of just moving on to something else.

"In fact, the princes are assuming that this plan he's engaged in now has been in the making for years, too. Clearly he has a taste for conspiracy."

Talk like this made her nervous. "What kind of plan could it be? And what will he do with the disaffected Cup Companion when he gets hold of him?" she wondered, aloud stroking his powerful, naked shoulder and wishing it didn't have to be Jaf. Wishing hard that she hadn't paused in front of that painting of Sheikh Daud on the night of the Grand Reception.

"It may never come to that, Lisbet. You're the one who will be in danger. Please don't do anything foolishly brave. Don't try to manipulate him into saying something incriminating. If he gets suspicious he may search you, and that would ruin everything. Just let him pay you off and go. I'll handle whatever comes after. Don't worry. Promise?"

She heaved a breath. "All right."

He kissed her. "Ready to start?"

A few hours later, they stood over their "favourite" roulette table, while Lisbet, charmingly female, all but ordered Jaf to play her lucky number. It was a last-ditch attempt to restore his fortunes. She had lost all track of the amount they had blown tonight. It was simply unbelievable.

She was looking dramatically beautiful, in a clinging metallic gold dress that hugged every curve to her ankles. It was slit to above the knee at the back. With it she wore gold strappy stilettos and no stockings on her tanned legs.

She was draped with emeralds, from the emerald-and-diamond star in her smoothly flowing hair to a tiny emerald-and-gold ankle chain. In between she wore earrings, a pendant, upper arm bracelet and two rings, all in the same dark, glowing green set off with flashing diamonds.

Her excited eyes flashed green fire, her tanned skin was smooth and bore all the signs of total pampering.

"Kiss me for luck," Jaf said, as he stacked all his

remaining chips on number twenty-two. In a black tuxedo, with a white burnoose thrown back over his shoulders like a cape, he looked like a nineteenth-century rake.

There was a glint in his eyes that melted her where she stood. He could always do it to her. However angry he might be underneath, when Jaf turned on the charm, she was jelly. Sweet, and wobbly, and ready to be gobbled up.

"Kiss me," he commanded, as the little ball began its fatal journey around the wheel.

The luck he wanted wasn't to win, of course, but to lose. They had made a show of this being his last hope. Everyone at the table knew that Jaf was down to his last barakati, and Lisbet had encouraged him to risk everything he had left on her intuition.

"I don't know how we'll get home!" he had warned her, but Lisbet had waved blithely and said, "On our winnings!"

And he had let the foolhardy bet stand.

Now he dragged her into his embrace with one strong, hungry arm, and his eyes gazed into hers from point-blank range. Behind them the wheel whirred and the ball spun, around and around.

"Kiss me, Lisbet," he murmured, "and tell me you love me."

He didn't mean it. It was all for show, but it would be a relief to say it. "I love you," she breathed.

His mouth covered hers with a rough passion that made the world disappear. Lisbet felt herself spinning as helplessly as the little white ball.

"I love you," he whispered when he lifted his mouth.

Behind them there was a collective gasp from the

crowd around the table, and they remembered and broke apart and turned to see their luck.

"Twelve," intoned the croupier.

"Noooo!" Lisbet cried in dismay. Jaf was silent, but she felt him stiffen in well-acted dismay.

The rake came out and inexorably dragged the massively stacked chips on number twenty-two across the green board. They fell into the maw where the house profits went, with a rattling *thunk*.

Jaf muttered a quiet curse and finished off the champagne in his gold-traced flute glass. "Right," he said, slightly unsteadily, setting the glass down on the edge of the roulette table. "That's the end of me. Let's go."

He took her arm and turned around, but Lisbet snatched her elbow away from his touch with a laugh. "You can't quit now!" she cried. "Our luck is turning, can't you see? Twelve, that's just one digit away from twenty-two! One more try, Jaf."

He resisted, she implored. The other players began to shift away in discomfort. "Come on," she cried at last. "For me, just one more little try?"

He was getting annoyed. "There is no more," he told her. "That's the last of it. You'll have to sell one of your trinkets if you want to play, darling." He flicked the emerald at her ear.

Staff of the casino were hovering, hoping to quiet them without taking more extreme measures. A bouncer was making a carefully unaggressive approach. A Cup Companion was still a Cup Companion, and besides, Jafar al Hamzeh was in peak condition, and even drunk his reflexes were probably lightning.

"I didn't realize you were such a coward!" Lisbet cried. "I thought you were an adventurer."

"Shhh!" he complained. "Come on, darling, don't make a fuss. We'll go home now."

"I'm not going anywhere! I'm staying right here! Are you going to place a bet or not?"

"Not," said Jaf, swaying slightly, but determined. "Have to borrow from Gazi as it is. You've cleaned me out, baby."

Lisbet's eyes and mouth opened in shocked outrage. "I cleaned you out? *I* cleaned you out? How dare you say a thing like that to me?"

The staff moved closer, the volume of her voice feeding their determination. Lisbet Raine, previously so fun-loving and good-natured, was starting to sound like a housewife being cheated in the *souk*. Her voice climbed, and the green eyes looked dangerous.

"Miss Raine," one murmured bravely, foolishly attempting to grasp her arm.

"Take your hands off me!" the actress cried, snatching her arm away so violently that they all watched fascinated for her breasts to come tumbling out of the low-cut dress. There was a collective sigh when it did not happen.

She was still shrieking at Jaf as members of the staff herded the couple to the door of the room, and finally she gave in to their force majeure.

"Don't bother to come with me!" she cried to Jaf. "You've seen the last of me!" And with one final imprecation, she stormed out.

Jafar al Hamzeh, his eyes dark with shock, straightened his suit jacket, twitched his burnoose over his shoulders, nodded elegantly at those who stood staring, and followed his lady love.

* * *

"I will give you an address," said the voice she recognized. "Come at once."

In the darkened limousine, Lisbet held her cell phone to her ear and took a deep breath. They hadn't been sure what course he would take. He might easily have put her off at this point, promising her a reward that never arrived.

"All right," she said.

"Tell your driver to take you to Mukaafa Road, the corner nearest the Jamaa al Fannun *souk*. From the casino it will take you no more than fifteen minutes. Someone will meet you there."

Lisbet disconnected with a steady hand. Now that it was happening, she felt very cool.

"Mukaafa Road?" the driver repeated. Behind the concealing keffiyeh was Arif al Rashid.

"The corner near the Crafts Market. Someone will meet me."

The Cup Companion nodded. "Thank you." The limousine swung out of the casino parking lot into the light traffic along the coastal highway, and headed back into the capital.

At her feet in the darkened car, Gazi said, "Let's test your mike, Lisbet."

"There is one small thing I require of you, Miss Raine," said Yadeth al Najaz. "Would you be so kind as to call Jafar al Hamzeh and ask him to meet you here."

His voice was flat with disdain. She was reaping the reward of traitors throughout time—the contempt of those whom the betrayal benefits.

"Call him! Are you kidding me? I'm not going to call him," Lisbet exclaimed. Her overt defiance was a cover for real dismay. What did they want Jaf here for? What were they going to do to him? Were the princes all wrong about this? Was it a personal vendetta against Jaf after all?

"I am afraid you must."

"There's no *must* about any of this," she told him angrily.

"*Laa ikraa,*" the man murmured. "No compulsion, Miss Raine, but your reward depends upon it."

"That isn't what you told me. That wasn't the deal. You never said Jaf had to know what I was doing."

She was fighting for time to think. A dozen different scenarios passed through her imagination. Would they make him a fake suicide, saying he had been unhinged by her rejection? Stage a domestic murder? Have him stabbed in one of the less salubrious streets of this neighbourhood?

"But sadly, it is necessary. It is part of the shock treatment I spoke of. Only when he fully realizes the emptiness of his way of life and the untrustworthiness of the Westerners he so loves to mingle with will the full shock take effect. Call him, Miss Raine."

"No." Lisbet leaned back against the cushions on the divan and crossed her arms. She thought of the Cup Companions, who were listening to this from the car, and felt their urgency. Of course they would want her to do as Yadeth al Najaz said. They were Cup Companions. No doubt, as far as they were concerned, risking their lives in the service of their princes was no more than a duty.

But she was a woman who loved a man. How could she summon Jaf into unknown danger?

Yadeth al Najaz smiled. "You know how to bargain," he said with false admiration. He nodded to the other man in the room, a younger man who might be his son. He was the one who had met her at the car and escorted her half a block to a small apartment building. Now he went into another room and returned. A silver suitcase was lifted onto the low table between them. With a calm smile Yadeth al Najaz clicked open the locks, lifted the lid, turned the case to face her.

It was filled with cash. She bit back her reaction.

"This case contains one million American dollars, Miss Raine. It is for you."

She couldn't help her startled intake of breath then, but didn't move from her adamant posture. "Real, or counterfeit?" she asked cynically.

He inclined his head with respect for her business acumen. "You see for yourself, they are all used notes."

With a knowing grin, she leaned forward and carelessly reached out to riffle through the neat piles of hundred-dollar bills, making sure it was all money. She sat back, flicking her hand.

"What good is cash going to do me? People ask questions, you know, when someone walks into a bank with a boatload of used American dollars."

"Arrangements will be made for you at a bank here," he said. "Now, Miss Raine. I know you have your mobile phone with you. Please use it."

She stared at him for a long moment, miming sulky resistance while her brain whirled, looking for a solution. With the phone in the little gold mesh handbag was the transmitter for the remote microphone that was taped under her breast. It was inexpertly disguised as a mirror case.

Yadeth al Najaz's assistant was now sitting beside

her on the sofa. How much danger was she in, if they realized she had set them up? Yadeth al Najaz might not guess that they already knew his name. Might they hope to escape by killing her and fleeing?

If she failed now, everything was lost. The princes knew who he was, but they had no idea what he planned, and no evidence to bring this evil man to justice. It was up to her, and no one else. The future of the Barakat Emirates might be in her hands.

But so was her own future, and Jaf's.

Lisbet heaved a breath. "All right!" she exclaimed mulishly, picking up the little gold bag and snapping it carelessly open. "But it's not exactly fair, is it?"

"What a very English sentiment, Miss Raine. Life is seldom fair. That is why religions inevitably promise justice in the other world."

Thirteen

"I don't understand," Jaf said, glancing from Yadeth al Najaz to the case full of money and back to Lisbet again. She sat on the sofa, her arms crossed, looking defiant. "How are you involved in this, *Sadin al Qasr?*"

"It is simple, Your Excellency. Betrayal always is. Miss Raine brought you to us for a price. Isn't it so, Miss Raine?"

"Call it what you like!" she sneered. "Why would you pay a million dollars for a meeting with Jaf? All anyone has to do is book an appointment. But if Jaf wants to believe it, he can."

Jaf frowned. "A million dollars? Why did you wish to organize a meeting in this way, *Sadin al Qasr?*"

"Ah, but it was more than a meeting, wasn't it? You agreed to bring him to ruin, did you not?" the old man said to Lisbet.

"Lisbet?" Jaf whispered disbelievingly.

"Believe that and you'll believe anything!" she snapped. "Now, can I please get out of here?"

She made to stand up, but Yadeth al Najaz held up a hand. "Not yet, please. You see where you are, Excellency. Did you think she loved you? I bought that love for a million dollars. You have spent much more than that on her, I am sure." He spread his hands helplessly. "But women are such changeable creatures.

"And you have lost everything, after all. What will be next? Miss Raine had to ask herself, as a practical woman. Her lovely jewels? Women such as she do not like to make sacrifices of that nature."

Jaf was looking stunned. "Lisbet, is it true? But why? I love you! I would do anything for you. You know it."

Lisbet sniffed and turned her head. "I didn't know it was going to turn out like this," she said sulkily. "It's not my fault you didn't win."

Jaf sank forward and put his head in his hands. "I've drunk too much. I can't think straight. What is it you want, *Sadin?*"

"Only to help you."

"You aren't leaving me, Lisbet? You can't. I can't live without you!" Jaf said, in a desperate voice that made her heart beat hard. Oh, if only that were true!

"Don't worry, Your Excellency. If you play your cards right, you can still win. Miss Raine will have no reason to leave you if you win, will she?"

"What do you mean?"

"I want you to make a phone call. One phone call. If you do that—" he flicked the silver suitcase "—you may take this money and go."

"Wait a minute!" Lisbet cried angrily. "You said that was mine already!"

"But we have already agreed, haven't we, that life is not fair?" Yadeth al Najaz turned to Jaf.

"Make the call and you may consider this—" he flicked the cash contemptuously "—a mere down payment. Your lifestyle will be guaranteed from now on. Your losses restored to you. How many millions have you thrown away? Never mind, Excellency. They will be yours again."

Lisbet sat a little forward in unconscious interest.

"You see?" said al Najaz.

Jaf rubbed his eyes, as if trying to clear his head. "What phone call?"

A card was placed on the table before him.

"Call this number. Ask for this man."

Jaf's eyes narrowed as he read the scrawled name. "I know this name. The man is a journalist," he said. "An English newspaper."

"You will tell him you want an immediate meeting with him. And give him this address."

Jaf tossed the card onto the table with easy contempt. "No."

Yadeth al Najaz smiled and signalled his younger henchman. "In that case—"

The other man closed the suitcase, snapped the locks, stood up.

"Wait a minute!" Lisbet shrieked in alarm. "That's mine!"

"If His Excellency makes the call, it is yours."

Jaf waved an arrogant hand. "Take it away. We don't want your money."

"Wait a minute, darling," Lisbet said quickly. "It won't hurt to ask what it's all about, will it?"

"Nobody uses bribes and blackmail to achieve any legitimate purpose," Jaf told her grandly. "Now, let's get out of here."

She smiled seductively at him. "I'm sure you're right, but at least let's ask." She turned to Yadeth al Najaz. The younger man hesitated, holding the shiny aluminum case as if uncertain what to do. "What's the call about, actually?"

"It is of no import, Miss Raine," al Najaz said, waving his henchman away. "If he will not do it, he will not. Someone else will be more willing."

"Just a minute, I said!" Lisbet shouted. All three men looked at her. "What is the call about? What does Jaf have to say to him?"

"Nothing beyond what I have already said. He asks the man to come here. Then you can go, with the money. And there will be more to follow."

Lisbet's eyes narrowed. "What are you going to do to the man? Is he going to be hurt in any way?"

The old man laughed. "On the contrary. He will be given the scoop of his career!"

Lisbet sat back, blinking. "Oh! Well, that's not bad, is it?" She turned to Jaf. "You can do that, can't you, darling?"

Jaf shook his head suspiciously. "What scoop? What story, *Sadin?*"

"I wish you two would stop calling each other by your titles in that ridiculous way!" Lisbet interjected. They ignored her.

"Nothing that nearly concerns you, or yours, I assure you."

Lisbet smiled and tilted her head. "You could do it, couldn't you, Jaf? It's enough money to be going on with, isn't it? And if you don't, you said yourself you'd have to ask Gazi for funds. I know you won't like that, and neither will he.''

"I want to know what the story is,'' Jaf said doggedly.

Lisbet sank down beside him, her thigh touching his. His body heat burned her, and for the first time since her arrival she felt how deeply her system thrilled to the danger they were in.

She stroked a lock of hair back from his forehead. "What difference does it make? A story's a story, whoever calls the journalist. It's not going to go away because you don't make the call.''

He grasped her upper arm, and she shivered at the power in his hold. The side-by-side presence of danger and safety made her blood rush through her like electricity.

"Lisbet, don't.''

"Do you love me, Jaf?'' she asked, and suddenly her voice quivered on tears, and the question was real.

"Lisbet—''

"Do you?''

"You know I love you,'' he said roughly, gazing into her eyes, and to her starved soul it sounded like the truth. She closed her eyes, smiling. It was an act, but she was glad she had heard it one last time. Something to remember.

"I love you, Jaf. I always have.''

They were still for a moment, gazing at each other. Behind them, Yadeth al Najaz cleared his throat.

"Please do this for me,'' she whispered.

He put her to one side and stood up. "Let's get out of here.''

"Jaf!'' she cried, a woman playing her trump card. "If you leave now, I'll never speak to you again.''

He turned and glared down at her. "You will," he said, trying for firmness.

She picked up her mobile. "Make the call for me, Jaf. Never mind him." She nodded towards the old man. "Do it for my sake."

"You sold me out," he muttered, like a man who has lost his footing and knows he will not regain it. "I know damned well you'll walk out on me as soon as you get your hands on that money."

"No," she cried softly, as he took the phone. "No, never, Jaf. How can I ever leave you? Please!"

Jaf, with the self-loathing of a man driven to do what he should not for an end he knows he will never achieve, took the phone and made the call.

"It was a majestic plan, Lord," Jaf explained to the three princes and several Cup Companions as they sat again in the King's Pavilion.

"Tell us," said Prince Karim.

"The file I was to pass on to the journalist documents a complete production line for heroin, from the seed all the way through to the distribution of the final product in Western Europe.

"All that was needed was someone to link that complete body of evidence with the Princes of Barakat, to say that you were producing and selling heroin to the West to boost your export revenues.

"That was why a Cup Companion was necessary. Someone whose word alone would be compelling evidence."

"But you did not give the file to the journalist?"

"No, Lord. Fortunately, both my microphone and Lisbet's continued to transmit throughout the evening. The task force in the street was able to detain the journalist and send in a ringer. Yadeth al Najaz fell for it.''

''How do investigations stand now, Hashem?'' Rafi asked.

The Cup Companion cleared his throat. ''Poppy fields have been discovered in the Noor Mountains, just where the documentation showed, on the border between Central and Eastern Barakat. The refinery also exists. So much we know. We are moving very carefully, Lord, so as to retain the element of surprise. We expect to make arrests within twelve hours.''

Lisbet and Jaf walked along the beach under starlight.

''So Ramiz is coming home now?''

''Soon, we hope. The princes were very complimentary about you, Lisbet.''

''What did they say?'' Lisbet asked.

''They asked me to pass on their deep gratitude and admiration for your courage. Of course, that is not the end of it. They made it clear that they intend to reward you, but want to know first what you would consider a suitable recompense.''

''Oh!'' She hadn't thought of that.

''They've asked me to sound you out. The sky is the limit, I think, Lisbet.''

''But what sort of thing do they mean?''

''You might ask for property here or abroad, or money, or an honorary title, I suppose. They are very determined that your reward should fit your courage. Of course, they will see you and express their gratitude in person.

''The proceedings in Yadeth al Najaz's place were taped, by the way, and the princes have listened to the entire scene with great interest. They are deeply impressed with your abilities, and Prince Rafi suggested that, if we could not convince you to join the police, you might undertake to set up a permanent British-Barakati film unit, with the aim of producing more joint productions.''

Lisbet laughed and shook her head incredulously. ''I can't believe this is happening!'' She looked up at the ever-magical night sky. ''You're right. It's not the same sky at all as the one in London. I think I'm on a totally different planet.''

Jaf laughed lightly. ''You have time to get used to it. There is no rush to make up your mind. Think it over, Lisbet. This moment may affect all the rest of your life, if you choose wisely.''

She kicked at the wet sand, exposing the paler sand beneath, and dug her toes into the cool softness. ''I don't think that the princes have the power to give me what I want,'' she murmured.

Jaf raised startled eyebrows. ''I would be very surprised if they did not. What is it you want?''

''It's something only you could give me,'' she said, her heart beating hard enough to kill her. ''And I doubt you'd be willing.''

''If it's the piece called the Concubine's Tears you wish for, it is yours, Lisbet. Do you think me so ungenerous?''

''Not that.''

He frowned. ''What, then?''

She looked up into his shadowed face and felt how much more dangerous this moment was than the one in which they had played their game for the traitor. Now, truly, she felt she risked everything. Life and limb was nothing compared to the risk to her heart.

"I want to hear you say you love me again," she whispered. "The way you did in front of Yadeth al Najaz. Only…I'd like you to mean it."

His mouth tightened, and her heart sank. She had known it would be too much to hope that the adventure they had been through would have softened him, but still the death of hope hurt.

"And what would you do with such a reward, Lisbet?"

She shook her head, because tears were burning her throat too painfully for speech. "Never mind," she managed.

She turned away, but he caught her shoulders in a hard hold and kept her there. "What would you do with such a rebirth of love, Lisbet? Run from it again? If I loved you, what then?"

She looked up, too scared to hope, too hungry to despair. Her eyes were bright with tears.

"I've changed, Jaf. I've learned so much about myself, about life…about love. If the princes were willing, I'd ask them—to let me marry one of their Cup Companions."

"Do you love me, Lisbet?" he asked harshly.

"Yes, *yes,* I love you. I adore you. I didn't know it before, because I was so afraid. But I've loved you from the beginning, just the way you always said, Jaf. You were right, it was magical and special, and there will never be anyone in the world for me but you.

"It's killing me that I didn't find it out until I'd lost your love. Please try to love me again, Jaf! Please believe that that love may still be alive in you, underneath. Please try to find that love in your heart, because I want to marry you and have children with you, and lots of grandchildren. I want them to learn that service is the duty of privilege, and grow up to be Cup Companions like their father.

"But most of all, I want to love you and be loved by you. Jaf, please say it's not hopeless. Please say I haven't killed your love forever!"

"This is what I have been waiting to hear from you, Lisbet," he whispered, his hands clasping her upper arms, pulling her close.

She gasped, feeling as if one of the stars had fallen to earth and hit her. "What?" she breathed.

"Am I a weakling, whose love dies with one small blow?" he growled. "Can you believe such lies?" His arms wrapped her and he pulled her close. "Kill my love? You didn't kill my love for so much as a minute, my beloved, my wife!"

Then his mouth covered hers and her body sank into his, and they tasted joy.

"Why did you tell me it was too late for us?" she protested later, as they lay looking out at the sea and the stars.

Jaf smiled. "You see, I had a problem. If I chased you, I only proved your fears, that I would overrule your real needs for the sake of my own. The more I told you I loved you, the less chance there was of winning you.

"When I came back to the Barakat Emirates last spring having failed to bring you with me, I understood that I needed a strategy. And the strategy I chose was to let you believe that I no longer loved you."

"But you said, *It's too late for us,*" Lisbet protested, in remembered pain.

"Yes. I thought that it was the way to get you to recognize love and throw away fear. If I pounced on you, I would lose you again. Like a wild animal watching for its prey, I had to wait until you came out of hiding all the way, by yourself. Then there would be no way back for you.

"But it was more difficult than I imagined."

"Was it?"

"I could not resist making love to you. It was not part of my strategy, but I was powerless to resist. So I told you it was a purely physical passion. And you were foolish enough to believe it."

He smiled at her, melting her heart.

"So your anger was an act?" she said, lifting her head.

He kissed her ruthlessly again. "It was no act. I was very deeply angry with you, but I was also in love and fighting to keep myself in check. It was not easy to be around you and pretend indifference. But I had one advantage."

"Which was?"

"I was already forced to live one lie. That made it easier for me. I had to act the part of a fool. Whenever I was in danger of telling you the truth, there was always the necessity to go to the casino to help me overcome it. And the fact that you could not sway me would always convince you that I didn't love you, no matter how dangerously I had slipped."

"And now?"

"And now, my strategy has finally paid off. You have left fear behind, and there is no way back," he promised her, in a tone that thrilled her.

She kissed him, and his strong arms wrapped her, protecting, possessing. Her heart leapt.

Lisbet rolled over on her back. "And are we going to get married?"

Jaf rose onto one elbow above her. His eyelids drooped and his hand slipped up over the tender throat. "You know we are," he said. "And very soon. I have waited for too long, Lisbet. I will not wait much longer to call you my wife."

"Will you promise, as the princes have, never to take another wife?" she teased.

"You are behind the times. It is against the law here, except in exceptional circumstances."

He stroked her flank, her side, her arm. His hand caught her upper arm in a firm clasp and he drew her up a little for his kiss. "But even if it were not against the law," he said, "there will never be another woman for me, Lisbet."

"You know," she said later, sighing in satisfaction, "there's one thing I've realized about myself in all this."

"What is that?"

"That I didn't really accept that it was over when I broke up with you. I think I was testing you, or something. I think that's why I kept sending you those cheques. Really, I was trying to stir you to action."

Jaf lay back with a little laugh, as though she had hit him. "Of course!" he exclaimed. "Why didn't I see that? Months of misery might have been spared."

"Were you miserable? But you never tried to see me, never called, never came after me. I really thought you'd forgotten me when I came to do the movie. And when you didn't visit Gazi and Anna in that first week, I was sure of it."

"I didn't forget you for one day," he assured her. "One hour."

"But—you didn't do anything about it, either. If I hadn't got this film when would we ever have met again?"

Now he was laughing gently. He lay back and drew her onto his chest, stroking her hair and all the length of her back with a firm, possessive hand that thrilled her.

"Lisbet, did you never guess? Never suspect? Not once?" he demanded, amused.

"Suspect what?"

"Masoud al Badi is an old, old friend, Lisbet. He was looking for financing for his film. He failed to get it off the ground last year and he had put the project on hold."

"No!" Lisbet cried. She broke out of his hold to sit bolt upright.

"You didn't! You couldn't have! Oh, Jaf, don't tell me—you mean that newspaper story was *right?*"

Jaf shouted with laughter. "Of course it was right! Who do you think was feeding all those stories to the press from the beginning, if not Gazi?"

"You bought my way into Masoud's film?"

"He did tell me it was no deal if he didn't think you were up to the weight," he said.

"Jaf, you *monster!*" she cried. "How can you laugh about it? How could you *do* it? Oh, my God! How humiliating! Who knows about this? Does everybody know except me?"

He was still laughing. "But Masoud loves you. He says he only wishes he'd cast me as the sultan. We would burn up the screen, he says, as we did on the beach."

"I was so right about you!" she cried. "It's the apartment all over again, isn't it? Manipulating me for my own good, I suppose you call it! But it's really just—"

"But you can't have it both ways, Lisbet! You can't complain that I never lifted a finger to win you in one breath and then in the next complain because I did!"

"But you didn't have to do it *this* way!"

"What else would have brought you in my way? If I had come to London, you'd have run away screaming."

"But—"

He caught her head between his two hands. "No, my darling, I am sure we will have many, many enjoyable arguments in future, but tonight I refuse to fight with you. Tonight is for love, Lisbet. Tonight we celebrate the mystery of how, out of all the stars in the universe, you and I found each other."

Epilogue

Actress Honoured in Barakat Emirates

Lisbet Raine, the British actress, and her fiancé Sheikh Jafar al Hamzeh, are to receive the country's highest honour from the Princes of the Barakat Emirates, it was disclosed today. The "playboy" Cup Companion and his bride have each individually been awarded the coveted title *Qalb al Maliki,* or King's Heart.

The honour is a rare one, historically awarded for service above and beyond the high degree of service normally expected from a Cup Companion in the Barakat Emirates. It is rare for the award to be made to anyone not a Cup Companion. Miss Raine is the first woman, and the first foreigner, so honoured.

The reputation of the renegade sheikh, who until

recently appeared to be on the brink of being stripped of his Cup Companion status, seems to be fully restored by the announcement.

The sheikh is widely rumoured to have taken an active part in the recent highly publicized cracking of a heroin-producing ring in the country.

Sources say that it is impossible that Miss Raine would have been given the award merely as a reflection of her fiancé's services.

Palace sources, however, refuse to disclose the precise reason for the awards.

*   *   *   *   *

The Sheikh and the Runaway Princess

SUSAN MALLERY

SUSAN MALLERY

is the bestselling author of over forty books. She makes her home in the Pacific Northwest with her handsome prince of a husband and her two adorable-but-not-bright cats.

To Terry who, after reading the first three sheikh books, kept saying that there just *had* to be a bastard brother.
Here he is…enjoy!

Chapter One

Sabrina Johnson had sand in her teeth and a lot of other places sand wasn't supposed to be.

She'd been an idiot, she told herself as she huddled under her thick cloak and listened to the storm howling all around her. Only someone incredibly foolish would have driven four hundred miles out into the desert *by herself,* and then left all signs of civilization behind, traveling with only a horse and a pack camel, looking for a stupid, mythical city that probably didn't even exist.

A particularly vicious gust of sand and wind nearly toppled her. Sabrina clutched her legs more firmly to her chest, rested her head on her knees and swore that no matter how long she lived—assuming she survived her current predicament—she was never, ever going to be impulsive again. Not even a little.

All impulse had gotten her was lost and trapped in the middle of a sandstorm.

Worse, no one knew she was out here, so no one would be looking for her. She'd stalked off without saying a word to her father or her brothers. When she didn't show up for dinner, they would probably assume she was either sulking in her room or had taken off for Paris on a shopping trip. They would never think she was lost in the desert. Her brothers had warned her more than once that her crazy ideas were going to be the death of her. She'd never thought they might be right.

Heat and dryness pressed against her. She coughed, but couldn't seem to clear her throat. How long would the storm go on and would she be able to find her way when it was over?

She didn't have answers to her questions, so she tried not to think about them. Instead she wrapped her thick cloak around herself more tightly, staying low to the ground, hoping the storm wouldn't sweep her up in its power and blow her away. She'd heard stories about that sort of thing. Of course her brothers had been the ones telling the stories and they didn't always stick to the truth.

After what could have been hours, she thought she noticed a slight lessening of howls. Gradually she became aware that the gusts weren't quite so strong and that it was getting easier to breathe. A few minutes later she risked peeking out from under her cloak.

There was good news and bad news. The good news was she wasn't dead. Yet. The bad news was her horse and the supply camel were gone, along with her food, water and maps. Almost worse, the storm had buried the makeshift road she'd been following and had erased all the landmarks she'd noticed on her way into the desert from the outpost where she'd left the truck and horse trailer. The truck that wouldn't be found until someone else journeyed to the abandoned old building. That event could be weeks or even months away. How would she survive until then?

Sabrina rose and turned in a slow circle. Nothing looked familiar. In the distance, the storm still raged. She watched clouds of sand reach up toward the sky as if trying to obliterate the sun. She swallowed. The sun was surprisingly low in the horizon. It was late. Apparently the storm had lasted longer than she'd realized.

Her stomach growled, reminding her she hadn't eaten since a very early breakfast. She'd been so eager to get started on her journey that morning, that she'd left the capital city well before dawn. She'd been convinced that she was going to find the fabled City of Thieves she'd been studying for ages, and prove its existence to her father. He'd always teased her about her fascination with it. She'd been so darned determined to have the last word. Instead she'd ended up here.

Now what? She could continue to search for the lost city, she could try to return to Bahania and her life of being ignored by her father and brothers or she could simply stand here and die of thirst. Actually while the third choice wasn't her favorite, under the circumstances it seemed the most likely.

"I'm not going without a fight," Sabrina muttered as she tightened the scarf tied around her head. She shook out her cloak, then folded it and slung it over one shoulder.

West, she thought and turned so the setting sun was on her right. She needed to retrace her earlier journey by heading south and a little west to find the outpost. There was food and water in her car, because she'd brought more than she'd been able to fit onto the camel. Once she had something to eat and drink, she could think more clearly and figure out what she was going to do.

Ignoring her hunger and thirst, she set off at a steady pace. Fear dogged her heels, like a desert jackal, but she mentally kicked the beast away and reminded herself that she was Sabrina Johnson. She'd faced much worse in her life. She was lying, of course. She'd never faced physical danger before. But so what? There was no one around to point out that fact.

Thirty minutes later she wanted to call a cab. Forty-five minutes later she realized she would have sold her soul for a single glass of water. An hour later, the fear won and she knew she was well and truly going to die in the desert. Her eyes burned from the dryness. Her skin felt as if it were a size too small and her throat was raw and on fire.

She wondered if death in the desert was like death in the snow. Would she simply get tired and go to sleep?

"Not with my luck," she muttered between parched lips. "My death will be much slower and more painful."

Still she continued to put one foot in front of the other, ignoring the tempting mirages appearing directly in front of her as the sun slowly set. First she saw a wavering oasis, then a waterfall. Finally she saw a half-dozen men on horses riding closer and closer.

Horses? She stopped walking. She blinked, then squinted. Were they real? As she paused, she realized she could feel the thunder of the horses' hooves on the ground. Which meant there was a possibility of rescue. Or something less pleasant.

Sabrina spent summers in Bahania with her father, supposedly learning the ways of his people. Not that he could be bothered to teach her anything, but some of the servants took pity on her and she'd picked up a thing or two. One tidbit had been that hospitality was guaranteed in the desert.

However, she spent her school years in Los Angeles, California, where her mother's maid had warned her never to speak to strangers. Especially men she didn't know. So should she stand her ground or run for the hills? Sabrina glanced around. There weren't any hills.

She studied the men as they galloped closer and seemed to get larger. They were dressed traditionally in burnoose and djellaba. Their long cloaks swept along behind them. As a way to distract herself from her growing apprehension, she tried to admire the strong yet elegant horses they rode. Bahanian horses, bred for the desert.

"Hi," she called as the men approached, trying for a breezy, confident tone. Between her dry throat and growing fear, she wasn't entirely successful. "I'm lost. The sandstorm caught me flat-footed. You wouldn't have happened to have seen a horse and a camel anywhere would you?"

No one answered her. Instead they circled her,

speaking in a tongue she recognized but didn't understand. Nomads, she thought, not sure if the men being nomads was good or bad for her.

One of the men pointed at her and gestured. Sabrina stood in place, even when several moved their horses very close to her. Should she tell them who she was, she wondered as she turned slowly. Nomads would respond to her father's name, but what about outlaws? Of course outlaws would want to hold her for ransom and she might impress them by telling them that even though she didn't look like much, she was actually Sabrina Johnson, aka Princess Sabra of Bahania. Or they might just kill her and leave her bones to bleach in the desert.

"I have want of a slave girl, but I doubt you'd do well at the job."

She spun toward the speaker. His clothing hid most of his features. She saw that he was tall in the saddle, with tanned skin and dark eyes. Lips curled up in a smile as he laughed at her.

"You speak English," she said stupidly.

"You do not speak the language of the desert," he replied. "Nor do you know its ways. She is not a forgiving lady." The humor fled his face. "Why are you out here alone?"

"That's not important," Sabrina said with a dismissive wave. "But maybe you could loan me a horse. Just to get me back to the outpost. My truck is there."

The man jerked his head. One of the others scrambled off his horse. For a second Sabrina thought she was going to get her wish. The man had actually listened. Most unusual in a Bahanian male. They generally ignored—

The nomad reached for her head covering and pulled it free. She screamed. The circle of men around her grew still. Sabrina sighed.

She knew what they were looking at. Long, curly red hair tumbled down her back, a legacy from her mother. The startling combination of brown eyes, red hair and honey-colored skin often caught people's attention, but no more so than here.

The men talked amongst themselves. She strained to understand what they were saying.

"They think I should sell you."

She glanced toward the English-speaker. She had the impression he was their leader. Panic fluttered inside of her, but she didn't let it show. Instead she squared her shoulders and raised her chin.

"Do you so need the money?" she asked, trying to fill her voice with contempt...or at least keep it from shaking.

"It makes life easier. Even out here."

"What happened to the hospitality of the desert? The laws of your land won't let you mistreat me."

"Exceptions are made for one as foolish as you."

He motioned to the man still standing next to her. In the split second before he reached for her, Sabrina spun on her heel and began to run. She had no destination in mind, just a burning need to be as far away from her captors as possible.

She heard hoofbeats behind her. Fear added speed, but not enough. She'd barely gone twenty yards when she was swept up onto a horse and held tightly against the hard, unforgiving chest of the nomad.

"Where, exactly, did you plan to go?" he asked.

She squirmed, but he didn't release her. Instead she found herself getting tangled in his robes.

"If you continue to try to get away, I'll tie you and drag you behind my horse."

She could feel the strength of him, and his heat. He was as unyielding as the desert. Just her luck, she thought glumly, and stilled.

Tossing her hair out of her face, she glared at him. "What do you want from me?"

"First, I would like you to remove your knee from my stomach."

She glanced down and saw that her jean-clad knee was indeed pushing against his midsection. It felt as if she were butting up against a rock, but she didn't share that thought with him. Instead she shifted slightly, so that she was sitting on the saddle, facing his left.

She sucked in a deep breath. The sun had slipped below the horizon. There was no way she could escape now. Not at night. She was lost, thirsty, hungry and held captive by who knows who. At least it wasn't raining.

"Ah," he said softly. "So you can be reasoned with. A most pleasant attribute in a woman. And rare."

"You mean beating all your wives doesn't keep them in line? What a surprise."

She glared at him as she spoke, telling herself that she didn't care if his gaze narrowed slightly.

His features were dark and hard, like a rock shaped by the blowing winds of the desert. His headdress covered his hair, but she suspected it would be dark, perhaps to his collar, perhaps a little shorter. He had broad shoulders, and he carried himself like a man used to the weight of many burdens.

"For a woman completely at my mercy, you are either incredibly brave or incredibly foolish."

"You've already accused me of being foolish," she reminded him. "Rather unjustly if you ask me."

"I did not ask you. Besides, what would *you* call someone who heads out into the desert without a guide, or even the most basic of supplies?"

"I had a horse and—"

He cut her off with a slight tilt of his chin. "Or the skill to keep them," he finished.

Rather than answer, she glanced over his shoulder. The men he'd left when he'd chased her had started to set up camp. Already they had a small fire burning and were setting a pot to boil.

"You have water?" she asked, licking her dry lips.

"Yes, and food. Unlike you, we kept possession of our supplies."

She couldn't seem to tear her gaze away from the liquid being poured into the pot. "Please," she whispered.

"Not so fast, my desert bird. Before you partake of our meager offerings, I want to make sure you don't fly away again."

"As you already pointed out, where would I go?"

"Not having a destination didn't stop you before."

He dismounted. Before she could slide to the ground, he pulled a length of rope from his voluminous robes and grabbed her wrists.

"Hey," she protested, tugging against his actions. "You don't have to do this. I'm not going anywhere."

"I intend to make sure of that."

She tried to pull her arms away so he couldn't

reach her wrists, but he moved too quickly and tied her. Then she shifted too far back in the saddle and started to slide off the horse. The man caught her by the front of her shirt and pulled her toward him. She lost her balance and fell heavily against him. He didn't even grunt.

Wrapping one arm around her waist, he lowered her to the ground. While she was still trying to catch her breath, he secured her ankles together, then straightened.

"Wait here," he told her and led his horse toward the makeshift camp.

"What?" she yelled, wiggling on the ground, unable to get up on her own. "You can't leave me here."

He studied her with his dark eyes, then smiled. "I would say that I can."

Stunned by disbelief, Sabrina watched as he joined the other men. He said something she couldn't hear and they chuckled in response. Anger replaced the fear burning in her chest. She would show him, she vowed, tugging on her fastenings and kicking at the sand. She would get free and find her way back to Bahania and have him shot. Or hanged. Or maybe both...at the same time. Her father might not pay much attention to her but he wouldn't be happy about her being kidnapped.

Unable to free herself, she shifted until her back was to the camp. Bad enough that she could smell them cooking dinner, she didn't want to have to watch it, too. Her mouth and throat felt so dry, they seemed swollen. Her stomach had never been so empty. Was the stranger just tormenting her or was he really not going to give her dinner? What kind of monster was he?

The desert kind, she told herself. Men like him didn't see women as anything but chattel.

"I would have been better off with the troll prince," she muttered.

Tears burned in her eyes, but she refused to give in to them. She never showed weakness. What was the point? Instead she vowed to stay emotionally strong enough to survive, so that she could take her revenge. She closed her eyes and tried to imagine herself somewhere else.

As the smell of the food continued to drift toward her and her stomach clenched painfully, she couldn't help wishing she was still at the palace. Okay, so her father rarely noticed she was around and her brothers ignored her, except when they were teasing her, but was that so bad?

She remembered her rage the previous day when her father, the king of Bahania, had announced that he'd betrothed her. Sabrina had been in shock.

"You can't be serious," she'd told her father.

"I am *most* serious. You are twenty-two. More than of an age to marry."

She'd glared at him. "I turned twenty-three last month. And this is the modern world. Not medieval Europe."

"I am aware of the time and the country. You are my daughter. You will marry the man of my choosing because you are a Bahanian princess and alliances must be made."

The man didn't even know how old she was, so why on earth would she trust him to pick out a husband? She could only imagine the horrible old man with three wives and bad breath whom King Hassan would consider suitable.

For the past twenty-three years her father had been content to ignore her. While she'd spent every summer in the palace, he'd rarely spoken with her. Although he took his sons on trips, she had been left behind. And when she spent the school year with her mother in California, he never phoned or wrote. So why would he think that she would do what he wanted now?

Rather than stay and meet her troll prince, she'd escaped, hoping to find the City of Thieves. Instead she'd been captured by nomads. Maybe the troll prince wasn't so bad.

"What are you thinking?"

The voice startled her. "That I need a vacation and this isn't what I had in mind."

She opened her eyes and saw her captor standing in front of her. He'd removed his headdress and outer robes. Dressed only in cotton trousers and a tunic, he should have looked less formidable. Unfortunately he did not.

He loomed like a deity, silhouetted by a beautiful, inky-black night sky. While she might not be completely comfortable in Bahania, she'd always admired the perfection of its stars. But tonight something other than twinkling lights captured her attention.

The man was tall. His thick dark hair was short and layered. In the darkness of the evening, his features blurred, although she saw a flash of white teeth when he smiled.

"You have the courage of a camel," he told her.

"Gee, thanks. Camels aren't brave."

"Ah, so you know that much about the desert. Fine. How about the courage of a desert fox."

"Don't they run away all the time?"

He shrugged. "You see my point. Good."

She had the most childish urge to stick her tongue out at him. Instead she took a deep breath and smelled something wonderful. Her stomach growled loudly as she realized he held a plate in one hand and a cup in the other.

"Dinner?" she asked cautiously, trying to keep the hope out of her voice.

"Yes." He crouched in front of her and set the plate and cup on the sand before helping her into a sitting position. "But can I trust you enough to untie you?"

It was all Sabrina could do not to throw herself at the food and start eating directly from the plate. Her mouth watered so much she had to swallow twice, and her throat ached at the thought of water.

"I swear I won't try to run away."

He settled next to her on the sand. "Why would I trust you? I don't know anything about you except you have the sense of a flea."

Her gaze narrowed. "I really hate all these animal comparisons. If you're discussing the fact that I misplaced my horse and my camel, it's not my fault. I tried to tether them when the sandstorm approached. I covered myself with a thick cloak and stayed low to the ground. I would say the fact that I survived the storm at all is a testament to my good sense."

He did not appear the least bit impressed by her argument. "What about the fact that you're in the desert by yourself?" He picked up the cup. "Or would you rather discuss the fact that you *lost* both your horse and your camel?''

''Not really,'' she muttered, then leaned forward to sip from the cup he held out to her.

The water was cool and clean. She swallowed greedily, taking in the life-giving moisture. Never had anything tasted so sweet, so perfect.

When she finished the cup, he put it on the ground and picked up the plate.

She looked from the strips of meat and pieces of vegetables to his hands. ''You aren't seriously considering feeding me, are you?'' She held up her bound wrists. ''If you don't want to untie me, at least let me feed myself.''

The thought of him touching her food was too weird. Although she was pretty hungry and he looked clean enough. Despite the heavy robes and the heat of the desert, the man in front of her didn't smell.

''Allow me the privilege,'' he said mockingly, and picked up a piece of meat.

She probably should have been brave and stubborn and refused. But her stomach was so very empty. Instead she leaned forward and took the meat from him, making sure her mouth never touched his fingers.

''I am Kardal,'' he said as she chewed. ''What is your name?''

She took her time in replying. After she'd swallowed, she licked her lips and stared eagerly at the plate. For reasons that weren't completely clear to her, she didn't want to tell him who she was.

''Sabrina,'' she answered, hoping he wouldn't connect that name with Princess Sabra of Bahania.

"You don't sound like a nomad," she said in an effort to distract him.

"Yet I am." He offered her another piece of meat.

"You must have gone to school somewhere else. England? America?"

"Why do you say that?"

"The way you speak. Your word choices and syntax."

One corner of his mouth lifted. "What do you know of syntax?"

She chewed and swallowed. "Despite what you think, I'm not an idiot. I've studied. I know things."

His dark eyes seemed to take possession of her soul. "What things, my desert bird?"

"I, ah—"

She was saved from having to answer by him feeding her a grilled bit of vegetable. This time, however, she wasn't so very cautious and the side of his index finger touched her lower lip. At the moment of contact, something odd shifted inside of her. Food poisoning, she told herself. No doubt he'd laced the food with something horrible.

But she was hungry enough not to care. She continued eating until the plate was empty, then drank the second glass of water Kardal gave her. When they were finished, she expected him to return to the men sitting around the small fire. Instead he continued to sit across from her, studying her.

She wondered how bad she looked. Her hair was a tangled mess and she was sure she had smudges of dirt on her face from the sandstorm. Not that she wanted to be attractive for her captor. This was generic female vanity—nothing specific about the man in front of her.

"Who are you?" he said quietly, staring into her eyes. "Why were you alone in the desert?"

With food in her belly, she felt a little less vulnerable and scared. She thought about lying, but she'd never been very good at that. Refusing to answer might be an option, except there was something compelling about Kardal's steady gaze. The easiest course of action was to tell the truth. Or at least part of it.

"I'm looking for the lost City of Thieves."

She expected a reaction of interest or disbelief. What she didn't expect was for him to lean his head back and laugh. The low chuckling drifted across the desert. The men at the fire turned to look at them, as did the horses.

"Laugh all you want," she snapped. "It's true. I know exactly where it is and I'm going to find it."

He raised his eyebrows. "The city is a myth. Adventurers have been searching for the city for centuries. What makes you think one slip of a girl will find it when they have not?"

"Some of them have," she insisted. "I have maps, diaries."

He lowered his gaze to her body. She wore a T-shirt and jeans, along with hiking boots. Behind her, on the sand, lay her cloak. She would need that cloak later. Already the temperature was dropping from stifling to pleasantly cool.

"Where exactly are these maps and diaries?" he asked sounding oh so polite.

She gritted her teeth. "They're in my saddle bags."

"I see. On your runaway horse?"

"Yes."

He paused. "You do realize it will be more diffi-cult to find this fictional city without the maps."

She curled her fingers into fists. Irritation swelled inside of her. "I've already figured that out."

"Yet you continue to seek the city?"

"I don't give up easily. I swear I'll come back and find it."

He rose to his feet and stared down at her from his rather impressive height. "How determined you sound. But your plans are based on an interesting assumption."

She frowned, barely able to see him in the dark-ness of the night. "What's that?"

"For you to return anywhere, I must first let you go."

Chapter Two

Kardal kept his eyes closed, trying to ignore the squirming of the woman next to him. The ground beneath was hard, but not uncomfortable, although he doubted Sabrina would appreciate that fact. While he'd unbound her feet, he'd kept her wrists tied and connected to a rope anchored to the belt around his waist. He knew that without a deterrent of some kind she was impulsive enough to try to escape in the night.

She was less than amused by their sleeping arrangements.

"This is ridiculous," she hissed, her words barely audible over the snores of his men. "It's the middle of the night in the middle of the desert. Where exactly do you think I'm going to go? Untie me at once."

"How imperious you sound," he replied, not

bothering to look at her. "If you continue to speak, I'll put a gag in your mouth. I assure you, after a time it grows most unpleasant."

He heard her sharp intake of air, but she didn't talk anymore, for which he was grateful.

She shifted again, drawing her thick cloak more tightly around her. The night temperature continued to drop. Kardal knew that in time she would welcome the heat of his body next to hers. Left on her own, she would be shivering by dawn. But he doubted she would thank him. Women were rarely sensible creatures.

As for trusting her enough to release her—he would rather trust his fortune to a gambler. He couldn't believe she'd been foolish—or foolhardy—enough to be traveling by herself in the desert. Didn't she realize how dangerous the vast emptiness could be?

Obviously not, he thought, answering his own question. At first he'd been shocked to see a lone traveler in the distance. He and his men had quickly changed course to offer assistance. As they'd approached, he'd realized the traveler was a woman. And then he'd seen her face and known exactly who she was.

Sabrina Johnson—otherwise known as Princess Sabra, the only daughter of King Hassan of Bahania—was everything he'd feared. Willful, difficult, spoiled and lacking the intelligence the good Lord gave a date palm.

He supposed the sensible course of action would be to return her to her father, even though he knew the king wouldn't do anything to mend her wayward ways. From what he'd heard, King Hassan ignored his only daughter, allowing her to spend much of the year with her mother in California. No doubt living in wildness as the king's former wife did.

Kardal opened his eyes and stared up at the heavens. Stars twinkled down at him. He was as much a product of the new century as any man in his world could be. Trapped between tradition and progress, he attempted to find wisdom and act accordingly in all situations. But when he thought about Sabrina wasting her time in Beverly Hills, having affairs and living who knew what kind of hedonistic lifestyle...

He swore silently. She might be uncomprehendingly beautiful but she had the heart and soul of a spoiled and willful child. She was not a traditional desert wife, nor was she a sparkling gem of a woman produced by the best western culture had to offer. She fit nowhere and he had no use for her. If life were fair, he could simply return her and be done with her.

Unfortunately life was not fair and that course of action wasn't open to him. The price of being a leader, he supposed.

Sabrina flopped onto her back, tugging at the rope that bound them together. He didn't move. She sighed in disgust and was quiet. In time, her breathing slowed and he knew she'd found sleep.

Tomorrow would be interesting, he thought wryly. He would have to decide what to do with her. Or perhaps he already knew and didn't want to admit it to himself. There was also the matter of her not recognizing him, although it was possible she hadn't been told his name. That thought made him smile. If she didn't know, he wasn't about to tell her. Not yet.

* * *

Sabrina woke slowly to an unusual combination of hard bed and warmth. She shifted slightly, but the mattress didn't yield at all. Nor did the heat source surrounding her. It was specifically on one side. Like a—

Her eyes popped open. She looked up into the rapidly lightening sky and realized she wasn't back in her bed in the palace, nor was she in her room in her mother's house. Instead she was in the desert, tied by a rope to a man she didn't know.

The previous day's events returned to her memory with all the subtlety of a desert storm: Her excitement at finally starting the journey she'd been dreaming about ever since she'd first heard of the lost City of Thieves. How she'd been so darn careful to pack her supplies sensibly, even taking a more docile horse than usual so that she wouldn't have to worry about a riding accident. She'd had a compass, maps, diaries and determination on her side. What she hadn't counted on was a conspiracy by the elements.

Which was how she'd come to find herself in her present predicament. Tied to a nomad who was going to do who knows what to her.

She risked glancing to her right. The man was still asleep, which gave her the opportunity to study him. In the soft light of morning, he still looked hard and powerful—a man of the desert. He held her fate in his hands, which alarmed her, but she no longer believed her life was in danger. Nor had she worried for her virtue. Even as she'd protested and then seethed at the thought of being tied up, she'd never once thought he would actually physically attack her. Which didn't make any sense. She *should* have been afraid.

Now she looked at the thick lashes resting on his

cheek and the way his mouth relaxed as he slept. His skin was tanned, adding shadows to sculpted cheekbones and a strong jawline. Who was this Kardal of the desert? Why did he hold her prisoner rather than simply offering to escort her to the nearest town?

Suddenly his eyes opened. They stared at each other from a distance of less than eight inches. She tried to read his expression, but could not. It was very strange, but if she had to pick a word to describe what was in his dark eyes, she would have said disappointment.

He rose without saying a word. As he did so, she realized that he must have loosened the rope holding them together, because it lay on the blankets he'd spread over the sand. With a quick movement, he bent down and untied her wrists.

"You may have a small bowl of water for your morning ablutions," he said by way of greeting. "Don't try to escape. If you do, I'll give you to my men."

And then he turned his back on her. "Not much of a morning person, are you?" Sabrina called out before she could stop herself.

He kept walking away and didn't bother responding. She sighed. So much for friendly chitchat.

She did as he instructed, taking her small bowl of water to the far side of the camp. Covering herself with her cloak, she did her best to freshen up. Between the sandstorm, the night of sleeping in her clothes and the prospect of wearing them again for an unspecified length of time, she would have given a lot for a shower.

Ten minutes later, she cautiously approached the fire. Two men were making breakfast. She ignored the food and gazed longingly at the pot of coffee sitting close to the flames. Food wasn't a priority for her until later in the day, but coffee was life.

She caught Kardal's attention and motioned to the pot. He nodded without saying anything. She sidled closer to the men and took an unused mug from an open saddlebag, then poured herself a full cup of the steaming liquid. It was hot and strong enough to grow hair.

"Perfect," she breathed.

Kardal moved around the fire to stand next to her. He wore his robe open over his shirt and trousers. The long covering flowed behind him with each step.

"I'm surprised you like it," he said. "Most westerners and many women find it too strong."

"Too strong isn't possible," she said after sipping again. "I like coffee I can stand a spoon in."

"No lattes or mocha cappuccinos?"

What? Humor from the great and mysterious Kardal? She smiled slightly. "Not even on a bet."

He motioned for her to follow him to the edge of their camp. Once there he put his hands on his hips and stared down at her as if she were a particularly unappealing bug. So much for the moment of bonding over coffee.

"Something must be done with you," he announced.

"What? You don't want to spend the rest of your days traveling with me throughout the desert? And here I thought you enjoyed tying me up and making me sleep on the hard ground."

He raised his dark eyebrows. "You have more spirit than you did last night."

"Not surprising. I'm rested, I have coffee. Despite

rumors to the contrary, I'm a creature of simple wants.''

The curl of his mouth indicated that he didn't believe her.

''We have three choices,'' he told her. ''We can kill you and leave your body here in the desert. We can sell you as a slave or we can ransom you to your family.''

She nearly choked on her coffee, barely able to believe he meant what he said. Although the edge of determination in his voice told her that he did.

''Can I see what's behind curtain number four?'' she asked when she could finally speak. Here she'd been thinking ol' Kardal wasn't so bad and he was talking about killing her and leaving her remains for whatever animals lived out here.

Of course if they *were* going to kill her wouldn't they have already done it? Sleeping with her tied up next to him had to have been just as uncomfortable for Kardal as it had been for her.

''Eliminating death as an option,'' she said cautiously, ''I don't think I'd make an especially good slave.''

''I had considered that. Of course a good beating would change that.''

''And what would a bad beating do?'' she murmured.

''Which would you prefer?''

She stared at him. ''A good or a bad beating? Neither, thank you.'' She couldn't believe they were discussing this. She couldn't believe this was actually happening. That she was standing in the middle of the Bahanian desert discussing the physical abuse of her person.

"I meant," he said slowly, as if she weren't very bright, "which of the three do you prefer?"

"It's my choice? How democratic."

"I am trying to be fair."

She grimaced. Obviously he'd missed the sarcasm she'd attempted to interject into her words. "Fair would be giving me a horse and some supplies, then pointing me in the right direction."

"You've already lost your own horse and camel. Why would I trust you with stock of mine?"

She didn't like the question so she ignored it. There was no point in protesting that the loss of her horse and camel had been more because of the storm than because she'd done something wrong.

"I do not want to be killed," she said at last when it became apparent he really was waiting for her to choose her fate. "And I have no desire to be any man's slave." Nor did she want to return to the palace and marry the troll prince. Unfortunately there wasn't much choice.

She wondered if her father would bother to pay a ransom for her. He might if for no other reason than it would look bad for him if he didn't. Now if one of his precious cats had been kidnapped, the entire kingdom would be in an uproar until it was returned.

It was very sad, she thought to herself, that her place in her father's affection was far below her brothers and well under the cats. Unfortunately it was true. However, Kardal didn't know that. There was no other choice. She was going to have to tell him who she was and hope that he was a man of honor, loyal to the king. If so, he would happily return her to her father. Once there, she would deal with her betrothal to the troll prince.

She drew herself up to her full height—all of five feet four inches and tried to look important. "I am Princess Sabra of Bahania. You have no right to keep me as your prisoner, nor may you determine my fate. I demand that you return me to the palace at once. If you do not, I will be forced to tell my father what you have done. He will hunt you and your men like the dogs that you are."

Kardal looked faintly bored.

"You don't believe me?" she asked. "I assure you, it's the truth."

He studied her face. "You don't appear very royal. If you're really the princess, what are you doing out here in the desert by yourself?"

"I told you yesterday. Searching for the City of Thieves. I wanted to find it and surprise my father with treasures I discovered there."

That much was true, she thought. Not only had she wanted to study the fabled city, but she'd figured finding it was a surefire way to get the king's attention. Once he realized she was a real person, she might be able to talk him out of her engagement.

He considered her words. "Even if you are the princess, which I doubt, I don't see why you would have been out alone. It is forbidden." His gaze narrowed. "Although they say the princess is willful and difficult. Perhaps you *are* her after all."

Talk about a no-win situation, Sabrina thought glumly. She could accept the character assassination or not be believed. Once again she was left grasping for an alternative. Why was it people always assumed the worst about her? Didn't anyone understand that she hadn't had a normal life? Splitting time between two parents who didn't really want her around hadn't given her anything close to a happy childhood. People who thought she was fortunate saw only the physical trappings of her station. No one saw the endless hours she'd spent alone as a child.

But there was no point in explaining all that to Kardal. He wouldn't believe her and even if he did, he wouldn't care.

"I will consider what you have told me," he said at last.

"What does that mean? You believe that I'm really the princess? Are you going to take me back to the palace in Bahania?" Compared to her recent desert experience, the troll prince might not be such a bad choice after all.

"No," Kardal told her. "I think I will keep you for now. It would be most entertaining to have a princess as a slave."

She tried to speak but could only splutter. He couldn't mean it, she told herself, hoping she wasn't lying.

"No," she finally said. "You couldn't do that."

"It appears that I could." Kardal chuckled to himself as he walked away, leaving her openmouthed and frothing.

"You'll regret this," she yelled after him, fighting the fury growing within her. If she hadn't treasured her coffee so much, she would have tossed the steaming liquid at his retreating back. "I'll make you sorry."

He turned and looked at her. "I know, Sabrina. Most likely all the days of my life."

Forty minutes later, she knew a flogging was too good for him. She was back to wanting him both hanged and shot. Maybe even beheaded. It wasn't enough that he threatened her and insulted her. No. Not only had he tied her up, but he'd blindfolded her as well.

"I don't know what you think you're doing," she announced, practically vibrating with rage. The sensation of being blind while on a moving horse was completely disconcerting. With each step, she expected to tumble under the horse's hooves.

"First," Kardal said, his voice barely a whisper in her ear. "You don't have to shout. I'm right behind you."

"Like I don't know that."

She sat in front of him, on his saddle. As much as she tried to keep from touching him, there wasn't enough room. Holding herself stiffly away from him only made her muscles ache. Despite her best effort to prevent contact, her back kept brushing against his front.

"What's the second thing?" she asked grudgingly.

"You're about to get your wish. Our destination is the City of Thieves."

Sabrina didn't respond. She couldn't. Her mind filled with a thousand questions, not to mention disbelief, hope and excitement.

"It's real?"

Behind her, Kardal chuckled. "Very real. I've lived there all my life."

"But you can't— It isn't—" What he was saying didn't make sense. "If it truly exists, how come I've never heard about it except in old books or diaries?"

"It's how we prefer it. We are not interested in the outside world. We live in the old tradition."

Which meant life for women was less than agreeable.

"I don't believe you," she told him. "You're just saying this to get my hopes up."

"Why else would I blindfold you? It is important that you not be able to find your way back to our city."

Sabrina bit her lower lip. Could Kardal be telling the truth? Could the city exist and did people really live there? It would almost be worth being captured just to see inside the ancient walls. And his statement about finding her way back implied that he would— despite his posturing to the contrary—eventually let her go.

"Are there treasures?" she asked.

"You seek material wealth?"

There was something in his tone. Contempt, maybe? What was it about this man and his assumptions?

"Stop talking to me like I'm some gold digger," she said heatedly. "I have a bachelor's degree in archeology and a master's in Bahanian history. My interest in the contents of the city are intellectual and scientific, not personal."

She adjusted her weight, trying to escape the feeling that she was going to fall from the horse at any moment. "I don't know why I'm bothering," she grumbled into the darkness. "You're hardly a sympathetic audience. Just believe what you want. I don't care."

But she did care, Kardal thought with some surprise when she was finally quiet. He had heard about her going to school in America. It had never occurred to him that she would actually complete her studies, nor had he thought she would study something relevant to her heritage. He wasn't sure she didn't want the treasures of his homeland for herself, but he was willing to wait and let her show her true self on that matter.

She leaned forward, as if holding herself away from him. He felt the tremor in her muscles, the result of her tension.

"Relax," he told her, wrapping an arm around her waist and pulling her against him. "We have a long day's ride. If you continue to sit so stiffly, you'll spend much of the time in pain. I promise not to ravish you while we're upon my horse."

"Remind me to never dismount then," she muttered, half under her breath, but she did let herself sag against him.

Sabrina was more trouble than any other three women Kardal had ever known, but he found he didn't dislike her as much as he would have thought. Unfortunately he also found her body appealing as it pressed against his own. During the night he'd managed to ignore the sweet scent of her, but not while they rode pressed so closely together. When he'd first placed her in the saddle, he'd only thought to keep her from running off. By tying her hands, he'd attempted to both restrain and punish her willfulness. Now he was the one being punished.

With each step of the horse, her body swayed against his. Her rear nestled against his groin, arousing him so that he could think of little else. It was a kind of trouble he did not need.

She was not the traditional desert woman he would have chosen. She was neither deferential nor accommodating. Her quick mind allowed her to use wit and words as a weapon and there was no telling how her time in the west had corrupted her. She was disrespectful, opinionated and spoiled. And even if he found her slightly intriguing, she was not whom he would have chosen. But then the choice hadn't been his at all. It had all been proclaimed at the time of his birth.

He wondered why she didn't know who he was. Had her father not told her the specifics or had she simply not listened? He would guess the latter. Kardal smiled. He doubted Sabrina listened to anything she didn't want to hear. It was a habit he would break her of.

He could almost anticipate the challenge she would be to him. In the end he would be the victor, of course. He was the man—strength to her yielding softness. Eventually she would learn to appreciate that. In the meantime, what would the ill-tempered beauty say if she knew he was the man to whom she had been betrothed?

Chapter Three

Eventually Sabrina found the rhythm of the horse hypnotic, even with the chronic sensation of falling. Despite her desire to, if not prove herself then at least be somewhat independent, she found herself relaxing into Kardal's arms. He was strong enough to support her and if she continued to hold herself stiffly, she would be aching by the end of the day.

So instead she allowed herself to lean into him, feeling the muscled hardness of his chest pressing against her. He shifted his arms so that he held the reins in front of her instead of behind her. Her forearms rested on his.

The sensation of *touching* him was oddly intimate. Perhaps it was their close proximity, or perhaps it was the darkness caused by her blindfold. She'd never been in a situation like this, but that shouldn't be a surprise. Not much of her life had been spent with her being kidnapped.

"Do you do this often?" she asked. "Kidnap innocent women?"

Instead of being insulted by the question, he chuckled. "You are many things, princess, but you are not innocent."

Actually he was wrong about that, but this was hardly the time or the place to have that conversation. She could—

The horse stumbled on a loose rock. There was no warning. For Sabrina, the blackness of her world shifted and the sensation of falling nearly became a reality. She gasped and tried to grab on to something, but there was only openness in front of her.

"It's all right," Kardal soothed from behind her. He moved his arm so that it clasped her around the waist, pulling her more tightly against him. "I won't let anything happen to you."

She wanted to take comfort in his words, but she knew the real purpose behind them. "Your concern isn't about me," she grumbled. "You don't want anything to happen to your prize."

He laughed softly. "Exactly, my desert bird. I refuse to let you fly away, nor will I allow you to be injured. You are to stay just as you are until I can claim my rightful reward."

She didn't like the sound of that. No doubt he believed everything he read in the papers about her, so he thought he knew her.

"You're wrong about me," she said a few minutes later, when the horse was once again steady and her heartbeat had returned to normal.

"I am rarely wrong."

That comment made her roll her eyes, although with her wearing a blindfold he couldn't tell.

"I know you are not a dutiful daughter," he murmured in her ear. "You live a wild life in the west. But that is no surprise. You are your mother's daughter, not a woman of Bahania."

She told herself that he was a barbarian and his opinion didn't matter. Unfortunately those words didn't stop the sting of tears or the lump in her throat. She *hated* that people judged her based on a few reports in newspapers or magazines. It had happened to her all her life. Very few people took the time to find out the truth.

"Did it ever occur to you that sometimes the media gets it wrong?" she asked.

"Sometimes, but not in your case. You have lived most of your years in Los Angeles. Picking up that lifestyle was inevitable. Had your father kept you here, you might have learned our ways, but that was not to be."

She didn't know which charge to answer first. "You're making it sound as if my father letting me go was my fault," she told him. "I was four years old. I didn't have any say in the decision. And just in case you forgot, Bahanian law forbids a royal child being raised in another country, yet my father let my mother take me away. He didn't even try to stop her."

She couldn't keep the bitterness out of her voice. All her life she'd had to live with the knowledge that her father hadn't cared enough about her to keep her around. She didn't doubt that if she'd been a son, he would have refused to let her go. But she was merely a daughter. His *only* daughter, but that was obviously not significant to him.

She felt her frustration growing. It wasn't fair. It had never been fair and it was never going to be fair in the future. One day she would figure that out. Maybe on the same day she would cease caring what people thought about her. Maybe then she would be mature enough not to worry when they formed opinions and judged her before even meeting her. Unfortunately that day wasn't today and she hated that Kardal's low opinion stung more so than usual.

"You can say what you want," she told Kardal. "You can have your opinions and your theories, but no one knows the truth except me."

"I will admit that much is true," he said, his deep voice drifting around her and making her wonder what he was thinking.

"Relax now," he continued. "We will travel for much of the day. Try to rest. You didn't sleep much last night."

She started to ask how he knew, then remembered they had been tied together. Although she'd fallen asleep right away, she'd awakened several times, tossing and turning until she could doze off again. No doubt she'd kept him awake as well. What with being kidnapped, blindfolded and left with her wrists tied, Sabrina wasn't sure she was even sorry.

She drew in a deep breath and tried to relax. When the tension in her body began to ease, she allowed her mind to drift. What would it be like to be someone as in charge of his world as Kardal? He was a man of the desert. He would answer to no one. She'd always been at the beck and call of her parents. They were forever sending her back and forth, as if neither really wanted her around.

"Do you really live in the City of Thieves?" she asked sleepily.

"Yes, Sabrina."

She liked the sound of her name on his lips. Despite her predicament, she smiled. "All your life?" she asked.

"Yes. All my life. I went away to school for a few years, but I have always returned to the desert. This is where I belong."

He spoke with a confidence she envied. "I've never belonged anywhere. When I'm in California, my mother acts like I'm in the way all the time. It's better now that I'm older, but when I was young, she would complain about how she wasn't free to come and go as she wanted. Which wasn't true because she just left me with her maid. And in Bahania..." She sighed. "Well, my father doesn't like me very much. He thinks I'm like her, which I'm not."

She shifted to get more comfortable. "People don't appreciate the little things in their lives that show they belong. If I had them, I would appreciate them."

"Perhaps for ten minutes," Kardal said. "Then you would grow weary of the constraints. You are spoiled, my desert bird. Admit it."

Her sleepiness vanished and she sat up straight. "I am not. You don't know me well enough to be making that kind of judgment. Sure, it's easy to read a few things and listen to rumors and decide, but it's very different to have lived my life."

"I think you would argue with me about the color of the sky."

"Not if I could see it."

"However you talk around me," he said, "I'm not removing the blindfold."

"Your attitude needs adjusting."

He laughed. "Perhaps, but not by you. As my slave, you will be busy with other things."

She shivered. Did the man really intend to keep her as his personal slave? Was that possible? "You're kidding, right? This is all a joke. You think I need a lesson and you're going to be the one to teach it to me."

"You'll have to wait and see. However, don't be too surprised when you find out I have no intention of letting you go."

She couldn't get her mind around the idea. It was crazy. This wasn't fourteenth-century Bahania. They were living in the modern world. Men didn't keep slaves. Or maybe in the wilds of the desert, they did.

She swallowed hard. "What, ah, exactly would you want me to do?"

He was silent for several heartbeats, then she felt him lean toward her. His breath tickled her ear as he whispered, "It's a surprise."

"I doubt it will be a very good one," she murmured dryly.

Sounds awakened her. Sabrina jerked into consciousness, not aware that she'd been asleep. For a second she panicked because she couldn't see, but then she remembered she was both bound and blindfolded.

"Where are we?" she asked, feeling more afraid than she had before. There were too many noises. Bits of conversation, yells, grunts, bleats. Bleats?

She listened more closely and realized she heard the sounds of goats bleating and the bells worn by cattle. There were rooster calls, clinks of money, not to mention dozens of conversations occurring at the same time. The fragrance of cooking meat competed with the desert animals and the perfumed oils for sale.

"A marketplace?" she asked. Her stomach lurched. "Are you going to sell me?"

A coldness swept over her. Until this moment, she hadn't really thought through her situation. Yes, she'd been Kardal's prisoner, but he'd treated her well and she hadn't felt more than inconvenienced. Suddenly things were different. She was truly his captive and at his mercy. If he decided to sell her, she couldn't do anything to stop him. No one would listen to the protests of a mere woman.

"Don't think you have to throw yourself in front of the next moving cart," Kardal said calmly. "Despite the appeal of the idea, I'm not going to sell you. We have arrived. Welcome to the City of Thieves."

Sabrina absorbed the words without understanding them. He wasn't going to sell her to some horrid man? Her life wasn't in danger?

She felt his fingers against the back of her head, then her blindfold fell away. It took several seconds for her eyes to adjust to the late-afternoon light. When they did, she could only gasp in wonder.

There were dozens of people everywhere she looked. Hundreds, actually, dressed in traditional desert garb. She saw women carrying baskets and men leading donkeys. Children running between the crowds. Stalls had been set up along a main stone street and vendors called out enticements to come view their wares.

It was a village, she thought in amazement. Or a town. The City of Thieves really existed? Did she dare believe it?

She half turned in her saddle to glance at Kardal. "Is it real?"

"Of course. Ah, they've noticed us."

She returned her attention to the people and saw they were pointing and staring. Instantly Sabrina was aware of feeling dirty and mussed. Her cloak lay across her lap, hiding her bound hands, and a thin cloth covered her hair so no one could see the bright red color. Still, she was a woman sharing a saddle with a man. Worse, she had western features. Her skin wasn't as dark as a native's and the shape of her eyes was all wrong. There was also something about her mouth. She'd never quite figured out exactly what bow or curve set her apart, she only knew that she was rarely mistaken for a *true* Bahanian.

"Lady, lady!"

She glanced toward the high-pitched voice and saw a small girl waving at her. Sabrina started to wave back only to remember at the last second that her hands were bound. She had to settle for nodding pleasantly.

"Where is the treasure kept?" she asked. "Can I see it? Do you have it inventoried?"

Before he could answer, she heard a most peculiar sound. Something familiar, yet so out of place that she—

She turned toward the noise and gasped. There, on the edge of the marketplace, was a low stone wall.

On the other side, a lazy river flowed around a bend and disappeared from view.

"Water?" she breathed, barely able to believe what she saw.

"We have an underground spring that supplies all our needs," he told her, urging his horse through the crowd. "On the east side of the city, it returns underground, here it provides irrigation for our crops."

Sabrina was stunned. In the desert, water was more valuable than gold, or even oil. With water, a civilization could survive. Without the precious commodity, life would end very quickly.

"I read several references to a spring in some of the diaries," she said, "but no one mentioned a river."

"Perhaps they weren't allowed to see it, or chose not to write about it."

"Maybe. How long has it existed?"

"Since the first nomads founded the city."

She jerked her attention away from the flowing river and focused again on the marketplace. "These people can't all be nomads. By definition, they would want to spend some portion of the year in the desert."

"True enough. There are those who live permanently within the city walls. Others stay for a time and move on."

Walls? Sabrina searched the far edges of the marketplace for the beginnings of walls. It was only then that she noticed they appeared to be riding through a giant courtyard. She turned in the saddle to glance behind them. Nearly a quarter mile away were massive stone walls.

"It's not possible," she breathed, amazed by the sheer size of the city.

"And yet it exists."

They approached an inner set of walls. She raised her gaze to study the thick stone, taking in the massive wooden arch that was actually a frame for the largest set of double doors she'd ever seen. They had to be at least fifty or sixty feet high.

She longed to jump down from the horse and study the doors.

"How old are they?" she asked, barely able to speak through her excitement. "When were they built? Where did the wood come from? Who were the craftsmen? Do they still work? Can you close them?"

"So many questions," Kardal teased. "You haven't seen the most magnificent part yet."

She was about to ask what could be better than those incredible doors when they moved through the arch. On the other side of the inner wall was a second courtyard. Sabrina glanced around with great interest. The walls continued to circle the city, probably surrounding it completely. How big was the walled city and how long was the wall? Two miles? Ten? Were there—

She raised her head and nearly fell off the horse. Kardal reined the animal to a halt and let Sabrina look her fill. In front of them stood an awe-inspiring twelfth-century castle.

Sabrina tried to speak and could not. She wasn't sure she was even breathing. The structure rose to the sky like an ancient cathedral, all towers and levels, complete with arrow slits and a drawbridge.

A castle. Here. In the middle of the desert. She

couldn't believe it. Not really. And yet here it was. As she continued to study the design, she recognized that it had been built in sections, modernized, added to and modernized again. There were western and eastern influences, fourteenth-century windows and spires, along with eighteenth-century towers. People walked across the main bridge. She could see shapes moving inside.

A real live, to-scale working castle.

"How is this possible?" she asked, her voice breathy with shock. "How has it stayed a secret all these hundreds of years?"

"The color, the placement." Behind her Kardal shrugged.

Sabrina studied the sand-colored stones used to build the castle and noticed the low mountains rising up on either side of the city. It *was* possible, she supposed, that the city could not be seen from the air. At least not with the naked eye or conventional photography.

"Other governments must know about the city," she murmured, more to herself than to him. "They've seen it from satellite photos, infrared."

"Of course," Kardal murmured from behind her. "However, it is to everyone's interest to keep our location a secret."

They stopped just in front of the entrance to the castle. As Sabrina glanced around, she recognized descriptions from the diaries she'd read. She was absolutely right in the middle of the City of Thieves. She felt almost dizzy from excitement. There was so much to study here; so much to learn.

"I will dismount first," Kardal said, easing himself off the horse.

Sabrina waited for him to help her down. It was only then that she noticed they'd gathered a crowd. She felt disheveled and dirty, but fortunately very few people were paying attention to her. They were busy watching Kardal and murmuring to themselves.

As he walked around the horse to help her, several men in traditional dress bowed slightly. Sabrina swallowed against a sudden lump in her throat. She had a bad feeling about this.

"Why are they watching you?" she asked. "Did you do something wrong?"

He grinned up at her, then put his hands on her waist and pulled her off the horse. "What a suspicious mind you have. They're simply greeting me. Welcoming me home."

"No. That would mean waving as you rode by." She glanced at the collecting crowd. "This is more than that."

"I assure you, this is very common."

He started to lead her up the stairs toward the entrance to the castle. The crowd parted as they walked and everyone bowed. Sabrina stopped suddenly.

"Who are you?" she asked, knowing she wasn't going to like the answer.

"I have told you, I am Kardal."

He waited, obviously expecting her to start walking again, but she stood her ground. She glanced around at the happy, almost reverent crowd, then back at him. "Uh-huh. Okay, Kardal, what am I missing?"

He tried to make his expression innocent and failed badly. If her hands hadn't still been bound, she would have planted them on her hips.

"Look," she said, both fearful and irritated. "You

can call me a spoiled brat if you like, but I'm not stupid. Who are you?''

An old man stepped forward and smiled at her. He was stoop-shouldered and barely came to her chin.

"Don't you know?'' he asked in a quavering voice. ''He is Kardal, the Prince of Thieves. He rules this place.''

Sabrina opened her mouth, then closed it. She'd heard of the man, of course. There had been a prince of the city for as long as the mysterious place had existed.

"You?'' she asked in disbelief.

Kardal shrugged. ''I suppose you had to find out sometime. Yes, I'm the prince here.'' He motioned to the castle and the desert beyond. ''I am ruler over all we survey. The wild desert is my kingdom…my word is law.''

At that, he jerked the cloak from her bound hands and grabbed her fingers in his. He pulled her up the stairs to the entrance to the castle, then turned to face the murmuring crowd.

"This is Sabrina,'' he said, motioning to her. ''I have found her in the desert and claimed her as my own. Touch her and you will have breathed your last that day.''

Sabrina groaned. Everyone was staring at her, talking about her. She could feel herself blushing.

"Great,'' she muttered. ''Death threats to those who would help me escape. Thanks a lot.''

"I say these words to protect you.''

"Like I believe that. Besides, you're treating me like a possession.''

"Have you forgotten that you're my slave?''

"I would if you'd give me a chance.'' She glared

at him. "Next you'll be putting a collar around my neck, the way my father does with his cats."

"If you are very good I might just treat you as well as your father treats his cats."

"I won't hold my breath on that one, either."

Kardal laughed as he led her into the castle. She followed, her mind whirling with a thousand different thoughts. Too much was happening at once. She was having trouble keeping up.

"If you're the Prince of Thieves," she said, "have you really spent your entire life stealing from other people?"

"I don't steal. That practice went out of style some time ago. We produce our income in other ways now."

She wanted to ask what, but before she could, they stepped into the castle. Everywhere she looked she saw beauty. From the perfectly even stone walls to the intricate tapestries to the elegant mosaic tile floor. There were candleholders of gold, frames decorated with gems, paintings and antique furniture.

The main room of the castle was huge, perhaps the size of a football field. It stretched up at least two stories and there were stained-glass windows and skylights to let in the light. She motioned to the candles and gas lamps.

"No electricity?" she asked as Kardal cut the bindings on her wrists.

"We generate some, but not in the living quarters. There we live as we have for centuries."

Again he took her hand in his, tugging her along. She tried to take everything in, but it was impossible. Everywhere she looked, she saw something old, beautiful and very likely, stolen. There were paintings by old masters and impressionists. She recognized the style but not the subject. There were some she'd seen in books, rare photographs of paintings missing and long thought destroyed.

Kardal led her through a maze of corridors, up and down stairs, twisting and turning until she was completely lost. People passed them, stopping to smile and bow slightly. If she hadn't been sure of his identity before, by the time they finally stopped in front of double wooden doors, she was convinced. The Prince of Thieves, she thought in amazement. Who knew such a man existed?

It could be worse, she told herself as he pushed open one of the doors. He could be the troll prince. With that thought, she stepped into the room. And gasped. When Kardal released her, she turned in a slow circle, taking in the spacious quarters.

Each item of furniture was huge. The four-poster bed could easily sleep six or seven. There was a fainting couch, covered in the same thick burgundy as the bedspread and a fabulous Oriental carpet on the stone floor. A brilliant mosaic of a peacock displaying for his peahens graced one humongous wall. There was a fireplace as large as her dorm room and books. Hundreds, perhaps thousands of old, leather-bound books.

She crossed to them and reverently ran her fingers along their spines.

"Are they cataloged?" she asked, opening an old copy of *Hamlet* by Shakespeare, then gasping when she saw an inscription dated 1793. On the small table in front of her sat a hand-illustrated text of the Bible. She'd never seen such bounty.

Still holding the slim volume, she turned to face

him. "Kardal, do you know what you have here? It's priceless. The knowledge and history."

He dismissed her with a wave. "Someone will see to you. A bath will be brought, along with appropriate clothing."

She could barely force her attention away from her book to concentrate on what he was saying. "Appropriate?"

Something dark sparked to life in his eyes. "As my slave, you will have certain…responsibilities. To fulfill them you will need to dress to please me."

She blinked at him. "You can't be serious." She replaced the book and for the first time really *looked* at the room. At the chaise and the very large bed. Her throat tightened.

"Uh, Kardal, really. This is a game, right?" She backed up until she pressed against the far wall. "I mean, I'm Princess Sabra. You have to think this through."

He walked over to her, striding purposefully until he was directly in front of her. Close enough to touch. Which he did by cupping her jaw.

"I am aware of your identity so there's no need to play the innocent with me."

The implication of his words hit her like a slap. She flinched. "Did it ever occur to you that I'm not playing?"

One corner of his mouth turned up. "Your lifestyle in California is well documented. I might not approve of what you've done, but I intend to take advantage of it…and you."

His fingertips barely grazed her cheek, yet she felt his touch all the way down to the pit of her stomach. He stood too close—it was nearly impossible to breathe. Fear combined with a sense of disbelief. He couldn't really be saying all this. He couldn't mean to...to—

"We can't have sex," she blurted.

"I will not be a selfish lover," he promised. "You will be well pleased."

She didn't want to be pleased, Sabrina thought frantically. She wanted to be believed. Tears burned but she blinked them away. What was the point? Kardal would never listen, no matter how she protested. He thought she was some party girl who slept with every man who asked. Telling him she was a virgin would only make him laugh.

"I doubt my pleasure will be enough payment for what you have in mind," she said bitterly.

"You're making that judgment before you've had your way with me."

"The only thing I want is to go back to the palace."

He dropped his hand to his side. "Perhaps in time. When I grow tired of you. Until then—" He motioned to the room around them. "Enjoy your stay in my home. After all, you've finally found your heart's desire. You now reside in the City of Thieves."

He turned and left.

Trapped, she thought dully. She was well and truly trapped. She had no idea where she was, and didn't know a soul to help her.

Sabrina slid down the wall until she sat crouched on the stone floor. He was right. She had found what she'd been looking for. Which reminded her of that old saying. The one about being careful about what one wished for. The wish might come true.

Chapter Four

"I can't believe it," Sabrina muttered as she stared at her reflection in the gilded full-length mirror in her bedroom. "I look like an extra in a badly made sheik movie."

"The prince was most insistent," said Adiva, the soft-spoken servant sent to help Sabrina "prepare herself" for Kardal's return.

"I'll just bet he was," Sabrina said, then sighed. There wasn't anything to be done and she refused to get angry at the young woman who had been so kind.

She glanced at Adiva. The young woman, barely eighteen, stood with her eyes averted. She wore a conservative tunic over loose trousers and had pulled her thick, dark hair back in a braid. No doubt the teenager had all the retiring qualities that Kardal admired in women. He would think nothing of defiling Sabrina, while he would treat Adiva like a saint.

Sabrina returned her attention to her reflection and tried not to choke. She wore gauzy, hip-hugger trousers that were fitted at her ankles. Except for the scrap of lining low on her belly, she was practically naked from the waist down. The thin fabric concealed nothing. The top half of her outfit wasn't any better. The same pale, gauzy fabric draped over her arms, while all that covered her breasts was a bra-style lining in gold. Adiva had caught her long, curly red hair up in a ponytail that sat high on her head. It was held in place with a gold headband.

Adiva stepped back and bowed slightly. "I will leave you to await our master," she said quietly.

"I really wish you wouldn't," Sabrina told her, trying to ignore the nervous jumping in her stomach. All costumes aside, she wasn't in the mood to be ravished. Not that the Prince of Thieves was going to ask her opinion on the matter.

Adiva either didn't hear her plea, or didn't believe it. Or maybe there was nothing the girl could do. She bowed again, then turned and left Sabrina alone.

The long room turned out to be perfect for pacing. Sabrina stalked from one end to the other, cursing Kardal, calling herself an idiot for setting out yesterday alone. If only the storm hadn't come up. If only she hadn't lost her horse and her camel. If only Kardal weren't going to force her to have sex with him.

He was in for a surprise, she told herself, trying to keep her sense of humor and not panic. He was expecting Bathsheba, and instead he was about to get the virgin Sabrina. At least she would have the satisfaction of knowing that after he defiled her, he would be killed. However, that was small comfort.

What would please her more would be a way to prevent the situation from occurring at all.

She reached the window and tried to find beauty in the view of the courtyard below and the marketplace in the distance. It was growing late and most people were hurrying home. She wished she could do the same. She turned to retrace her steps.

''Stand still so that I may look upon you.''

The words came out of nowhere and startled her into freezing in place. Kardal stood just inside the door. He had entered as quietly as a ghost. She'd heard neither the door open nor close. Darn the man for being so stealthy.

He'd cleaned up, she thought, looking at him and trying to still the rapid thundering of her heart. The man cleaned up pretty good. He still wore loose trousers and a linen shirt, but they were freshly pressed. His hair gleamed damply in the lantern light and his jaw was freshly shaved. Not wanting to know what he was thinking, she avoided glancing at his eyes, but she couldn't help notice the elegant sweep of his nose or the strength inherent in his jawline. Were he not a kidnapper and a potential defiler of women, she might think him very handsome.

She had tried to make her study of him surreptitious, but he did not share her good manners. Instead he gazed at her as if he were considering the purchase of a mare. He stalked around her, looking at her from behind, then returning to stand in front of her again.

His attention made her shiver. She felt both his power and her near-nakedness. She liked neither. Fear took up residence low in her belly, making her chest tighten and her fingers curl toward her palms.

"You can't do this," she said, trying to make her voice strong, but sounding scared instead. "I'm a royal princess. The price of doing...*that* to me would be death. Besides, as the Prince of Thieves, you owe allegiance to the king of Bahania. To so insult his daughter would be an insult to him."

Kardal folded his arms over his chest. "You're forgetting that the king of Bahania doesn't care about his daughter."

She fought back a wince. "Actually I have trouble forgetting that, as much as I would like to."

"Do you really think he would be angry?" he asked, stepping closer.

He reached for her right hand and took it in his. The contact startled her. She tried to pull away, but he would not release her.

"He might be annoyed," Kardal conceded even as he ran a single finger along the length of her palm. Something unexpected skittered up her arm, as if a nerve had been jolted. "He might stomp about the castle, but I doubt he would kill me."

"It doesn't matter what he thinks about me," she said, hating that those words were true. "But if you defile me, you defile a woman of his household. Regardless of his lack of concern, he would not let that go unpunished."

Kardal shrugged. "Perhaps you are right. We'll have to find out together."

He moved with a swiftness that defied physics. One second he was lightly stroking her hand, the next he'd snapped something heavy around her wrist. She'd barely had time to gasp when he did the same to her left arm.

The air fled her lungs. She tried to scream in outrage, but had no breath. Slave bracelets. The man had claimed her with slave bracelets.

"You—" She searched her mind for an appropriate slur and was disgusted when none came to mind. "How dare you?"

Instead of being afraid—which was obviously too much to ask with this man—he grinned at her. "You appreciate that which is ancient and valuable. You should be honored."

Honored? Her gaze dropped to the gold encircling the five inches of her arm just above the wrist. The slave bracelets were obviously old and handsomely made. A swirling pattern had been etched into the gold—the design both intricate and beautiful. She knew that somewhere was a tiny latch which when pressed, would cause the locking mechanism to release. She also knew that it could take her weeks to find it.

"How dare you?" she demanded again, glaring at Kardal. "You mark me."

He shrugged. "You are my possession. What did you expect?"

The insult was nearly unbearable. "I am not a creature to wear a collar."

"No, you're a woman in slave bracelets."

She stuck out her arms. "I demand you remove them."

He turned away and walked over to a bowl of fruit left on a table near the door. He picked up a pear, sniffed it and then took a bite. "I'm sorry. Were you speaking to me?"

She jerked at the right bracelet, knowing it was useless. "I hate this. I hate being here. I refuse to be your slave. And there are times when I really hate being a woman. My father and my brothers ignore me, you think you can do anything to me. I will not be treated with the contempt you give a camel.''

At last he turned to face her. ''On the contrary,'' he told her, then took another bite of the pear and chewed slowly. ''I have great respect for camels,'' he said when he'd swallowed. ''They provide a lifetime of service and ask very little in return.'' He glanced at her, starting at her feet and ending at the top of her head. ''I doubt the same may be said for you.''

It was too much. She screamed, then reached for the bowl of fruit. Her fingers closed around an orange and she threw it at him.

''Get out!'' she shrieked. ''Get out of here and never come back.''

He headed for the door. The man was laughing at her. Laughing! She wanted him killed. Slowly.

''You see,'' he said as he reached the door. ''You are not going to be as well behaved as a camel. I'm disappointed.''

She threw a pear at him. It bounced off the door frame. ''I'll see you in hell.''

He paused. ''I've lived a most exemplary life. So when we are both in the great afterward, I'll try to put in a good word for you.''

She screamed and picked up the entire bowl. Still laughing, he stepped into the hall and closed the door, just as the bowl exploded against the wall.

Kardal was still chuckling as he entered the oldest part of the castle. He'd offered to modernize this section, but his mother protested that she preferred to keep things as they had been for hundreds of years.

He rounded a corner and saw an open arch, leading to what had been the women's section. Nearly twenty-five years ago, his mother had opened the doors of the harem. Eventually she had sold them. As they had been nearly fourteen feet high, twelve feet wide and made of solid gold, they had fetched an impressive price. She'd promptly taken the money and used it to fund a clinic for women in the city. Well-trained doctors now monitored the women's health, delivered their babies and took care of their young, all free of charge. Cala, his mother, had said the generations who had lived and died within the confines of the harem would have approved.

Kardal stepped through the open arch. What had been the main living area of the harem was now a large office. It was late enough in the day that her staff had left, but a light burned in his mother's office.

He crossed the elegantly tiled floor and knocked on the half-open door.

Princess Cala glanced up and smiled. Tall, slender and doe-eyed, she had an ageless beauty that affected any man still breathing. A year away from turning fifty, she looked to be much closer to his age than her own. Her long dark hair was sleek and free from gray. During the day she wore it up in a sophisticated twist, but when work was finished, she often put it back in a braid. That combined with jeans and a cropped T-shirt allowed her to frequently pass for a woman half her age.

''The prodigal mother returns,'' Kardal teased as he stepped around her desk and kissed her cheek. ''How long will you be here this time?''

Cala turned off her computer, then motioned to the

visitor's chair across from her own. "I'm thinking of making this an indefinite stay. Will that cramp your style?"

Kardal thought of his recently monastic life. His workload had been such that he hadn't been able to take time for female companionship. "I think I'll survive. Tell me about your latest coup."

She smiled with pleasure. "Six million children will be inoculated this year. Our goal had been four million, but we had an unexpected increase in donations."

"I suspect it's due to your persuasive nature."

Cala ran an international charity dedicated to women and children throughout the world. When Kardal had gone away to boarding school, she had begun to busy herself with her charity work, traveling extensively, raising millions of dollars to help those in need.

She touched the collar of her dark red suit. "I'm not sure of the cause of the generosity, but I am grateful." She paused to study him speculatively. "Is she really Princess Sabra?"

Kardal told himself he shouldn't be surprised. News traveled quickly within the walls of the city and his mother always knew everything.

"She goes by Sabrina."

Cala raised her eyebrows. "I hadn't thought you could still surprise me, but I find I'm wrong. I'm sure you have a reasonable explanation for kidnapping the daughter of a trusted ally."

He told her about finding Sabrina in the desert. "She was looking for the city, but there was no way she was going to find it. She would have died if we hadn't helped her."

"I don't dispute the fact that you should have offered assistance. What I question is you holding her captive. I heard that you brought her into the city on your horse, with her hands tied."

He shifted uncomfortably.

"Why was she looking for the city?" Cala asked, leaning toward him. "I can't imagine she's interested in the treasures."

"Actually she is. She said she has a couple of degrees. Archeology and something about Bahanian artifacts or history."

"You can't remember what she studied?" Cala shook her head as if silently asking herself where she'd gone wrong with him. "It was too much trouble to pay attention. Yes, I can see how a first conversation with one's betrothed could be tedious."

Kardal hated when his mother spoke as if she was being reasonable when in fact she was verbally slapping him upside the head.

"She is all I feared," he told her. "Not only doesn't she know we're betrothed, but she's willful, difficult and very much a product of the west."

His mother's dark eyes didn't show even a flash of sympathy. "You knew her reputation when you agreed to the match. Don't forget it was your decision. I wasn't even here when King Hassan approached you."

"I couldn't refuse him without creating an international incident."

Cala didn't bother answering that. He knew the truth as well as she. Tradition stated that he marry the oldest Bahanian daughter, but it wasn't a matter of law. Kardal supposed he could have insisted on finding a wife of his own choosing—a love match.

But he didn't believe in love. Not the romantic kind. So what did it matter who he married? The purpose of the union was to produce heirs. Nothing more.

"You and Sabrina have more in common than you realize," Cala told him. "You would be wise to seek out those things. Also, if she is truly willful, I suspect there is a reason. Much would be gained by finding and understanding her motivation."

"None of that is necessary."

"Kardal, your future happiness is at stake. I would think you would be willing to put in a little effort."

He shrugged. "To what end? Sabrina isn't the sort of woman who can make me happy." Except possibly in bed, he thought remembering how she'd looked in the costume he'd made her wear. There she could please him very well.

"A wise man would make peace with his future wife. If she is content, she will be a better mother."

"If only she were more moldable," he grumbled. "Why did King Hassan allow her to be raised in the west?"

"I'm not sure. I know that he married Sabrina's mother very quickly. Theirs seemed to be a match more about passion than affection. I have heard that if not for Sabrina, they would have divorced in a matter of months. Apparently when they did finally end the marriage, Hassan's wife wanted to take her daughter with her back to California and he agreed."

Kardal shook his head. "Why would a man allow his child to be taken from him? Bahanian law required Sabrina to stay with her father." While the law allowed for either parent to take custody of the children, in the royal house, the children stayed with the royal parent. Sabrina had been the only exception.

"Perhaps the king was being foolish," Cala said quietly. "Men act that way all the time. I know of a man who won't even bother to get to know his future wife. He also assumes they can never be happy together. All this based on a few hours in her company."

"Imagine," Kardal said dryly. "All right. You have made your point. I will spend more time with Sabrina before I pass judgment on her. However, I'm convinced I will find her wanting."

"Yes. Of course. As long as you keep an open mind." His mother gazed at him. "What am I to do with you?"

"Admire me."

She rolled her eyes. "I see I gave you your way too much when you were young."

He didn't doubt that was true, but what he remembered from his youth was his mother's loving attention. She was devoted to him, always there when he needed her, always stepping back when he needed room to experience life.

She was the most beautiful woman he'd ever seen. Kind, intelligent, wise beyond her years. Yet she'd lived her life alone.

"Was it because of me?" he asked.

Cala took several seconds to figure out what he meant. She rose and circled the desk, then crouched in front of him and touched his cheek. "You are my son and I love you with all my heart. My reasons for not marrying have nothing to do with you."

"Then it must be *his* fault."

Cala rose and stared down at him. "Kardal," she said warningly.

He recognized the tone. Restless, he stood and glared at her. "I do not understand why you refuse to see the truth about the man."

"Because there are things you can't understand."

There was no point in arguing about it. They'd had the same discussion dozens of times before. Instead Kardal kissed her cheek and promised to dine with her later that week. Then he left.

But his anger didn't ease. With each step it grew, opening old wounds that still had the power to make him ache inside. Perhaps it was wrong, but Kardal had always hated his father.

Thirty-one years ago, King Givon of El Bahar had arrived in the City of Thieves. Cala, the only child of the Prince of Thieves, had turned eighteen. With no male heir, tradition required her to have a son by the king of a neighboring kingdom. King Givon had been her father's choice. Her son would then be betrothed to the daughter of the king of Bahania, thereby cementing the relationship between the two countries and the desert city.

Givon had seduced Cala, stayed until she was pregnant and then had abandoned both her and her child. In the past thirty-one years he had never acknowledged her or his son. Kardal had been a teenager before he'd even known the identity of his father. But knowing the truth had only made his situation worse. He'd longed to meet the man, yet had stayed away. King Givon's behavior had made it clear he had no interest in his bastard son.

Kardal stopped in the middle of the stone corridor. There was no point in visiting these memories again.

Nothing had changed. So he forced himself to push down his rage. Over the years, he'd grown to be an expert at ignoring the past.

He continued down the hall, barely noticing the paintings, statues and tapestries that decorated this part of the castle. He pushed through a pair of wooden doors and entered into the "business" side of the castle.

Within the walls of a fourteenth-century addition existed a modern office complex and security center. A raised tile floor concealed miles of cable, electrical wires and fiber optics. Computers clicked, faxes beeped and telephones rang. He thought about Sabrina in the old living quarters and smiled. What would she throw at him if she knew the truth about this part of the castle? Perhaps if she was very good, one day he would show it to her and find out.

He nodded at his male assistant and stepped into his office. A large L-shaped desk sat in the center. At the far end of the room, French doors opened onto a courtyard.

He ignored the view, the blinking message light and the papers left for him. Instead he crossed to his desk and reached for the phone. He dialed the operator and asked to be connected to the king of Bahania. Even a disinterested father would want to know that his only daughter had survived her time in the desert.

"Kardal," a familiar voice said as King Hassan picked up the line. "Is she with you?"

"Yes. We found Princess Sabra yesterday. She'd lost her horse and her camel in a sandstorm."

Hassan sighed. "She took off without saying anything, which is just like her. I'm pleased she is safe."

Kardal tapped his desk. "She seems to be unaware of our betrothal."

"Yes, yes, that's true. When I started to explain that I'd arranged a match for her, she screamed at me and bolted from the room before I could give her any details." There was a slight pause. "She's flighty, like her mother. A woman without great depth or intelligence. I fear for the minds of her children. I don't suppose, now that you've met her, that you wish to continue the engagement."

Kardal had heard that the king of Bahania didn't pay much attention to his daughter, but he wouldn't have thought the man would insult her so freely. While Sabrina wasn't what he would have chosen for a wife, he'd seen no sign of her being slow-witted. Quite the opposite.

He might have toyed with the idea of ending the engagement, but Hassan's bald assumption that Kardal would dislike his daughter bothered him.

"I have not made any final decision," Kardal said at last.

"Take all the time you need. It's not as if we're eager to have her back at the palace."

They discussed a minor matter of security, then Kardal ended the call. Sabrina had hinted that things were not as she would like them at the palace, but he'd had no idea how her father thought of her. Not that Hassan's attitude should make any difference. Still, it might explain a few things.

"You're looking thoughtful. Are we going to war?"

Kardal glanced up at the tall, blond man standing in the entrance to his office. Rafe Stryker, former U.S. Air Force officer and now head of the city's security, moved forward and took the seat across from Kardal's.

"No such luck," he told his friend. "Although King Hassan is very enthused about the combined air force."

"Enthusiasm doesn't pay the bills," Rafe reminded him.

"No, but the king does. Do not worry that there won't be enough to buy all those expensive planes you covet."

Rafe grinned. "You want them, too."

Kardal nodded in agreement. In recent years it had become increasingly apparent that remote security cameras and irregular patrols by the nomadic tribes weren't enough to keep the desert safe. The oil fields were increasingly vulnerable. King Hassan had contacted Kardal about starting a joint air force. Rafe was in charge of coordinating with the Bahanians.

Kardal knew it was unusual for a man in his position to trust a foreigner with such an important job. Yet Rafe had earned his trust many times over. The blond officer carried a knife scar from a potentially lethal blow meant for Kardal. In return Kardal had permitted Rafe to wear the mark of the prince. As a result, the people of the city accepted Rafe as one of their own—honoring him with the title of sheik.

Today Rafe wore a uniform but just as often he swept through the castle in traditional robes, his blue eyes looking startlingly out of place against his tanned face.

Rafe's expression changed to one of mild amusement. "There's a rumor about a slave girl in the palace. The word is you found her in the desert and claimed her as your own."

Kardal glanced at his watch. "I've been back nearly four hours. When did you hear?"

"About three and a half hours ago."

"Word travels fast."

Rafe shrugged. "I have good sources. Is it true? I never thought slave girls were your style."

"They're not."

He hesitated. So far no one knew Sabrina's true identity and that was how he preferred it. But if she needed protection, there was no one he would trust more than Rafe.

"Her name is Sabrina. She's Hassan's daughter."

Rafe stared at him. "The one you're engaged to?"

"The same. She knows about the betrothal, but not the details. I don't want people finding out who she is."

"Or her finding out who you are?"

"Exactly."

Rafe whistled softly. "I knew this job would be interesting when I signed on. I can't wait to meet her. I've never seen an honest-to-God princess in person before."

Kardal knew his friend was joking, but that piece of information didn't stop the knot from forming in his gut or the sudden heat that filled him. He frowned. Anger? At what? Rafe would never bother Sabrina, and he, Kardal, shouldn't care if his second-in-command was interested. Sabrina was nothing but a thorn in his side.

"You're bound to run across her," Kardal said, rising to his feet. "I'll instruct her to stay in her quarters. I'm sure she won't listen. If you find her wandering around, please return her to her rooms."

''Where are you going?'' Rafe asked lazily.

''To prepare to do battle. If I am going to marry the wayward Princess Sabra, she must first be tamed.''

Chapter Five

Kardal entered Sabrina's quarters around ten the following morning. He'd given her the night to come to terms with her situation, although he doubted she would see reason on the matter. From what he could tell, Princess Sabra could be most willful.

Interestingly enough, he found himself looking forward to their encounter. She would complain and possibly throw things, they would battle verbally, and although he would best her in the end, she would make him work for his victory.

He was still grinning when he pushed open the door to her chambers. But before he stepped inside, some sixth sense that had saved his life more than once in the past, urged caution. He hesitated before entering, thereby avoiding a violent thrust of movement.

Sabrina sailed harmlessly past him, her right arm

extended, a small fruit knife in her hand. He caught her around the waist and lifted her from her feet.

"Put me down, you great oaf," she yelled.

Unceremoniously, he carried her to the bed and dumped her on the mattress. Before she could spring back up, he flung himself on top of her, pinning her thighs between his and wrists in his hands. She squirmed, but couldn't twist free.

"Good morning, my slave," he said, staring into her flashing brown eyes, then pinching her wrist until she released the weapon. "Did you really think you could be rid of me so easily?"

"Obviously not," she muttered, turning away from him. "It's a fruit knife, Kardal. I couldn't have done any serious damage. I was protesting being held prisoner."

"You could have expressed your displeasure with a sign. Perhaps a small demonstration or a strike."

"I preferred the knife."

She spoke through gritted teeth. He fought against a smile. She had attacked him. He respected that in anyone. She'd known she couldn't possibly best him and that she might make him angry, yet she'd been fearless…if inept.

He drew in a breath and inhaled the sweet scent of her. As he'd left her with no other clothes, she'd been forced to wear the ridiculous harem outfit he'd provided. How she must hate the scanty clothing. And how he enjoyed the sight of her breasts spilling out of the too-tight top.

He found himself wondering what she would taste like and how she would feel under him while they made love. His arousal was instant and insistent. Still, he ignored the throbbing in his groin. Taking a princess, even one who wasn't a virgin, was not something he could do lightly. There was also the matter of their betrothal. If he had his way with her, he would be sealing the match—something he wasn't sure he was willing to do.

"You are not a very obedient slave," he informed her.

She glared up at him, still squirming beneath him. He was surprised she didn't realize the pleasure he found in her movements.

"You didn't leave me any instructions," she said tartly. "Therefore I couldn't have disobeyed that which I hadn't been told."

"Not attacking one's master is implicit in the slave's covenant."

"Not from the slave's perspective."

He considered her words, then released her. "You have a point. From this moment onward I will provide you with detailed instructions. I do not wish you to attack me in any way."

She waited until he stood away from the bed, then she slid off the side and rose. "I'd rather discuss the disobedient part."

"I'm sure you would. But instead, I would request that you serve me. You need a lesson in subservience."

She folded her arms over her chest. "I don't think so."

He walked to the far wall and pulled a cord hanging there. "I would like a bath."

She blinked. "You taking a bath is supposed to make me subservient? What? You're going to make me drink the bathwater or something?"

"No. I'm going to make you bathe me."

Her eyes widened and color drained from her face. She took a step back, which caused her to bump into the bed. She dropped into a sitting position, then quickly bounced back to her feet.

"You can't be serious."

"Oh, but I am."

She opened her mouth again, but didn't say anything. Kardal studied her startled expression. She couldn't possibly be as shocked as she seemed. His gaze dropped to the curve of her breasts, then lower to the sweep of her hips and her long, nearly bare legs.

No woman raised as she had been raised, with such an attractive face and body could possibly be innocent. Sabrina thought to play him for a fool. Fine, he thought as there was a knock on the door. He would go along with her game...for as long as it suited him.

Sabrina told herself this wasn't really happening. No way was she dressed like an Arabian nights call girl, with Kardal insisting that she bathe him. Yet even as she inched her way toward the rear of the room, Adiva appeared in the doorway and nodded as Kardal instructed her to have a bathtub and hot water brought to the room.

It was all so fourteenth century, she thought, unable to believe there really wasn't running water for bathing in the castle. There had been a surprisingly modern toilet in a small room off her bedroom, but instead of a sink, there had been a basin and a drain, along with some handmade soap. Yesterday, she'd used a tub filled with water brought by several servants.

"Kardal, you can't be serious," she told him. "About the bath. You look really clean."

Kardal actually winked at her. "Come now. Don't play the shy virgin with me. I'm not going to insist that we become lovers, just that we play a little. You'll enjoy it." He lowered his voice. "I promise."

Her throat tightened until it was difficult to speak. "Did it ever occur to you that I wasn't playing? You can call me anything you'd like but that doesn't change my reality."

His eyebrows raised slightly. Great. The man didn't believe her. She stalked to the window. "Figures that you're just like everyone else," she complained, studying the view of the courtyard below without actually seeing it. "The horrible things they say about me in the tabloids and newspapers are a whole lot more interesting than the truth."

Kardal didn't answer. A few minutes later she heard the door open and several people came in with large buckets of steaming water. An empty tub was placed in front of the tiled fireplace across from her bed. Water filled the tub, and then they were alone.

"I am ready," Kardal announced.

"That makes one of us," she murmured under her breath, not moving from her place by the window.

"Sabrina, do not make me angry with you."

"Or what? You'll beat me? Tie me in chains? Starve me?"

"I have no desire to physically abuse you, but if you try my temper, I will be forced to remind you that you are my possession. I am a fair master, but I expect obedience from my subjects."

Her eyes burned, but she refused to give way to tears. They wouldn't do any good and she wouldn't give Kardal the satisfaction of knowing that he'd won. If he wanted a bath, she would give him a bath. If he tried anything, she would fight and claw and scream until he was sorry he hadn't left her to die in the desert.

With her shoulders back and her head held high, she marched over to the tub and stood next to him. "What do you want me to do?"

He smiled. "Nothing until I'm undressed."

Her resolve dissolved like sugar in boiling water. Instinctively she stepped back, then averted her gaze as he reached for the buttons on his linen shirt.

He chuckled. "Surely even the great virgin princess has seen a man's bare chest before."

"Yes, of course." But not while she was alone in the room with him, she thought, then forced herself to look at him.

He removed the shirt slowly, as if she would find the process appealing. He couldn't have been more wrong. Her desire was for him to get it over with so she could be done and he would leave her alone. But no. Inch by inch he slid the material down his arms.

She took in the impressive size of his muscles and the way they rippled with each small movement. There was an interesting scar on his left shoulder, and another along his rib cage.

"Another assassination attempt?" she asked, pointing to a mark on his midsection.

"An encounter in the desert. I was young and foolish and riding out alone. I was trapped by an unfriendly group. They thought killing me would be great sport."

He spoke easily, but his words made Sabrina shudder. Whether or not he was simply recounting a story or warning her about the dangers of the desert, she got the point. While most nomads were honorable and attacked only when provoked, there were renegades who cared naught for the laws of the desert. Those dangerous few killed with the ease of a horse using its tail to swat flies.

"You survived," she said, trying to act casual as he stepped out of his shoes.

"Don't sound so sad," he told her. "You may yet find a use for me."

"I doubt it."

He reached for the waistband of his trousers. Sabrina instantly turned away. She busied herself rearranging the bowl of fruit on the table and it was only when she'd heard the splash of him stepping into the water that she dared to turn back.

But she'd looked too soon. Kardal had not submerged himself in the tub. Instead he stood naked in the water. Facing her.

Sabrina blinked and tried to turn away, but she couldn't seem to make her feet obey her. Nor could she tear her gaze from him.

He stood casually, as if nothing of great import had occurred, arms relaxed, one leg slightly in front of the other. She told herself that if she couldn't seem to look away, she could at least look at *something else,* but no. Her attention was firmly fixed on that most male part of him. The part that had, until now at least, been a complete mystery to her.

His hips were narrow, his legs long and powerful. Dark hair bisected his belly, drawing her attention to that which she most wanted to avoid. His, ah, maleness seemed much as she had observed on various statues and in old paintings, although it looked more threatening in person. And it was getting bigger by the minute.

So that part of a man was supposed to fit inside of her. Sabrina squinted slightly, hoping to make it look less imposing. She considered herself a modern woman, quite clear on the ways of the world. But there was something about being a virgin and looking at a naked man for the first time. She felt... intimidated.

"Perhaps I should have specified a cold bath," Kardal drawled as he lowered himself into the tub. "You may begin bathing me whenever you would like."

"That may be never," she answered before she could stop herself. Bathe him? He had to be kidding. She couldn't touch him. Not while he was naked and certainly not *there*.

"Let me change my instruction. Sabrina, I wish you to bathe me now. Pick up the washcloth and begin immediately."

She sighed. He had ordering people around down to an art form. She eyed the distance to the door. She could probably make it out of the room before he could jump out of the tub. However, she didn't doubt that he would come after her, naked or not, and that he would catch her. There would be trouble after that. Besides, even if she got away from him, no one was going to help her. She would be left wandering the castle, dressed like a stripper sing-o-gram.

"I wish you'd left me in the desert," she grumbled. "I would have been fine."

"You would have been dead." He glanced at her. "Tell the truth. You would rather be my slave than dead."

"Maybe."

She picked up the washcloth and soap Adiva had left on a small table next to the tub, then moved to stand behind his head.

"Lean forward. I'll do your back."

"But that is not the part that most interests me."

"I'll bet, but it's the part I'm going to do first."

"Ah. Anticipation. How well you play the game."

This wasn't a game to her and she wasn't playing. Nor could she prevent herself from blushing.

She dipped her cloth into the warm water, then rubbed on soap. Kardal obliged her by leaning forward and she ran the cloth up and down his back.

"If you joined me, you would find the job easier," he told her.

She had a sudden image of herself as naked as him, stepping into the water. A shiver rippled through her. Something warm and sort of melty filled her chest and made her squirm.

"If this is your best material, I'm not impressed," she said, trying to sound calm.

Kardal surprised her by laughing. When she finished with his back, he leaned against the tub and held out his left arm. "You may not be a well-trained slave, but you do entertain me."

"Oh, joy. Because I live to serve." She ran the washcloth along the length of his strong arm. "While we're chitchatting about my place in your world, let's talk about my clothes. Can't I wear a dress, or even jeans? Where on earth did you find this costume?"

He turned his head so that their eyes met. They were too close, she thought as she leaned away.

"I find your appearance delightful," he said.

"I think it's awful. Aside from the fact that I'm cold half the time, I feel like an idiot."

"But it pleases me."

She wanted to point out that didn't matter, however she stopped herself in time. "Kardal, be reasonable."

He lowered his gaze to her half-exposed breasts. "I will decide after my bath. If you please me here, I may please you later."

Another shiver moved through her. Sabrina had a bad feeling they weren't talking about her harem costume anymore. She knew what he thought about her. That wasn't difficult to figure out because she read what they wrote about her in those magazines and newspapers. Half-truths, almost-facts and outright lies. The press made her sound as if she attended a party every other night and spent her days in the arms of various men. They judged her by her mother's standard. It wasn't fair.

"Sabrina, your expression grows most fierce. What are you thinking?"

She shook her head. No way she would make herself vulnerable to a man vying for "slave owner of the month" honors. She moved to the other side of the tub and reached for his right arm. Her thumb brushed against a scar.

"How did you get this?" she asked, hoping to distract him.

"A knife fight. I believe I was ten or eleven. I went to the Bahanian marketplace by myself. A mistake."

She frowned. "Earlier you said you were out in the desert by yourself. Did you spend all your time looking for trouble?"

"Yes. And I frequently found it."

Humor darkened his eyes. Humor and something else. Something almost angry.

"I would have thought you'd enjoy growing up here."

"Much of the time I did. But there were occasions when I chafed at the rules. My grandfather was loving, but also stern."

"How did he feel about the slavery issue?" she muttered.

"He would not have approved."

"Really?" She dropped the washcloth. "I don't suppose he's still around."

"No. He passed away five years ago."

Sabrina touched his damp arm. "I'm sorry. I didn't mean to be disrespectful."

"I understand. There's no need to apologize. I often wish he was still with us. Until his death, I was merely the heir to the city. I had more freedom. Now I have a greater responsibility."

She knelt on the floor. "What's the governmental structure here? Is there a parliament of some kind?"

"A tribal council that advises me. However, they do not have power unless I grant it to them. The city is a complete monarchy."

"Just my luck."

"You could always appeal to my mother. She has much influence with me."

Sabrina gestured to herself, then to him in the tub. "This might not be the time. She would get the wrong idea."

"Actually she would understand exactly what I was after."

His voice had turned low and seductive. Sabrina

swallowed. "Yes, well, perhaps later when I'm more formally dressed."

He took her hand and placed it on his chest. "I would prefer you not to be dressed at all. I want to see my prize."

She felt like a bird trapped in the compelling gaze of a cobra. As much as she wanted to shriek and run away, she couldn't. Her fingers curled into the hair on his chest. Warm water lapped against her wrist and his heartbeat pulsed against her palm.

Was it her imagination or was he getting closer? Was Kardal leaning toward her, or her toward him? The shivers turned to honest-to-goodness trembling and she knew that if she'd been standing, her legs would have given way.

Fire filled Kardal's eyes. She felt the heat down to her bones. It melted her resistance. His gaze settled on her mouth and she knew he was going to kiss her. What would it be like to be kissed by a man such as him? He would expect her to understand the ways between a man and a woman. He would expect her to be an expert, when in fact most sixteen-year-old girls knew far more than her. She'd never really been kissed—not the way she'd read about in books.

Kardal watched the various emotions flash through Sabrina's eyes. He read curiosity and fear, confusion and desire. The combination intrigued him...and made him wonder. If he didn't know better, he would think she was as innocent as she claimed.

But that wasn't possible. She'd been raised in Los Angeles. There was her lifestyle, the parties she attended, the men she'd been associated with.

But the seed of doubt had been planted. Kardal found himself wanting to know the truth. He touched her soft cheek with one hand and with the other, drew her fingers under the water, toward his arousal. He'd been fully erect for some time and welcomed the thought of her touching him.

But she barely brushed against him before pulling free and jumping back as if she'd come in contact with an open flame. Color flared on her face and her mouth trembled slightly.

"You're going to have to finish your bath yourself," she said, turning away from him. "I can't do this anymore."

Interesting, he thought to himself. Sabrina might not be a virgin, but she wasn't as experienced as he'd thought. She might be able to play at certain things, but she couldn't invent a blush, or the haunted expression in her eyes.

"Hand me my towel," he said, preparing to rise. When she didn't move, he sighed. "The towel is by the fire, which is across the room. I will walk there naked, if you would prefer. If not, hand me the towel and avert your gaze."

She did as he suggested, keeping her back to him as he stepped out of the water. After covering himself, he collected his clothes and headed for the door.

"We will have dinner tonight," he told her. "Both in clothes."

She glanced at him, appearing unsure of his purpose. Kardal didn't understand it, either. It seemed that he wanted to get to know Princess Sabra. Perhaps because she might not be exactly who or what he'd first imagined.

"A girl's school?" Kardal asked in disbelief.

Sabrina leaned her elbows on the low table be-

tween them. Humor brightened her brown eyes.
"Well, duh. Eastern fathers aren't the only ones trying to protect their daughters. Rich people do it, too.
Also, a lot of studies have been done showing that
girls learn more and perform better in school when
they aren't in mixed classrooms."

"I don't dispute that," he said, dismissing her
with a wave. "I had never heard that you attended
such an establishment."

She wrinkled her nose. "Like you would have believed it. You only want to know that I went to wild
parties and dated lots of guys. That's far more interesting than the truth."

She had a point. He'd been guilty of assuming the
worst about her.

He studied the woman lounging on pillows across
from him. As a concession to her complaints about
her costume, he'd had Adiva bring Sabrina a dress
of cobalt-blue. The long sleeves and high neckline
were so modest, even the sternest father would approve. Yet he found sensual pleasure in watching her.
The supple silk covered her curves, but did not hide
their existence. He watched the turn of her neck and
the way her breasts shifted as she moved.

Tonight Sabrina wore her long red hair down
around her shoulders. The loose curls tempted him.
He wanted to let them twist around his fingers to
discover if they were as soft as they looked.

"So you did not live the hedonistic life of a wanton western woman?" he asked as he reached for a
strawberry in the bowl between them.

Sabrina sighed. "All that muck about me and men
doesn't come from me." She ducked her head but

not before he saw color staining her cheeks. "It's my mother. She's a bit of a flirt."

"That bothers you?"

She shrugged. "It was weird when I was little. There were different men around all the time. I missed my father, but she didn't want me to talk about him. Of course when I was with him, I wasn't allowed to speak of her, either. I always wanted her to find one person and marry him. But she said she'd been married once and she'd hated it."

She picked up a slice of pineapple, then put it on her plate. "When I turned fourteen, she told me it was time for me to have a boyfriend."

Kardal had heard stories of Sabrina's mother's wildness, but he had never thought she would push her own daughter in that direction. "What did you say?"

"That I thought life should be about more than body parts."

Kardal bit into his strawberry. He wasn't sure he believed Sabrina, but he liked her answer.

"School was important to me," she continued. "Especially after I went to college, but Mom never got that. The irony is I maintained an A average in college, which meant I spent a lot of time studying. I couldn't physically have attended all those parties and still gotten my grades. But no one bothered to figure that out."

More and more interesting, Kardal thought. Sabrina was a woman of many surprises. Some of them were turning out to be quite pleasant.

"Perhaps it was not a mistake to rescue you in the desert," he told her.

She rolled her eyes. "I cannot even begin to tell you how your words make me quiver with joy."

Chapter Six

"You have a most disagreeable personality," Kardal said, rebuking her as he took another strawberry. "A slave should be more docile. I do not approve of sarcasm in a woman."

"Hey, I don't approve of being kidnapped, but no one asked me," Sabrina told him, somewhat pleased to be holding her own with the Prince of Thieves. Of course the fact that he was fully dressed helped her situation considerably. Naked, he was the hands-down winner.

He dismissed her protestation with a flick of his wrist. "You are enjoying your time in my city and most especially in my company. Would you prefer to be meeting your betrothed?"

She stared in surprise. "How do you know about the troll prince?"

Kardal nearly choked as he swallowed, then glared at her. "The what?"

"Troll prince. My father has betrothed me to some horrible man."

"How do you know he is horrible?"

"Because my father has never been concerned about me. This is—as he put it—an alliance, not a marriage." She shrugged. "I suppose the good news is that you're slightly better than the troll prince, but not by much. So how did you know about my betrothal?"

"I hear rumors." He passed her a strawberry. "Returning to our former subject, you did not attend your mother's infamous parties?"

Sabrina wrinkled her nose. "Not if I could avoid it. She and I are so different, I have trouble believing we're related. However, I do look like her, so there's no question that she found me under a rock and took me home."

"I have seen pictures of your mother," he told her. "I find you more attractive."

The man was holding her captive, she reminded herself. He'd taken her from the desert, forced her—until tonight—to dress like a harem call girl. She still had on her slave bracelets and who knew what other tortures he had in mind for her. So she should absolutely not care that he thought she was prettier than her mother. Yet she did.

"Yes, well, isn't that interesting?" she mumbled, not looking at him as she pleated the napkin on her lap.

They were sitting by the fireplace in her bedroom. Their meal had been set on a low table, with cushions serving as seats. When Adiva had reverently announced that the great Kardal was being gracious enough to dine with her, Sabrina had thought she might show him her appreciation by throwing the dishes at his head. But somehow she'd never found the right moment. Maybe it was because she sort of liked having someone to talk to. It wasn't as if she had any friends at the palace in Bahania.

"In addition to your boarding school in Los Angeles, did you also study when you were with your father?" Kardal asked.

"No. I only stayed with him in the summer. He mostly shuffled me off with nannies or companions." Sabrina held in a sigh. Thinking about her father always made her sad. "A few of them were from different countries, so that was interesting. I learned about their customs and a bit of their native language."

She set her napkin on the table and drew her knees to her chest. "Moving between the two worlds was more complicated than people might think. When I first arrived for my summer stays, I was always startled by the palace and how everything was so different here. My father was busy running the government and training my brothers. I felt out of place and not very welcome."

"A household of men," Kardal said. "I'm sure they did not know what to do with you."

"I guess I can see that, although at the time I simply felt unwanted. I would spend a lot of time reading about Bahanian history and talking with the servants. Just as soon as I started to feel like I finally belonged, I had to go back to California. Then I had the same sort of adjustment all over again. My friends would talk about their summer vacations and all the things they did. What was I supposed to say? 'Gee, I went to stay in my palace by the sea and practiced being a princess'?" She grimaced. "It sounds wonderful to someone on the outside, but it wasn't. Besides, I really didn't want anyone to know who or what I was. All they knew was that I visited my father in the Middle East. I never said who he was."

Kardal stared at her. His intense gaze made her uncomfortable.

"Is this boring you?" she asked, wondering why she would have thought he would be the least bit interested in her life.

"Not at all," he said slowly. He leaned toward her slightly. "Your story isn't unfamiliar. I, too, grew up caught between two worlds."

He paused as if he wasn't going to say any more. Sabrina didn't interrupt. She couldn't possibly imagine what she and the Prince of Thieves would have in common.

Kardal stared past her toward the door. She wondered what he was really seeing.

"I was a child of the desert," he said at last. "I could ride as soon as I could walk and my days were spent with the other children of the city. We had great adventures, first within the protective walls surrounding us, then out in the desert."

A slight smile tugged at his mouth. "I could ride like the wind and hunt with the skill and cunning of a desert fox. Part of each year, I traveled with the tribes and learned their ways."

"Sounds wonderful," she breathed.

"It was. Until I turned ten and my mother decided it was time for me to become educated. She sent me to a prep school in New England." The smile faded and his mouth formed a straight line. "I did not fit in with the other boys."

She winced. "I can't even imagine what that was like. You don't strike me as a coat and tie kind of guy."

"I had never worn such garments," he admitted. "I knew nothing of their ways, I barely spoke their language. My reading skills were minimal. I'd always had a head for mathematics, but no formal training." He raised one shoulder. "I spent much of that year being punished for fighting."

"The other boys teased you and you reacted the only way you knew how."

"Exactly. I was nearly expelled."

"What happened?"

"I came home for the summer. My grandfather explained that I could only be the prince of the city with the proper education. That to keep the city a secret, no one at the school could know who I was. They thought I was the son of a wealthy sheik. He told me that it was my responsibility to learn all that I could, so that I would be a wise and honorable ruler to my people. I promised him I would try to fit in and dedicated myself to my studies."

She studied the stern lines of his handsome face. "So you returned in the fall and this time instead of kicking actual butt you kicked academic butt."

"I would not have phrased it that way, but yes."

"Did the situation improve?"

He grinned. "When I turned fifteen and we had several joint activities with the neighboring girl's boarding school."

Sabrina couldn't help laughing. "Let me guess. You were wildly popular with the opposite sex."

"I did well," he admitted. "Also, I'd grown taller and stronger. No one wanted to take me on anymore. And I had learned how to fit in. But like you, each summer I returned to the desert. It took several weeks until I felt at home here, and then I had to return. I was pleased when I graduated from college and was able to always live in the city."

"Who would have thought we'd have that in common," she said, feeling suddenly awkward. She pressed the fingers of her right hand against the slave bracelet on her left arm. "Kardal, do you really mean to keep me as your slave?"

"Of course. Nothing has happened to change my mind."

"But you can't. I'm a princess. We've already established that my father doesn't care about me too much, but he would never let someone hold me against my will."

Kardal's dark gaze turned unreadable. "I have informed him that I'm holding you for ransom."

Shock and outrage filled her. She sprang to her feet. "You can't be serious."

"Why not?"

"Because the king of Bahania will not negotiate with you. He'll crush you like a bug."

Kardal looked unconcerned as he put his napkin on the table and slowly rose. "He cannot. A symbiotic relationship exists between his country and the City of Thieves. He cannot afford to anger me."

"What about *you* angering *him?* You're crazy. This will never work."

"Of course it will. Occasionally it is important for

me to remind my larger neighbors that I have power as well. That we each need the other.''

She planted her hands on her hips. ''Are you trying to tell me that you kidnapping me is simply political?''

She couldn't believe it. Nor did she understand why the information should upset her.

''I rescued you from the desert because I did not want to leave you there to die,'' he told her. ''However, there were many reasons for me keeping you. Yes, one of them is political.''

''What are the others?''

His gaze swept over her. ''Perhaps I find you attractive.''

She'd been thrilled when Adiva had shown up that afternoon with a selection of dresses. Anything was better than the uncomfortable costume. But even knowing she was covered from collarbone to ankle, Sabrina still felt exposed. Something about Kardal's intense stare made her wish she had several more layers of clothing between her and nakedness.

''I'd rather you let me go,'' she said.

He stepped around the table, toward her. She backed up.

''I told you, my desert bird. You are my slave. The proof of your status rests around your wrists.''

''This is crazy. You can't hold a royal princess captive.''

He continued to move toward her. She kept stepping away. Unfortunately she soon found herself pressed up against the stone wall.

Kardal loomed over her. He raised one hand and touched her cheek. Just a light brush of his knuckles against her skin. She should have barely felt it. Instead heat seemed to fill her as a shiver rippled all the way down her spine.

"I choose to keep you here," he murmured, lowering his head slightly. "Perhaps, if you are lucky, eventually I'll choose to let you go."

She tried to inch away along the wall, but he placed a hand on her waist, holding her still.

"Maybe I'll get a bigger knife and stab you in your sleep," she said recklessly.

"You may certainly try. I would welcome you seeking me out in my bedchamber. I am eager to know all that you've learned about pleasing men."

There was information that would fill a pinhead, she thought grimly as he moved closer and closer until his mouth was less than an inch from hers.

"I don't know anything," she insisted, pressing her hands against the wall, as if she could scratch her way to safety. "Not about men or sex or any of that."

"We shall see," he breathed and pressed his lips to hers.

Sabrina steeled herself against the contact. It was going to be gross. She would endure, but if it went on too long, she would kick him in the shin and bite his lip until he screamed. Then she would run out of the room and find a way to escape.

His mouth touched hers as lightly as a feather. His breath smelled of strawberries and the heat from his body seemed to settle over her.

"How was that?" he asked.

"Awful."

He chuckled. "I'll add liar to your list of sins."

She bristled. "I don't have a list. I would like to

point out that I'm the innocent party here—in more ways than one.''

"Prove it," he said and settled his mouth on hers.

Prove she was innocent while he was kissing her? What was she supposed to do?

Sabrina was still trying to figure out what he'd meant when she became aware of him moving back and forth, his lips rubbing lightly against hers. It was not the contact she'd expected. She'd thought he would be rough as he took, attacking and acting like a macho jerk. Instead Kardal was almost tender.

Despite the stories in the papers, she'd had remarkably few boyfriends. She'd been determined not to be like her mother, so she'd waited until someone really engaged her heart before she went out with him. Unfortunately she'd told two of her boyfriends the truth about her parents, especially her father, and the fact that it was a big deal for her to have sex before she was married. They'd been so terrified of what her father would do to them, they'd dumped her. Her third significant boyfriend had turned out to be a two-timing jerk. So they'd never gotten as far as the "why I can't have sex" conversation.

Despite being twenty-three, she hadn't had much experience at all. It was humiliating. It also made her nervous about Kardal's kiss.

Fortunately he wasn't moving very fast. He kept one hand on her waist while the other continued to touch her face. He traced the shape of her jaw and tickled her ear, which was actually pretty nice. His lips were firm, but not pushy. She found herself enjoying the light contact. When he drew back, she sort of leaned forward because, well, it seemed the thing to do.

"Sabrina," he breathed against her mouth.

The sound of her name in that husky voice did odd things to her stomach. Her chest felt tight and there was a faint pressure between her legs. Nothing sexual, she assured herself. Probably just some issues with her lunch.

He tilted his head and kissed her again. This time his tongue swept against her lower lip. She jumped slightly but didn't pull back. Her fingers curled into her palms. She felt stupid, standing there with her hands at her sides. When he moved his hand from her waist to her shoulder, she lightly pressed her right hand against his side.

His tongue continued to stroke her lip. Sabrina understood this part. He wanted to deepen the kiss. Which was all right with her. She'd never found that particular act especially exciting but it wasn't too awful, either. She opened her mouth slightly. He slipped inside, teasing the inside of her lip before touching the tip of her tongue with his.

A jolt of electricity shot through her. She jumped, not sure what had just happened. Her bare toes curled toward the floor and she rested her left hand on his chest. Kardal cupped her face in his strong hand and swept his tongue over hers.

The reaction in her body startled her into forgetting to breathe. It was like being on fire, but in a really good way. Heat filled her. Heat and pressure. She ached all over and the tightness in her chest increased until it wouldn't have mattered if she'd remembered to breathe because she couldn't physically do it anymore. She was going to die right here in Kardal's arms and she found she didn't really mind. Not if he kept on kissing her.

She shifted so that she could wrap her arms around him and hold him close. When he retreated, she followed him, liking the feel of him, the heat and the taste. He pulled her to him so that they touched intimately. Her breasts flattened against his chest. His thighs pressed against hers. She wanted... The exact "what" wasn't clear, but there was a hunger in her she'd never experienced before.

He broke the kiss so that he could press his mouth against her neck. The contact both tickled and made her cling to him. He licked her ear, then bit the lobe. Breath returned as she gasped.

Hesitantly she opened her eyes and found him staring down at her. She saw bright fire in his dark irises. Tension tightened the lines of his face.

"Do you still want to fly away, my desert bird?" he asked, his voice sounding husky.

Yes, of course, she thought, but wasn't able to form the words. Her plan of kicking and running suddenly didn't seem so necessary. Not if he was going to kiss her again.

He rested his hands on her shoulders, then moved them lower. Still dazed from his passionate kisses, she wasn't prepared for him to cup her breasts. His thumbs swept against her suddenly tight nipples.

Desire poured through her but with it, icy shock. Sanity returned. She pushed his hands away and shoved until he took a step back.

"You can't do that," she told him, barely able to catch her breath. "It's one thing to kidnap me, but it's quite another to defile me. My father may not care about me, but he will kill any man who touches me. As will the troll prince. He's expecting a virgin."

She braced herself for his laughter. ''Defile'' was a pretty old-fashioned word. Besides, Kardal didn't seem to have much respect for her or her family.

But he wasn't smiling. Instead he frowned at her, as if she'd just become a puzzle he couldn't solve.

''It is not possible,'' he said more to himself than her. ''A virgin?''

She grabbed him by the front of his shirt. ''Have you been listening to me?'' she demanded, speaking loudly and directly into his face. She wanted to shake him but he was about as unmovable as a mountain.

''I did not know,'' he said quietly.

She released him. ''Yeah, well, I've been trying to tell you. Next time pay attention.''

He wasn't even listening, she thought in disgust as Kardal continued to stare at her. Then he turned on his heel and stalked from the room, leaving her standing by the wall, out of breath and still trembling from the power of his kiss.

Sabrina pressed her back against the castle hallway wall and tried to hear if anyone was approaching. For the first time since she'd arrived five days before, she'd found her bedroom door unlocked after breakfast. Not knowing if Adiva had simply forgotten to secure it after delivering the meal or if Sabrina was now allowed to roam at will, she'd taken the opportunity to leave her room while trying not to be seen.

At this point she didn't care if Kardal would be furious if she was caught. She couldn't stand to stay inside those four walls for another second.

Sabrina drew in a deep breath and listened. There was only the sound of distant voices and the rapid pounding of her own heart.

Usually she enjoyed being by herself, she thought as she continued down the hallway. There were plenty of wonderful books to read and Adiva brought her newspapers and magazines every day. But ever since two nights before when Kardal had kissed her, Sabrina had found her world had shifted on its axis.

She couldn't forget the way she'd reacted to his kiss and his touch. She'd enjoyed everything he'd done and found herself longing to repeat the experience. Although there hadn't been many men in her life, she had kissed a few and not one of them had left her so aroused and shaken. Was her reaction specifically about Kardal or was it something more sinister?

Ever since Sabrina had begun to understand her mother's relationship with men, she'd feared turning into the same kind of woman. She didn't want to be driven by passions, making bad choices because of a man's ability to please her in bed. If she were to fall in love, she wanted it to be because of a meeting of the minds and an understanding between souls. She wanted to respect her lover and have him respect her. Passion appeared to be both fleeting and dangerous.

She came to a set of stairs leading down to the left. The corridor in front of her stretched on for several feet before bending to the right. Sabrina paused. If she continued on her current path, she might find her way out of the castle. If she went down, she was more likely to find the treasure stores. As much as she wanted to get away from here and stop thinking about what had happened with Kardal, she wanted to see the plunder more. Telling herself she was an idiot, she hurried down the stairs.

Since the kiss, she'd seen Kardal twice, once when he dined with her for lunch and once late last night when he'd invited her to watch a movie with him and several of his staff. She'd refused the latter invitation because she felt strange about being seen as his slave.

Just being in the same room with Kardal was enough to get her heart racing. She wasn't sure how she managed to have sensible conversation when her brain could only focus on how his mouth had felt against hers and was he planning to do that again?

"I need a vaccine," she murmured to herself, taking another staircase down, then pausing to study a beautiful seventeenth-century tapestry showing an elegant Queen Elizabeth greeting a visiting Spanish delegation.

She raised her fingers toward the intricate work but didn't touch it. There was a slight fraying at the edges and more dust on the cloth than she would like.

"It needs to be cleaned," she said aloud. "Then put under glass and protected from the elements."

What Kardal was doing here was a crime, she thought as she continued moving down the stairs. The dry desert air offered a measure of protection but so many of the stunning artifacts needed to be protected. She would take him to task the next time she saw him.

She turned at the bottom of the stairs. In front of her was an open area leading to several rooms. All the rooms had thick wood doors and massive locks. The good news was she'd found the treasure of the City of Thieves. The bad news was she'd never learned to pick a lock.

"Visiting or stealing?"

The voice came from behind her so unexpectedly that Sabrina screamed. She turned and saw a tall, blond man in a dark uniform standing on the bottom stair. He loomed nearly as well as Kardal. Despite being as fair as a California surfer, there was something spooky in his midnight-blue eyes.

She touched her fingers to her chest and tried to catch her breath. "I'm visiting. I'd hoped to see some of the treasures of the city. I have a great interest in the city's past. Who are you?"

The man stepped down on the stone floor. "Rafe Stryker. I'm in charge of security here in the City of Thieves."

"You're American," she said in surprise. "What are you doing here?"

"Prince Kardal hires the best."

"And that's you?"

Rafe nodded.

He was good-looking but in an icy way that made her think twice about making this man angry. Kardal could be dangerous but there was fire in his blood and she understood heat far more than cold.

His steady gaze never left her face. "I understand that you're the princess Kardal found wandering in the desert."

She couldn't help smiling. "That's one interpretation of the events." She glanced at the gun holstered at his waist. "Are you here to escort me back to my room?"

"Not at all." Rafe moved toward the first of the heavy doors and drew a key from his trouser pocket. "My instructions are to show you your heart's desire."

She thought about telling him that seeing the trea-

sure inside wasn't her heart's desire so much as ful-
filling an intellectual curiosity. However, when the
door swung open and she saw inside, she couldn't
speak.

Her body trembled the way it had when Kardal
had kissed her, but this time for a different reason.
At least a dozen cases stood in a darkened room.
Electrical light illuminated the insides of the glass
containers. There were no labels, no explanation, but
she recognized many of the pieces and stones.

Exquisite Fabergé eggs sat in satin nests in one
case. She gasped over the perfection of the workmanship, while itching to hold at least one of them
in her hand. But before she could ask, a glitter of
diamonds caught her attention. A dozen tiaras filled
the next display.

There were gems and set jewels, treasures from El
Bahar, Bahania, France, England, Russia and the Far
East. A ruby the size of a small melon glittered in a
case of its own.

There was too much to take in and this was only
one of the locked rooms.

"This can't be possible," she breathed, facing
Rafe who continued to watch her with his cold eyes.
"Kardal must return these at once."

Rafe shrugged. "You'll have to take that up with
the boss. My job is to make sure no one takes any
of it without his permission."

"I see. We mustn't steal from the thieves, is that
it?"

"On this one, I agree with Kardal." He flicked his
wrist in dismissal. As he did so the sleeve of his dark
jacket rose far enough for Sabrina to see a small
mark on his right wrist.

Involuntarily she gasped. Without thinking she reached for his wrist, capturing it in her hands. Rafe didn't stop her, nor did he offer an explanation.

''The mark of the prince,'' she breathed.

A small tattoo of the City of Thieves coat of arms stood out against his tanned skin. She touched the desert lion, the castle, all perfectly rendered in their miniature form. While she understood the significance, she'd never seen such a thing outside of history books.

She stared into fathomless blue eyes. ''You speak for the prince,'' she said, not asking a question. ''You bear on your body a scar—proof of a death blow meant for Kardal. You are trusted above all and have been made a sheik.''

Rafe tugged his wrist free. ''You know your history.''

''Yes.''

An American speaking for the prince? Who had ever heard of such a thing? ''You have land?''

He shrugged. ''Some. A few goats and camels. I was offered a couple of wives, but I declined.''

''Who are you?'' she asked.

''Someone who does his job.''

He was obviously much more than that. A shiver rippled through her. Without saying anything more, she walked out of the vault, still reeling from all she had seen and learned. Something had to be done, she told herself as she headed back to her room. The next time she saw Kardal, she would insist that he see sense in the matter. She would also ask him several pointed questions about his second-in-command.

Chapter Seven

Kardal left his office shortly after six that evening. He generally worked later but since Sabrina had arrived at the castle, he'd found himself stopping earlier and earlier.

It was simply a matter of wanting to train her, he told himself as he walked along the stone corridors of the castle. The more clearly she understood what would be expected of her, the better chance of success for their marriage. *If* he married her. He still hadn't decided.

Their kiss earlier in the week had showed him that physically they got along exceptionally well. He'd hoped for passion, but that single word didn't begin to describe what had occurred between them. It had been more of an explosion. He'd been seared down to his soul by a need he'd never experienced before.

All that from a kiss. What would occur if they became intimate?

His initial plan had been to find that out for himself...if he decided to continue the engagement. But now he wasn't so sure. From the first Sabrina had claimed to be innocent. He hadn't believed her but now he wasn't so sure she lied. There had been a hesitancy when he'd touched her. An awkward eagerness. While she could fake shyness, her blushes had been real, especially those during his bath. If he didn't know better, he would swear she'd never seen a naked man before.

A virgin. He shook his head as he approached the door to her room. How could that have happened, given the life she'd lived? Yet he was more and more convinced she was untouched. Which meant he had no right to claim her as his own until they were married. Doing so before, even with the betrothal, invited the well-deserved wrath of her father.

Kardal pushed open the heavy wooden door and stepped into Sabrina's quarters. As usual, she was waiting for him, but this time she did not greet him with a smile.

"I can't believe it," she announced, darting toward him, her hands clenched in fury, her eyes flashing with fire. "They're not yours and you have no right to keep them."

"Them?" he questioned. "I thought you were the only slave in the castle."

"I'm not talking about myself. I've seen some of the treasure. You can't mean to keep it. That would be unconscionable. It must be returned."

"Ah, yes. The treasure. Rafe told me about your wanderings in the dungeon."

He walked to the tea cart by the window. Adiva had already been by to leave a tray of drinks. Kardal had been raised to respect the ways of his people, so he did not drink alcohol when he was among them. When he was with someone from the west, he occasionally indulged. Around Sabrina, he seemed to drink more than he ever had.

"They have to be returned," she told him, planting her hands on her hips. "They belong to their respective nations. They're a part of the country's heritage."

He poured scotch over ice and took a grateful sip. "An interesting notion. But to whom should I return them? The nations in question have changed."

"Not all of them."

"Enough. What about the Imperial Eggs? The czars are long gone. The Russian government has changed several times in the past ninety years. Who owns the eggs? Do I find a long-lost relative of the czar? Or should I hand them over to the current regime?"

Sabrina hesitated. "Okay, the eggs are a problem, but what about the tiara owned by Elizabeth the First, or gems you stole from El Bahar and Bahania?"

He put down his drink on the tray and held up both his hands. "I have not stolen anything. I am simply holding those items in trust. If the nations who let them go want them back, they should come steal them, as my relatives did."

"Not everyone wants to be a thief."

Color stained her cheeks. She looked even more attractive than usual when she was furious with him. Her chest rose and fell with each angry breath. He watched the movement of her breasts under her dress. While he had enjoyed seeing her in her silly harem costume, he preferred her in the conservative dresses he had provided. In some ways, imagining how she looked underneath was more interesting than simply being able to see it.

Today she wore her long red hair pulled back into a thick braid. A few curls brushed against her cheeks. Wide brown eyes glared at him. She had the most unusual coloring, he thought. The deep red hair, brown eyes and skin the color of honey. Not a single freckle marred her beauty. She would produce attractive children.

"Are you even listening to me?" she demanded.

"With bated breath," he assured her. "My heart beats only to serve you."

She turned to the window and stared out at the approaching twilight. "I hate it when you're sarcastic. My point is illegally taking things isn't a tradition to be proud of. It's a disgrace."

"It has been our way for a thousand years. In the past generation or so the thieving has stopped, but the legacy is still there. In time we can discuss returning some items, but not yet." He took a sip of his drink. "Since you have so much interest in the treasure, perhaps you would like to begin cataloging it."

She glanced at him over his shoulder. "No one's done that? You don't even know what you have?"

He shrugged. "I know we have enough. But no. There's no detailed inventory. Also, I believe some of the items might require special treatment to prevent them from being destroyed as they age."

"You're right. There's a tapestry in one of the halls that is turning to dust. It needs to be protected."

She turned to face him. "But you're talking about thousands of items. Jewels and paintings. It would take years."

"Perhaps your father will be slow to pay for you."

He'd expected some kind of teasing response, but instead Sabrina sighed, then nodded slowly.

"I don't doubt that he'll be happy to have me out of his way," she said. "I'll begin in the morning."

Kardal frowned. "I hadn't meant to remind you of something unpleasant."

"My lack of relationship with my father is hardly your fault." She crossed to the tea cart and poured herself a soft drink. "At least working with the treasure will give me something to do. What about the royal watchdog? Is he going to trust me?"

"I will speak with Rafe."

"I saw the mark."

Kardal was not surprised. "Don't worry. He will not speak for me in matters of slavery."

She smiled slightly, then grew serious. "He nearly died for you."

"And I rewarded his loyalty."

"So now he's a sheik."

"You know the ways of the city. Rafe has a fortune of his own and my trust."

She glanced at him. "He doesn't strike me as the type of man who would be content watching over a bunch of vaults. What is he doing here?"

The newspapers and tabloids had given Sabrina many characteristics, but they'd never mentioned that she was intelligent.

"There's more to running a hidden city than simply stealing from the neighbors," he told her. "Rafe has many responsibilities."

"Which is a tidy statement, but doesn't answer my question."

A knock on the door interrupted them. Figures, Sabrina thought. Kardal always seemed to have a lucky escape planned. He crossed to the door and opened it.

"Thank you for coming," he said by way of greeting, then stepped back to let a beautiful woman enter the room.

She was a couple of inches taller than Sabrina, with dark hair swept up in an elegant chignon. She wore a dark purple pants suit with a gold-and-pearl pin on her lapel. Wide brown eyes twinkled with humor as she took in her surroundings.

"At least you put her in a nice, large room," she said, glancing from Kardal to Sabrina. "I would hate to think you'd chosen one of the dungeons."

"I'm difficult," Kardal said, "not a barbarian."

"Sometimes I can't see the difference," the woman murmured before turning her attention to Sabrina. "How nice to meet you at last."

Kardal stepped between them. "Mother, this is Princess Sabra of Bahania. Sabrina, my mother, Princess Cala of the City of Thieves."

Sabrina blinked in surprise. She took in Princess Cala's unlined face and youthful features. She was beautiful and couldn't be more than thirty-five.

Cala laughed. "Your shocked expression makes me feel positively youthful. I was nearly nineteen when Kardal was born."

"Practically an infant yourself," Kardal said, urging both women toward the low table that had been set with their dinner.

For the first time Sabrina noticed that Adiva had

provided three places. She waited until Cala was seated, then settled across from her. Kardal sat next to his mother. Cala sat on the cushions as if she'd been doing it all her life, which she probably had. Sabrina studied her, noticing the similarities between the two in the shape of their eyes and their smiles.

Cala motioned for Kardal to open the wine sitting at the end of the low table. She leaned toward Sabrina.

"I want you to know that I don't approve of my son's behavior. I would like to blame someone else for his bad manners, but I fear the fault is mine. I hope you can find some enjoyment during your stay in the City of Thieves, despite the circumstances."

"She wants for nothing," Kardal said firmly. "She has books to entertain herself during the day. I dine with her each evening and I have just agreed to let her catalog the city's treasures."

Sabrina traded a wry smile with Cala. "As your son points out, Princess, my life couldn't be more perfect."

Cala held out her glass to Kardal as he poured the wine. "Tell me, Sabrina, are you as much trouble to your mother as Kardal is to me?"

"Not really." Sabrina thought about mentioning that her mother barely noticed when she was around, but didn't see the point.

"I thought not." Cala glanced at her son. "You could learn from that, Kardal."

"You adore me," he said, unruffled by his mother's complaints. "I am the sun and moon of your world."

Cala laughed. "No. You are an occasional light-bulb in a dim room."

Kardal gave her a brief hug, then kissed her forehead. "You must not lie. Untruths damage the perfection of your soul. I am your world. Admit it."

"You can sometimes be a charming son. Other times, I think I should have been far more firm with you."

Sabrina watched the exchange between mother and son. They were obviously close and had great affection for each other. She envied that.

Kardal poured her wine and she took a sip. "I didn't know you lived here, Your Highness," she said.

"Call me Cala," Kardal's mother said, lightly touching her hand. "Despite my son's highhandedness, I hope that we can be friends. I don't usually spend much time within the city walls, but I have just returned and plan to spend a few months here."

"Mother runs a large charity," Kardal said. "It provides health care for children."

Cala reached for the first serving dish and passed it to her son. "When Kardal left for school in America, I found I had too much time on my hands. I began to travel. Everywhere I went I saw need. So I started the children's charity as a way to address that." She smiled. "I was quite wicked. The initial funding for the charity came from some of the stolen treasure. I was careful to choose pieces that could not possibly be returned to a government or family. Still, I expected to be struck by lightning every time I sold something."

Kardal passed the vegetable dish to Sabrina. "Sabrina believes the treasure should be returned."

Sabrina glared at him. Figures he'd bring that up

now. "I understand there are difficulties with some of the items, but not with all of them."

"I agree," Cala said easily. "Perhaps that will happen eventually. The city has not encouraged thievery for many years, but there are still those who remember and long for the old ways."

"Oil is more profitable," Kardal pointed out.

Cala passed her son another dish and leaned toward Sabrina. "He says that now. But when I insisted he go off to school, he protested for weeks. Threatened to run away into the desert so that I couldn't find him. He didn't want to learn western ways."

Sabrina glanced at Kardal. "I understand that. When my mother took me from Bahania, I didn't want to go, either. The transition was difficult. I had the advantage of having lived in California for nearly a year before I started school."

Some of Cala's humor faded from her eyes. She turned to Kardal. "You know I didn't have a choice in the matter. You were to be ruler of the city. You needed an education."

He smiled at her. "Mother, all of your actions were based in what was best for me. I do not regret my time in America."

"But it was hard on you."

He shrugged. "Life is hard. There were adjustments. I made them."

Sabrina waited for him to say more but he didn't. Had he never told his mother the details of his first few years at the boarding school? He'd told Sabrina. Was that because she was so insignificant as to not matter or because they shared the experience?

Cala turned back to her. "You had much the same

situation, didn't you?'' she asked. ''You spent your school year with your mother and your summers in Bahania?''

Sabrina nodded. ''It was always a shock to go from one place to the other. For security reasons my mother never told anyone who I was. As I grew old enough to tell my friends on my own, I didn't say anything because I thought they either wouldn't believe me or things would change.''

Cala glanced at her son. ''I believe you shared her opinion.''

''It was a secret city, Mother. I couldn't talk about it.''

Cala changed the subject, mentioning the opening of a new wing in the medical clinic. They discussed the unusually cool spring weather and the latest nomadic tribal council meeting. Sabrina found herself liking Kardal's mother. The woman was gentle and kind without being spineless. Kardal treated her with great respect. He also glanced at Sabrina from time to time, his eyes almost twinkling, as if she shared a secret with him.

She wasn't sure what it could be, but she liked the feeling. It made her shiver nearly as much as his kiss had.

''I've issued an invitation,'' Cala said when the meal had finished. Sabrina collected the last of the plates and put them on the tray.

''Do I need to be concerned?'' Kardal asked lazily. ''Will twenty women be invading the castle? Should I plan a trip into the desert?''

His mother busied herself folding her napkin. ''No women. Just one man. King Givon.''

"The king of El Bahar," Sabrina began. "Why—"

Kardal rose to his feet. His expression turned dark and forbidding as he glared down at his mother. "How dare you?" he demanded. "You know he is not welcome here. If he tries to step one foot in the City of Thieves, he will be shot on sight. If necessary, I will do it myself."

He stalked from the room and slammed the door behind him.

Sabrina stared after him, bewildered. "I don't understand," she whispered. "King Givon is a wonderful ruler. His people adore him."

Cala sighed. "Kardal would not care about that. I had hoped time would heal the wound, but I see that I was wrong."

"What wound? Why does Kardal hate King Givon?"

Cala bit her lower lip. "Because Givon is his father."

Cala stayed for several minutes before excusing herself, but when Kardal's mother finally left, Sabrina saw tears glinting in her eyes.

King Givon was Kardal's father? Sabrina couldn't believe it. The king of El Bahar was known to have been a devoted father all his life, and before his wife's death, they were supposed to have been wildly in love.

She paced the length of her room for a few minutes, then headed out to find Kardal. She ran into one of the servants and got directions to his private quarters.

The imposing wood doors with an enamel seal

nearly made her turn back, but she had the feeling that Kardal would need to talk to someone tonight. They had more in common than she would have thought so maybe she could help with this. Squaring her shoulders for courage, she knocked once, then entered.

Kardal's rooms were large, filled with incredible antiques. She entered a tiled foyer with a fountain trickling in the corner. To her left was a dining area with a table that seated twenty. She recognized the ornate style of eighteenth-century France—a time of excess that produced beautiful furniture. She crossed the living area and saw the balcony doors were open.

Some inner voice drew her out into the evening coolness. Below were the lights from the city and in the distance, the darkness of the desert. She sensed more than saw movement and approached the man leaning against the wooden railing.

"Kardal?" she whispered, not wanting to startle him.

He didn't say anything, nor did he move away. She walked toward him and stopped when she was next to him. His face was expressionless. As twilight turned to night, his features blurred.

They were silent for a long time, but she found she didn't mind the quiet. There was something restful about the desert. The occasional voice drifted up to them. Laughter. So much life all around them, hidden from the rest of the world in this fabled city.

"I've only been here a few days," she said without thinking, "yet I can't imagine being anywhere else."

"I never wanted to leave," Kardal replied. "Even when I knew it was for the best."

He leaned forward and rested his forearms on the wood railing. "You don't understand, do you?"

"Not any of it," she admitted. "I never knew King Givon was your father. Of course I didn't know much about the city or its inhabitants so I suppose that's not a complete surprise. But I thought…" Her voice trailed off. "I don't know what I thought."

"It's a long story," he warned.

She glanced at him and gave him a slight smile. "I might be your slave, but I have amazingly few duties. So I'm free to listen."

He nodded briefly, then began. "Centuries ago, before the discovery of oil, there existed what was called the silk road. It was a path through the desert, linking India and China with the west. Trade between the near and far east supported dozens of economies. When the silk road was open, many flourished. When it was closed, countries suffered. Over time the nomads found they could made a good living by offering protection for merchants. Those who dwelled in the City of Thieves learned they could make more by preventing theft than by stealing."

"Quite a change in the way of doing business," she said, listening intently.

"Agreed. El Bahar and Bahania have been good neighbors for hundreds of years. What most people don't know is that the City of Thieves is intimately involved with the two countries. There is a symbiotic relationship between the three governments. Five hundred years ago the prince of the city controlled the nomads. He collected a percentage of all goods passing through the desert. Today I collect a percentage of the oil. In return my people keep the desert safe from terrorists and the oil fields free from attack.''

"Rafe," she said softly. "He's not here for castle security at all.''

"The castle is part of his responsibility," Kardal told her. "But not the main part. My nomads can only do so much to protect the desert. The use of technology has been growing over the years.''

She touched his arm, resting her fingertips on his shirt. She could feel the heat of him, and his strength.

"What does this have to do with your father?''

He glanced down at her, then returned his attention to the night sky. "El Bahar, Bahania and the City of Thieves are bound by more than economics. There is also a blood tie. When there is no male heir for the city, either the king of El Bahar or the king of Bahania joins with the oldest daughter, staying with her until she is pregnant. If the child is a boy, he's the new heir. If the child is a girl, the king returns each year until a son is born. My grandfather had only one child...a daughter.''

Sabrina withdrew her fingers and pressed them against her chest. "That's barbaric," she said, shocked by what he was saying. "He just shows up and sleeps with her? They don't even get married?''

Kardal shrugged. "It is the way it has been for a thousand years. The kings alternate so that the blood lines stay connected but still healthy. Two hundred years ago the king of Bahania performed his royal duty. It was King Givon's turn this time.''

Sabrina shook her head. Nothing made sense. "But your mother was so young.''

"Just eighteen.''

She tried to imagine herself in that position, having to take a stranger into her bed for the sole purpose of getting pregnant. "It could have just as easily been my father," she breathed. "That would have made us half brother and sister."

She wasn't sure but she thought he might have smiled briefly. "That would have made things more interesting," he told her. "But we are not related. Although I'm not sure your father would have treated my mother any differently."

His anger returned. "Givon never cared about her. He simply did his duty and walked away. Not once in the past thirty years has he been in touch with either of us. He never acknowledged me."

Sabrina felt his pain. "I know," she said softly, leaning toward him but not touching him. "I know exactly what it feels like to be rejected by a parent. There's a horrible combination of not wanting to care and desperately wanting to be noticed."

"My feelings don't matter," he said into the darkness. "Thirty-one years after the fact, my father is finally ready to admit I exist." He shook his head. "It's too late. I won't receive him."

"You have to," she said urgently. "Kardal, please listen to me. You have to see him, because if you refuse, everyone is going to know the rejection still hurts and you don't want that. Your people will assume you're sulking. That is not the measure of a good leader. Face him because you don't have a choice. Don't let him see that he still matters."

He turned on her. "He doesn't matter. He never mattered."

She held her ground and met his furious gaze. "He matters a lot and that's what makes you so angry. Whatever you tell yourself, he's still your father."

He continued to glare at her. Eventually some of the heat left his gaze. ''You are not as I imagined,'' he said.

Despite the tension in the air, she couldn't help chuckling. ''I know what you thought of me before so that's hardly a compliment.''

''I mean it as one.'' He touched his fingers to her face. ''I have much to consider. Your counsel is most wise. I will not dismiss it simply because you're a woman.''

''Thank you,'' she murmured, knowing he was actually being sincere. The man might have gone to school in the west, but desert sand flowed through his veins. He made her crazy.

Worse, she wasn't sure she would change even one thing about him.

Chapter Eight

The next morning Kardal's assistant, Bilal, knocked on his door, then stepped inside to announce that Princess Cala was here to see him. Kardal hesitated. For the first time in his life, he didn't want to see his mother. He'd spent most of the last night and this morning trying to forget what she'd told him. That King Givon was coming to the city.

He nodded at Bilal and told the young man to show her in.

Cala swept into the office. She wore jeans and a T-shirt, and looked more like a western teenager than a nearly fifty-year-old mother. Her long hair hung in a braid down her back.

"I thought you might refuse to see me," she said as she plopped down in the seat across from his. "You were in quite the snit last night."

"Snit?"

She shrugged. "You were obviously upset with both the situation and with me."

"Upset?"

"Do you plan to repeat everything I say?"

"No." He placed his hands on his desk. How could he explain what he was feeling? Why did he have to? Shouldn't his mother understand?

Cala crossed one leg over the other and smiled at him. "I liked Sabrina. She's very nice."

It took him a second to catch up with the subject change. "Yes. I was surprised as well, although I'm not sure I would use the word 'nice' to describe her."

"What word would you use?"

"Spirited. Intelligent."

He thought of her advice the previous evening. That he couldn't refuse the king's visit because then he would be showing that Givon mattered to him. Not that he did. Kardal had stopped caring about his father a long time ago.

"I had suspected you two had much in common. I'm pleased that's true," Cala told him. "Have you decided what to do about the betrothal?"

"No." Although the thought of being married to Sabrina was less distressing than it had been. "She is willful and still has much to learn."

"And you can be a real idiot sometimes. I tried to raise you to believe women are the equal of men."

Kardal raised his eyebrows. "I do not recall that lesson."

"Of course you don't." Cala put both feet on the floor and leaned toward him. She drew in a breath. "Kardal, I'm sorry you're upset about Givon's visit. I had hoped that you would be willing to listen and understand now that you're older."

He sprang to his feet. "I have nothing to say on the subject."

His mother's dark eyes pleaded with him. "What about what I have to say?"

"It is not important."

She stood and glared at him. "I hate it when you get this way. You talk about Sabrina being stubborn, but you're the worst in that respect. You didn't even ask me why."

"Why what?"

"Why King Givon is coming for a visit. Why after all this time he's finally making an appearance."

Kardal didn't want to know, but he also wasn't about to admit that to his mother. Instead he inclined his head, indicating she could tell him.

"I asked him," she said simply. "He stayed away because I told him he wasn't welcome in the city. Last month I sent him a message requesting his presence here."

He could not have been more shocked if she'd slapped him. "You invited him?" The sense of betrayal left a bitter taste on his tongue. Cala? "After what he did to you?"

She took a step toward him. "I've told you dozens of times, Kardal. There's more to the story than you know. I invited him because it's time we laid the past to rest."

"Never," he announced. "I will never forgive him."

"You have to. It's not all his fault. If you'd just let me explain."

He turned to his computer and touched several keys. "Please excuse me, Mother. I have much work to do."

She hesitated for a minute or two, then left his office. Kardal continued to stare unseeingly at the computer screen. Finally he swore, stood and left the room as well.

Sabrina consulted the dictionary on her lap, then returned her attention to the ancient text on the small table in front of her. Old Bahanian was a difficult language in the best of circumstances. When written in a curvy script and seven-hundred-year-old ink, it was practically impossible.

Picking up a magnifying glass, she brushed away some dust with her gloved fingers. Was that an *r* or a *t*, she wondered. Did the—

The door to her quarters flew open and Kardal stalked into the room. She stared at him thinking that he never walked or stood like a normal person. He was forever looming and pacing and sweeping around. Even as she watched, he unfastened his cloak and tossed it on the bed, then moved to stand next to her.

"What are you doing?" he demanded.

She set down the magnifying glass, then pulled off her gloves. "Trying to read this text. Unsuccessfully," she added. "It's something about camels, but I can't figure out if it's a bill of sale or instructions for care."

He looked at the paper. "Why does it matter which?"

"Because it's an old document related to a way of life that is lost to us. We'll discover the truth about that time through the mundane. Which, by the way, is not why you came to see me. What's wrong?"

He threw up his hands and paced to the window

in her room. Once there, he stared out into the desert. "My mother invited him. That's why he's coming. She actually wrote him. What was she thinking?"

Energy poured from him, filling the room and making Sabrina wish there was something she could do to ease his suffering. Kardal was a strong man. From what she'd heard on her walks through the castle, he was well respected and honored as a wise ruler. But in this matter of his father, he was as confused as anyone else would be.

She put the dictionary on the table and went to stand next to him. "Which bothers you more?" she asked. "That he's coming or that your mother invited him?"

He turned his dark eyes on her. His mouth twisted. "I don't know. It's been thirty-one years. I've never met him. What am I supposed to do now?"

"Pretend he is just another visiting dignitary. Have a state dinner with fabulous food and wine. Talk about world events and don't let him see that you care."

"I don't care."

He spoke forcefully, but she saw his pain and confusion. A part of her wanted to reach out to him. After all, they had a version of this circumstance in common. But she didn't know him well enough to predict how he would react to an offer of comfort. And the thought of being physically close to him made her nervous.

Instead she crossed to her desk and pulled out a drawer. Taking a modern pen and paper out, she pushed aside the text and dictionary, then sat.

"We need a plan," she said firmly. "I'm serious about the state dinner. What else do you want to do while he's here? What about a tour of the castle? It's been thirty-one years, right? I'm sure there have been changes.''

''We've modernized,'' Kardal admitted, moving toward the table.

She glanced around at her room, her gaze lingering on the lanterns and the lack of running water. ''Obviously the remodeling didn't get this far,'' she said dryly. ''Okay, item one, the dinner.'' She wrote. ''Item two, tour of the castle and that security stuff that Rafe is in charge of.''

Kardal pulled out a chair and sat next to her. He wore a loose linen shirt and dark trousers. Even casually dressed, he appeared powerful and just a little scary. At least that's what Sabrina told herself to explain the rapid beating of her heart. It couldn't possibly be because he was sitting close to her, could it?

''The air force,'' Kardal said.

Sabrina opened her mouth, then closed it. ''Excuse me?''

''The air force,'' he repeated. ''That is why Rafe is here. He's working with another American in Bahania. In the past few years it has become apparent that nomadic tribes and electronic surveillance isn't enough to keep the desert safe. We need airplanes to patrol the area. Rafe and Jason Templeton, who is Rafe's counterpart in Bahania, both have military experience. Your father and I hired them to get our air force up and running.''

''You're kidding,'' she said, still in shock. ''You're going to have a military presence here in the City of Thieves? And my father is doing the same?''

"We have valuable resources to protect. Not just the oil. Minerals are being mined. When tensions run high, we are vulnerable. My grandfather was a wise man in many ways, but he resisted technology. I don't share his view."

"I guess not."

Sabrina supposed that when she thought about it, some way of protecting the country made sense. Bahania, like El Bahar, had remained neutral as much as possible throughout the past several hundred years. But situations arose that forced action. Or at least protection.

"What about El Bahar? Will they participate?"

Kardal frowned. "Hassan wants to invite Givon, but I have resisted. With my father coming here, I may not have a choice in the matter."

"At the risk of starting trouble, wouldn't everyone be safer if the three of you presented a united front?"

"Perhaps." He looked at her. "Yes, of course. But for now I would rather be stubborn."

"Just so you're willing to admit it."

They were sitting closer than she'd realized. She could see the flecks of gold in Kardal's irises and the dark line where his whiskers began on his cheeks. Her gaze drifted to his mouth and she remembered what it had felt like against her own. He hadn't tried to kiss her again. Was that because he hadn't been pleased with what had happened before? Was he angry because she'd pushed his hands away?

She wasn't going to get any answers to her questions, she told herself. There was no way she was going to ask them and he wasn't likely to volunteer the information. Time to return to the subject at hand.

"Do you think the air force is the reason Cala

invited Givon here? So that you would have to include him?''

"Perhaps. My mother rarely interferes with issues of state, but she understands the ways of the world. I frequently seek her counsel.''

"But not in this matter.''

"No. We disagree about King Givon.'' He tapped the table. "You are right about the state dinner, however. It is necessary to act as if this visit is no different from any other. Would you plan that for me?''

His request surprised her. Her father rarely let her plan more than her own wardrobe. "Yes. Of course.''

"I'll instruct the household staff to consult with you on every detail.''

She nodded, more pleased than she could say. "I'll put together a menu, then discuss it with you.'' A thought struck her. "If you like, I could find some El Baharian treasures in the vault and use them to decorate the dining room and the king's rooms.''

Kardal grinned. "Tweaking Givon's nose?''

"Just a little. Do you mind?''

He smiled at her. "Not at all, although I'm beginning to see that while it's very pleasant to have you on my side, I would not want you for an enemy.''

She made a few more notes, then set down her pen. "Kardal, you have to really be prepared for this. Seeing your father is going to be a bigger deal than you imagine. If you don't get ready, you won't be able to do more than react when you see him.''

He stared into the distance. "I know. But how does one prepare for such an event? I can imagine it, as I have dozens of times in my life. I see him in my mind's eye, but he doesn't speak. After all this time, what is there to say?''

''I wish I knew.'' Sabrina thought about her own father whose greetings to her usually consisted of an absent, ''Oh, you've returned.''

''What do *you* want to say to *him?*'' she asked.

Kardal leaned back in his chair. ''I don't know. I have many questions, but I'm not sure I still care about the answers. It was different when I was younger. However, I will consider your advice.''

She wanted to point out that considering and taking were two different things. She also thought he was wrong. He might be older, but she doubted his feelings for his father had changed very much over the years.

''Will King Givon come alone or bring his sons with him?''

''My mother didn't say and I have not clarified that with her.'' Tension filled his body. ''I will speak with her today and let you know so that you may plan accordingly.''

''Thanks. I'll make sure the appropriate number of rooms are ready.''

Kardal shook his head. ''His sons,'' he repeated slowly. ''My half brothers. I have never met them. They are married, they have children. Nieces and nephews.''

''I know,'' she told him. ''It's weird. I have four half brothers. Of course most of them are only half brothers to each other. My father wasn't like yours. He didn't see the need to stay loyal to one woman.''

She stopped and pressed her fingers to her mouth. ''Sorry,'' she said quickly. ''I didn't mean…'' Because King Givon *hadn't* been faithful to one woman and Kardal was the result of that indiscretion.

"I know what you mean," he said.

Sabrina shuffled her papers. "Are you sure about this?" she asked. "About me? Isn't there someone better qualified to handle these arrangements?"

"You do not want the job?"

"No. I'm happy to help. I just don't want to make any mistakes."

He touched her arm. She felt the contact all the way to her thighs. It was as if fire flickered inside of her.

"You are the one I want," he said.

She knew how he meant the words. She was the one he wanted to prepare for King Givon's visit. But for one heartbeat, she took his statement a different way. A more personal way. Her chest tightened, as did her throat. In that split second, she wondered what it would be like to hear those words from Kardal and having the meaning be romantic. What would it be like to be wanted by this man?

But she would never know. She was betrothed to another. It was her duty to guard her innocence to present to her husband on their wedding night. Oddly enough, she'd never been tempted before. She'd never thought about being with a man. Why did Kardal change all that?

A knock on her bedroom door made them both look up.

"Come," Kardal called.

Rafe stepped into the room. He nodded at Sabrina, then turned his attention to his employer. "It's nearly time for the conference call."

Kardal nodded. "Ordering a dozen jets is not as

simple as one might imagine,'' he told Sabrina as he rose. ''Thank you for your assistance.''

Then, in an act that surprised her more than anything since her capture, he bent down and lightly brushed her mouth with his. He was gone before she could do more than open her eyes and wonder if the kiss had even occurred.

Why had he done that? she wondered when she could finally drag herself out of her chair. Did it mean anything? She knew it was possible he'd reacted without thinking, but for some reason, she wanted the brief kiss to be significant. She wanted it to matter.

Feeling both silly and unexplainably happy, she put away the text she'd been reading when Kardal had arrived. She would spend the afternoon planning the king's visit. She would need to tour the guest rooms and pick one for King Givon. She would also have to find out how many were in his party. Which would probably mean speaking with Princess Cala.

Sabrina wondered why Kardal's mother had invited Givon to the City of Thieves after all this time. What did she think about the man who had seduced her when she'd been barely eighteen? Tradition might demand that he do his duty, but Cala had been five years younger than Sabrina was today. She didn't think *she* would be very happy about sleeping with a stranger.

And what about King Givon? He'd been married at the time, with two sons of his own. She frowned as she tried to remember the age of his youngest. Was it possible his wife had been pregnant while he'd been staying in the City of Thieves? Why would he have agreed to such a thing?

Still mulling over the question, Sabrina picked up Kardal's cloak from the bed and walked over to her closet. She would keep it here until she next saw him and could return it.

As she walked, something banged against her leg. Something small and square. Curious, she put her hand in the pocket and drew out a cellular telephone. What on earth? She stared at the flip phone, running her fingers along the cover. What was he doing with one of these out here in the middle of the desert? It couldn't possibly work...could it?

She hung the cloak, then turned her attention to the cell phone. Her fingers trembled as she opened it and pressed the on button. The phone screen lit and beeped softly. The screen flashed several messages, including the name of the service provider and the cell phone's telephone number. She blinked. There was a small *D* in the upper left corner indicating there was digital phone service, and the lit bars showed she had full reception. How was that possible?

Then she remembered what Kardal had said about the oil fields and using technology to protect them. Her bedroom in the palace might still be from the fourteenth century, but obviously there was modern life elsewhere in the castle.

Without thinking, she pushed the numbers for her father's office. Seconds later, his assistant answered the phone.

"This is Princess Sabra," she said hesitantly. "May I speak with my father?"

"Yes, Your Highness. One moment please."

There was a click, followed by silence. Sabrina bit her lower lip. Was she doing the right thing by calling? What was she going to say? Was she ready to return to Bahania? Would Kardal be in trouble for kidnapping her?

She grimaced. There was a silly question. Of course he would be. Her father might not think the sun rose and set because of her but he was hardly going to condone someone abducting her.

But was that what she wanted? What about the joint air force? Would this ruin everything? And if her father did indeed come to her rescue was she prepared—

"Sabrina?"

She jumped at the sound of the familiar voice. "Yes, Father. It's me. I'm—"

"I know where you are," the king said, cutting her off. "I've known since you arrived. I'm not surprised Kardal wants to get rid of you so quickly. I had hoped it would be different." He sighed heavily. "You're not much use to anyone, are you? Well, I'm not taking you back. Stay in the City of Thieves until you've learned your lesson."

The phone clicked in her ear as her father hung up.

Sabrina walked to the bed and sat on the mattress. She didn't remember releasing the phone, but suddenly it was on the nightstand and her hands were curling into tight balls that she pressed into her stomach. Pain filled her. Ugly, dark, humiliating pain that made the rising sobs stick in her throat.

Her own father didn't care about her. Kardal was playing his own game with the kidnapping, but what if he was being cruel to her? What if he'd attacked her? Obviously her father didn't care. He never had.

She'd known, she thought rolling onto the bed and

drawing her knees up to her chest. She pressed her face into the pillow and didn't bother fighting the hot tears that spilled onto her cheeks. She'd known that she didn't matter. Or at least she'd believed, but had hoped she'd been wrong. But now she couldn't deny the truth. Not anymore.

Her body shook with the intensity of her sobs. Her mother had made it clear that Sabrina was no longer welcome. Sabrina no longer looked like a young girl, which made it more difficult for her mother to lie about her own age. Now her father didn't want her around, either.

Emptiness filled her, making her feel sick. She closed her eyes and wondered what she was supposed to do now.

Unexpectedly, something warm brushed against her cheek and the mattress dipped. She opened her eyes in time to see Kardal sit on the edge of her bed.

"What's all this?" he asked, his voice low and gentle.

She tried to answer but instead cried harder. He didn't rebuke her or complain. Instead he drew her into his arms and held her tight.

"Everything will be fine," he promised.

Sabrina couldn't believe how desperately she wanted his words to be true.

Chapter Nine

Kardal pulled Sabrina into his arms. She resisted at first, then allowed him to raise her into a sitting position. Her body shook with the force of her sobs and he freed one hand so that he could stroke her hair.

"I am here," he told her quietly.

She didn't respond right away and he was content to wait for her to calm before speaking. Her tears should have bothered him. His mother had never cried in front of him, so his only experience with females and tears had come from the women in his life. It had seemed to him that tears were often a way to manipulate him into giving them what they wanted. But he didn't think that of Sabrina. She'd had no way of knowing he would enter her quarters at that particular moment.

He also felt strangely protective of her, wanting to keep her close until he knew what was wrong, then leave only to take care of the problem. He frowned. Why would he care about what made her cry? She was a woman and the complaints of her life should be of little consequence to him. And yet he did not feel impatient, nor did he want to tell her that she needed to deal with whatever it was on her own.

Gradually her tears lessened. Eventually she raised her head and wiped her face. He pulled a handkerchief from his trouser pocket and handed it to her. She gave him a wavering smile of thanks, then unfolded the neatly pressed square of cotton and touched it to her eyes.

"I f-found your phone," she said, her voice shaking slightly.

When she turned and pointed, he noticed the small cellular telephone on the nightstand by her bed. He swore silently. "I left it in my cloak."

She nodded. "I wasn't looking through your pockets. I went to hang it up in the closet so that it wouldn't wrinkle. As I carried it across the room, something bumped against my leg. I was curious. Then I found the phone." She sniffed. "I didn't think it would work, but it did. I called my father."

Kardal tensed. What had Hassan said? Had he mentioned the betrothal? Did Sabrina now wish to leave?

Fresh tears spilled from her eyes. She tried to shift away, but he kept his arms around her, hugging her to him.

"Tell me," he instructed. "What happened?"

"I c-called my father," she whispered hoarsely. "You had said you were waiting for ransom and I thought if I spoke to him…" Her voice trailed off.

"I thought he would be worried about me. I was wrong."

Kardal felt uncomfortable. "I did not mean to cause you distress."

"You didn't. I don't want to know what my father said when you called him." She raised her chin and looked at him. "I don't think he's going to pay any ransom. He told me that he wasn't surprised you wanted to get rid of me so quickly and that he wasn't going to take me back. He said I had to stay here and learn my lesson."

She ducked her head as more tears filled her eyes. Kardal swore under his breath and hugged her tight.

He understood that the king was disappointed with his daughter, but Hassan had no right to treat Sabrina so heartlessly. Not only was she the child of his loins, but she was not all the newspapers made her out to be. Kardal had been just as guilty of judging her based on the words of others. As he got to know her better, he found that most of his assumptions were incorrect. Surely her own father knew that as well. But he wasn't convinced Hassan had ever bothered to spend enough time with her to find out for himself.

"What is he waiting for me to learn?" she asked. "What lesson? Does he want me to become a good slave?" She shook her head. "I'm his daughter. Why doesn't that matter to him?"

"Both our fathers are idiots," he announced. "What is it they say in the west? They need attitude adjustments."

She gave him a tiny smile, then swiped at her tears. "I always knew I wasn't very important to him. My brothers were what mattered, and his cats, of course. I thought I'd made peace with that, but it still hurts to find out he doesn't care about me at all.''

Kardal smoothed her hair away from her face. The thick red curls wrapped themselves around his fingers. He drew his thumbs under her eyes, brushing away her tears.

''King Hassan doesn't know what he's missing by not getting to know you better,'' he told her. ''In just a week I have learned that you are nothing like the young woman in the tabloid stories. You are intelligent and stubborn. Despite the lack of amusements, you seem very content here in the city. You have a vast understanding of our history, you even read ancient Bahanian.''

''Not very well.''

He smiled. ''I don't read it at all.''

Some of the pain left her eyes. ''Thank you,'' she told him. ''Your words mean a lot to me. I just wish my father shared your opinion. Maybe then he wouldn't have betrothed me to a man I've never met.''

Kardal stiffened. ''Did you discuss that when you spoke with him on the phone?''

''No. There wasn't time.'' She eased away and shrugged. ''Besides, what is there to say? I doubt we'll ever like each other, let alone fall in love. How could I possibly be happy marrying a stranger?'' She blinked back tears. ''For all I know he's a disgusting old man and has three wives.''

''The troll prince.''

She nodded.''

''Your father would not permit such a union,'' he told her.

"If it offered political gain, I believe he would subject me to anything."

Sabrina sat in the center of the bed, her spine straight, her chin held high. Despite her swollen eyes and damp cheeks, she looked regal. Every inch the princess. Kardal wanted to tell her that her fate wasn't to be as horrible as she imagined. That he had no other wives, nor was he that old. Barely thirty-one. But he was not yet ready to reveal the fact that he was her betrothed. Not before he was sure.

"All I wanted was to find someone who cared about me. Someone who wanted me." She twisted the handkerchief in her hands. "No one ever has," she said softly. "Neither of my parents, my brothers. No one."

He thought of telling her that he wanted her very much, but he did not speak the words. The desire he felt was not what she meant. Sabrina wanted a longing of the heart. Why did women care so much about love? Didn't they realize that respect and shared goals mattered so much more?

"Besides," she said, "it's the twenty-first century. Arranged marriages are barbaric."

"You are of royal blood," he reminded her. "Arranged marriages are a fact of life. You have a duty to your country."

"What about you? Will you go easily to the slaughter?"

"Of course. Tradition states that my marriage be advantageous to my people."

Her eyes widened. "You can't be serious. You'll agree to an arranged marriage?"

"Within certain parameters. I will meet my prospective wife first and see if I think we can have a productive marriage with many sons.''

''What? You want to make sure she'll only have sons? You do understand the biology of pregnancy, don't you? It's not the woman who decides gender.''

Her combination of outrage and earnestness made him smile. ''Yes, Sabrina. I know where babies come from and how their sex is determined. By productive I didn't just mean having children. I need a woman who can rule at my side, understand my people and be a part of the rhythm of the city.''

She glanced down at the handkerchief in her hands. ''I might be willing to go through with an arranged marriage if I got to pick all that, too,'' she muttered. ''You get Princess Charming and I get the troll prince. It's hardly fair.''

''Perhaps he's not so very horrible,'' he teased, thinking that the more he learned about Sabrina, the more he found her appealing. He could tell her the truth and ease her fears, but he found himself reluctant to change their current relationship.

''Do you think I should do my duty and just agree to the betrothal?'' she asked.

Kardal hesitated. ''Duty is always important.''

''Whatever the circumstances?''

''I have already said that I will agree to an arranged marriage.''

She returned her attention to him. ''That's not what I meant. King Givon was only doing his duty when he came to the City of Thieves. He was only doing his duty by fathering you.''

Kardal started to protest, then stopped. ''You have a valid point,'' he said grudgingly. ''I will consider it. However, it will be some time before I can reconcile duty with the fact that my father turned his back on his bastard son.''

Unexpected tears returned to Sabrina's eyes. She leaned toward him and touched him arm. ''I'm sorry,'' she whispered. ''I didn't mean to bring up something so unpleasant. Believe me, I know what it's like to be rejected by a parent. For what it's worth, I think King Givon is an idiot for not wanting to know you and being proud that you're his son. You're a really good prince, Kardal.''

Her words touched him more than he could have imagined. Kardal wouldn't have thought the opinion of a spoiled, wayward princess would have mattered, but now that he knew the truth about Sabrina, he found he respected her view of the world.

''Thank you,'' he said, reaching out to touch her face. ''I know that you *do* understand. I'm sorry your parents have treated you this way. You deserve more.''

''Really?''

Sabrina couldn't keep the surprise out of her voice. No one had ever seen her side before. When she'd dared to confront her father about him ignoring her, he always told her about his responsibilities as king. He made it sound as if he barely had time to sleep an hour a night and that she was a selfish child for demanding his attention. Her mother never stayed in one place long enough to listen at all. But Kardal understood.

In a way she supposed it made perfect sense. Who else had lived with a foot in each world?

He swept his thumbs across her cheeks again. ''No more crying,'' he told her. ''Your eyes are much too pretty to be filled with tears.''

He thought her eyes were pretty?

Before she could ask, or even revel in the compliment, Kardal moved closer. She suddenly realized they were alone in her room, on her bed. But instead of getting scared, she found herself filled with anticipation. Was he going to kiss her again? Heat flared inside of her at the thought.

He wrapped his arms around her and eased her back onto the mattress.

"Sabrina."

He breathed her name before he touched his lips to hers. The shivers began as he lowered himself next to her. There was a tiny flicker of fear, but she ignored it. Need and curiosity were much greater.

His mouth brushed against hers, moving back and forth. The movement was familiar—he'd done it before—and allowed her to relax slightly. The pillow was soft beneath her head. Her hair fanned out across the white cloth. Kardal twisted his fingers in her curls, tugging slightly, making her feel as if she wouldn't be allowed to escape. The thought should have terrified her. Instead it made her reach up and rest her hands on his shoulders.

The pressure of his mouth increased. She tilted her head to the left, then parted her lips, allowing him entrance. But instead of dipping inside and touching her intimately, he nibbled on her bottom lip.

Fire shot through her. Intense flames licked at her breasts, making them swell, then moved lower, between her tightly clenched thighs. One of her hands moved to his head where she ran her fingers through his silky, dark hair. Her other hand moved to his back where she felt the thick strength of his muscles.

He gently bit down on the fullest part of her lower

lip, then rubbed her with the tip of his tongue, as if easing some imagined pain. His teasing made her want more. She wanted the deep kisses from their previous encounter. She wanted to feel herself melting again.

Restless energy filled her as he continued to nibble and kiss. Finally she couldn't stand it anymore and she grabbed his hair to hold him still. She was the one who thrust her tongue into his mouth. She stroked him, circled and danced.

She felt his chest rumble as he groaned. One of his legs slipped over hers, pinning her to the bed. His hand came to rest on her shoulder.

"You seek to tame me?" he asked, drawing back slightly.

Sabrina was embarrassed by her boldness. She wouldn't meet his gaze. "No. Of course not. I just…"

He touched her chin, forcing her to look at him. "Don't be ashamed. I am excited by your desire. Your passion fuels my own until we are in danger of going up in flames." He smiled slightly. "Perhaps it is because I've never kissed a princess before."

"I haven't kissed a prince."

"Then let me show you how wonderful that can be."

She thought about pointing out that she knew from their last kiss, but already his mouth was claiming hers and she found she didn't want to interrupt the experience with something as boring as words.

This time he swept his tongue inside her mouth, discovering her, making her strain against him. The heat grew until her bones nearly melted. But as parts of her relaxed to the point of being unable to move, tension filled other places. Her breasts swelled and ached. Her bra seemed uncomfortable. Between her legs there was an odd pressure that made her want to shift on the mattress.

She wrapped her arms around him and held him close. If she pressed more tightly against him, perhaps she would feel better. Kardal seemed to understand what she was doing because he moved his leg so that his thigh pressed between hers. At the same time he drew away from her mouth and began kissing her neck. His hand moved from her shoulder down her chest toward her breasts.

There was too much going on, she thought frantically, not sure where to put her attention. His leg between hers should have felt awkward and embarrassing. No one had ever touched her *there.* Instead the increased pressure helped. If she arched her hips and rubbed against him she felt both better and worse.

His hand gently closed over her left breast, even as he licked the inside of her ear. His thumb swept across her tight nipple, making her gasp. His touch was more amazing than she could have imagined. There was an instant connection between her breast and a spot between her legs. The more he touched one, the more the other ached.

She'd never gone this far before, she thought hazily. She should probably make him stop—except she didn't want to. She felt vulnerable, but not scared. Kardal might be the man who had kidnapped her from the desert, but she was no longer afraid of him. Nor of what he would do. All her life she'd tried to live in a way that honored her family and her heritage, yet her phone call to her father made it clear that he didn't care. What did it matter if she let Kardal have his way with her? What did it matter if she wasn't a virgin?

He shifted, moving so that he was between her thighs, supporting himself on his forearms. Sabrina felt the first fluttering of panic.

"Kardal, I don't..."

He hushed her with a quick kiss. "I know, my desert bird. You are still innocent and I'm not willing to accept the consequences of defiling a princess." He grinned. "I'm very fond of my head and wish to keep it upon my shoulders. I will not go too far."

His smile faded. He tugged on her dress until it was up to her hips, then pressed himself against her.

Something hard pushed into the apex of her thighs. Something she'd never seen until Kardal's bath, never touched, but there was no doubt as to its purpose.

"I want you to know how much I desire you," he said fiercely. "How I ache for you. Do you feel my arousal?"

She nodded, unable to speak. There were several layers of clothing separating them. Her panties, his trousers and whatever he wore under them. But the pressure of his need was unmistakable. He moved slightly, rubbing against her. Something quickened inside of her. She caught her breath.

His smile returned. "So you like that? If I do more will you tell me what you want?"

She frowned. "I don't understand."

He flexed again. Pleasure shot through her. She gasped.

"Perhaps this is not such a good idea," he said

through slightly clenched teeth. He shifted so that he was lying next to her.

Before she could ask what he was doing, he slid his hand up her thigh and settled it between her legs. The pleasure returned, although she wasn't completely sure they were supposed to be doing this.

He must have read her concern in her eyes. "Don't worry," he murmured, pressing kisses to her face. "You will be as untouched as before." He pressed in, only the barrier of her panties between them. "All right, perhaps not *as* untouched, but still a virgin."

She wanted to ask him why he was doing this. What was so special about touching her *there*. But before she could form the words, he began rubbing her, circling around. He favored one small spot that made her entire body stiffen in a very good way.

"Kardal?" she breathed.

He nuzzled her neck. "Enjoy, my innocent princess. There are many delights of the body. This is just one."

As he spoke, he continued to touch her. Her legs fell open. She thought she should be embarrassed, but she couldn't think about anything except how wonderful he made her feel. When he leaned over her to kiss her, she found herself sucking on his tongue and biting his lips. She needed deep, passionate kisses and the continued stroking of his fingers.

Pressure built inside of her. Her breasts felt so tight that the slightest brush of his forearm against her nipple made her gasp.

Her hips began to pulse in time with his ministrations. The tension increased and she could barely breathe. Kardal muttered something under his breath, then stopped what he was doing.

"What?" she asked, dazed, lost and feeling as if she would die if he didn't continue.

"I have to touch you," he growled and quickly jerked off her panties.

With her dress up around her hips, she was naked from the waist down. No man had ever seen her this way, yet she didn't care that Kardal looked upon her. Not if he started touching her again.

Thankfully he did. But this time was so much sweeter. His fingers parted her curls and found that one spot again. This time he rubbed her, circling her swollen and damp flesh until she found she could not breathe. All of time stood still as he continued to touch her over and over again.

Then, when she knew she was going to die from the wonder of it, he thrust a single finger inside of her. The shock, or the pleasure, thrust her into an unfamiliar universe. The glory of it filled her as her very first release crashed through her.

She clung to him. He kissed her, urging her to continue, holding her close, touching her until the last bit of paradise had faded and she was filled with a lethargy she'd never known. It was an effort to keep her eyes open.

Kardal smiled down at her. "I will not ask if you enjoyed it."

He was being an arrogant male. She found she no longer cared. "Is it supposed to be that wonderful?"

"Yes. It will also be better next time."

"That's not possible."

He kissed her cheek. "Of course it is. I could touch you again and bring you close to your release. Then, when you were so close as to be shaking, I could enter you, filling you completely. With each thrust you would climax a tiny bit, but build as well until there was nothing for us to do but fall together.''

His word picture made her blush. She pushed down her dress so that she was covered to her thighs. ''Yes, well, is that what we're going to do?''

''No. I meant what I said. As much as I want to make love with you, this isn't the time.''

''Then why did you touch me like that?''

''To show you the possibilities.'' His eyebrows raised. ''Now you can dream about me while you sleep.''

He stretched out on his side, then drew her toward him until she was facing him. He pressed a kiss to her forehead.

''Was that truly your first time?'' he asked.

Heat flared on her face as she nodded. ''I didn't get out much.''

''How is that possible? You're very beautiful. Western men are not blind.''

His compliment made her glow.

''I was always careful about dating. I had a few boyfriends, but…'' She shrugged. How to explain the strangeness that was her life? ''I didn't want to be like my mother, going from man to man. So I was more particular. There was also the whole virgin princess thing. I didn't want the responsibility, but there it was. I always thought that I was supposed to save myself for my husband.''

''No young man tried to change your mind?''

She couldn't believe they were having this calm conversation lying on her bed. She might be wearing a long-sleeved dress but her panties were somewhere on the floor and just a couple of minutes ago, Kardal had been touching her in a way she'd only ever read about.

"A couple of boys tried to, you know." She bit her lower lip. "Most of the time I wasn't interested and it was easy to say no. When I was interested, I felt obligated to tell them the truth about me. They didn't take it well."

Humor brightened his dark eyes. "I imagine they did not."

She laughed, then gathering her courage, pressed her fingers against his high, sculpted cheekbone. When he didn't protest, she slowly traced his features. The sweep of his eyebrows, the firm line of his jaw. She lingered longest on his mouth, outlining his lips, then laughing when he unexpectedly nipped at her fingers.

"Did you tell people who you were?" she asked.

"No. The city is a secret. I had to protect it. Besides, telling people I was a prince made them act differently."

"I know what you mean. Keeping that part of me from my friends meant there was always something between us. I wanted to be close...I wanted to confide the truth, but I couldn't."

Kardal rolled onto his back and pulled her along with him. When he wrapped an arm around her, she rested her head on his shoulder.

"I could talk to my grandfather," he said. "He understood because he'd led the city for nearly forty years."

"You still miss him."

"Every day. It's been four years and I still long to hear his voice. I have so many questions and no one has answers. No one who understands."

She thought about pointing out that King Givon would understand. But even if Kardal and Givon could make peace with the past, it would take time to build a relationship based on trust.

"It's too bad about your father," she said.

"I agree. I do not approve of how he handled things here, but in El Bahar, he has been a good and strong leader for his people."

Sabrina ached for him. "I wish there was something I could do," she said. "I'd listen, if it would help. I don't know much about running a city, but I get the whole royal thing. More than I want to."

Kardal raised his head and looked at her. "Thank you. I would like to speak with you about my concerns."

"Really?"

He nodded. "I am surprised as well, but then you are nothing like I imagined."

"Don't even pretend to tell me what you thought before. You got all your ideas out of those stupid articles. I'm nothing like that."

"I know." He sat up. "The troll prince is a most fortunate man."

He started to say something more, then turned and rose. "Thank you," he said, leaning forward and kissing her mouth. "I was most honored this afternoon."

He straightened and adjusted the front of his bulging trousers. "And most aroused."

He gave her a smile, then turned and left. Sabrina stared after him. When the door closed, she pressed her head to her pillow and sighed. What a strange encounter. She didn't understand Kardal at all, yet she liked him. A shiver rippled through her as she wondered how long it would be until he touched her again.

Chapter Ten

Sabrina, Kardal, Rafe and Cala sat around an antique oval table in a small anteroom outside the old throne room in the palace. Despite the importance of the meeting, Sabrina found it difficult to focus on what everyone was saying. She was too busy admiring the room.

It wasn't large, maybe sixteen feet square, with tall, narrow windows on one wall. Instead of a view of the desert, she could see a beautiful garden. Lush and green with exotic flowers from around the world. The bougainvillea tree looked ancient and she wondered where it had originally come from. What Prince of Thieves had requested it be carried by camel to his secret palace? Or perhaps one of the princesses had wanted something beautiful to gaze upon while waiting for her husband to finish his business for the day.

There were several stunning tapestries on the wall, although she winced when she saw bright sunlight falling directly on a length of cloth depicting Queen Victoria attending an elegant picnic. There were faded patches and frayed threads. The tapestry needed immediate attention if it was to be saved.

"Sabrina?"

Kardal spoke her name with some impatience, as if he'd been trying to get her attention for some time.

"What? Oh, sorry." She turned her attention away from Queen Victoria and settled it firmly on those in the room.

Cala smiled at her. "Kardal and I have grown up in the palace so we're used to its splendors, but it can be overwhelming for someone seeing it for the first time."

"It's not just that," Sabrina said heatedly. "So many of the treasures are in serious danger. These tapestries—" she pointed to the cloths on the wall "—should never be exposed to sunlight. They're being destroyed."

Kardal glared at her. "You may deal with them later. Right now we need to plan for the visit."

Instead of arguing, Sabrina simply nodded. Kardal had been growling like a lion ever since he'd agreed to allow King Givon to visit. She couldn't blame him for his temper. No doubt he was fighting nerves, not to mention second and third thoughts about the whole thing. Meeting one's father after all this time couldn't be easy.

She reached for her pad of paper and pointedly ignored the sideboard covered with small ivory figurines just begging to be cataloged. "How many will be in the king's party?" she asked. "Oh, and how are they arriving? Will there be extra animals to house in the stables?''

Kardal, Rafe and Cala all stared at her. ''I assure you the king of El Bahar will not arrive by camel,'' Kardal said dryly.

Sabrina thought about sticking her tongue out at him, but restrained herself. ''Like that was something I should know intuitively,'' she grumbled. ''The palace is in the desert. From what I can tell, there aren't any big roads. A convoy would have difficulty with the terrain and call attention to the location of the palace.''

Kardal leaned toward her. He sat next to her, with Cala across from her and Rafe on her right. She was fairly comfortable with Kardal's mother, but Rafe still gave her the willies. The man seemed dangerous when he was just sitting in a chair and breathing.

''I understand your point about the convoy and it is well taken. Still, the king will not arrive by camel. Or horse.''

''Fine. Then how?''

''Helicopter,'' Cala said, consulting a notepad in front of her.

Rafe did the same, only instead of a pen and paper, he had an electronic device the size of a paperback book. ''The king will travel with the pilot and one security agent. We'll be responsible for his security once he arrives in the city.''

''No entourage?'' Sabrina asked, even as she felt Kardal stiffen. As clearly as if he'd spoken, she knew what he was thinking. Why so few people? Was Givon being trusting or showing disrespect?

''My father always travels with at least a dozen people,'' she continued. ''Even family vacations included staff. Is the king keeping the number down because this is a 'getting to know you' kind of visit?''

Cala glanced from her to her son, then understanding dawned in her brown eyes. "Exactly," she said quickly, flashing Sabrina a grateful smile. "He didn't want a lot of extra people around to call attention to the visit, or to get in the way. We discussed it and thought this would be best."

Kardal stared at his mother. "You've spoken with him?" He made it sound as if she'd been selling state secrets to a mortal enemy. Perhaps in his mind, she had.

"Yes, Kardal," Cala said evenly. "I've spoken with him. We've had several conversations. How do you think this visit got arranged in the first place?"

He didn't answer. Sabrina searched for something to say to ease the tension in the room. Instinctively she shot Rafe a pleading glance. The blond security agent surprised her by filling the silence.

"Keeping the king safe here won't be a problem," he said as if he hadn't noticed the tension between mother and son. "I understand Sabrina is planning the social portion of his visit, so I'll coordinate things with her. You'll want him to see the security center, of course, and perhaps tour the air force facility."

Sabrina had known about the fledgling air force for several days. "Where is all that stuff?" she asked. "I mean, is it far from the city?"

The corner of Rafe's mouth tilted up slightly. "I can't give you the exact location of the air force facility, ma'am."

"Because I'm such a security risk," she said,

glancing at Kardal. "Let me guess. If he told me, he'd have to kill me."

Kardal turned his attention from his mother. Some of his anger faded. "Yes, and that would displease me."

"I wouldn't be too thrilled about it, either. So how long do you need to show off this secret air force and security center?"

Kardal shifted in his seat. Sabrina stared at him thinking that if she didn't know better, she would swear he was suddenly uncomfortable.

"Give us an afternoon for the air force," Rafe said, consulting his tiny computer. "We can do the security center whenever we'd like. What works for you, Sabrina?"

Kardal continued to look uneasy. She glanced at him, then at Rafe. Comprehension dawned. "It's here, isn't it?" she asked as outrage filled her. "The security center is in the castle."

Rafe shrugged. "Sure. Where else would it be?"

She turned her attention to Kardal. "Let me guess. There's electricity and computers. Fax machines, telephones and all kinds of weird Internet stuff."

Kardal didn't meet her gaze. "I had planned to mention it."

"When? Two weeks after you released me?"

"No. At first I didn't want you to know and then I simply forgot." He finally met her gaze. "You are my slave. You have no right to question me. I am the Prince of Thieves and here, within the walls of this city, my word is law."

"You're a slimy creep," she protested. "You let me live like some fourteenth-century sex slave in a room that doesn't even have running water. Do you realize that—''

Sabrina suddenly realized that all three of them were staring at her. She mentally replayed her last few sentences and felt herself go scarlet when the phrase ''sex slave'' crossed her consciousness.

She'd done her best to forget what had happened between Kardal and herself three days ago. Actually she'd thought she'd done a good job. Except for strange dreams in which he touched her as he had before, and the occasional moment of inattention as she worked her way through cataloging items in the vault, she'd practically put it out of her mind. Well, not when he joined her for dinner or when she bathed in the large tub delivered to her room every day. There was something about being naked and in steaming water that set her mind to wandering to what it had been like in Kardal's arms. And often when she was alone, flashes of what had happened appeared in her mind. But other than that, it was as if the incident had never occurred.

''I see,'' Cala said at last, gazing at her son. ''Is there something you want to tell me?''

''No.'' He didn't seem the least bit embarrassed when he turned to Sabrina and said, ''I had meant to tell you about the remodeled section of the castle. However, with all that has happened the past few days, I forgot. Would you like to move to a more modern room?''

She thought about the beauty of her quarters, the ancient books and the large four-poster bed upon which… She cleared her throat. ''No. I like where I am. However, I would like access to a real bathroom.''

"Of course. Tell Adiva to show you where the closest one is located." He inclined his head as if to say the matter was closed. "About the king's visit."

Sabrina returned her attention to her notes. "How long is he staying?" She glanced from Rafe to Cala as they seemed to be the ones in the know on the subject of Givon's visit.

"I'm not sure," Cala murmured. Now she was the one looking flustered. "A few nights. I don't think it's necessary to have a formal state dinner. Perhaps just one with a few close friends."

Kardal appeared uneasy at the suggestion. Sabrina knew he was wondering what they would all discuss. The reasons he, Givon, abandoned his family? Why he'd never acknowledged his bastard son? She sighed. While her summers in Bahania had not allowed her to move in royal circles beyond Bahania, she'd met King Givon several times. From her personal experience, not to mention all she'd heard about the man, he was a decent person. Stern, but not cruel. So why had he treated Cala and Kardal so badly?

"What about a small dinner the first night," Sabrina said. "Just you, the king and Kardal."

Cala nodded slowly. "Yes. That would work. Rafe, you are welcome to attend, and of course you'll be there, Sabrina."

She wasn't so sure she wanted to participate in what promised to be a most awkward meal, but felt it was important for her to be there, at least for Kardal.

"As for the meal itself," Sabrina said, "I'll discuss several options with the chef and come up with a tentative menu. There is also the matter of entertainment. I was thinking of background music more than an actual show.''

They continued to discuss different ideas. At least Cala, Rafe and Sabrina did. Kardal was no longer participating in the conversation. Sabrina wished there was a way to make this easier for him. She wished a lot of things. She wished that she understood why she cared if Kardal was apprehensive about meeting his father. She wished she knew why she wasn't anxious to leave the City of Thieves. While the opportunity to study the stolen treasure was not to be missed, she was here on the whim of a man who claimed her as his slave. Not that he'd treated her badly. He obviously had no plans to abuse her or mistreat her. So why exactly was she here? What did Kardal intend for her?

Cala asked a question, forcing her attention back to the conversation at hand. Fifteen minutes later everyone stood.

''I think we have a basic understanding of what we plan to do,'' Cala said brightly, although her eyes looked more haunted than happy. ''Kardal, you are pleased?''

He took his time in answering. Sabrina could practically read his thoughts. He wasn't pleased about any of this, but he didn't want to make his mother more uncomfortable. She wasn't surprised when he replied in a reassuring tone.

''Yes. Well pleased.''

He walked to the door and held it open. Cala went first. Rafe hesitated. Kardal murmured something to him that Sabrina couldn't hear. The American nodded and stepped into the hallway, leaving Kardal and Sabrina alone.

She collected her notes. "Are you all right?" she asked.

Instead of answering, he crossed to the window and stared out at the elaborate garden. Today he wore western garb—a well-tailored suit in dark gray with a white shirt and red tie. She wasn't used to seeing him dressed like a businessman. In some ways she found that she preferred Kardal in more traditional clothing.

He motioned for her to join him at the window, then pointed to the stone benches circling a large tree.

"This is a replica of a French garden," he said. "From some time in the eighteenth century."

"Early or late?" she asked, following his gaze and staring at the neatly trimmed shrubs.

"Late. When being a member of the royal family put one's head at risk." He touched the glass. "It takes more water than it is worth, yet I cannot find it in myself to instruct the gardeners to dig it up. Sheer folly."

"I'm surprised the heat doesn't destroy everything."

"It would, however in the summer the gardeners hang tarps to provide shade." He looked at her. "As I said, a waste of time and resource. There was an English maze on the other side of the palace. It had taken nearly fifteen years for the hedges to grow tall enough. Every fall and spring there were festivals in the maze. The children loved it."

"What happened?"

He shrugged. "During the Second World War there were more important concerns than caring for the maze. It, too, required protection from the desert summer. The decision was made to dig it up. The land is now a park. Something easier to maintain within the walls of the city.''

"This world is so different from any I've ever known," she said, wondering how it was possible that something so magical existed within a few hundred miles of the capital of Bahania.

"I hope you are pleased with it."

"I am." She smiled. "Although I still think you should return some of those treasures."

He dismissed her with a wave, then rested his hand on her shoulder. The slight weight was most pleasant, she thought dreamily, wishing that he would kiss her. While she was a little nervous about repeating their previous intimacy—the one she barely thought of anymore—she wouldn't mind repeating their kisses.

"I should have told you about the rest of the palace," he said. "You may change rooms if you wish."

"No. I already told you, I like where I am." She tilted her head. "Besides, if I'm your slave it would be inappropriate for me to choose my own room."

He slid his hand down her arm, making her tremble slightly. Her thighs felt too weak to support her weight. He stopped at her wrist where he fingered the gold slave bracelets binding her to him.

"Are you my slave?" he asked softly.

His eyes flared with a light she didn't understand. Although she often knew exactly what he was thinking, at this moment, Kardal was a mystery. A looming, slightly intimidating *male* mystery.

"I wear the bracelets," she hedged.

"I see that. But do you embrace their philosophy? Is your purpose in life to serve me? Will you do whatever you must to provide me with my heart's desire?''

It was as if he'd run a feather along the length of her spine. The hairs at the back of her neck rose and she felt goose bumps on her arms.

''Are you asking if I'll die for you?''

''Nothing so dramatic.''

His fingers continued to rub the bracelet with occasional forays onto her forearm and the back of her hand. She found herself wishing he would spend more time caressing her and less time polishing the gold.

''I simply wondered how far you would go to fulfill your duties. If you *are* my slave.''

''You mean there's a question? I'm free to leave if I want to?''

His dark gaze never left her face. She found herself leaning toward him, wanting to be closer. The need for him to kiss her grew until it was difficult to breathe. She wanted to be in his arms, feeling the male strength of him. She wanted the forgetfulness she found when they were together.

''Do you want to leave?'' he asked.

It was, of course, a completely logical question. She shouldn't have been shocked by the inquiry. Yet she was. Stunned, actually. Leave Kardal? Leave the City of Thieves?

She turned away from him until she was staring out the window. But she didn't see the beautifully landscaped garden. Instead different images filled her mind. The ride out into the desert. Her first view of the city. The way her father had barely bothered to greet her when she'd arrived in Bahania.

''Sabrina?''

She squeezed her eyes tightly closed. "I don't know if I want to go," she whispered.

"Then don't decide now," he suggested. "You are welcome to stay in the City of Thieves for as long as you like. Should you grow tired of our company, there is always the troll prince."

She opened her eyes and glared at him. "Talk about threatening me with something horrible."

"He may not be as bad as you think."

She shook her head. "With my father arranging things, he's probably worse." But she didn't want to think about that. Instead there was something more important to consider. "Why do you keep me here?"

Kardal smiled. "I come from a long line of men who collect beautiful things. Perhaps you are to be my greatest treasure."

If her knees hadn't been in danger of collapsing before, they certainly were now. Whether or not he meant them, she appreciated his words. Did he really think of her as a treasure? She'd never been valued before. In the past she'd only ever been in the way.

"Why did you lie to me about the city?" she asked. "Why didn't you want me to know there were modern conveniences?"

He grinned. "You are known to be spoiled and willful. I thought to teach you a lesson."

She knew he was teasing, but the words still stung. "You were wrong about me."

"I know."

"It was not your place to teach me anything."

He shrugged. "I am Kardal, the Prince of Thieves. My place is what and where I choose it to be."

She rolled her eyes. "Don't go all royal on me. I get enough of that with my brothers."

''You cannot change my nature.''

''No, but I can insist on retribution. I should be compensated for your lies.''

''They were little more than omissions.'' The humor fled his gaze. ''What would you like for your compensation?''

Her ability to read him was back. She knew exactly what he was thinking. That she would pick some bauble from the vault. Perhaps a priceless necklace or earrings.

Disappointment filled her. Just when she thought he finally understood her, she realized that he didn't. Frustration filled her voice. ''I'm not her,'' she insisted. ''I'm not the spoiled brat from the papers. Why can't you see that?''

And why did it matter that he didn't? Except she was afraid to answer that question.

He folded his arms over his chest. ''What are you talking about?''

''You. Right now you're assuming I want one of the treasures. Haven't you figured out that all the gold in the world can't buy me what I want?''

''What is it you want?''

She returned her attention to the garden. Tears filled her eyes, but she blinked them away. What was the point? Kardal wouldn't understand and she would never make herself so vulnerable as to speak the words. What would a man who had been well loved all his life know of not being wanted anywhere? She and Kardal shared a past of being torn between two worlds, but he'd always had his mother's support. She, Sabrina, had been unwelcomed by both her parents. What she wanted more than anything was to be loved for herself. To be accepted, welcomed, cherished.

He touched her cheek. "Ah, my beautiful desert bird, you are wrong about me. I may not know your heart's desire, but I can guess what you would like to compensate you for my omission of certain details about the castle."

"I doubt it."

"You have so little faith." He tapped one of her slave bracelets. "While it is your duty to please me in all things, it is my duty to protect you and care for you."

How she wanted the words to be true. "You haven't a clue about me."

He leaned close until his breath tickled her ear. "You are wrong and in the morning, I'll prove it."

Darn the man. He'd gotten it right in one. Sabrina thought about being annoyed at the fact the next morning when they left the city on horseback, but she was too happy to be riding in the desert to want to quarrel with Kardal.

"I feel as if I haven't been outside in weeks," she announced when they'd cleared the gates and cantered toward the rising sun. "This is wonderful."

Kardal didn't reply with words. Instead he urged his horse forward until they were racing across the smooth desert floor. The air still contained a hint of coolness, but that would soon burn away. It was spring in the desert, which meant the intense, killer heat lurked around the corner. But Sabrina didn't want to think of that. This morning there was only the rush of air in her face as her robes flew out behind her.

Kardal had appeared at her door shortly after five thirty that morning. He'd brought traditional clothing for her, explaining that in robes and a headdress she would not call attention to herself. She'd seen the sense of his suggestion right away. Now, flying over the sand as the sun rose higher above the horizon, she felt at one with the glory that was the desert.

After a half hour or so, they slowed to a walk. Sabrina glanced around at the endless empty land.

"You do know how to find your way back, don't you?" she asked, her voice teasing.

He met her gaze. "I have been out here a time or two. I believe I will manage quite well."

She remembered what he'd told her about growing up with his people. "Did you really spend months at a time out in the desert?" she asked.

He nodded and moved his horse closer to hers. "Until I was sent away to school, I lived in the desert. I only went to the city to visit my mother and grandfather, although sometimes he rode out with me as well."

He stared toward the horizon. Sabrina looked in the same direction and saw nothing, but she suspected Kardal could see a thousand adventures from his past.

"I would guess it's a difficult life," she said.

He looked back at her. "The desert does not tolerate weakness or fools. But it honors those who know its ways. I learned. The elders taught me, as did my grandfather. By the time I was eight, I could find my way across the length and breadth of the El Baharian and Bahanian desert."

He pointed to the north. "There is an oil field. You should be able to make out the pumps."

She squinted slightly and saw several metal pumps, along with a few low buildings.

"There are many more stations, such as that one. We take from the desert, but we do carefully. If there was an attack, the fragile ecosystem would be destroyed. After the Gulf War, oil fires raged for months. I do not want that for my land or my people."

Sabrina nearly pointed out that the land wasn't really his. It belonged to the two neighboring countries. However, while Kardal's territory might technically end at the borders of his city, in truth it stretched for thousands of miles. Neither King Givon nor her father could begin to control the vastness of the desert. It was here that Kardal reigned supreme.

"Perhaps it is time to change your title," she said. "You are no longer the Prince of Thieves."

He smiled. "Perhaps not, but I have no desire to acquire a new title."

He looked especially dangerous on horseback. She had seen him slip a gun into a holster before they left and she doubted that was his only weapon. Should they be attacked, Kardal was prepared. She'd been more than stupid heading out on her own the way she had. She was lucky to have been found alive.

"What are you thinking?" he asked.

"That I should have stayed home instead of going off looking for the City of Thieves. It wasn't my finest hour."

"But if you had not ridden into the sandstorm, I couldn't have taken you as my slave."

She wanted to say that wouldn't have been tragic to her at all, but the words got stuck in her throat.

"Yes, well, you did and here I am." She pulled at her head covering, removing it so the breeze could stir her hair. "Where exactly will the air force be located?"

Kardal gazed at her for a full minute, letting her know that he didn't *have* to accept her change in topic. But eventually he responded to her question.

"The main base will be in Bahania, but there will be airstrips all over the desert. I believe your brother, Prince Jefri, is in charge of the development of the air force."

Sabrina shrugged. "Maybe. No one has mentioned anything to me, not that I'm surprised. As a woman, I'm not considered bright enough to follow any kind of meaningful conversation."

"Obviously they have not spent much time in your company."

She smiled. "Obviously."

Their horses were practically bumping shoulders, they were so close. Sabrina liked the feeling of being next to Kardal. He was unlike anyone she'd ever met.

She stared out at the desert and tried to imagine a jet cutting through the silence. "The planes are going to be very out of place in the middle of all this," she said thoughtfully. "Are any pilots going to be stationed in the City of Thieves?"

"Probably not. They will be at different bases in the area."

"Is Rafe going to coordinate all that?"

"Yes."

"Because you trust him."

"He has given me reason."

In the process Rafe had become a rich, powerful

man. "I can't imagine him as a sheik in traditional robes. I would guess—"

Without warning Kardal reached toward her and grabbed her by the hair. He wrapped her long red curls around his fist and held her tight.

"Make no mistake," he growled, pulling her close, forcing her to lean toward him. "I may be willing to give you some freedom, but you are still mine. All the men of the city, including Rafe, have been warned."

He held her firmly, without hurting her. She listened to his words and stared at the fury in his face. Energy poured from him.

"What on earth is wrong with you?" she demanded. "I asked a simple question."

She supposed she should have been afraid, but she was not. Not of Kardal. Nor of his power or his possession.

He released her, then ran his palm along the length of her hair. His dark eyes glittered. "You asked about another man."

"We were discussing the air force. Rafe is in charge of security and getting the whole thing off the ground, so to speak. I didn't think inquiring as to whether or not he would be coordinating it for the city was out of line."

Kardal urged his horse to take a step away from hers. "I see." His voice was tense. "He is an American. Many of the women find him attractive."

Sabrina stared at him. "You can't be worried I'm going to do anything with Rafe. Kardal, I've avoided men and romantic entanglements all my life. Why would I give in now?"

He shrugged. "I do not know. We will speak of something else."

"Aren't we being Mr. Imperious?"

She wanted to pursue the topic, to find out what he thought she might do with his chief of security. She found she sort of liked the idea of Kardal being a little bit jealous. He'd never said how he felt about their kissing and the touching. She didn't want to be the only one affected by the experience. Apparently she was not.

Kardal felt restless as he approached Sabrina's room that evening. He normally didn't allow himself to feel ill at ease. Not since those first disastrous years at the American boarding school. He'd taught himself all he needed to know in order to fit in. Since then he had not experienced the nagging sensation of needing to be doing something else.

But the feeling was with him tonight. Perhaps it was because he was going to dine with his betrothed, speak with her, look upon her and perhaps touch her. But he would not be able to *have* her.

He had thought he might grow to like his future wife, although he had doubted the possibility. He'd thought they might find some common interests...eventually. He'd hoped to find her somewhat easy to talk to. He had never thought he would ache for her. Ache in a way that haunted his sleep until he was reduced to dreaming about her like a teenage boy dreaming of a film star.

He was the Prince of Thieves. Custom stated that it was an honor to be chosen for his bed. Like his grandfather before him, he had been careful not to abuse the privilege, taking only the willing and experienced. A young widow of an unhappy arranged marriage. A divorced computer technician trained in the west. No married women, no innocents. The Prince of Thieves did not defile virgins.

Nor did he take innocent princesses to his bed, however much he might like to. Which left him wanting and unable to satisfy that want. It was a most uncomfortable and unfamiliar circumstance. One he would like to change as soon as possible. Yet he could not. Not without setting both himself and Sabrina on a course from which there was no escape.

Did he want to marry her? Was the wanting simply a desire to tame a beautiful woman who challenged him, or was it something more? Love was an emotion created by women for their own use. It had no place in a man's world, except for the love a man might have for his children.

Kardal paused in the corridor and frowned. Children? Had he thought "children" and not just sons? Would he love his daughters as well?

The image of a red-haired girl riding fearlessly across the desert filled his mind. He heard her laughter and felt pride in the strong, sure movements of her small body. Yes, he thought in some surprise. He *would* love a daughter. Perhaps even as much as a son. Five years ago he could not have imagined such a thing. What had changed?

Not wanting to know the answer, Kardal stalked toward Sabrina's room, then entered without knocking. He found her curled up in a chair in front of the fire, comparing a gold and ruby bracelet with some pictures in a large textbook.

"I knew you would be unable to resist taking some of the treasure for yourself," he said by way of greeting. "As you see, it's easy to say 'give it back to the rightful owners' when it is not yours to own. But put the items in your hand and things change."

She laughed. "Good try, Kardal, but not even close to the truth. I'm trying to place the age of this piece. It's a blend of styles." She closed the book and set it on the table next to her chair, then put down the bracelet as well. "I'm thinking that the artist was originally from El Bahar or Bahania and then moved to Italy at some point. Maybe the late 1400s."

She rose and crossed toward him. "How was your day?"

She moved with the grace of a hawk—her body curved and swaying. The ancient rhythm of the female called to him so strongly it was all he could do to resist her siren song. The ache returned and with it the desire to claim her as his own. To be her first— her only. To touch and taste her innocence, then to change her into a woman and discover all the possibilities they could create together.

However, this was not the time. Kardal ignored the fire inside of him and instead handed her the saddlebags he'd slung over his shoulder.

"Your horse and your camel were found wandering in the desert. I believe these belong to you."

She laughed and took the bags from him. "My maps and diaries," she said with delight. "Not that I need them to find my way to the city now. Thank you for bringing them to me. And I appreciate knowing my animals are all right. I've been worried about them."

"They were found by a tribe of nomads right after

the storm,'' he told her, watching her open the saddlebags and pull out the contents. ''They have been safe since then. The tribe was making its way to the city and turned them over to me as soon as they arrived.''

He walked to the tray of refreshments Adiva always kept ready in Sabrina's room, then poured himself a glass of water. ''The information in the diary is mostly accurate, but the maps would not have brought you anywhere near the city.''

She flipped through the pages of the diary. ''You looked through my things?'' she asked, then glanced at him. ''What happened to me being a free woman and all that?''

He moved toward her and stared into her dark eyes. ''You had your chance at freedom, Sabrina, and you chose to stay in the City of Thieves. You are mine once again. To do with what I will.''

She shivered slightly at his words, but didn't turn away. ''You're forgetting about the troll prince. He might want me enough to fight for me.''

Kardal was grateful she didn't know the truth of her words. ''I know he would fall on a sword for you...if he knew you. But he will only know what he has read in the paper and what your father has told him. I think I am safe from him.''

''You can't know that,'' she said, but they both knew she was bluffing.

''Is it so awful, to be my slave?'' he asked.

She sighed and turned away. ''No. I'm not ready to return to Bahania and face my fate, but it's going to happen eventually. You have to know that, Kardal. You can't keep me here forever.''

''I know.''

He spoke the words even as he wondered what she would say if she knew the truth. That he *could* keep her forever, if that was what he desired. What exactly did Sabrina think of him? And why did he care? She was only a woman. His betrothed, if he chose to have her.

He tried to tell himself that it was only his desire for her that made him interested in her opinion, but a voice in his head warned him it might be more serious than that. He might be close to admitting that Sabrina's opinions, needs and happiness just might matter.

It was a most disconcerting state of affairs. One he wasn't sure he liked at all.

Chapter Eleven

The afternoon temperature was surprisingly warm. Sabrina found herself wishing her cloak weren't so thick and long, but she didn't have a choice. She also wished she weren't sneaking around the halls of the palace like some common criminal, but that wasn't to be helped.

As she had every day since Kardal had said she could begin cataloging the treasures of the city, she kept careful hold of the items bundled together under her cloak. When she met someone in the hall, she did her best to act as natural and normal as possible, praying no one would guess the truth. Kardal would kill her if he knew what she was doing.

Sabrina saw the door to her room at the end of the hall and sighed with relief. Another secret mission completed without incident. She slipped into her room and hurried over to the small trunks arranged against the far wall, next to the window. She'd requested them from Adiva, supposedly to store her personal belongings. Fortunately Adiva had never realized Sabrina had very little of her own to store.

Sabrina shrugged out of her cloak and let it fall to the ground. Lengths of white cloth were wrapped around her middle, holding her precious cargo safe. She released the tie in back, then pulled out three velvet bags and a small jade statue. In the bags were various gems and pieces of jewelry. The jade statue had once belonged to the emperor of Japan. At least the residents of the city had been equitable thieves, she thought humorously. They had stolen from nearly every country in the world.

After examining the contents of the first bag—the tiara from the reign of Elizabeth I, she opened one of the small trunks and deposited everything inside. Pausing to admire her bounty, she calculated that given just another month she could make quite a sizable dent in the—

"I know for a fact you can't be stealing," a woman's voice said from behind her. "So what *are* you doing?"

Stunned, Sabrina spun on her toes and watched as Cala stepped out of the shadows. Kardal's mother had been sitting in a chair in the corner, obviously waiting. She'd seen everything. Questions filled her dark eyes, but it was impossible to read her expression or know what she was thinking.

Sabrina felt the heat that instantly flared on her face. She knew she was turning the color of a pomegranate seed. Words failed her as she met the questioning gaze of someone she had come to think of as a friend.

"I..." She cleared her throat. "It's not what you think."

"I don't know what *to* think."

Sabrina glanced at the small chests lined up against the wall and knew their contents could damn her. "It's just—" She began speaking very fast. "Kardal won't listen to me and I don't understand his position. If the city no longer steals, why can't some of the treasures be returned? But he won't speak of it. He says that if those countries want their treasures, they should come and take them back themselves. Except how can they when they don't know that they're here?"

She twisted her hands together. "I see his point about some of the treasures. He's right about the Imperial Eggs. Who owns those? But there are other items that are easily identified. I pointed that out to him, but he just laughed. So I, ah, well, I decided to return some of the items myself."

She pointed to the chests. "Most of the things I've taken are from El Bahar and Bahania. Those are the easiest for me to identify and the ownership is clear. There are a couple of things that belong to the British crown and some other countries. They're not for myself," she finished, feeling lame.

Cala didn't say anything for a long time. She walked over to the open trunk and stared inside. "I think I told you my charity was first financed by stolen goods."

Sabrina exhaled in relief. Cala didn't sound angry. At least not *too* angry. "Yes, you'd mentioned that."

Cala smiled slightly. "My father indulged me. He gave me diamonds and rubies, emeralds the size of your fist. All stolen. He made sure that what he gave me was untraceable. They were at least a hundred years old and no one knew the rightful owners. So I went out and sold them. In time the charity grew large enough to attract attention. Donations now support the causes. But the seed money was the result of the city's tradition.''

She bent down and pointed to a diamond tiara. ''This has always been one of my favorites,'' Cala said. ''Where does it belong?''

''Great Britain. It was created for the first Elizabeth. She's wearing it in one of her portraits.''

Cala straightened and touched her arm. ''Kardal can be most difficult when he doesn't agree with someone. He tends to be stubborn to the point of wearing one down. I'm glad you've found a way to circumvent him.''

Sabrina tried to keep the surprise out of her voice. ''You're not going to tell him what I've been doing?''

Cala laughed. ''Kardal is the Prince of Thieves. Surely one with such a title should know when he himself is being robbed.''

She walked to the sitting area next to the fireplace and rested her hands on the back of the brocade chair. Today Cala wore her casual clothes, jeans and a T-shirt. Her long hair had been pulled back in a braid. She wore no jewelry save a pair of gold hoop earrings and a gold bracelet.

''What do you think of my son?'' she asked, staring into the fireplace, as if the unlit logs could show her a most desired truth.

The question surprised Sabrina. What did she think of Kardal? ''He confuses me,'' she said honestly, walking over to stand closer to her guest. "I agree that he can be stubborn, but he can also be kind."

She thought of the way he touched her. How he'd kissed her. He was a passionate man, but she wasn't comfortable saying that to his mother.

"You're his prisoner," Cala said. "Shouldn't you hate him?"

"When you put it like that, I want to say yes. But I don't. Mostly because at this point in time, I have no desire to go home. So as long as Kardal lets me, I will stay in the city, cataloging the treasures." She paused, then smiled. "Stealing those small enough for me to carry to my room, with the intent of returning them when I finally leave."

Cala moved around to the front of the chair and settled herself. Sabrina sat opposite her.

"Why must you go home?" Cala asked.

Why indeed? Sabrina had begun to suspect she might like to stay for a very long time. But to what end?

"My father and I aren't very close," she began carefully. "However, he does have certain expectations. I am betrothed."

Cala looked surprised. "To whom?"

"I don't know. I was so angry when he told me he'd arranged a marriage that I left before hearing the details. I refer to my future husband as the troll prince. My biggest fear is that my description is going to be accurate."

"Perhaps he will not be as bad as you fear." Kardal's mother leaned back in her chair.

Sabrina didn't want to think about that. She didn't want to think about not being with Kardal. She knew she was here on borrowed time and eventually she would have to leave. And then what? Would he miss her? Would he think about her after she was gone? Sabrina didn't understand her relationship with the Prince of Thieves. He could be both passionate and caring, funny and dictatorial. She still didn't know why he'd brought her here nor why he kept her. She wasn't his slave, yet a few days before he'd told her that she wasn't allowed to leave.

"I suppose if I were a different kind of person I would want to leave," she said more to herself than to Cala. "I should hate being held here."

"As prisons go, it *is* very nice," Cala teased. "One with a remarkable treasure."

Sabrina smiled. She supposed the problem was that she liked Kardal. Perhaps too much. He was unlike anyone she'd ever known. Perhaps her half brothers—also princes—had similar personalities, but she'd never spent enough time with them to know.

"There is also the matter of Kardal," Cala said, completely serious now. "I think you like him a little."

"Yes."

Sabrina was willing to admit to that. Perhaps even more than a little. He made her think of things, want things, she'd never thought of before. When she remembered how it was when he kissed her and touched her, she nearly went up in flames. But they had no future. She could not allow them to make love. However angry she might be at her father, she couldn't defy tradition or the monarchy. Not in that way. She had to stay a virgin. If she did not—if she allowed Kardal to make her his own—her father would kill him. She did not want to think of a world without the Prince of Thieves.

"Life is complicated," Cala said quietly. "After nearly thirty-two years, King Givon returns to the city and I can't think of what I'm supposed to say to him."

Cala's obvious distress distracted Sabrina from her own thoughts. "You invited him. Have you changed your mind?"

Cala looked at her and laughed. The sound was more strangled than humorous. "A thousand times. Every morning I wake up determined to withdraw the invitation. I reconsider that over breakfast, then around ten in the morning, decide to call and tell him not to come. Then I switch again." She shrugged. "It goes on like this all day and long into the night."

She leaned forward and wrapped her arms around herself. "What am I supposed to tell him?"

Sabrina tried to imagine what it must be like—to meet the father of one's child after a thirty-one-year absence. "What do you want to tell him?" she asked. "Is there any unfinished business between the two of you?"

"Too much. Perhaps none. I don't know." Cala shook her head. "I was so young. Just eighteen. I knew the tradition, the expectation. I knew there had to be heirs for the city, but in my heart I never thought my father would make me bed a stranger for the sole purpose of becoming pregnant. And if the resulting child was a girl, I would be expected to do it again and again, until I had a son."

She closed her eyes as if she could not stand to see into her past.

"I threatened to run away," she continued. "I believe I even threatened to kill myself. My father stood firm and told me I was the princess of the city. I had a responsibility to my people, my heritage and the future." She glanced at Sabrina. "At eighteen, I wasn't very moved by his arguments. But I had never defied my father, not significantly. So I didn't run away or take my life. I waited. Then one day he arrived."

Cala stood and walked to the fireplace. She touched the uneven stones. "In a room much like this one, I met him for the first time. He was old." She laughed. "He *seemed* old to me. He was at least thirty and he was married, with two sons and a third child on the way." She paused, then turned to face Sabrina. "He was kind. I could tell that the situation made him as uncomfortable as it did me. Perhaps more, because he had a wife and a family. But duty required that we produce a son together."

Cala fingered a slender gold chain on her wrist. "That first night we only talked. He said we had time and that he would not rush me. I had imagined being raped and abandoned so his consideration did much to ease my fears. Over the next couple of weeks, we became friends. When we were finally lovers, I was the one who went to him."

Cala turned away, facing the stones again. Her shoulders stiffened. "As I already told you, I was very foolish. I didn't think about his wife or his sons. I only thought of myself and how Givon made me feel when he touched me. I only thought of the laughter, how we danced together. How we made love each morning as the sunlight crept across the room. I fell in love with him."

Sabrina's chest tightened at the words. Cala

painted a picture of a doomed relationship, one in which an innocent young woman lost her heart to a man she could never have. Recognition made her squirm. Until this moment, she hadn't bothered to name her growing feelings for Kardal. She'd found him annoying and charming, dictatorial and a great companion. She knew that she liked him when he wasn't making her crazy. But she hadn't thought beyond that. She hadn't considered there might be danger for both of them.

"One month turned into two," Cala said. "I knew I was pregnant, but I didn't want to tell him because I didn't want him to leave." She glanced at Sabrina and smiled, despite the tears sparkling in her eyes. "It turns out he knew, but didn't want to say anything because he'd fallen in love as well."

Cala sighed and returned to her chair. "When we finally confessed all, I was so happy. Givon loved me and would never leave me. Because I was young I could convince myself that it would work out. I didn't think of his kingdom, his wife or his sons. I only thought of the man who was the light of my world."

"But he left," Sabrina said. "What happened?"

Cala fingered the slender bracelet again. "His wife arrived. She brought with her his newborn son and placed the child in his arms. 'Will you abandon us all?' she asked. I was standing in an alcove of the foyer and I heard her words. I saw the indecision in Givon's eyes and I saw the moment he chose." She glanced at Sabrina. "He didn't pick me."

Cala pressed her hands together. "I raged at him. I accused him of toying with me, of tricking me, of never loving me. I'm not proud of my behavior. My only excuse is that I was very young and in love for the first time in my life. I told him if he left I never wanted to see him again. He crushed the last piece of my heart when he agreed that would be best. Neither of us would be comfortable with an ongoing affair.''

She curled her feet under her and closed her eyes. ''In a final attempt to punish him, I told him I would forbid him to see his son. That the heir to the city would be raised by me and my father. Givon was not to approach the child ever. I made him swear.''

Cala opened her eyes and looked at Sabrina. ''So you see, I have many sins to atone for. I have kept Givon and Kardal apart all these years. I nearly destroyed a king and I did serious damage to his marriage. So what, after all this time, am I supposed to say?''

Sabrina had no easy answer. ''There were circumstances you couldn't control,'' she told Cala. ''You didn't seduce him from his marriage. Your father arranged it and Givon agreed. Aren't you the innocent party in all this?''

''Perhaps I was once, but not anymore. What about Kardal? He hates his father. How am I supposed to explain the truth?''

Sabrina bit her lower lip. She had thought her situation was complicated and difficult, but Cala's had been much worse.

''Do you want me to speak with him and try to explain?'' she asked.

Cala nodded. ''I'll admit I'm willing to take the coward's way out of this. I don't want to see the hate in my son's eyes when he finds out it was my fault he never knew his father.''

Sabrina didn't think Kardal was going to hate his mother when he found out the truth, but he wasn't going to be happy with the information. She wondered if it would change his attitude toward Givon. She wondered if her impossible story was going to have as unhappy an ending.

"So you see," Sabrina said that evening when she and Kardal had finished dinner. "It's not all Givon's fault. Cala made him swear he wouldn't contact you."

Kardal stared into his coffee, but didn't speak.

Sabrina shifted on the cushions in front of the low table. "Don't you believe me?"

His dark gaze settled on her. "I don't question that you are repeating the story as it was told. However, that does not make it the truth. Givon had a choice in the matter. He could have come to see me when I was at school. He could have invited me to visit him in El Bahar."

"But he'd given his word!"

Kardal raised his eyebrows. "He had given his word to his wife, yet he bedded another woman."

"That's not the same thing at all. His being with Cala was a matter of state."

She could tell that Kardal was not impressed by her argument. She wanted to reach across the table and shake him. Didn't he understand how important this was to her?

"What are you thinking?" he asked suddenly.

"Nothing." She stared at the napkin draped across her lap.

"Sabrina?"

She slowly raised her gaze. "I don't understand

why you're being so difficult," she admitted. "I'm not saying that Givon wasn't wrong, but there might have been mitigating circumstances. I think you should talk to your mother about this. Hear her side of the story."

"No." He rose to his feet. "I do not wish to discuss this anymore."

She stood, also. "Maybe that's not your choice. You said you wanted my help in this matter. You can't pick and choose when you want me to participate. Either we each have an equal voice in this matter or there isn't any matter between us."

He glared at her. She thought he might be trying to loom over her but she was too upset to notice.

"We are not equal in this circumstance or any other," he announced. "I am Kardal, Prince of Thieves."

"That's hardly news. I've been aware of your title practically since we met. And while we're on the subject of titles, I happen to be a princess, which makes us pretty much the same. And if you dare to get into some macho conversation about you being a man and me merely being a woman, I won't just scream at you, I will come into your room while you're sleeping and cut out your heart."

Thick silence filled the room. He glared down at her and she didn't even blink. Finally one corner of his mouth turned up.

"With what?"

"A spoon."

He chuckled. "Ah, Sabrina, don't fight with me."

His voice was low and husky as he moved around the table toward her. She recognized the danger signs and took a step back.

"I'm not fighting with you—*you're* fighting with me. If you would just listen with an open mind you would see the sense of what I'm s—"

His lips pressed against hers, cutting her off before she could complete her sentence. In the half second before passion claimed her she knew that Kardal would never see anyone's view but his own on the subject of his father. She could speak for a thousand years, but his mind had long since been decided.

Then she gave herself up to the glory of his body pressing against hers, the feel of his strong arms wrapping around her body, and the sweetness of his mouth claiming hers.

Being with him felt so incredibly right, she thought dreamily as she parted her lips to welcome him home. Fire began, as it always did, heating her breasts before settling between her legs. She longed to feel his strong hands on her body. She was embarrassed to admit—even to herself—that she wanted him to touch her again, the way he had before. She wanted to feel that amazing release and this time she wanted to put her hands on *his* body. She wanted to know what he would feel like and look like. She wanted him to take her.

Unable to resist the need growing inside of her, she rose on her tiptoes and pressed against him. If only there was a way to crawl inside of him, she might at last feel that she belonged. When his tongue touched hers, she answered with more intensity, following him back, tasting him, circling him, silently begging him never to stop. She ran her hands up and down his back, then boldly pressed her palms against his rear. The action forced his hips forward, thrusting his arousal against her belly.

She might never have seen a fully aroused man before, but she knew exactly what that bulge meant.

''Sabrina,'' he growled when he dragged his mouth from hers. His breathing was as heavy as her own. ''I want you.''

Unwelcome tears sprang to her eyes and before she could blink them away, they spilled onto her cheeks.

He frowned. ''What is wrong? You cannot be shocked by my declaration.''

''I'm not.''

A sharp pain thrust through her chest. She didn't know what it meant, nor could she state its cause. For some reason his words had stung.

I want you. Not—I love you.

Time froze. Sabrina couldn't breathe, couldn't think, couldn't do anything but stand there as harsh reality sank into her being.

She wanted Kardal to love her. But why? The situation was impossible. They could never be together. She was betrothed to someone else. Her father would never forgive, never understand. Kardal had responsibilities. She should be pleased that his desire was only physical.

But she wasn't. Because…because… Because she wanted more. She wanted Kardal to long for her heart as much as her body.

''Sabrina?'' He touched the tears on her cheeks. ''Why do you cry?''

She couldn't tell him the truth so she searched for something that would satisfy him. ''We can't do this,'' she said quickly. ''Be together physically. If you take my virginity you'll be killed, or at the very least, exiled.''

He surprised her by smiling. "How like my little desert bird to worry. But you must let that be my concern."

"I can't. I won't be responsible for something bad happening to you."

She felt confused. Her words were the truth; she didn't want him hurt in any way. Even though he didn't care about her the way she cared about him, she wanted only the best for him. So they couldn't become lovers.

She was both pleased and dismayed by his recklessness. Would he really risk his life to play in her bed? She thought that he might. Yet he wouldn't let her touch his heart.

She was confused and afraid.

"You have to go," she said, pushing him away. "We can't do this anymore."

For a number of reasons, some of which she would never explain.

Kardal watched as Sabrina turned from him. Fresh tears trickled down her cheeks. Her distress pleased him. Things with her were going exactly as he had planned.

"As you wish," he said formally. "I will see you in the morning."

He left her bedroom and headed for his office. Sabrina had obviously come to care about him. Her fear for his physical safety was proof. While at first he had resisted the betrothal, now he found that she was nearly the perfect wife. Her intelligence meant that their sons would be good leaders. She cared for the people and the castle. She had adjusted well to life within the city walls. The marital connection to Bahania was an advantage, of course. Her body aroused his and he didn't doubt they would do well in bed. Yes, she would be a fine wife. He would call King Hassan this very evening and tell him that he agreed to the match.

He paused in the hallway. When would he tell Sabrina? Not now, he thought. Not until after Givon's troublesome visit. Then he, Kardal, would be free to deal with her. They would plan the wedding together. She was a sensible woman and would be most honored to know that he found her worthy.

He remembered the fear in her eyes. How concerned she'd been about his safety. Perhaps she was even falling in love with him. He resumed walking, pleasure lightening his step. He would like Sabrina to love him, he told himself. She would love with the same fire and determination she brought to all her other occupations. Yes, he had chosen well.

Chapter Twelve

Kardal called the king of Bahania and was quickly connected with Hassan.

"You are sending her back," Sabrina's father said as soon as he came on the line. "I suppose I should not be surprised. She has never been very good for—"

"Be very careful about what you say," Kardal told the monarch in a low, deadly voice. "You speak of my future wife."

"What?" Hassan spluttered. "You can't mean to marry her."

"That is my intention. I have not informed her of the fact yet, so while you may go ahead with the plans, I wish you to keep them quiet for now."

"But—"

"You have been wrong about Sabrina," Kardal said. "Very wrong. I do not know her mother, but I can tell you your daughter is a treasure. She is loyal, determined, caring and even intelligent.''

"Yes, well, perhaps.'' Hassan sounded stunned. "Kardal, you realize that I can't vouch for her virtue.''

It was the final insult. Kardal rose to his feet, still clutching the telephone in his hand. "I will vouch for her virtue. I know that she has been untouched by any man.'' Then, because he couldn't resist tweaking the tiger's tail he added, "Until now.''

"Kardal!'' Hassan's outrage traveled the nearly thousand miles between them. "If you have defiled my daughter, I'll have your head on a platter.''

"Don't you think it's a little late to pretend you care?'' he asked contemptuously. "She is no longer your concern. Despite your neglect, she is all I desire in a bride. I accept the conditions of the betrothal. See that your staff prepares a wedding fitting for your only daughter and the Prince of Thieves.''

Then, without saying goodbye, he hung up the phone. Satisfied he'd captured Hassan's attention, he turned to the work waiting for him.

The helicopter appeared in the sky, first as a small bird, then growing larger and larger against the impossible blueness of the desert afternoon. Kardal stood alone, watching the security personnel that Rafe had assembled rather than the approach of his father.

Sabrina stood behind him, next to Cala who was practically hyperventilating from nervousness.

"I can't do this,'' Cala murmured, turning as if to leave.

Sabrina put a reassuring hand on her arm. "You'll

be fine. You look beautiful. He'll be too stunned to speak.''

She was telling the truth, Sabrina thought. Cala wore an elegant suit in deep purple. She'd swept her long hair up into a chignon. Diamond earrings glittered. They were her only adornment and didn't distract from the loveliness of her features.

Rafe stood to their left. He looked calm, but then Sabrina doubted anything ever ruffled the city's head of security. As for herself, she was prepared to do whatever she must to make this visit a success for Kardal. He was her main concern. Despite the times they'd talked about it, she knew he wasn't prepared for the impact of meeting his father for the first time. He said he didn't care, that Givon would have no effect on him, but she knew he was wrong.

Wind swept around them as sound filled the air. Sabrina tried to imagine what it would be like to meet a man who had ignored her for her whole life. What was Kardal feeling now? While she had problems with her own father, at least he had acknowledged her from the beginning.

But when the helicopter's doors were opened by two of Rafe's men and King Givon stepped out into the afternoon, she was surprised to find he didn't look like an evil man. He wore a tailored suit, which made him look more like a European businessman than the El Baharian king. He was a couple of inches shorter than Kardal, strong looking with dark eyes he'd passed onto his son. She saw wisdom lurking there, and sadness. There was something about the set of his mouth that made her wonder—for the first time—if he'd been suffering, too.

Had he missed the opportunity to get to know his

son? Kardal didn't believe Givon had stayed away because he'd given his word to do so, but Sabrina thought it might be the truth.

She sighed. There were no easy solutions to this situation. What a thing to realize in the first thirty seconds of Givon's visit.

The king stepped away from the helicopter. A single security agent stepped out after him. The pilot shut off the engine. As the noise wound down, Sabrina waited for Kardal to say something. As the leader of the city, it was his job to greet his father first. Yet he didn't move or speak.

Cala solved the problem by stepping around her son. She walked slowly and proudly toward a man she hadn't seen in over thirty years. Sabrina watched as his expression changed. Emotions followed each other—gladness, pain, longing. In that moment, Sabrina knew that Givon had loved Cala with all his heart.

"Welcome to the City of Thieves," Cala said warmly. "It's been a long time, Givon."

"Yes, it has. I had begun to wonder if I would ever see this place again."

Or you.

He didn't say the words, but he didn't have to. Sabrina heard them and judging from the hesitation in Cala's step, she heard them, too.

Sabrina's throat tightened as the older couple stood in front of each other. There was a moment of awkwardness as Cala thrust out her hand to shake his, then withdrew it. Givon took a half step forward. Cala cried out softly and opened her arms. The king stepped into her embrace.

The naked longing on his face was so private and

intimate that Sabrina quickly looked away. She glanced at Kardal. He, too, had found something else to interest him. What was he thinking? she wondered. Was he beginning to understand that no one person was to blame for their current circumstances?

Cala released Givon and stepped back. "It is time for you two to meet," she said.

The king approached his son and held out his hand. "Kardal."

Kardal nodded as he took his father's hand. "King Givon, welcome to the City of Thieves."

While Givon continued to smile, Sabrina saw the flicker of pain in his eyes. He had hoped for a more personal greeting.

Give it time, she said silently to herself. Kardal needs more time.

"And this, of course, is Sabrina. Perhaps you know her by her more formal title—Princess Sabra of Bahania."

Givon bowed to her. "Sabrina. A pleasure. I did not know you were staying here." Confused, he drew his brows together. "I spoke with your father just yesterday. He didn't mention anything."

"She is my guest," Kardal said quickly. "She is here, ah, studying our treasures."

"Oh, sure," she said with a laugh, hoping to ease some of the tension. "You say that now." She held up her arms, allowing the full sleeves of her dress to fall back and reveal the gold slave bracelets around her wrists. "That wasn't your story when you captured me in the desert and took me as your slave."

Givon looked shocked. "You took a Bahanian princess as a slave?"

Kardal shot her a look that warned her she would

answer to him later. Sabrina merely smiled. She didn't care if he was angry with her or not. All that mattered was that he'd forgotten about being distant toward his father.

"The story isn't quite so simple," Kardal said stiffly, still glaring at her.

"Actually it is," she said breezily to the king. "I'll give you all the details as I show you to your room. This way, Your Majesty."

Givon hesitated. He glanced at his son, then at Cala. Finally he nodded and moved next to Sabrina. "Please, call me Givon," he told her as they walked toward the open doors of the palace.

"I'm honored. I mean what with being a mere slave and all."

Givon looked at her. A smile played across his mouth. "I see that you have probably been more than Kardal bargained for, however you came to be in the City of Thieves."

Finding herself starting to like Kardal's father, she linked her arm through his. "I believe you are right. At times I frustrate him immensely. Let me tell you all about it."

Kardal watched them leave. He hated that Sabrina had been so easily blinded by his father's practiced charm. He would have expected more of her.

"What do you think?" Cala asked. Her voice quivered slightly as she spoke.

"I do not know what to think. It is always stressful to have a visiting dignitary in the city. The security concerns, the disruption of the routine."

Cala faced him, her eyes stormy. "Don't play that game with me, Kardal. I'm your mother. I'm not asking about the inconvenience of the visit, I'm asking what you think of your father. You've never seen him in person before, have you?''

Of course he'd known what she was asking but he hadn't wanted to answer the question. "No, I've never seen him before.''

At joint conferences, he'd always managed to avoid King Givon and the man had never sought him out. When there was direct conversation between the city and El Bahar, representatives had been sent.

"So, what are you thinking?'' she persisted.

"I don't know.''

In that he told the truth. Givon was not the devil, nor even a bad man. Kardal felt confused and angry and hurt. He couldn't explain why he felt such emotions, nor did he know how to make them go away.

"I'm sorry,'' his mother said, touching his arm. "I shouldn't have kept you apart all these years.''

"It wasn't your fault.''

She met his gaze. "Yes, it was. You don't want me to have any blame in the matter, yet so much of it is mine. I was young and foolish. When Givon returned to his family, I was destroyed. I ordered him out of my life, which was my right, but I also ordered him out of yours, which was wrong.''

Kardal shrugged off her concerns. "He had a wife and sons of his own. He would not have been interested in me.''

"I think he would have been. While it would have been difficult for him to openly acknowledge you, there could have been private meetings. You needed a father.''

He didn't like that her words made him ache for what he'd never had. "My grandfather was the best man I have ever known. He was more than enough.''

"I'm glad you think so and I hope it's true because I can't change the past. I can only tell you that I'm so sorry."

He pulled his mother to him and kissed the top of her head. "You have no need to apologize. What is done is done. The past is behind us."

"I don't think it is."

He straightened and looked at her. Color stained her cheeks and she wouldn't raise her gaze past his chest.

"What are you saying?" he asked.

She swallowed. "I'm afraid my worst fear has come true. Despite the time that has passed and different people we have become, I'm still very much in love with him."

Sabrina opened the door to the guest quarters she had prepared for the king. As Givon followed her, she gave the room a once-over, taking in the elegant sitting area with its view of the desert from all three large windows. A tile mosaic showed marauders thundering across the desert, arms held high, swords at the ready.

There were several sofas and occasional tables. Small pedestals had been set up around the room, each displaying a different treasure. She had chosen them herself.

Givon stepped into the center of the room. He glanced around, saw a small golden statue of a horse and crossed to the display. After picking up the animal, he turned it over, then looked at Sabrina.

"Are these to honor me or mock me?" he asked.

"I had wondered if you would recognize some of your country's history."

"I have a full-size version of this in bronze in my garden."

"Ah, that would make it easier then."

She cleared her throat. What had seemed like a good idea at the time suddenly didn't. Would King Givon be angry with her choices?

"I didn't intend to mock you…exactly."

Kind eyes crinkled as he smiled. "What was your intent?"

"Perhaps I simply wanted to get your attention."

"Something my son has wanted to do all his life?" he asked, then returned the horse to the pedestal.

Sabrina took a step toward him. "I'm sorry," she told him. "I didn't mean to make this situation any more difficult than it needed to be."

He crossed to the window and stared out at the desert. "I've always thought the city a most beautiful place," he said conversationally. "How much of the story do you know?"

"Some of it. Cala told me what happened but only you and she know the details. I doubt anyone knows the entire truth."

"I suspect you are correct."

He nodded. There was much gray in his hair and lines by his eyes, but he didn't appear to be an old man. There was still an air of vitality about him. Did Cala find the king attractive? Sabrina thought she might.

He turned away from the window and walked to the far end of the room where an ancient tapestry showed several women being gifted to the king of El Bahar.

"That was a long time ago," he said.

For a second Sabrina thought he meant the tapestry. "Yes, it was."

He kept his attention on the tiny stitches. "Choices had to be made. Difficult choices. Ones that no man should have to make. Is he very angry with me?"

She ached for his pain. "You'll need to discuss that with him," she murmured.

"I shall." He glanced at her over his shoulder. "But your lack of answer gives me the information I need. Kardal *is* very angry. I can't blame him. From his perspective, I abandoned him. He was never acknowledged. I had no place in his life. There were reasons, but do they matter?"

"No," she said before she could stop herself. "Children don't care about reasons. They only know the results of actions. When a parent isn't there, or makes it clear the child isn't important, then the child is hurt and feels betrayed."

He walked toward her, studying her. Sabrina kept her chin high and her shoulders square, but her manifestation of pride didn't erase the fact that Givon knew her life story. He would know that she wasn't just speaking about Kardal.

When he was standing in front of her, he took one of her hands. "I was a fool. Partly because I was hurt when Cala demanded that I never contact her or her child again, and partly because it was easier. I could suffer silently when I was alone, and no one else had to know. If I had acknowledged Kardal, questions would have been asked. Questions that I did not want to answer."

He squeezed her fingers, then released them. "Expediency is never the answer. I should never have promised Cala. Or having promised, I should have broken my word. Kardal was more important than both of us.''

Sabrina followed him to the sofa and settled next to him. "King Givon, it's not too late. Seeing the truth is the first step in making it right."

"This can never *be* right."

"Perhaps, but it can be better than it is now." She leaned toward him. "Why did you come if not to make peace with the past?"

He was silent for a long time. "I came because I could no longer stay away. The pain of being without was too great. I wanted to know if there was a second chance." He shrugged slightly. "Perhaps with both of them."

"Cala, too?"

Was it possible that after all this time they would rekindle their romance? Sabrina felt pleased at the thought.

King Givon smiled. "You think I am too old?"

"No. I think things are going to be very interesting around here."

"Kardal will not approve."

"Perhaps not at first," she admitted. "But I don't think it's going to be his decision. His mother can be just as determined."

"Tell me about Kardal. What is he like?"

She drew in a breath. "Obviously the best thing would be for you to get to know him yourself. But until that happens, I can tell you that he is a wonderful man. You'll be proud of him."

Givon shook his head. "I have no right to pride. I had no part in forming the man he has become. Is he a good leader? Do his people respect him?"

"Yes to both. He does not shy away from difficult

decisions. He is strong, yet fair. You know about the joint air force with Bahania?''

''Yes. El Bahar will be a part of that as well. We will contribute financially as well as having airfields out in the desert.'' He touched her slave bracelets. ''I suspect you and Kardal met under most unusual circumstances.''

She laughed, then told him about getting stranded in the desert. ''He brought me here, so I have found the City of Thieves after all.''

''You have not known him very long, yet you seem to understand him.''

''I try. In some ways we make each other crazy, but in other ways we get along perfectly.''

King Givon's expression turned knowing. Sabrina shifted uncomfortably. ''It's not what you think,'' she said, refusing to remember the kisses they had shared. ''We're friends. There's not all that much royalty running around so we understand each other.''

''Does he know what he has in you? Does he know what is in your heart?''

Heat flared on her cheeks, but she refused to be embarrassed. ''I assure you, there's nothing to know.''

''Ah. So you have not yet admitted the truth even to yourself.''

''There's nothing to admit.''

And even if there was, she thought to herself, and there wasn't, it all meant nothing. Because no matter what she might dream about, reality was very different. Her destiny lay elsewhere, and not here with the Prince of Thieves.

* * *

Sabrina did not return to her own quarters after leaving King Givon in his. She had too much to think about. Too much to consider.

The king had been wrong, she told herself for the hundredth time. He'd been wrong about her having feelings for Kardal. She couldn't think of him as anything but a friend because that's all he was to her. A good friend. Someone with whom she had a lot in common. Someone…

She hadn't realized where she'd been walking to until she found herself in the anteroom overlooking the formal garden. Spring was rapidly approaching summer and already the gardeners had hung wide awnings to protect the delicate plants from the strong desert sun.

Sabrina moved to the window and pressed her fingers against the three-hundred-year-old glass. It was less smooth than what one could buy today, and thicker. But it had a beauty no factory could produce. She thought of the treasures in the vaults and the magnificence of the castle. There was so much to see and understand here in the city. She could happily make it her life's work.

And in a few short weeks, she would never see it again. She knew her time here was limited. She felt like Dorothy in *The Wizard of Oz,* watching the time of her life flow like the sands in an hourglass. How long before her father insisted she return home? How long until she had to pledge herself to the troll prince? How many more days in the City of Thieves?

She ran her finger along the ledge, where lead held the glass in place. A sharp point caught the skin of her thumb, piercing her. She winced and pulled back.

Instantly a single drop of blood formed in the shape of a teardrop. As if her body wept.

But not for the city, she thought as she finally accepted the truth. While it intrigued her and excited her imagination, she would not miss the castle nor the streets nor even the treasure when she left. She would miss the man who was the heart of the city. The man who had stolen *her* heart.

She'd fallen in love with the Prince of Thieves.

Sabrina rubbed at the drop of blood, as if by erasing it from her body, she could erase the truth. Except the truth could no longer be denied. She was in love with a man she would never see again. Even if she went to her father and confessed her feelings, she knew he wouldn't care. He had married for the sake of his country twice and he would expect no less of her. Perhaps if he cared about her, she might have a chance, but he did not. He had made his feelings abundantly clear.

Kardal, she thought suddenly. She could go to Kardal and tell him. Perhaps he had come to care for her as well. They could run off together and…

And what? Where would they go? Even if he *would* leave the city for her, she could never ask that of him. He was as much a part of this place as the castle itself, or the sand of the desert.

So he would stay where he belonged and she would return to Bahania to marry someone else…a man who could never hold her heart because she had already given it away.

Chapter Thirteen

"The security area is through here," Kardal said the next afternoon, trying to sound more gracious than he felt.

After more than twenty-four hours of ducking his father and when that wasn't possible, making sure they weren't ever alone so they would have to speak directly to each other, he was finally trapped with Givon.

After lunch, both his mother and Sabrina had claimed appointments that could not be broken. Even Rafe had deserted him, stating he had an important staff meeting to attend. Givon had been left to Kardal, and Kardal didn't doubt for a second that there was a conspiracy afoot.

However, there was no time to round up those involved and complain. Instead he had to show his father the security section of the castle.

"We have taken advantage of improved technology," Kardal said as they stepped through wide glass doors that opened silently, admitting them into an alcove. When the doors closed behind them, they did so with an audible *snick* of an activated lock.

"As you can see," he said, indicating the glass room, "we are trapped. The glass is bulletproof and explosion resistant. Should we try to make our way into the security area without proper clearance, forces on duty will respond within thirty seconds. To prevent us from trying something aggressive in that short period of time, a nontoxic sedative will be dispensed into the atmosphere." He pointed to small spray nozzles extending down from the ceiling.

Givon looked around at the glass enclosure. "Most impressive," he murmured. He glanced at Kardal. "Do you plan to sedate me?"

Kardal ignored the humor in the other man's voice along with the question. "The doors are released by a combination of thumbprint and retinal scan."

He touched the security pad and stared into the scanner. Seconds later the inner doors opened and they stepped into the heart of the operation.

Television screens lined one entire wall of the huge room. Remote cameras sent back views of every oil pump in both El Bahar and Bahania, except those within twenty miles of the main cities.

"All the information gathered is collected here," Kardal said, walking over to a row of monitors opposite the television screens. "We regulate oil flow, check for any potential safety problems with the equipment and notify the nearest crew if something breaks. Over here—" he led the way to a different cluster of monitor screens "—we use infrared to find trespassers. And of course the remote cameras provide us with the majority of our information.''

Givon crossed to those screens and watched a group of nomads seen on one television. They rode camels and appeared not to notice the large oil pump behind them.

''Internal security?'' he asked.

Kardal nodded. ''They patrol the desert regularly. We also have helicopter patrols, but it's not enough. The area is too large and those who wish to make trouble are growing more sophisticated. The technology which aids us, assists them as well.''

Givon circled the room, pausing to speak with several technicians. Kardal stayed still, watching his father, wishing the visit would end quickly. He didn't like being uncomfortable, but that was how he felt around King Givon. If they weren't discussing matters of mutual political and economic interest, he didn't know what to say.

His father was not as he had expected. Kardal hadn't realized he even *had* expectations until they were not met. He'd thought Givon would be more arrogant and brusque. Instead he found the king to be a thoughtful man who didn't pontificate or insist his opinion be the only one.

He wore western-style dress rather than traditional robes. He could have been a visiting executive rather than a reigning monarch.

Givon returned to his side and smiled. ''You are doing an extraordinary job. Your unique blending of traditional methods with new technology has given your security an edge.''

Kardal led them out of the security monitoring station and into one of the conference rooms. Unlike the ones by the old throne room, this space was completely modern and impersonal.

"The City of Thieves receives a percentage of the oil profits from both your country and Bahania. In return we provide security for the oil fields. It is to our advantage that there is no trouble, or any delays in production."

Givon took a seat on the far side of the table. "I agree, but there are degrees of excellence. You aim for the top."

Kardal settled in the chair opposite his father. Was that pride in Givon's voice? Kardal felt both pleased and annoyed.

"You have a natural affinity for leadership," Givon continued.

"I suppose you want to take credit for that," Kardal growled before he could stop himself.

"Your grandfather raised you and you are now your own man. I think any praise should be shared equally between you and him." Givon paused, then pressed his hands on the table. "Whatever you might have inherited from me could have easily come to nothing. So no, I do not believe I am entitled to take credit for your success. I will admit to feeling some sense of pride, however misplaced. That is a father's right. Even a father who has done as badly as me."

Kardal didn't know how to answer that. He wanted to storm out of the conference room and not have this conversation, however he didn't think he would. He and Givon had been heading toward this moment ever since Cala had issued the invitation to the king.

There was a pitcher of water in the center of the table, along with several glasses. Givon turned one of them right-side up and poured the water. He took a sip.

"I should have come sooner," he said, studying Kardal.

"Why? What would have changed?"

Givon shrugged. "Perhaps nothing. Perhaps everything. We will never know."

"You wouldn't have received any better security service."

Givon set the glass on the table. "This is not about your work, Kardal. It is about you and I. However much you do not wish us to discuss these matters, we must. I can tell you that I have learned over my life that some things can be delayed, but few can be escaped entirely. I don't blame you for being angry with me."

Kardal continued to sit in the chair. He forced his features to remain calm, but both activities took all his strength of will. He wanted to spring to his feet and rage against the man sitting across from him. He wanted to shout his frustration and demand Givon explain his arrogance in coming here after all this time. He wanted to yell that his father was nothing to him—less than dust and no words were going to change how he felt.

Anger, frustration and deep, ugly hurt filled him. Emotions he'd never acknowledged before bubbled to the surface. He could barely breathe from the intensity of it. Sabrina had warned him, he thought suddenly. She had said he must prepare himself for what would happen when he finally met his father. That if he didn't consider the impact the meeting might have, he could be overwhelmed.

She was more wise than he had been willing to admit.

"I know you are angry," Givon said.

"Anger is the least of it." Kardal spoke between clenched teeth.

"Yes. That must be very true. I wish…" He sighed. "I want to explain. Are you willing to listen?"

Kardal wanted to shout that he was not. But he refused to storm out of the room like an angry adolescent. Instead he offered his father a curt nod and wished fiercely that Sabrina was with him. He could use her gentling presence.

"Thank you." Givon leaned back in his chair. "I am sure you know the story of how I came to be here. When your grandfather produced no male heirs, tradition dictated that either King Hassan or I provide Cala with a son. The tradition also stated that the king of Bahania and the king of El Bahar would alternate. The last time there had been no heir had been over a hundred years before. It was my turn, so I left my wife and sons and came here."

"I am familiar with the history of the city," Kardal said impatiently.

"Perhaps, but this isn't just about history. This is about the people involved. We are not talking about cold facts. I was married, Kardal. I had two sons. I cared for them very much. None of them wanted me to come here. *I* did not want to come here. The thought of seducing an eighteen-year-old girl was repugnant to me." He paused and stared directly at Kardal. "I was the same age you are now. How would you feel about taking one of the elder's daughters?"

Kardal shifted uncomfortably. He understood his father's point at once, but didn't want to admit that. "Go on," he said instead.

"Whatever you may think of me," Givon continued, "know that I was never unfaithful to my wife. She was pregnant with my third son. We were happy together. But duty called. I came to the City of Thieves and met Cala."

As he spoke her name, Givon's entire face changed. A softness filled his eyes and the corners of his mouth turned up. Kardal frowned, refusing to allow the old man's emotions to sway him.

"She was not what I expected," Givon said simply. "She was beautiful, but it was more than that. She might only have been eighteen, but she and I got along from the first. I found myself mesmerized by her, feeling things for her I had never felt for anyone before. I had arrived with the intention of doing my duty and leaving. But after meeting her, I could not imagine simply taking her into my bed without some kind of understanding between us. We spent time together and began to enchant each other."

He leaned forward and picked up his glass. "I was a king, a powerful man, completely enthralled by a slip of a girl. I felt like an idiot and more happy than I had ever been in my life. I loved her and in loving her realized I had never truly loved my wife. Not the same way. So Cala and I decided that I would stay."

Kardal stiffened in his seat. "You were going to stay here?"

Givon took a sip of water, then nodded. "I did not want to leave her. What other choice did I have?"

"But you didn't stay."

"No." He set his glass on the table. "A month

slipped into two. I knew I would have to give up my monarchy, my sons, everything. I was prepared to do so until my wife arrived. In my absence, my third son had been born. She placed the infant in my arms and asked if I was planning to abandon them all. In the baby's eyes I saw my future and knew it could not be here. I had been playing a game but it was time to return to my responsibilities. The people of El Bahar mattered more than the state of my heart.''

Kardal didn't want to think about how difficult the leaving would have been. He knew his mother well enough to know that she would not have handled the disappointment with quiet dignity.

''Cala told you never to come back,'' he said, believing the words for the first time in his life.

Givon nodded. ''I agreed, but I had no intention of keeping my word. I promised I would return. But within a year, my wife had died. I was left alone with three young boys. I couldn't leave them to be with you and Cala. They were the heirs, so I could not take them with me, nor would I have forced my oldest son to rule at such a tender age. I sent word to Cala asking her to bring you and join me. She said that you were to be the Prince of Thieves and had to be raised within the city walls. I think she was still very hurt and angry. I don't blame her. Mine was not a world she trusted. I was not a man she trusted.''

Kardal didn't know what to think. He hadn't wanted to hear his father's words, but now that he had, he couldn't erase them from his mind. Nothing was as he had imagined.

''She never hated you,'' he said before he could stop himself. ''She never spoke ill of you.''

''Thank you for telling me.'' Givon's dark eyes

turned sad. ''For myself, I never stopped loving her.''

That was more than Kardal wanted to know. He mumbled an excuse to his father and quickly left the room. Hundreds of thoughts tumbled around and around in his brain, but there was only one that mattered. He had to get to Sabrina. Once he was in her company, everything would be better.

He hurried down the halls of the palace, slowing only when he reached her door. He stepped inside without knocking.

She sat at the table, several old books opened in front of her. She looked up at him and smiled. He took in the long red hair tumbling around her shoulders, the welcoming light in her eyes, the curves of her body more hidden than revealed by the cotton dress she wore.

She rose and walked toward him. ''Kardal. What's wrong?''

''I spoke with my father.''

He tried to say more, tried to explain how difficult it had been to find out that Givon wasn't the devil at all, but a man who had been forced, by circumstance, to make difficult decisions. Kardal didn't feel the older man was absolved from blame. Givon still could have contacted him. But the areas of blame and guilt were less clear than they had been.

Sabrina watched the emotions chasing across Kardal's face. His confusion and pain called to her as clearly as if he'd spoken her name. She didn't know exactly what had been discussed, but she could guess.

Her heart ached for the proud man standing in front of her. The man she loved but could never be with. Without considering the wisdom of her actions, she crossed to him and wrapped her arms around him. He hugged her back. Their bodies pressed together, comforting them both. When he lowered his mouth to hers, she had no thought of refusing him or pulling back.

The passion was as instantaneous as it was familiar. Sabrina felt her bones begin to melt as she pressed against Kardal. He was all hard planes to her soft curves and she thought about how right it was to be in his embrace. His lips, always tender yet firm, pressed against hers. There was something hungry about his kiss. This time he didn't tease her or play by nibbling. Instead he plunged inside of her, circling her, taking her as if she were necessary for his very being. His desire—almost a desperation—fueled her own growing excitement. She clung to him, letting him take what he would and then following the movements of his tongue, showing him how much she wanted as well.

His large hands moved up and down her back. One slipped to her derriere and he pressed her to him. She arched her hips forward, and settled her belly against the thickness of his arousal. As she felt his maleness, she shivered from equal parts of excitement, curiosity and apprehension.

"Sabrina," he breathed, breaking the kiss long enough to press his mouth against her jaw. He bit the tender skin just below her ear, then licked her lobe and made her squirm.

When she moved, his need flexed, as if he'd enjoyed the contact. She suddenly wanted to see him without his clothes. She wanted to touch him and understand what happened between a man and a woman. It wasn't that she didn't have theoretical knowledge, it was that her practical skills were sadly lacking.

Just the thought of them lying naked together was enough to make her breath quicken. Her breasts were already swollen and tender. Her nipples pressed against her bra in a way that was almost painful. Between her legs dampness and pressure grew, making her wish he would touch her there as he had before.

She wanted him. She wanted them to make love. Her bodily needs blended with her emotional connection to this man. Combined they were a force impossible to deny.

"I want you," he said, kissing his way down her neck. "Sabrina, I need you."

I love you.

But she only thought the words. She didn't speak them. For loving Kardal would only bring heartache.

"We can't," she whispered even as he found the zipper at the back of her dress and tugged it down. "Kardal, I'm a virgin."

Her dress slipped off her shoulders. She pressed the fabric to her breasts. He cupped her face in his hands and gazed into her eyes. She saw the tightness of his expression—the need flaring there.

"I want you," he repeated. "It would be worth any price to touch you, to teach you, to make love with you. Please, do not deny me the glory of making you mine."

Had he demanded, she might have found the strength to say no. Had he teased or cajoled she would have had some recourse. But the dark pleading, the raw need he exposed to her left her unable to deny him anything. Even when she knew they would both pay a price for this moment.

He reached for the dress she clutched to her chest. Reluctantly she released the cloth and he drew it away. The garment fell soundlessly to the floor.

Underneath she wore silk panties and a bra. The peach lace exposed as much as it concealed. Before Sabrina could react to being nearly naked in front of him, Kardal glanced down at her and caught his breath. He made an audible sound—a gasp of pleasure. As if her body were as beautiful as the ancient treasures that filled the castle. Reverence joined need in his eyes. Suddenly she wasn't embarrassed. She was proud to be the woman he desired.

"I would die for you," he breathed and stunned her by dropping to his knees.

Sabrina didn't know what to think. Kardal kneeling before her? What did it mean? But before she could figure out an answer, he pressed an open-mouthed kiss to her belly and all rational thought fled. Sparks seemed to flare inside of her, leaping through her body in all directions. Goose bumps erupted on her arms and legs and her breasts swelled even more.

He ran his tongue around her belly button before dipping inside. A trembling started in her thighs, then moved both up and down, making it nearly impossible for her to stay standing. Without thinking, she pressed one hand to his shoulder and the other on his head. She slipped her fingers into the thick layers of his dark hair and gasped when he moved lower, kissing her just above the elastic of her panties. Then lower still, nibbling along her thighs.

It tickled. It was perfect. She trembled so much,

she could only remain upright by clinging to him. He wrapped one of his arms around her waist, holding her in place. Kisses and bites and tantalizing licks—all up and down her thighs. Finally he tugged at her panties, drawing them down her legs.

She was confused by what was happening. Shouldn't they be in bed? Shouldn't it be dark in the room? Or at least more dim than it was with sunlight streaming in through the windows? They were up high enough in the castle that no one could see in, but she felt exposed and awkward as he urged her to step out of her panties. Exposed and very vulnerable.

"Kardal, I don't think we should—"

He kissed her. Not on the stomach or the leg, but in that most private place. A kiss of lips and tongue that made her stop breathing. Pleasure shot through her with an intensity she'd never felt before. Without meaning to, she parted her legs so he could do it again. She held on tighter and prepared herself for the next wonderful kiss.

He did it again, parting her curls and licking her deeply, finding that single point of pleasure and flicking it with his tongue.

She cried out and her knees gave way. He caught her easily and pulled her against him.

"Sweet desert bird," he murmured, shrugging out of his suit jacket, then gathering her in his arms and carrying her to the bed. "I wish to make you fly."

She had no objection. She had no will. She would have done anything he told her, said anything, promised the world. If only he would touch her that way again.

He lowered her onto her mattress, then reached behind her and unfastened her bra. When she was completely naked, he settled next to her on the bed and bent down to take one of her nipples in his mouth.

Sabrina had never felt the soft, damp warmth of a man's mouth on her sensitized breasts. She'd never felt the gentle tugging that pulled all the way down to her most feminine place. She hadn't thought she was capable of feeling more, but she'd been wrong.

Over and over he licked her breasts, discovering the shape of them, the sensitive places. His fingers worked on the opposite nipple, making her pant and toss her head. The bottoms of her feet burned, her toes curled into the bedspread.

She didn't know how long he touched her that way. Finally, when every muscle in her body had tensed with anticipation of a release—any release— he began to move lower.

This time she knew what to expect. This time she nearly wept with the glory of anticipating his tongue on her body. He moved between her thighs and she parted to admit him. When he lowered his head, she caught her breath.

Then screamed his name. He licked her from the entrance of the place that would forever make her his to the tiny point of pleasure hidden within her slickness. Again and again. First slow, then moving faster. She clutched at the bedspread, unable to catch her breath or focus or do anything but exist through the most amazing pleasure she'd ever experienced.

No one else could ever do this to her, she thought hazily as her body tightened even more. No one would ever touch her body or her heart the way Kardal had. She wanted to tell him. She wanted to cry out that she loved him, that she would always love him. But words required air and she could not breathe. She couldn't do anything but hang on for the sudden rush that overwhelmed her.

The whisper of a ripple slipped through her. Then another and another until she was no longer in possession of herself. It was perfect. It was better than her wildest fantasy. It was impossible, and yet the pleasure continued until she was limp, exhausted and more content than she'd ever been in her life.

She opened her eyes and found Kardal looming over her. Let him loom, she thought with a smile. Right now he could do anything he wished and she wouldn't protest.

"There's more," he murmured, kissing her neck, then sitting up and unfastening his tie.

As she watched, he removed the length of silk, then his shirt. Next he pulled off shoes and socks, finally standing to unfasten his trousers and step out of them, along with his briefs.

In a matter of seconds, he was as naked as she. Naked and…oh, my. She tried to notice how his honey-colored skin seemed to reflect the light, but she could not. Instead her gaze was drawn down the thin line of hair bisecting his belly, lower until she gazed upon the proof of his arousal.

He was beautiful in a way only a man desiring a woman would be beautiful. He smiled slightly as he knelt on the bed and lightly kissed her still-tight nipples.

"I would ask you to touch me, but the results would be most disastrous. I find myself in the embarrassing situation of having to admit that my control is not what it should be." He stroked her face. "I would like to tell you that it is because I have not been with a woman in a long time, which is true, but the truth lies elsewhere.''

He reached between her legs and began to rub her sensitized flesh. Instantly tension began to fill her.

''It is you,'' he said lazily, slipping one finger inside of her. ''You, Sabrina. You make me want with a fire I cannot control.''

She hadn't thought it was possible for her body to need him again so quickly, but in less time than it took him to finish his sentence and her to clutch the words tightly to her heart, she found herself ready for him to take her back to paradise.

''Kardal,'' she breathed, opening her arms.

A warning sounded in her head. A small voice whispered that once done this act could not be recalled. They would both be changed forever. But she couldn't pull away or demand that he stop. She wanted him. She *needed* him. She loved him and she wanted to lose her innocence in his arms.

He didn't take much persuading. He slipped between her thighs and she felt him pushing against her. She was slick from her recent release and at first he moved inside her easily. But then her body began to stretch to accommodate him. Pressure increased— a different kind of pressure from the pleasure she had felt before.

He paused and reached between them, finding her point of pleasure and rubbing it. She was quickly aroused. He pushed in a little more. And so they went until he reached the barrier that defined her innocence. With a kiss of apology, he pushed through, making her wince at the slight pain.

And then he was inside of her. Supporting himself on his arms, he began to move in and out of her in a rhythm as old as time itself. She clung to him, feeling her body respond to each thrust. Tingling began. Odd flares of heat filled her. She found herself pulling him closer, straining toward him. Wanting more, wanting him. Knowing that—

Deep contractions started low in her belly. They moved out like ripples in a pond. She was caught unprepared and found herself drowning in the sensation.

"Yes," Kardal growled, thrusting in her again and again. With each movement, another ripple began. Then he stiffened and called out her name. She felt the powerful shudder that shook his body.

They lay tangled together until their breathing slowed. He touched her face and smiled at her. "You are mine," he told her. "I have made you so and nothing will ever change that."

Chapter Fourteen

Sabrina lay curled in Kardal's arms and tried to think only of how contented she felt. How this had been right from the very first moment he had touched her.

She had finally done it—she was no longer the innocent virgin she had been just an hour before. The realization surprised her because it didn't frighten her. She'd been so terrified that if she allowed herself to want a man, she would turn into her mother—going from relationship to relationship, her life ruled by sex.

She recalled a conversation she'd overheard between her mother and another woman. They'd talked about how being with one man made them want to be with all of them. Sabrina hadn't understood their feelings then and she still didn't. As far as she was concerned, she would be happy to have Kardal be the only man in her life for always.

For so long she had tried to be unlike her mother and now she knew that she'd succeeded. Perhaps they had always been different and she had never noticed before.

"What are you thinking?" Kardal asked as he gently stroked her hair.

She snuggled closer, savoring the heat of his body and the way the hair on his legs tickled her skin. "That I don't have to worry about turning into a wanton."

He was silent for a moment, his expression confused, then he smiled. "You were worried that making love with me meant you were like your mother. You see that you are your own person instead?"

She nodded, her chin brushing against his bare arm. "I have no interest in another man."

He shifted so that she was on her back, her head pressed into the pillow. He bent down and kissed her.

"That is as it should be," he said arrogantly. "I have told you—you are mine. No one else will ever have you." He grinned. "Not even the troll prince."

His words broke the fragile protective wall she'd erected. While they'd been making love she'd been able to ignore the fear gnawing at her but it crashed into her, filling her with apprehension.

"Kardal, you can't joke about that," she said frantically, pushing him away and sitting up. She pulled the sheet with her so that she could cover herself. "You don't understand."

He sat up as well. "Do not trouble yourself. All will be fine."

"Will it? What do you think will happen when my

father finds out about this? And the troll prince? He's not going to be happy that I'm not a virgin.''

Panic filled her. She tugged the sheet free and wrapped it around herself while she hurried to her closet.

''Why are you pretending this doesn't matter?'' she asked as she reached for her clothes. There had to be a solution. What would her father do to Kardal? Would he simply threaten him or would there be actual violence? And what about the troll prince? What kind of man was he? If he had a temper…

She spun back to face Kardal. Tears burned at her eyes. ''You have to do something. Go away. Maybe just for a little while until all this blows over.'' She pulled on panties and a bra, then slipped into a sleeveless dress.

Kardal didn't seem to appreciate the seriousness of the situation. Instead of getting up and dressing, he stretched out on the bed and beckoned her to his side.

''I have told you,'' he said lazily. ''You need not worry. I will be fine.''

He was so handsome, she thought as the first of her tears fell. So strong and such a good leader for his people. She'd never met anyone like him and she never would again.

Sabrina leaned over him. ''Kardal, you have to listen to me.''

He touched a tear on her cheek. ''You cry for me?''

''Of course.'' She wanted to shake him. ''Don't you get it? I love you and I don't want anything bad to happen to you.'' The tears fell faster. ''Dammit, Kardal, get up, get dressed and get out of here.''

She hadn't thought about what would happen if she confessed her feelings, but she never expected him to sit up and start laughing. His reaction was so unexpected, she stopped crying and stared open-mouthed at him.

He kissed her cheek. "How sweet you are to worry about me." A smile curved his mouth. "And I'm glad that you love me. It is always important for the woman to love the man. Loving him makes her happy. Obedient as well, but I doubt you will ever be that. Still, you have many good qualities and you will be an excellent wife for me."

She heard the words. They physically entered her ears and moved to her brain. She was even somewhat confident that he was speaking English. Yet nothing made sense.

"W-what?" she asked, barely able to form the question.

"Haven't you guessed?" His smile turned into a grin. "I am the troll prince." He chuckled. "At first I was quite insulted that you would call me by such a disrespectful name, but now I find it charming."

"You?"

She took a step back from the bed. She tried to recall her conversation with her father. The one during which he'd announced her engagement to a stranger. She hadn't stayed around long enough to find out anything about the man. But Kardal?

He shrugged. "I know. You are happy now. That is as it should be." He got out of bed and reached for his clothes.

A large object sailed toward him. Kardal barely had time to duck out of the way before a vase crossed the place where his head had been just the second before. He stared at Sabrina who stood by the table at the foot of the bed. Fury darkened her face and fire flashed from her eyes.

"You bastard," she said in a tone of outrage. "How dare you?"

He quickly pulled on his trousers, then held up his hands in protest. "What's wrong? Why are you angry? You should be happy that there is no troll prince."

"You knew!" She pointed at him as if he'd just stolen something precious. "You knew we were engaged, but you never told me."

Her mouth opened, then closed. "That's why you claimed me as your slave. You wanted to know what I was like. And that's why my father didn't come get me. It's not that he didn't care that I'd been kidnapped. I hadn't been kidnapped at all."

"Sabrina, you are overreacting. You said you loved me and now we will be together. I told you it would be fine, and it is."

"Like hell." She picked up another vase, glanced at it, then set it back on the table. A fruit bowl flew at him next.

"You played with me, you bastard," she spat. "You deliberately kept this information from me and let me feel horrible about everything. How dare you presume to decide if you want me around without consulting me?"

"Why are you angry? I will be your husband."

"What makes you think I want anything to do with you?"

He still didn't understand why she was so upset. "Sabrina—"

"Don't you 'Sabrina' me," she yelled. "All this

time I was worried about you. I was afraid to be with you and make love with you because I thought you were going to get killed because of me. You used me and you kept the truth from me.'' She crossed her arms over her chest and turned away. ''I thought we were friends. I thought we mattered to each other.''

''We are friends…and lovers. Soon we will be married.''

She spun back to face him. ''Don't for one second think I'm going to marry you. I'll never forgive you for this, Kardal. You treated me badly. You're still doing it.''

''How?'' he asked, genuinely baffled. ''What have I done wrong?''

''You don't love me.''

''You are a woman.'' Love? A woman? Him? ''I am the Prince of Thieves.''

''You're a man. I have to tell you, I'm really sorry there isn't a troll prince, because I would much rather marry him than have anything to do with you. I can't believe I was stupid enough to let myself care about you. Well, you can be sure that I'm never going to make that mistake again and just as soon as I figure out how not to love you anymore, I'm going to do it.''

She stalked toward the door and before he could stop her, she was gone.

Sabrina ran through the halls of the palace. Adiva saw her and tried to find out what was wrong, but Sabrina couldn't think. She couldn't do anything but keep moving because it all hurt too much.

She ached inside, as if someone had ripped out her

heart. Perhaps they had. Kardal had thought all of this was a great joke. He'd been laughing at her expense. So many things now made sense. She should have realized. Somewhere along the way, she should have known the truth.

Without realizing where she was, she found herself in front of Cala's quarters. She walked through the arch that used to lead to the harem and knocked on the closed door of Cala's private chamber.

"Cala," she called as she knocked again on the door. "Cala, are you there?"

"Just a moment."

There was a rustling sound from inside the room, then the door opened a few inches.

The normally perfectly groomed and unruffled princess wore a thin robe. Her long hair was mussed.

"Sabrina." Cala sounded distracted. "What's wrong, dear?" Her gaze sharpened. "Have you been crying?"

A movement in the rear of the room caught Sabrina's attention. She saw a partially dressed King Givon pulling on his shirt. Color flared on her cheeks. She pressed one hand to her chest.

"I'm sorry," she said quickly. "I didn't mean to interrupt you while you were… That is, I didn't want to bother you."

Apparently Givon and Cala had picked up the pieces of their relationship. The information should have made Sabrina happy, but instead it was very hard not to cry.

"I'm sorry," she repeated, and started to leave.

"Wait." Cala glanced at Givon who nodded slightly. She drew Sabrina into the room. "Tell us what's wrong."

Sabrina felt uncomfortable discussing her personal life in front of King Givon. She tried to retreat, but Cala's grip on her arm was firm. When Cala and Sabrina were seated on the sofa, Cala took her hands and squeezed them gently.

"What happened?"

Givon sat in a club chair at right angles to the sofa. His concerned expression combined with Cala's kindness was Sabrina's undoing. She found herself stumbling over her story, starting with her father telling her that she was engaged to someone she'd never met and ending with Kardal's admission he was her betrothed.

"He laughed at me," she finished, barely able to keep from crying. "All the time I worried about him and loved him, and he was laughing at me. Plus he doesn't love me at all. He thinks I'll be a decent wife, but that's not the same thing. He's talking about the fact that I'll be happy loving him. I guess that's supposed to be my reward as his wife. Pleasure in service."

She looked at Cala. "What did I do wrong? How can this have happened?"

Kardal's mother sighed. "It seems I do no better in my relationships today than I did thirty years ago. I'm sorry, Sabrina. I knew who you were, but I didn't say anything. I didn't want to interfere with my son's life, but I see now that was a mistake."

Sabrina tried not to feel even more stupid than she already did, but it was impossible. She started to rise to her feet.

"I see. I'm sorry I bothered you."

"Don't," Cala implored. "Please, don't run off. I feel terrible about what's happened. I'm sorry my son is an idiot. I want to do what I can for you. I know you and Kardal have a lot in common. I think you would do well together.''

Great. Cala was offering a lifetime of companionship. Sabrina wanted love.

"Perhaps I can help," Givon said, speaking for the first time.

Sabrina sniffed. "I don't think anyone can. I don't care if Kardal is willing to marry me. I won't have him. He treated me as if my feelings were only there to be convenient for him. If he doesn't love me back, I don't want anything to do with him."

Givon nodded. "I understand what you are saying. However, I have recently watched all three of my sons fall in love with wonderful women. Not one of them did it right. In fact they all came perilously close to losing the loves of their lives. Thirty-one years ago, I lost mine. So I have some experience in this matter. Kardal needs to learn what is important."

Sabrina swallowed. "You know how to teach him that? Because I don't."

"I have a good idea." He smiled. "Men often do not realize the importance of what they have until it is taken from them. With that in mind, I would very much like to offer you sanctuary from both your father and Kardal."

She blinked. "You can do that?"

"Young lady, I am Givon, king of El Bahar. I can do anything I wish."

Less than thirty minutes later Sabrina, Cala and several servants crossed toward Givon's waiting helicopter. In addition to suitcases containing clothes, they carried with them several small trunks. Inside were the stolen artifacts Sabrina was determined to return to their rightful countries.

The helicopter blades circled lazily in the early-evening twilight, stirring up dust and the sweet scents of the desert.

"Princess, are you sure you want to do this?" Adiva asked, sounding worried and yelling to be heard over the engine. "The prince will miss you very much."

"I hope you're right," Sabrina said as Cala kissed Givon goodbye and stepped onto the helicopter.

"What is going on here?"

At the shouted question, Sabrina glanced back and saw Kardal striding toward her. He'd changed into traditional garments and the front of his robe flapped with each step. He looked dark, angry and very dangerous. Sabrina thought about ducking into the helicopter, but instead she squared her shoulders. Kardal couldn't hurt her any more than he already had.

"What are you doing?" he asked when he stopped in front of her.

"Leaving."

Dust swirled around her, making her squint but she could still see the frown as Kardal planted his hands on his hips and stared down at her.

"Why?"

She wanted to scream with frustration. The man honestly didn't know. When had he gotten so stupid?

"Because I fell in love with you and you played me for a fool. I was worried about you *dying* and you laughed at me. I'm leaving and I'm never coming back."

"But if you love me, you must want to marry me. I will consent to the union. I wish us to be married."

Givon moved close and put his hand on his son's shoulder. "Tell her you love her."

Kardal glared. "I do not need your fatherly advice at this late date." He reached for Sabrina's arm. "Enough of this game. Return to your rooms at once."

"Not even on a bet."

She jerked free of him and hurried to the helicopter. As she settled in her seat next to Cala, a man appeared in the door. Rafe! She gasped.

But he didn't grab her or haul her out. Instead he stared at her for several seconds.

"He's a stubborn man," he said finally.

"I don't expect him to change. I simply refuse to play his game anymore."

Rafe surprised her by smiling. "You have backbone. I always figured you were exactly what he needed."

She knew that Rafe was only trying to be kind, but his words were a knife to her heart. Why did everyone see that she and Kardal belonged together *except* Kardal?

"I can't wait around until he figures that out," she said.

Rafe nodded. Kardal approached. Rafe quickly shut the door, then stepped back and gave the pilot a thumb's-up. Seconds later they were in the air, moving away from the City of Thieves.

Sabrina glanced out the window at the ancient castle. She'd been happy there. She'd fallen in love there. And now she was leaving and would probably never come back. She couldn't remember ever feeling so broken and sad.

Cala touched her arm. "Things will work out. You'll see."

Sabrina didn't say anything. Words of comfort from a woman who had lost the love of her life for thirty-one years didn't make her feel better.

"I will not stand for this," Kardal raged.

He paced the length of his office, unable to believe what was happening. One moment everything had been fine with Sabrina. The next she was in tears and threatening to leave him. More than threatening. She was gone.

"How could you help her?" he demanded of Rafe as he walked past the other man. "You work for me. You should have stopped her from leaving."

Rafe shrugged. "So fire me."

Kardal didn't want to lose the other man, so he ignored his impertinence. He turned his anger on his father.

"Where are they? Tell me this instant."

Givon leaned against a corner of the desk. A gleam of humor lit his dark eyes. "You're not the only one with a secret castle. Both Sabrina and your mother are perfectly safe. When you've figured out what the problem is and how to fix it, I'll take you to them. Until then, you're on your own."

"Problem?" Fury filled him. He understood Sabrina's need to throw things. Right now he wanted to throw both these men across the room. "There is no problem except Sabrina is gone. I wish her to be returned to me, immediately."

He paused in front of his father and glared at him. "We are engaged. You have no right to keep her from me."

"The lady does not want to marry you," Givon said calmly.

"I can't blame her," Rafe offered helpfully. "You're being an idiot, Kardal."

He stared at the two of them. Had the entire world gone crazy? "I am Kardal, the Prince of Thieves. I have made no mistake."

"So why did Sabrina leave you?" Givon asked.

"Because she is a woman and prone to hysterics."

"Then one would think you are better off without her."

One *would* think so, Kardal thought grimly. Yet he couldn't imagine the palace without her. In the past few weeks, she'd become a part of his life. Almost of his very being. He needed to hear her voice and her laughter. She was someone he could talk with. She understood so many things.

"I will find her," he announced.

"Good luck," Rafe said cheerfully. "I've heard rumors about Givon's secret palace. It's way the hell and gone out in the Indian Ocean. You ever try finding an island in an ocean before?"

Before Kardal could respond, there was a knock on his office door.

"Go away," he yelled, but instead of doing as he requested, his secretary stepped into the room.

"I'm sorry to bother you, sir," Bilal said, obviously uncomfortable. "However, I've just been informed that King Hassan of Bahania has arrived. He says he's here to check on the welfare of his daughter."

Chapter Fifteen

Chaos exploded upon them. King Hassan burst into Kardal's office. He was not as tall as Givon or Kardal, but he had about him an air of authority that spoke of many years of being the respected leader of a sovereign nation.

"I heard she's not even here," Hassan announced by way of greeting. He paused to nod at Givon, then turned his steely gaze on Kardal. "I trusted you with my daughter and you have misplaced her."

"She is perfectly safe," Givon said mildly, walking over to Hassan and shaking his hand. "She and Kardal's mother flew out a few minutes ago on my helicopter."

Hassan frowned. "Why? Where are they going?"

"That's what I want to know," Kardal growled, thinking that he didn't need to be dealing with Sabrina's father right now.

Givon shrugged. "She is going to a private island that I own."

Hassan folded his arms over his chest. "What is going on here? Givon, why are you in the City of Thieves?"

"I am visiting my son."

Hassan raised dark eyebrows. Kardal tried to find some likeness of Sabrina in her father, but except for her brown eyes, he didn't see any.

"I was not aware that you acknowledged your son."

"I do now," Givon said.

"It is about time," Hassan announced.

The three of them were standing in the center of the room. Rafe was the only one who had bothered to claim a seat on the sofa. Kardal thought about playing the polite host, but he found he didn't care about good manners or what the other men thought of him. He leaned toward Hassan.

"You have no right to lecture anyone on fatherly responsibilities. What about your own failures with Sabrina?"

Hassan stiffened. Anger flashed in his eyes. "You forget yourself."

"Not for a minute." Kardal narrowed his gaze. "Your daughter is a beautiful, intelligent woman. You assumed she was like her mother, but that is because you never bothered to get to know her. She could have been the most valuable flower in the garden that is your children, but you ignored her in favor of your sons. You ignored her because it was easier." He turned to Givon. "Much as you ignored me."

Givon nodded. "I cannot deny the truth of your

words. However, I would remind you that you grew to be a fine strong leader who has done well for himself.''

''That doesn't erase your responsibilities.''

''Perhaps not, but it explains my choice. You had your mother to raise you and love you. Had I left El Bahar, I would have been required to abandon my children to be raised by ministers. They had no mother.''

Kardal refused to see any validity in Givon's argument. ''What about Cala? Did you ever think about her?''

''Every day of my life. I thought about you as many times. I wanted to be with both of you. Meaningless to know now, perhaps, but true.''

Givon spoke the words with such profound sadness that Kardal almost forgot to be angry.

Hassan waved his hand. ''This is all very nice. Now father and son can reconcile. However, my question remains unanswered. Where is my daughter?''

''She has run off,'' Kardal said flatly. ''Givon won't say where.''

Givon smiled slightly. ''You are leaving out the most interesting parts of the story.''

Kardal shifted, suddenly feeling uncomfortable. ''What parts?''

''Tell him about her falling in love with you,'' Rafe offered helpfully from his place on the sofa. ''And about this afternoon. You know, when you...''

Kardal glowered at Rafe, but his friend simply shrugged.

"I will deal with you later," Kardal said, then turned his attention to Hassan.

The king of Bahania nearly vibrated with rage. He might be wearing a western-style suit, but he had been born in the desert and the blood of vengeance ran in his veins.

"This afternoon?" he repeated icily.

"We're engaged," Kardal reminded him. "You're the one who said you couldn't vouch for her virtue."

"And you're the one who told me she was innocent. Until you had your way with her. I had assumed you were bluffing. Trying my patience to get my attention."

Kardal drew in a breath. "It is important that Sabrina and I are married right away." He squared his shoulders. "This afternoon I made her mine."

Hassan lunged at him. Givon grabbed for Sabrina's father, and Rafe sprang up from the sofa, but Kardal waved them both off. He moved even closer to Hassan.

"What are you going to do to me?"

"Behead you," Hassan spat out. "If you are lucky. Or perhaps I'll simply make sure you aren't able to be with another woman again."

"Why?" Kardal challenged. "You have never cared about Sabrina before."

Hassan opened his mouth, then closed it. "You were wrong to take her," he said at last.

"I know. I want to make it right by marrying her."

Rafe shoved his hands into his trouser pockets. "I think this is where the argument started, King Hassan. The trick is Sabrina no longer wants to marry him."

"What?" Hassan looked surprised. "Why would she refuse you?"

"Who knows the mind of a woman," Kardal said, trying to sound casual, but inside he felt uneasy. He knew that he could force Sabrina to marry him. Theirs was an arranged marriage and she did not have to be present for it to take place. Perhaps with someone else, he might have simply seen it done, but not with her. He found himself wanting her to *want* him.

"She loves him," Rafe said, earning another scowl. "But he doesn't love her back. So she left."

"Love." Hassan threw up his hands. "Women and love. They think it is both the moon and the stars."

"They are right," Givon said. "Thirty-one years ago I chose duty over love. While I cannot regret my decision because I did not feel that I had a better option, I have hated the outcome every day since then."

For Kardal it wasn't a matter of duty. It was practicality. Women loved and men… He frowned. What did men do? They respected their wives, treated them well, supported them and their children. But love?

He glanced at his father. Givon claimed to have never *stopped* loving Cala.

"Why?" he asked his father. "Why did you love my mother?"

Givon smiled. "To quote your future father-in-law, she was my moon and stars. There was passion between us, but more than that, there was a meeting of the minds. There was no one I wished to speak with more, no one else who understood me and whom I could understand. I would not have minded her seeing me ill or weak. I could trust her with my heart.''

''Yes, yes, all that is fine,'' Kardal said impatiently. ''But men do not love.''

Givon nodded. ''Perhaps you are right. Perhaps you will be content to live without Sabrina.''

''I do not want to live without her,'' he said. ''I want her here.''

''Why?'' asked Rafe. ''She's just some good-looking princess with a mouth the size of Utah. Frankly, I always thought she was a pain in the butt. I could easily get you a dozen, all of them better in bed.''

Kardal turned on him and grabbed him by the front of his shirt. ''Speak of her that way again and I will kill you with my bare hands.''

''Powerful words for a man not in love,'' his friend told him, not looking the least bit impressed by the threat.

Kardal released him. ''I do not—''

But he found he couldn't say that he didn't love Sabrina. He walked to the window and stared out at the vast emptiness. He tried to imagine a world without his desert bird. In his mind the walls of the castle became a cage. How could he survive without her laughter? Her beauty? Her sharp mind? The way she insisted he return treasures to governments long past caring about them?

He stalked to the door. ''Come,'' he said. ''We are going to find them. Hassan, you may join us if you promise to treat your daughter with respect. Givon, you must go with me because you are the one who knows the way.''

Hassan stepped toward him. "Not so quickly, my young prince. You still have to answer for your crime against my daughter."

Sabrina sat on her balcony and watched the sun rise over the Indian Ocean. Givon's island paradise was more lovely than anything she could have imagined. But the stunning profusion of colorful blooms and soft balmy breezes didn't wipe the tears from her cheeks or ease the pain in her heart.

"Kardal," she whispered, then gasped as the sound of his name inflicted new pain.

She was never going to see him again. She might love him for the rest of her life, but she refused to give her heart to a man who wouldn't love her back. Worse, Kardal wouldn't even admit that him loving her was necessary for them to have a successful relationship.

She'd been so stupid. How could she have let him trick her that way? Why hadn't she seen what was going on? She'd been so worried and he'd known the *entire* time.

"Did you sleep at all?" Cala asked as she walked onto the balcony.

Sabrina shook her head. She sniffed and brushed the tears from her face. "I would like to tell you that I spent the night planning painful ways for your son to die, but I can't quite wish him dead. I'm sure that will come in time."

"Although I believe my son is behaving very badly," Cala said, pulling up a chair and sitting next to her, "I don't wish him dead. Besides, if you truly love him, you won't want to live without him."

"I don't have a choice." She looked at Cala. "Would you tell me to go back and simply accept all that happened?"

"No. Of course not. However, walking away can be difficult." She stared out toward the ocean. "Forgiveness isn't easy, Sabrina. But sometimes it's the only alternative." She sighed. "Kardal always asked me why I never married. It wasn't for lack of offers. There were men in my life—good men. I wasn't holding out for Givon. Instead, after a period of mourning and growing up, I decided I would find someone I loved as much, and then I would get married."

"What happened?" Sabrina asked, intrigued despite her pain.

"I never met him. All I wanted was to love someone as much. Not more, just the same amount. But I couldn't. I had great affection and respect for many of the men I met. Some I took as lovers and we were together for several years. But I never loved the same way, so I never married. For the past thirty-one years, I've been haunted by a ghost."

"He's back now," Sabrina said.

"I know." She smiled. "And his feelings are exactly as they were. He has asked me to marry him." She turned toward Sabrina. "My choices are simple. I can forgive him and take the happiness he offers, or I can live with the bitter taste of knowing I finally have revenge when I refuse him."

"You're going to marry him," Sabrina said without doubt. For Cala there was no other choice.

"I am. I will go with him to El Bahar and we will begin a new chapter together." She tucked a strand of dark hair behind her ear. "Kardal was wrong to keep the truth from you. And if he can't admit that he loves you, then I believe you are right to walk away. For a man who will not tell the truth about the secrets of his heart will lie about other things. But if he comes to you and confesses his devotion, I would urge you to forgive and begin a new chapter of your own. If you do not, I fear you will regret it the rest of your life. And even if you are offered a second chance later, you may find that it is not as precious as the first."

Sabrina didn't know what to say. She respected Cala and her life's wisdom, but Kardal had made it clear that he didn't love her. He'd been playing her for a fool, not wooing a wife.

"I can't—"

A commotion in the hallway made them both turn. Loud voices called out. Sabrina pulled her robe closer around her as she rose to her feet.

One of the servants came running out to the balcony. "Princess," she said, looking at both women. "You must come at once."

Cala and Sabrina exchanged confused glances, then hurried after the servant. The young woman led them into the hallway, then back toward the entrance. Sabrina heard men yelling and what sounded strangely like the *clink* of chains. Chains?

They rounded the corner and stopped instantly. Sabrina's breath caught in her chest. She had to lean against the white walls of the small villa. Cala gasped out loud, then ran toward her son.

"Kardal!" she screamed.

Two armed guards captured her, keeping her away from the people just inside the main door.

Sabrina shook her head, convinced she was seeing things. But the image in front of her didn't go away. Kardal knelt on the floor, shackled and held by large, burly guards. Beside him were King Givon and...her father!

She blinked several times. "I don't understand."

Hassan nodded at the guards holding Cala. They released her instantly, but when she tried to approach her son, Kardal looked at her.

"Mother, stay back."

"But Kardal—"

Cala turned to Sabrina. "Help him."

Sabrina didn't know what to think. "I will. Of course, I just don't know what's going on."

She glanced at the two kings, then focused her attention on the Prince of Thieves. "Is this some kind of game? What are you playing at?"

"He's not playing," her father said, stepping toward her. Hassan crossed the tiled floor and took her hands in his. "How are you, my daughter?"

"Confused," she admitted. "Why are you here?"

"Because you are my child and I have behaved badly toward you."

Sabrina stared into her father's familiar face. They didn't look very much alike—she'd always taken after her mother—but she knew him. Now she gazed into his eyes and tried to tell what he was thinking.

"You don't believe me," he said sadly. "I suppose that is your right. For all these years I've ignored you and treated you as if you were little more than a bother. I'm sorry. I've learned that you're nothing like your mother. I was wrong to judge you as if you were."

She pulled her hands free. "That's a pretty crummy apology. What you should be telling me is that it doesn't matter if I'm like my mother or not. I'm still *your* daughter. Parental love shouldn't come with conditions."

Surprisingly Hassan bowed his head. "You are correct. I have been gravely at fault. I hope that with time, we can begin to rebuild our relationship."

She wanted to believe him. Perhaps she would...someday.

Hassan moved to stand next to her. He draped one arm across her shoulders. "On a different matter, Kardal, the Prince of Thieves has confessed to defiling you. Under normal circumstances, he would be put to death, but there are extenuating circumstances. The two of you are betrothed. Also, I have responsibility in the matter as I allowed you to stay with him."

Cala began to cry. It was the other woman's tears that convinced Sabrina this was really happening. She looked at Givon. "This is real, isn't it?" she asked.

Kardal's father nodded. There wasn't a flicker of humor in his eyes. "Kardal has been a law unto himself for many years. But even the greatest leader must answer to a higher power. Kardal took something that was forbidden. He is fortunate to still be alive."

She turned to Kardal. His steady gaze didn't show any fear. "It's not so bad," he told her. "You can either marry me and all will be forgiven, or you can refuse me and I will be banished."

Feeling returned to her body, and along with it, pain. "So this is another trick. You've got them all on your side. I'm not going to marry you, Kardal. No matter how many games you play."

His dark eyes continued to watch her. "Good," he said. "I do not wish you to marry me."

She hadn't thought he could continue to hurt her, but she was wrong. Another knife wound cut through her heart. "I see."

"No, you don't." He started to stand but the guards on either side of him pushed him back to his knees. He frowned at them, then returned his attention to her.

"Sabrina, I was wrong from the beginning. I shouldn't have kept the truth from you. My excuse is simple arrogance. I had read things about you, things that made me not like you. I had agreed to the betrothal, but I had second thoughts about the bride. I wondered if the alliance with Bahania would be payment enough."

"Gee, thanks," she muttered.

He shrugged. "Then I began to spend time with you. I learned the truth about your heart and your soul. I knew then that I would be proud to call you mine. I wanted to teach you a lesson—how to be a docile wife—yet I was the one who changed."

He paused and shifted on his knees. She thought that his bindings looked uncomfortably tight, then scolded herself for caring. Kardal deserved whatever happened to him.

"I love you," he said bluntly. "I who had thought men were above such emotions have realized you are my moon and stars. My father has loved my mother for thirty-one years, despite being apart from her. I fear that I would suffer the same fate should you cast me aside.''

Too much had happened too fast, Sabrina thought, still not sure what to believe. Her heart ached, desperate to be convinced by his words, but her spirit was not so sure.

''Kardal, how do I know this isn't just some way for you to get what you want?'' she asked.

''You don't,'' he said simply. ''So I ask that you refuse my proposal. Then I will be banished.''

Her lips parted. ''What? You would leave the city?'' The desert? The place he loved more than anything in the world?

''Yes. Once banished I would come to you and spend the rest of our days convincing you that you are my one true love.'' He smiled, then. A warm, open, loving smile that began to heal the wounds of her heart. ''I can live without the city, but I could never survive without you.''

Sabrina took a step toward him, then paused. What should she do? She so wanted to believe him, but could she?

''Follow your heart,'' Cala said, stepping into Givon's embrace and holding him close. ''Sabrina, trust what you know to be true.''

''Don't marry me,'' Kardal said. ''Please. Have them send me away. I swear I will come to you. I will prove it all. I will worship you as the sun worships the City of Thieves.''

''Kardal…''

''Sabrina, you were right. I didn't mean to play you for a fool, but that is what happened. You deserve to be sure of me and what I tell you here today. Banish me. Banish me and I will love you forever.''

His dark gaze seemed to see into her soul.

''You know we belong together,'' he continued, his voice low and heated. ''We are too much alike to ever be happy with anyone else. Let me prove my love.''

''No!''

Sabrina shook her head, then turned and hurried from the room. There was too much information. Too many questions. Banish Kardal? Have him lose everything to prove his love?

She reached her quarters and slipped inside. Footsteps sounded in the hall, then her father stepped into the room.

''This is not a bluff,'' Hassan said. ''Givon and I *will* have him banished.''

''I don't want that,'' she told him. ''I just want to be sure.''

''What would you have him do to convince you? Give up his heart's desire?''

Which is what Kardal had done. She thought of the beautiful city and how happy he was there. She thought of all the times he'd come to speak with her, seeking her advice, sharing secret fears with her. These were not the actions of a man who didn't care. He'd been arrogant and stupid. He was a prince— and a man—why was she surprised?

''I love him,'' she said, impulsively hugging her father. For the first time in her life, he hugged her back.

''I'm glad. After all, you could be pregnant with his child.''

Sabrina froze. "I hadn't thought of that." Pregnant? With Kardal's baby?

Joy filled her. Joy and a certainty that eased the pain in her heart and made her feel as if she could fly. She loved him. Cala had been right. It was time for her to follow her heart.

She ran across the room and opened the first of the small trunks she'd brought with her. Inside were dozens of priceless treasures.

"They're in here somewhere," she said, digging through the gold, diamonds and other precious stones.

She opened a second trunk, then third. Finally she crowed in triumph and pulled out a pair of slave bracelets. They were solid gold and intricately carved. They were also much larger than hers—designed to fit a man's wrists and forearms.

Hassan raised his eyebrows. "I am most impressed with your creativity."

"Thank you."

Still smiling she hurried back to the villa's foyer. Everyone was still there, including Kardal who remained on his knees. She crossed to him and motioned to the guards to release him.

"I have decided," she said.

Kardal waited until his wrists were unbound, then he rose and stood in front of her. She held out the slave bracelets. Kardal looked at her, then at the gold symbols of servitude. Without saying anything, he put his arms out straight in front of him. She locked the bracelets in place.

"Just as a reminder that I could have had you

banished," she said, watching his expression. "Although I've decided to marry you instead."

Love and pleasure lit his eyes. He touched her cheek. "Most couples prefer to exchange rings of some kind."

"We're not most couples," she told him.

He pulled her close and kissed her. "I will spend the rest of my life proving myself to you, Sabrina. I am deeply sorry that I hurt you. I did not intend to make you feel that I didn't care."

"I know."

"Then you forgive me?"

"I love you. I don't have a choice."

He gazed into her eyes. "You had one today. I would have come for you regardless of my fate."

"I know, but now you can have me and the city."

"I have loved the city all my life," he admitted, "but you will always possess my heart."

His lips touched hers again. Behind them she heard Cala sigh.

"I am relieved that is over," her father said. "I really thought she might banish him. And then what would we have done?" He cleared his throat. "Now I must go home and deal with the rest of my family."

Sabrina raised her head and looked at her father. "Are my brothers all right? Is something wrong?"

Hassan smiled. "Not in the way you mean. I have four sons in need of wives. It is past time they married and still they resist me."

"I could never resist you," Kardal whispered in her ear. "Are you ready to go home, my desert bird? We have a wedding to plan."

She smiled at him. "We have a couple of other

things to do as well. One of them is to find the keys to these slave bracelets.''

He laughed. ''I will love you forever, Sabrina. I will be as constant as the desert, for all of our lives and into the next.''

''That works for me,'' she told him.

They turned and headed out into the bright morning light, ready to begin the adventure of their lives.

* * * * *

Look out for the new DESERT ROGUES *book from* Susan Mallery *–* The Sheikh & the Virgin Secretary *– on sale in March 2007.*

MILLS & BOON®

*Super*ROMANCE™

MORE TO TEXAS THAN COWBOYS
by Roz Denny Fox
Home To Stay

Greer Bell is returning to Texas for the first time since she
left as a pregnant teenager. She and her young daughter are
determined to make a success of their new ranch – and the last
thing Greer needs is a romantic entanglement, even with the
helpful and handsome Reverend Noah Kelley.

PARTY OF THREE by Joan Kilby
Single Father

Ben Gillard finally has a chance to build a relationship with his
son, instead of being a weekend dad. But he and Danny can't
seem to find any common ground. Ben is surprised to find that it
is the straitlaced Ally Cummings who can make them a family.

THE MUMMY QUEST by Lori Handeland
The Luchetti Brothers

Now that Tim Luchetti has found himself the best dad in
the world, he needs a mum! Only, picking a wife for Dean is
proving harder than he thought. But when Tim ends up in his
headteacher's office, he decides Ms O'Connell might just be
perfect.

ALMOST A FAMILY by Roxanne Rustand
Blackberry Hill Memorial

Erin can't believe she has to work with Dr Connor Reynolds
– the man her family blames for what happened to her cousin.
As well as that, she has to contend with her recent divorce and
three children who don't understand why Daddy left. If only she
could act as if Connor was simply another colleague…

On sale from 16th March 2007

Available at WHSmith, Tesco, ASDA, and all good bookshops

www.millsandboon.co.uk

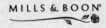

SPECIAL EDITION™

MARRIED IN HASTE by Christine Rimmer

Bravo Family Ties

When it came to grand fiery passions, Angie Dellazola
had been there, done that – and got burnt. Marrying
steady boy-next-door Brett Bravo seemed like a better
idea…until pent-up passions exploded between the
unsuspecting newlyweds!

HER BEST-KEPT SECRET
by Brenda Harlen

Family Business

Journalist Jenny Anderson had a great job in Tokyo
and a loving adoptive family, but she definitely had trust
issues related to her birth. For Jenny, it was a big step to
get close to Hanson Media lawyer Richard Warren. But
would their fledgling affair run foul of his boss Helen
Hanson's secret?

A TEXAS WEDDING VOW
by Cathy Gillen Thacker

The McCabes

When the bride skips town, maid of honour Laurel
McCabe has to face the fury of the bridegroom, and finds
herself promising to put things right. But never had she
imagined that Cade Dunnigan would whisk her up the
aisle instead!

MILLS & BOON®

0307/23b

SPECIAL EDITION™

WORTH FIGHTING FOR
by Judy Duarte

Single mother Caitlin Rogers knew exactly what her priority was – her little daughter, Emily. So when that relationship was threatened, Caitlin was lucky to be able to count on Brett Tanner, a man with scars in his past who made a family worth fighting for.

SECOND-TIME LUCKY
by Laurie Paige
Canyon Country

How ironic that family counsellor Caileen Peters was turning to her client Jefferson Aquilon, a foster father, for help with *her* daughter. But Caileen soon found something more in Jeff's arms.

THE PRODIGAL MD RETURNS
by Marie Ferrarella
The Alaskans

Things were really heating up, when Ben Kerrigan came back after leaving Heather Ryan Kendall at the altar seven years ago. Recently-widowed Heather and her six-year-old daughter had a surprise for the prodigal MD.

Don't miss out!
On sale from 16th March 2007

Available at WHSmith, Tesco, ASDA, and all good bookshops
www.millsandboon.co.uk

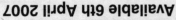